THE FORGOTTEN DAGGER OF AZULA

THE SHADOWLAND SAGA

BOOK TWO

STEPHANIE ANNE

THE FORGOTTEN DAGGER OF AZULA
Copyright © 2022 by Stephanie Anne

For information contact :
https://www.stephanieanneauthor.com/

Book and Cover design by Celin Graphics
Proofreading by E. Rose Books
Book Formatting by Derek Murphy @Creativindie
E-BOOK ISBN: 978-0-6488520-4-9
PAPERBACK ISBN: 978-0-6488520-3-2
HARDCOVER ISBN: 978-0-6455011-1-7
First edition: December 2022

*TO EVERYONE WHO MADE THIS POSSIBLE.
ELIZA'S JOURNEY WOULDN'T BE THE
SAME WITHOUT YOU.*

*THANK YOU FOR BEING PATIENT WITH
ME AND THIS BOOK.*

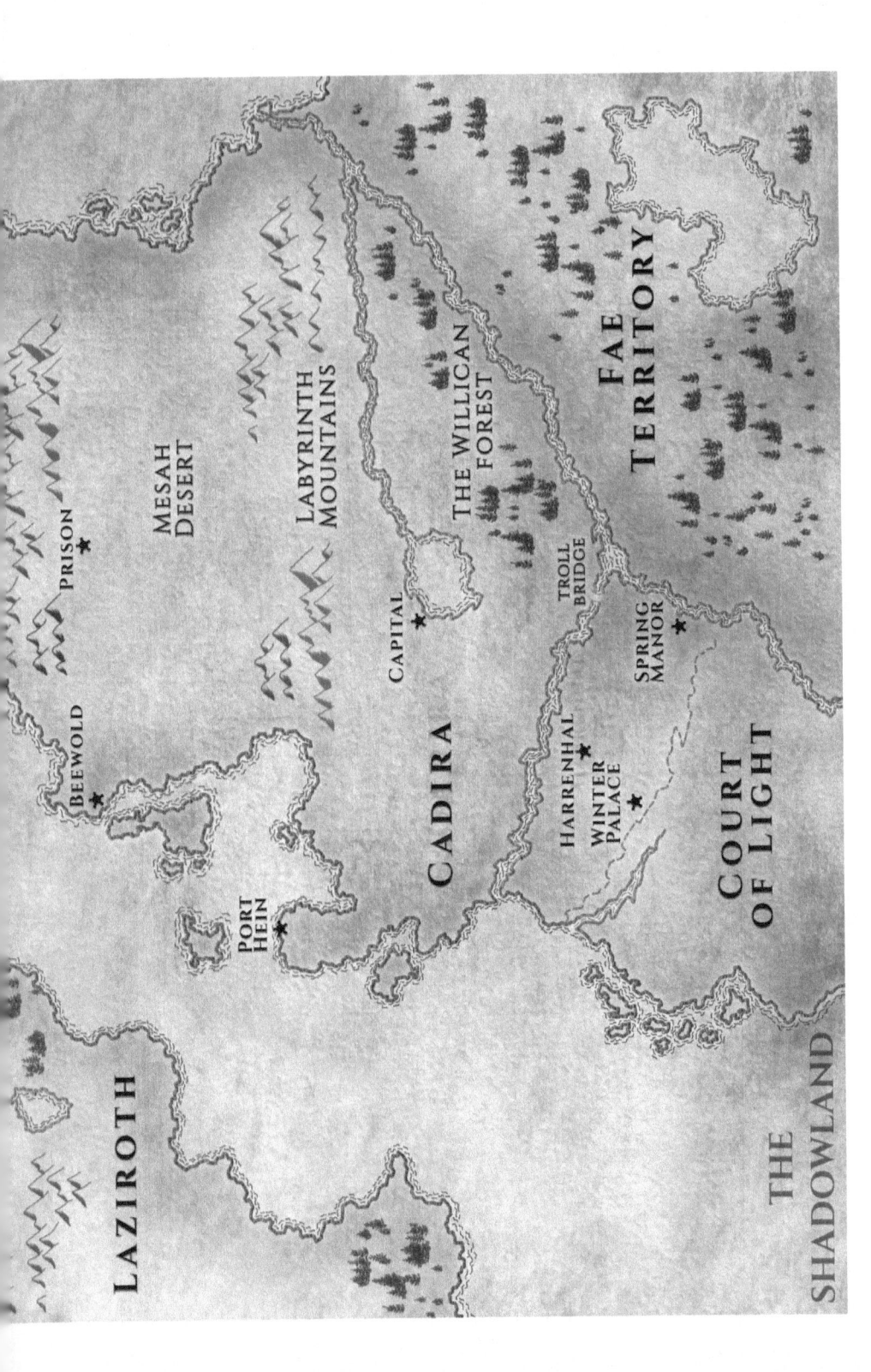

1

THE CAPITAL
ELIZA

Shadow Magic had a particular scent that made it easy to identify.

Sulphur permeated the air, joined by the lingering aftertaste of copper on the back of the tongue. To Eliza Kindall, it wove like a dark stream of smoke through the city. The dead—spirits caught in endless loops and unaware of the living—walked the never-ending path.

At the end of which she found *them*.

The two Shadow Soldiers were from a group she and her immortal commander friend, Brandon Thorne, had been tracking through the city after a failed attempt at locating one of the Dark Master's pawns. The streets were an unfamiliar maze of both tall and squat buildings, mismatched and built in no clear pattern. For Eliza, that was trouble enough; navigating the streets of the Cadiran capital without the help of Brandon Thorne or her Blood Witch sister, Celia, left her mildly defenceless against those she chased, but with every turn, a map formed in the back of her mind.

The Shadow Soldiers evaded her by slipping down narrow alleys and into the shadows. They were silent and skilled—every bit as terrifying as they had been during her last encounter with them, beneath the desert in Mesah. Created with a strange form of Blood Magic and Necromancy, the Shadow Soldiers were neither dead nor alive—a zombie, if she were thinking in terms of her home world—except the spirits that had once existed within the flesh now hovered close to their bodies, tethered by a string just strong enough to keep the soldiers moving.

That was how Eliza continued to track them; she didn't have to dig very far for her connection to the dead. It was a constant feeling in the back of her mind, an ability she'd had since she was a child. For as long as she could remember, she thought she'd been born with the power, exiled from Cadira because of it. Now, she knew better.

Now she knew she was a Blood Witch.

The Ecix; a powerful necromancer revered by the Blood Witches who trained her, feared by the rest of her world for the power building in her veins.

The presence of the Shadow Soldiers grew stronger, their darkness a tickle in her mind; something she'd learned to identify after two long months trapped in Cadira after finding the lost prince.

With help from Thorne and Celia, Eliza had figured out how to track the soldiers around the city using her connection to the dead. The deep magic that had once frightened her was now her only means of finding the Dark Master and his allies. So, she followed it down the maze of streets, heart in her throat.

It had been a while since she'd been left alone outside of the palace. Thorne trusted her, though he usually kept a watchful eye on her when they were beyond the palace walls. Celia worried too much, and her Blood Witch trainers... they didn't trust Eliza at all.

Eliza slowed to a stop and sucked in a breath. She let the shadows of the city encase her in a tight cocoon, hiding her from the darker parts of the capital: where criminals played and hunted throughout the night; magic was peddled to the less fortunate as cures and miracles; and the Dark Master whittled away at the foundations of the capital with his Shadow Soldiers and darkness.

Under her breath, Eliza swore, but she'd been determined not to let the Shadow Soldiers get away—not again. The Dark Master—a cunning adversary who had almost killed her in the desert, who had masterminded the kidnapping of the Cadiran prince, and who had been hunting her since she was a child—was out in the world, biding his time for *something*.

And she was determined to find out what he had planned—no matter the cost.

The Shadow Soldiers didn't speak. They wore cloths over the lower halves of their faces, leaving their blood-red eyes visible. To anyone else, they might have seemed strange, maybe poisoned by magic. But to those who knew what the Dark Master was capable of... They were her only shot at getting closer to the monster who haunted her dreams.

Eliza crept forward and stopped at the feel of a hand touching her wrist. Magic tingled at her fingertips as she whipped around to face Commander Thorne. He brought a gloved finger to his lips, stopping her. His eyes were on the two Shadow Soldiers she'd tracked.

Eliza released a heavy breath. "I could have killed you," she whispered, enclosing him in her blanket of darkness.

Behind her, Thorne chuckled. "It would take a lot more than that to kill me, Eliza."

She frowned, but returned her attention to the two soldiers. Their spirits clung to the flesh, barely visible thanks to the magic dampener wrapped around Eliza's wrist. The gold band—courtesy of her Blood Witch trainer and the king—not only lessened her connection to Blood Magic, but acted as a tracker to keep Eliza in line.

She knew she'd screwed up the moment she'd stepped out of the *safety zone*. By now, she was sure Celia would be looking for her. It tracked all her movements and meant she couldn't leave the confines of the city without her *handler*—a witch who disliked the capital more than Eliza did. It meant she couldn't entertain the idea of escaping.

If it wasn't bad enough that she was trapped in Cadira, being held hostage with her own magic made her situation a hell of a lot worse.

The soldiers entered what looked like an old market; stalls were set up around a crumbling fountain, with shoeless children running around the debris with toys made of straw. It was a stark contrast to the upper city, where nobility strolled around pristine gardens, the snow swept to the sides fashionably, the children were well dressed with heavy coats and thick shoes, with toys carved from the finest wood and enchanted with the spells of warlocks and Fae.

But down in the sectors Eliza *wasn't* permitted to journey, the city was a much darker place. Bodies were heaped where the snow met the dirt-packed streets, all frostbitten and frozen because there was no room left in the morgues. The houses, compact and built on top of each other, couldn't contain the influx of people swarming to the capital to see the lost prince, and escape the influence of the Dark Master, which seeped into the lands north and east of the capital.

Eliza saw the influence of the Dark Master during her scouting missions in the city; the dark underbelly slowly showing their support for the creature responsible for turning Cadira upside down. She saw it in the faces of those forgotten by the nobility, the shadows sneaking into their hollow cheeks and hunched backs. The city was overcrowded in one place, and almost empty in another.

And she could do nothing more than magically sprout food in places food did not grow, and hope that one day she could change it.

That meant the Shadow Soldiers were no more out of place than the smuggled dragon-scale daggers or the Fae swords. Over the last several weeks, their presence had grown more and more, but it hadn't been until that morning that Eliza had been able to locate them.

They've either gotten sloppy, or the Dark Master has something he wants me to see... Eliza's stomach churned at the second option. Everything she had done up to the moment she'd found Prince Alicsar had been a masterful ploy, some kind of trap for her. Only Eliza couldn't be sure the exact reason why.

She tightened the darkness around the commander and herself as the soldiers moved between vendors. It didn't take long for Eliza to realise the shady stall owners and the other patrons weren't all they seemed; magic—a barrier of some sort—surrounded the market, and gave away a false illusion of what was really transpiring within the circle of houses. Thorne's presence alone would send up all kinds of red flags, she surmised, but hers... she was the future princess of Cadira, and a witch.

She'd be found out the moment she stepped foot inside the market.

They were far enough away from the barrier that they wouldn't alert the magic wielder within to their presence. But just in case, Eliza whispered a spell beneath her breath and let the magic she had spill out around her and the commander; one that would hide them from detection and sight.

They crept forward, and she felt for the barrier, stopping when her magic recoiled. Eliza frowned, and hesitantly reached out with her magic once more.

There was something strange about the barrier, how it had been created. It took her a moment too long to realise it hadn't been created by just anyone—it was born of the Dark Master's shadow magic.

"He's behind this," she whispered, low enough for only Thorne to hear.

His breath warmed her ear as he spoke. "Shadow market. They don't usually get this close to the inner city. But since the return of Alicsar, we've seen an influx of mercenaries and traders from all over Cadira looking to make profit from the commotion."

She spared him a glance over her shoulder; their gazes locked for a moment, his irises a storm of greys and blues, filled with memories that were lost to her, but frighteningly clear for him.

"How bad is it?" Eliza asked, averting her eyes. Her cheeks heated as she returned her gaze to the market.

"It isn't good." He moved closer and lowered his voice, the heat of his body warming her back. "I suspect it has more to do with Alicsar than we may know."

"Like maybe he's letting the Shadow Soldiers into the capital?" She shook her head. "I doubt it, Thorne."

The commander released a heavy breath. "Not quite that."

The Shadow Soldiers continued to roam the small market, never once stopping to speak to any of the vendors, not even pausing to speak to one another. They never did say a word, Eliza thought, recalling two weeks before when the King's guards had successfully caught a soldier attempting to flee. No matter how hard she, the Blood Witches, and the guards worked, the soldier hadn't uttered a sound.

At the command of the Dark Master, the soldier had ceased to live—all magic keeping him alive severed.

Eliza had failed that day to create a blood connection to that magic. She swore she wouldn't fail again.

A figure appeared from the alley behind them. Thorne wrapped one arm around Eliza, forcing her to still, as a scrawny peddler searched the shadows and city above before entering the protected market. The barrier rippled ever so slightly around his lithe frame, almost silver in colour, but it disappeared just as quickly.

The peddler shuffled closer to the destroyed fountain, back hunched. The soldiers, who finished walking the perimeter of the market, turned to face the newest patron. Their eyes—a mix of crimson and darkness—caught the peddlers gaze; despite the distance, Eliza made out the colour as clearly as Thorne's.

"What do they want with *him?*" she whispered.

Thorne uncoiled himself from her and unsheathed the sword that permanently remained at his side. "We're about to find out."

Eliza tightened the shadows around them as they inched closer; a secure blanket that would do nothing against the Dark Master's magic. Regardless, she focused more of her energy on the protection spell, while also working furiously at the threads that tied the barrier together. If she could untangle the spell protecting the Shadow Soldiers, then she and Thorne could enter and capture the two before they could escape.

Or at least, she hoped that would be the case.

Sometimes her plans didn't quite work how she intended.

Eliza swallowed hard and, with quick fingers, worked the intricate spell in front of her. It was like a knitted rug, tightly knotted and beautifully crafted. Seamless, even, in the way it wove together to form a beautiful tapestry of spell work and magic. But somewhere along the way, a stitch had been dropped and forgotten.

Eliza searched for that missing stitch; that one thread that could undo everything the Dark Master had tied together. Her fingers moved along imaginary lines of stitches, counting rows upon rows of handcrafted spells.

The magic leapt at her, burning the bracelet around her wrist. Eliza flinched, biting the inside of her cheek, but she furrowed her brows and kept working. A bead of sweat raced down her cheek, but she squeezed her eyes shut, focused on the dark magic, the smell of sulphur, and the taste of copper as her finger worked to dismantle the spell.

This is the Dark Masters work, alright, she thought, fingers growing sore and magic running thin. *He doesn't make mistakes.* The bracelet—her shackle to the Blood Witches—grew warm and heavy with warning.

And yet...

She found the loose thread, and the entire spell unravelled before her eyes.

2

SHADOWS & SECRETS
ELIZA

The shadows that were once wrapped tightly around Eliza and the commander fell away as the barrier collapsed. Uncertain cries rang out in the cold afternoon as the stench of dark magic and potions perfumed the air.

Eliza breathed in once as her eyes locked on the Shadow Soldiers. She exhaled as the first dagger flew towards her.

The shield went up immediately; a barely visible wall that covered herself and the commander. The dagger collided with the magic and lodged itself within the threads of her spell. The blade, soaked in the remnants of Dark Magic, could have broken through her spell.

Instead, it dropped with the shield.

Eliza recalled all her lessons; the long nights spent in the barracks with Thorne learning how to wield a sword, the days in the games park mastering spell after spell with Celia at her side.

Magic warmed her fingertips. She lifted her hand at the approaching Shadow Soldier, fire burning the palm of her hand, and aimed the magic at his chest.

The soldier landed on his back, and as he slid, the other jumped in with his sword raised. Thorne met the second soldier's blow with one of his own, cutting through his armour like butter. The Shadow Soldier slumped, but it did not stop him from rising again.

Eliza focused on her soldier, who had climbed to his feet, smoke rising from the burnt fabric around his chest. A blade now hung loosely in his grip, the weapon dripping in Dark Magic. The Dark Master's power circled the sword, woven deep into the metal.

The soldier swung, the arc wide, narrowly missing her stomach. She clapped her hands together and a wave of magic sliced the air and threw the soldier back once more.

A loud bang from an alley across from her—not the one she and Thorne had been hiding in, but another that had been hidden by cloth—drew her attention. Stall owners were carrying their illegal wares into the darkness, but there was another figure hiding in the shadows.

The informant.

Shit.

Eliza had been too focused on the immediate threat that she hadn't even noticed the Dark Master's informant scurrying away.

She spared her friend a look; their eyes met over the chaos, and when she looked at the informant, he followed her gaze. The shallow nod was all she needed for her to duck under the Shadow Soldier's arm and chase after the peddler who was carrying away the Dark Master's secrets.

A set of stairs led into the alley, but she flew them and landed hard on the balls of her feet. The sellers still caught in the alley jumped aside for her, their shaky voices a dull murmur in her ears. The peddler had her full attention; the hood, now a discarded piece of cloth at her feet, could no longer conceal the weathered face of the man. Lines marred his scarred skin; his head smooth, save for a few tufts of hair.

He looked sick, dying. Not at all the type the Dark Master liked to keep in his control.

The peddler looked from the hood to her, and ran.

She whispered a spell beneath her breath, and the hood flew into her grasp. As she ran, she focused on the peddler's essence, the part of him attached the material. In New Orleans, as a girl, she'd learnt how to find people based on the trace they left on their belongings. Boredom during summer break had left her pickpocketing tourists and ultimately hunting them down later to return their wallets or cell phones.

In Cadira, however, she'd learnt how to hone the skill and use it like another sense. The connection to the land, as well as her growing connection to Blood Magic, gave the spells she'd learnt in the mortal world a whole new meaning—and a whole lot more power.

Eliza clutched the hood between near frozen fingers, and the intricacies of the spell ignited on her fingertips. Her palms warmed as the hood emitted a soft glow which led her down the winding streets of the Cadiran capital after the informant, who pushed through the busy streets without a care for the civilians who watched in confusion.

But as she passed, the people parted. They knew who she was— what her presence meant. The whispers followed her like a creeping darkness; something new always lurking over her shoulder.

No one, however, stepped in to stop the informant from escaping.

Eliza blew out a frustrated breath as her lungs screamed at her. The last few weeks, she'd done the necessary training to keep herself in shape. She never knew when she'd need to run for her life, so spending a few mornings every week running through the games-park like her life was on the line didn't seem so bad now, as she sprinted after the peddler.

The air was icy from the winter that never wanted to end. Spring seemed to be getting further and further away, pushed aside by the magic that coursed through the veins of this world. Dark Magic begged for dark souls, bred in the hopelessness of a long, harsh winter. Eliza saw the effect the never ending cold had on the people of the city; they were frozen, starving, and seeking heat where heat would not survive.

The crowd thickened and the informant disappeared amongst the people. Gone.

Eliza stumbled to a stop, breath heaving from her tight chest. The hood was still warm, telling her he was close, but she couldn't pick him out in the crowd. There were too many people wearing the same muted colours. Too many men with heads bare of any hair. There were too many people who looked sickly.

Shit.

Eliza ran a hand over her face as the hood swayed loosely from her fingertips. *Not again*, she thought, sweeping her gaze over the people. *Not again.*

The buildings surrounding her looked identical to the ones she'd passed while hunting the Shadow Soldiers. Houses of different colours—some red, others beige, another green—were built on top of one another, towering over the streets and the people lining them. Eliza spun in a slow circle; hidden between two brown coloured buildings, a tavern, painted black with windows darkened by smoke, offered some idea of where she might be.

But the residential quarter of the city, lined by those escaping famine caused by the darkness of the Dark Master and hope that the lost prince's return meant change, hid the peddler too well.

She closed her eyes and tightened her grasp on the hood. The bracelet warmed in warning, but she furrowed her brow and focused on the scratchy material.

Where are you? The limp fabric grew colder, heavy with the wet winter air.

And then the hood warmed once more, scalding her cold hands.

Eliza ducked as a fist appeared in her peripheral vision, a blur as it rushed towards her. The body belonging to the fist fumbled, careened, then snarled something Eliza would never repeat and ran again, entering a crowd of similar faces.

If she weren't already in pain from running, she would roll her eyes and shout something at him. But instead she took off, darting through the gathered civilians whose whispers guided her to the informant.

His looks were deceiving, she'd give him that. Upon first glance, he looked as if he could barely walk, let alone sprint through a city slick with snow and sludge so heavy it had turned the once packed earth of the roads to mud.

Her foot slid from beneath her, but she steadied herself, cursing under her breath.

The informant turned sharply down an alley; if he had continued straight, he would have made it to the frozen lake at the edge of the capital. Eliza spotted several small children skating along the thick ice, their laughs and screams audible despite the loud song of the city and the heavy thump of her heart pounding in her ears.

She swung into the alley, but wasn't sure what to expect when she stopped.

Certainly not the informant, pinned to the wall with ice.

Certainly not the man standing before her.

Certainly not the feelings that crashed into her upon meeting the golden eyes of Cadira's most respected—and feared—warlock.

It was like a hurricane crashing down on her; fear and anger and guilt and shame, happiness and relief and excitement, and something else that made her heart race and her mind foggy. The emotions swirled and pummelled her until she wondered if she'd lost her footing and was somehow lost to the thick mud at her feet.

Amitel, centuries old, yet looking no older than twenty, with messy golden blonde hair and sun-kissed skin. After weeks of wondering where he might be, what had happened once the Dark Master realised one of his most important pawns was gone, she half expected him to either be dead or in hiding. He certainly looked like he'd seen better days.

There were dark circles under his eyes, and a hollowness to his cheeks. His eyes—which were normally so beautiful, so wonderful and ethereal—were shadowed with a darkness that worried her. The rumpled shirt, the stench of alcohol... he looked as if he'd stumbled out of a tavern.

She wanted to feel sorry for him; wanted hug him and punch him for making her worry. For making her feel like that after all he had done to her.

Instead, she clenched her jaw and spared the Dark Master's informant the briefest of looks, if only to make sure he was still alive.

"What are you doing here, Amitel?" she asked, crossing her arms.

His throat bobbed as he swallowed. "You look good, love."

For a moment, she couldn't breathe. The sound of his voice was both a melody and a bad-dream, stolen away by the memories of hot wind and sand hiding between clenched, bloody fists. The feel of his blood coating her fingers was a whisper against her skin, warm and magical, terrifying and haunting.

"Don't call me that and cut the crap." She scowled, and ignored the rapid beat of her heart. He'd almost gotten her killed before. "You look like you crawled out of a sewer."

A smile cracked across his lips. "You're still a pleasure, I see." His gaze roamed her body. She wasn't sure if she'd changed much in his eyes after two months; she wondered if he noticed that her hair was darker thanks to a bottle of dye she'd found in her bathroom back in New Orleans, or that her body was denser, shaped by more muscle. She'd gained weight since moving into the palace, which she attributed to sleepless nights and eating stolen chocolates.

Most of all, she wondered if she looked older, more like the Ecixes he knew in his long life.

Eliza didn't respond.

Amitel met her stare, smirked. "It looks like you've been busy. Chasing down... the homeless? I didn't think the king would have you, his most prized possession, doing his dirty work."

The scowl deepened on her lips. "He's an informant of the Dark Master. Thought you two might already be acquainted."

Hurt flashed in the warlock's eyes, but only for a moment. He smothered all other emotions as he strode towards her.

She didn't have time to step away or move; suddenly, he was in front of her, their bodies inches apart. Eliza was forced to look up at him to meet his stare. Her breath caught in her throat as the burnt gold of his irises caught the meagre light of the dying sun.

His gaze burned with a fierceness that made her heart skip a beat. Standing before her, Eliza wasn't sure what to think. She wasn't even sure if she should breathe, he was so close.

"Sorry love, but you already know: the Dark Master and I cut ties the minute I chose to follow you into those damned tunnels. The only thing he wants from me now is a slow death." His eyes darkened, a splash of red bleeding into the gold. When he blinked, it disappeared, and confusion rippled across his stoic expression. He took a step back, putting enough space between them that Eliza could finally breathe again.

"And you know I don't believe you," she replied, putting more distance between them.

Before Amitel could respond, the informant made a sound. She'd almost forgotten why she was even *in* the alley in the first place.

Pushing past Amitel, she strode towards the informant, who was still locked in place with a harness made of ice. Without looking back, she asked, "Your doing?"

She felt his presence at her back before he spoke. "Had a feeling you might want to speak to him without worrying he might run." He leaned down, lips a whisper from her ear, the stench of whisky heavy on his breath. "You're welcome... *love.*"

It took too much self-control for her to *not* ram her elbow into his chest. *He's a drunken fool*, she thought, pursing her lips. And he likely wanted something from her.

With the scowl still set on her face, she eyed the informant. "What were you going to give the Dark Master's soldiers?"

The man didn't respond. Instead, he squeezed his eyes shut, like if he thought on it hard enough, she and Amitel would disappear and he could go free.

But Eliza waited, arms crossed, her impatience growing. It was cold, her lungs were burning, and all she wanted to do was curl up with a movie and forget she was the target of a mysterious psycho who wanted her for her magic.

A mysterious psycho with a worm inside the capital.

A worm she finally had her hands on.

"What does the Dark Master want?" she asked.

The peddler finally opened his eyes. "Nothing from you, you little bi—"

Amitel slammed his fist into the wall beside the man's head. Eliza tried not to flinch or wince, but the force rocked the building, rattling shutters and breaking free loose stone.

"Answer her," was all Amitel said. His boots scuffed the earth behind her as he paced. She tried not to look back and say something along the lines of *piss off.*

The peddler looked from her to Amitel, then back, eyes widening. "I—I don't, I d—don't know."

A frustrated breath left her lips. "What were you planning on telling the Shadow Soldiers? What were you giving them?"

"They-they wanted s—something about an Alastor Verendus. I was s—supposed to g—give them the name."

Eliza narrowed her eyes. "What's so important about him?"

The peddler's eyes unfocused for a moment; he looked behind her, and his lips formed words with no sound. Then he uttered, "He's the God of War."

Eliza didn't have time to react as the informant went limp. Amitel released him from his icy shackles, but the body dropped to the sludge in a heap, and did not move.

No. No!

She dropped to her knees and checked the man's pulse, but she felt nothing.

"He's dead," she whispered, eyes wide. She didn't see the human life at her feet. She didn't hear Amitel as he whispered something in her ear.

Her blood pounded in her veins, so loud it drowned out the busy song of the city.

Blood.

"Necromancy," she murmured, and stood.

Amitel reached for her, but she stepped out of his grasp. "Eliza, wait—"

But she was already cutting her palm and spilling blood on the snow. The bracelet was like a dull warning in the back of her mind, one she actively ignored as her access to the deep-rooted magic of Cadira exploded around her.

There were threads of magic spilling down the streets and through the stone walls around her. The arterial veins of Cadira's power focused the flow of spiritual energy; one snaked down the alley she stood in, another followed the street she'd sprinted down. With her were dozens of spirits, all different ages, shapes, and colours, some mortal and some half-Fae.

Eliza searched the sea of faces, blood pounding in her ears. The voices of the dead were louder now, insistent, forcing her to listen, to be wary.

But she couldn't find the face of the peddler.

Eliza knelt again, her movements like that of a marionette. Her physical body did what her spirit told it to do. The body drew the knife along the exposed hand of the informant, forcing blood from a heart that no longer beat. Her dagger dripped with it, mixing with her own.

A spell she'd been practicing with her Blood Witch trainer slipped from her lips, the ancient language of the Blood Witches forming on her tongue in a way that wouldn't seem natural if it weren't for the fact that deep in her mind, she knew every word and what they meant, because the Ecix always knew, her past lives a dim whisper in her mind.

The blood on the tip of her dagger darkened, turning to soot as it fell. Eliza hesitated before lowering the dagger from her line of sight. She racked her brain for what that meant; Lennox, her trainer, and her Blood Witch *Athir* had told her, but the memory danced on the edges of her mind...

She caught it, and flipped it open.

"When the blood turns dark, the spirit is no longer on this plane," her Athir *said.*

Eliza frowned. "Is there a way to guide the spirit back?"

"Yes. It is hard, something you should be able to do, but your training..."

The sigh slipped from Eliza's lips before she could stop it. "Right. I'm behind."

Her Athir *grimaced. "Very much so, yes."*

Eliza released her hold on the necromancy and Blood Magic. A scream of frustration threatened to tear from her throat. A splitting headache formed at her temples, pounding with the force of a wrecking ball.

"Eliza..." Amitel touched her shoulder, but she shook him off.

"It's too late." She stepped away from the body, from the warlock. A tingle in her wrist made her look down at the bracelet, which warmed, a calling card from Lennox.

Releasing a breath, Eliza shook her head. "I have to go."

"We need to talk," was all he said.

Before stepping out of the alley, she looked back. "Find someone else who will listen. I need to go."

And so she joined the masses, ignoring the small flare of magic that followed her departure.

3

THE WARLOCK'S TRUTH
CELIA

Celia watched her letter disappear, ash circling the small writing desk before floating through her open window and out into the dreary afternoon. It had been hard writing back, answering questions about her time outside of the mountains and the Blood Witches, but she wrote back each time the young witch called on her, even when it hurt to do so.

All is fine, Celia thought, standing. She smoothed the front of her pale-blue dress, biting her lip. *All will be fine.*

Her gaze drifted down to the stacks of books, the only company she'd been keeping since her arrival back in the Cadiran capital after the sickness took her. *A sickness born of the Dark Master*, she knew. Shadow Sickness, Lennox called it.

Celia pressed a hand to her abdomen where the dull ache originated. The pain would spread to her spine and head in only a matter of hours, but she knew she wouldn't be able to see Lennox until midnight, once the palace—and her friends—were asleep.

But that didn't make the pain disappear, or stop her fear from taking over.

The Shadow Sickness would dredge up too many questions—none of which she had answers for.

Closing her eyes, Celia sucked in a cooling breath and released it slowly. *Soon*, she thought. Celia only hoped her superior would have the tonic finished in time.

A low hum of magic, like a bee hovering by her ear, made her open her eyes. Blood Magic tingled over her flesh in warning, warming her chilled skin and cold fingers.

Celia rushed to her balcony, throwing open the glass doors. From her position, the entire city lay before her; a strange beast alive with magic and noise, which only grew as more people from around Cadira entered the capital. But even with the packed bodies, her Blood Magic was visible within the white and grey of the city.

Eliza had stepped out of the boundary, beyond where she was permitted to go.

The doors to the balcony closed behind Celia as she stepped away, returning to the desk. She pursed her lips and returned to an open book of herbology. The magic swimming in her veins, which connected her to the bracelet around Eliza's wrist, gave no indication that her sister was hurt or in danger.

Brandon is with her, and she is safe. Celia closed her eyes and rubbed a hand against her temples. She hoped Lennox wouldn't notice, but her superior always did.

Celia returned to her book, sketching symbols in her grimoire and ideas for spells, though she couldn't concentrate on the words in front of her or the magic in her grimoire. Instead, her magic, tethered to Eliza and the bracelet, made her heart race.

A brush of familiar magic made the hairs on the back of her neck stand on end. Her hands curled into fists as a calling card appeared on the table in front of her. Only four words, and yet her stomach squeezed with anger and fear that he had returned to do more damage.

We need to talk.

—Amitel

No location, no time.

Four words after months of silence. A small appearance at the gathering where King Bastian announced Eliza and Alicsar's engagement, but nothing more.

Celia clenched her jaw and stood. Dropping the letter on the desk, she donned a black cloak, leaving her hair unbound as she pulled the hood over her head. The magic of her blood swelled and rose to the surface, closing around her with a warmth she missed.

Closing her eyes, she called upon a portal. In her mind, she envisioned a silver light wrapping around her, like smoke, but warm, inviting. A building appeared in her mind; a common structure for the wealthier districts in the capital. A brownstone building wedged between identical structures, with a beautiful lemon tree in the front courtyard, always in bloom, always dropping fruit no matter the season.

Celia took a step and opened her eyes. A chilling breeze picked up loose strands of her dark hair and whipped them around her face. Wrapping her arms around herself, she frowned, taking in the dead lemon tree and unkempt courtyard.

The pavers were covered in a thick sludge that might have once been snow. She followed a set of footprints through the mush up to the front door, which sat ajar.

Leaves, dragged in by whoever had entered before her, littered the entryway. Celia called upon her magic as she stepped across the threshold. The apartment Amitel stayed in when he visited Cadira was empty of anything valuable. It smelt damp, like forgotten memories and lost time. The furniture was covered with white sheets, there was no food in the kitchens, and not even a servant caring for the place.

Amitel, who liked exquisite things and had expensive taste, looked like he hadn't touched his upper-city apartment in years.

Celia stopped in the doorway of the sitting room. Releasing her magic, she sighed. "Is he here?" she asked, crossing her arms.

Brandon Thorne spun, eyes wide. He reached for the sword at his side; a beautifully designed blade forged by the Brotherhood at the request of her sister, Isolde. The pommel was that of a raven, inlayed with jewels charmed to protect him.

His dark grey eyes found hers, and he dropped his hand from the sword. "Looks like he hasn't been here in a while."

Brandon tossed the message onto a coffee table and scrubbed a hand over his face. The same four words that had been on her own calling card appeared on the one before her.

"This could be some kind of ploy," she replied, entering the sitting room. She stalked to the letter as another line appeared. "*Down by the lake. Across from the King's Tavern.*" Celia looked up and handed Brandon the new message. "That doesn't sound like the Amitel we know."

Brandon's dark eyes drifted over the words, jaw ticking. "I don't think we know Amitel at all."

~

They arrived at the tavern just as the sky was darkening with another threat of snow. The weather had been growing worse. There was no sign of spring, nothing to indicate the icy suffering would end.

Celia stepped up to a window and looked in. She spied drunks and women from the brothel several doors up inside the tavern, and a couple of palace guards on their break. It was past midday, but the room was full, but none of the seats were occupied by a golden-haired warlock.

Brandon stepped up beside her, emotions masked. She sensed the anger boiling beneath the surface. "You think he's actually in there?" he asked.

Celia stiffened, then turned towards the shadows. "He has been. I sense his magic..." She hesitated. "Eliza was there too. Today. She used Blood Magic."

Brandon stiffened. "Amitel must have found her," he replied, running a hand through his dark hair. "I don't know if he hurt her—"

"He didn't." She touched his forearm. She opened herself up to the connection between her and Eliza, reaching for the bracelet around Eliza's wrist. She was far from their location now, back within the palace. "We would know by now. I feel her back at the palace, where she should be for her lessons with Lennox."

Brandon nodded, clenching his jaw. "Let's go see if Amitel is still waiting."

They stalked to the mouth of the alley, where the light of the city barely penetrated the darkness swarming within. She shivered, but not because of the cold; magic coursed over her. It was familiar, one she thought she knew well.

Amitel.

Celia waved a hand, and the magic dispersed. No Amitel waiting for them, but was she surprised? He liked to play games. There was, however, a body lying in the snow.

Celia waited as Brandon approached it cautiously, and knelt to look at the face.

"The informant." Brandon released a heavy breath. He rose, gaze burning into her, but she couldn't look at him.

Her eye caught a figure walking down the alley. Tall, lithe frame and mass of golden hair, deep and old magic used like a cloak to protect him. As he stalked closer, Celia could make out dark circles beneath his eyes, the gauntness of his cheeks, and the hollow look that passed over his face as he took her in. He looked like he'd been dragged through the nine realms of the netherworld, spat out by Kaia, the Goddess of Darkness, and stepped on by Azula herself.

The usual bright spark in his eyes was gone, something dark and dead seeping into his golden irises instead.

A smirk worked its way across Amitel's lips, but the arrogance didn't reach his eyes.

Brandon stiffened beside her, his hands going to his weapons. "Every fibre in my being is telling me to take Amitel's throat," he murmured, low enough for only her to hear.

Their long-time friend had betrayed them, and for what?

Calm down, Brandon, she thought, reaching out to brush her hand against his. Anger radiated like heat off her friend, swallowing his energy.

To Brandon, it didn't matter that Amitel had *tried* at the last minute to help Eliza. It didn't matter that he'd been stabbed in the gut—though, quite frankly, Celia decided the warlock deserved that.

Amitel stopped and looked between the two of them. "It's nice to see you, darling Celia," he said, looking her over. Those golden eyes flickered to Brandon's. "You look about ready to kill me."

"You called on us," Celia said, tensing as his eyes found hers again. "Why?"

Brandon stalked to Amitel and shoved him against the wet brick. Their faces were inches apart, Brandon's breathing harsh, while Amitel seemed unbothered. Celia rushed to Brandon's side and pulled on his arm, but the soldier remained still, glare locked on the warlock.

Amitel's dead stare met his. "What?"

"You betrayed us," Brandon hissed. He shoved his old friend harder. "You betrayed *her*."

The warlock's eyes narrowed slightly. "What exactly did she tell you about what happened under the mountain?"

"Enough, you coward."

Something burned in Amitel's eyes, and his irises swirled, a mix of crimson entering the burning gold. "Then you have *no idea* what happened. You stayed behind with Celia, leaving her alone with *him*." Amitel looked him over once and spared her a glance, before returning his darkening gaze to Brandon. "Is it me that you are mad at, or yourself?"

Brandon swung, but his fist met stone instead of the warlock's jaw. Amitel vanished, and reappeared behind them.

"Brandon!" Celia rushed forward, pulling him away. He'd broken the skin on his knuckle.

Amitel chuckled. "Get it out of your system?"

Brandon sent him a scathing look. In a couple of hours, his hand would heal completely, but Celia wondered if Amitel's words had left a far greater wound.

She sent Brandon a look, but from the rage that darkened his eyes, she knew he was contemplating going after Amitel again for good measure. Their eyes locked, and for a moment, she prepared to restrain him.

Instead, Brandon sucked in a breath and took two steps back. "What the hell do you want, Amitel?" he asked, clenching his jaw.

Celia moved to Brandon's side and softly took his clenched fist, wrapping her fingers around his knuckles. She focused on the split skin, the blood beading along his fingers, the ache deep within the bone left from striking the wall. She let her magic spill from her hands and into his, restitching the skin and cleaning the wound, numbing the ache by mending the damaged bone. There was a burst of warmth before she let go, and when he flexed his fingers, there was no evidence of the punch; the skin healed, blood gone.

Amitel crossed his arms. "Have you had a chance to speak to Eliza yet?"

Celia shook her head before Brandon could respond. "No. When I left, she was supposed to be at her lessons with Lennox." Celia wrapped her arms around herself as a chilling breeze tunnelled through the alley. "Why?"

The warlock looked down at the body. Celia had almost forgotten about the informant, who lay dead in the snow, reeking of Blood Magic and darkness. Hesitantly, she knelt beside it and lifted a hand over the man's dirty face.

The lines of his face were filled with deep sadness and depravity. The hollowness of his skin, burned by the frigid air, sagged off his bones—bones rusted with the influence of dark magic.

Celia snatched her hand back and held it to her chest. The poor man had been left with no other choice. Rising, she whispered a prayer to Azula and hoped that when he found peace, he would be greeted by forgiveness.

"Did you kill him?" Brandon asked Amitel, sparing her a concerned glance.

Celia offered him a small smile in return before focusing on Amitel once more.

"No." Amitel shook his head, gaze falling to the body. "The Dark Master did."

"Convenient," Brandon muttered.

Amitel narrowed his eyes. "True. Eliza probably thought so too. But I can assure you, I don't work for the Dark Master, not anymore." His gaze cut to Celia. "I never really did."

"I don't believe you." The words were automatic, almost like she'd rehearsed them over and over again in her head. They should have been enough, and yet... something in the pit of her stomach warned her to think otherwise.

Amitel released a heavy breath. "Do you remember when we first met?" Amitel asked Brandon. "Do you remember Laziroth and Enya, the Child?"

Brandon scoffed. "Of course I do."

Celia frowned and looked up to take Brandon in; the strong line of his jaw ticked, but the anger was gone from his storm grey eyes. Instead, shadows played within the flecks of blue, swirling with memories she'd never been privy to. A light flickered behind his eyes.

"It just *clicked* in your mind, didn't it?" Amitel smirked. "*There will be a girl with great power. An Ecix. And she will be hunted and broken before she can rise. But she will be betrayed. By me.*"

From what Celia knew, Brandon had spent years trying to forget what had happened in Laziroth almost two hundred years ago. He'd been trying to forget the Resurgence, and Isolde's death. He'd walked away from the Brotherhood, away from the only life he'd been willing to know. The war had sent fractures throughout Cadira and the rest of their world, which she now saw being filled with the darkness of the Dark Master.

"The Child gave me a whole prophecy. I wanted to ignore it, but you know the old stories..." Amitel chuckled to himself. "Ignore an oracle, face the wrath of ten angry Gods."

Celia frowned. Her gaze drifted over the man she had once considered a close friend, but she couldn't recognise the arrogant warlock she'd met two hundred years ago.

Instead, she saw a mess of a man; a shell. Celia wondered what else had happened in Laziroth.

"Why not tell me?" Brandon asked. The anger had burned down

to a dying ember, replaced by exhaustion.

Amitel met his stare. "Because I was sure you'd kill me before anything like that could happen." He shook his head. "It was my own burden to bear. You were angry and sad over losing the woman you loved. The last thing you needed was to know I would betray the next in her line of rebirths."

"You could have spoken to me," Celia murmured. She stepped up to Amitel; she was a head shorter than him, and when he looked down to meet her gaze, something in his eyes softened.

He shrugged. "You were also grieving. I'm an old warlock. I could handle it." Amitel spared Brandon another glance. "I did what I had to do to protect her."

"I don't understand why you didn't just say something sooner." Brandon ran a hand over his face, shaking his head. "You could have let us in on your plan."

"Perhaps. But I'd gotten so used to doing things on my own, that telling you two didn't seem... fair. It was my prophecy. *I* had to betray her. *I* had to stand by while she was hunted and hurt. *I* had to get in the Dark Master's good graces. And it disgusted me how easily I could do it. But I did it. Until I couldn't." Something new burned in the warlock's gaze. "The reason why I'd gone to Mesah in the first place was because I'd had a bad feeling. I didn't know Dorin and Alicsar were one in the same. That was new to me. But I had a feeling she was going to get hurt. So when I entered the destroyed city and *neither* of you were there, I knew what I had to do."

Celia pursed her lips. Uncertainty wared within her; the longer one lived, the easier it became to lie. She had learnt that from an early age. The Blood Witches wove lies into truths like spinsters. Their lies were intricate, a practice immortals had perfected.

"Dorin tricked us," she mused, head cocked. "But you betrayed the Dark Master and helped Eliza." Even the words tasted strange on her tongue.

"Thank you for going after her."

Celia's gaze snapped to Brandon. The commander's eyes dropped to the grey sleet covering the alley, his lips twisted down. She wanted to ask what he was thinking, but was afraid with Amitel so close. Guilt churned in Brandon's gaze; he blamed himself for what happened in Mesah, for Eliza being alone. And she knew, somewhere deep in his mind, he blamed her, too—for leaving Eliza, for the sickness taking over.

Celia swallowed the thickness in her throat and looked away. She hadn't been able to protect herself then, and it had almost cost them Eliza. It had almost cost her the chance of avenging Isolde.

Celia trusted Eliza—knew she was capable of protecting and saving herself—but she also knew she'd do anything to protect the ones she loved; to save innocent lives. Eliza had seen Amitel and rather than letting him die, she'd saved his life and managed to save herself. Cut, bruised, stabbed in the back, all the while holding onto the hope that maybe there was still good in the world.

Celia could not forget that, either.

Amitel stepped forward. "I did what needed to be done. Otherwise I would have stayed out of it."

Celia almost believed him, but said nothing.

"But I swear to Azula, if you do anything to hurt her again, I'll kill you myself," Brandon muttered, crossing his arms.

Amitel smirked, shaking his head. "I'm sure you will." He took a lazy step back, head cocked. "I did *everything* to protect her, so the Dark Master couldn't take her. I did what the oracle foretold."

And before either of them could say another word, Amitel was gone; slipping into the shadows as a new rain of snow drifted from the sky, leaving them to care for the dead informant, and Celia to stew on what both men revealed.

~

Celia knew better than to believe every word from Amitel's lips.

She wondered if believing Amitel first would help Eliza heal, just a bit. Whether it would give her the permission she needed to forgive him, too.

Celia turned to Brandon, who looked lost in the turmoil of his own thoughts. She opened her mouth to say something, but no words were forming on her lips.

Was he struggling with his own ability to believe and forgive, she wondered, or was he struggling with something else?

Finally, he shook his head. She touched his arm. "Brandon—"

He turned and looked at her, but shook his head again. "I'm sorry. We should return to the palace. You should talk to Eliza."

He left the alley before she could form a coherent thought. It took her a moment to realise he was leaving her with a corpse, so with a quick flick of her wrist and a shake of her head, the body disappeared—hopefully to reappear in the palace morgue. She rushed after her companion, who was disappearing into the thickening crowds.

Too many people were hurrying to find cover in case the casual fluttering of snow turned into a raging storm. Celia looked up into the darkening sky. It had been calm for several days; a storm was certainly close, brewing on the horizon.

Celia caught Brandon at the edge of the great lake. The channel that led out into the eastern sea was unfrozen, but much of the lake itself had a thick table of ice covering it. Dozens of children who had been out skating were being called back in by their parents, and stalls that had once lined the shoreline were packing up for the day.

Further along the lake, Celia spied the walls of the palace. It would take her a few minutes to walk to one of the many entrances, but she hesitated.

Brandon hadn't noticed her at his side. "Are you alright?" she asked, touching his arm.

He startled, blinking down at her. A moment passed, then he shook his head. "I'm fine," he murmured. "It was... it was something Amitel said."

Celia swallowed. "About the oracle?"

Brandon hesitated, but nodded. "Yes."

She wanted to ask more; his mission in Laziroth had always been a shadow in their friendship, something he spoke about rarely. She knew next to nothing about what had actually happened, aside from what he'd shared once he and Amitel had returned. And for nearly two hundred years, she'd kept her questions to herself.

Now, they threatened to break free.

"What really happened in Laziroth, Brandon?" she asked. "What did Amitel say to have you so... spooked?"

Her friend shook his head. "Nothing."

She clenched her jaw, and watched him shut down. "Brandon—"

"Celia." She stopped and met his gaze. Something in the storming greys and blues of his eyes made the fight leave her completely.

Finally, she nodded. "I'll see you back at the palace, then."

As she turned to leave, she noticed the war in his eyes. Since returning from Mesah, there had been something different about him. She hadn't said anything, but she knew he was fighting something inside himself. Something to do with Isolde and Eliza, or his own guilt; she wasn't sure.

Celia wrapped her cloak around herself tightly as a sharp breeze cut over the lake, swirling snowflakes around her face. She lowered her head so that her cheeks were covered by her hood, protecting her from the icy wind.

The Laziroth mission had changed Brandon as much as the Resurgence had. It had been only weeks since Isolde's death when he'd walked away from the Blood Witches and Brotherhood. When he'd started taking jobs from mercenaries and other unsavoury characters. Seeing him after the Laziroth job had been her first time seeing him since the Resurgence.

Celia shook her head and released a heavy breath. Guards at one of the smaller entrances looked up as she approached. She said nothing, not even when one man's eyes widened. For most, it was clear she was a Blood Witch; immortal and beautiful and eternally young. She'd spent enough time at the palace to have earned a reputation, and most guards had, in some capacity, crossed her path.

The two at the door bowed, and without a word, opened the door for her. A blast of warmth hit her face as she entered a small hallway within the wall. There were several more soldiers within; some looked up at her appearance, but others kept their heads down.

The wall was several feet thick, with at least ten stories worth of walkways and staircases leading into darkness. Torches with flickering flames cut through the shadows, but they illuminated only a small patch of the wall.

Celia crossed to the other side and pulled open a wooden door leading into the palace gardens. Winter air split through the warmth, so she opened the door just enough to slip out into the darkening day. She let it close behind her, spared the two guards on this side of the door a glance, and started for the palace.

The gardens were enchanting in winter. The great hedges and bushes of crystal roses looked even more magical with a dusting of snow. On the other side of the gardens, Celia spied the top of the mighty golden dragon from the Great War, who continued to sleep despite the darkness clawing at their world.

The palace was alive when she finally made it inside through a side door Eliza had found. Her sister used it often to escape into the gardens, and it was otherwise forgotten by most. It led into a main hallway, close to a set of stairs up into the princes wing, and to the main library where Eliza spent most of her days.

Celia started for the study chambers that spread like honeycomb off the main library. One of the larger rooms had been claimed by the Blood Witches for Eliza's training. All texts on Blood Magic had been taken from the library proper and moved into the study room for easier access.

Whispers from servants followed Celia as she pushed back the hood of her cloak. No one stopped her though. She needed to talk to Eliza, especially after seeing Amitel. She needed to know what they had spoken about, what Eliza had learnt.

Had Amitel told her the truth of Laziroth? Celia hoped he hadn't. It would be too overwhelming, especially if neither she or Brandon had been there to confirm Amitel's story.

She shook her head, and stopped outside the study chamber. Waiting at the door, King Bastian of Cadira watched through a small window, his hands clasped behind his back. It was strange seeing him out of his office or meeting hall, especially with none of his personal guard surrounding him. Celia rarely saw him without his assortment of swords.

But there he was, watching Eliza.

As if sensing her there, King Bastian turned and regarded her with calm eyes. "Blood Witch Celia." He offered her a pleasant smile. "I was beginning to wonder where you were. You rarely miss Elizabeth's lessons."

Celia smiled in return. "I had to meet with Commander Thorne in the city. We had to deal with an... issue."

The king raised a brow. "I assume it concerns the Dark Master, then?"

She nodded. "There was an informant captured. He was dead before I arrived."

"That seems to happen often with the Dark Master's men." The king returned his attention to the window. "Did you learn anything new?"

"I'm not sure," she replied slowly. "There were some... difficulties understanding the information. Commander Thorne and I intend on working with Lennox." Lies were easy when it came to protecting Eliza. If the king knew what she was doing...

King Bastian remained quiet for a moment. Celia thought he might leave, but instead he turned to her completely. "How is Elizabeth's training? She spends so much time here and in the training halls that I fear she has little time for her etiquette lessons. She looks... tired."

Celia picked her next words carefully. She wasn't sure what the king was planning, but the last thing she wanted was for her words to be twisted against Eliza.

"She is doing exceptionally well, and everything new she learns, she applies to her training," Celia said, clutching her hands to her stomach. "She tires only because she rarely sleeps, and she rarely sleeps because she is afraid. Of the Dark Master."

And if she were allowed to actively join the search, she might feel more in control. Celia didn't dare say those words aloud though.

"Interesting." He nodded as if he understood, but she knew he didn't. Even though of all the people who would, it should have been him. He, who made a deal with the Blood Witches to hide a young Ecix in the mortal world so that she may later find his son. He, who made a deal with the Blood Witches that changed the trajectory of Eliza's life.

But King Bastian refused to see the similarities. "You are very devoted to your sister," he noted, gaze flickering to hers.

Celia swallowed hard, forcing a smile to her lips. "I have always dedicated myself to the Ecix. It is my job to protect her."

"Indeed..." The king's eyes darkened. "Be careful, Blood Witch Celia. You spend too much of your life dedicated to someone else, you lose sight of what is truly important. You lose sight of yourself."

Celia opened her mouth to answer, but no sound passed her lips. His words struck a chord inside her, deep in her chest. But he seemed less focused on her and more so on himself, gazing down at his gloved hands. Had he been speaking the words to her... or to himself, she wondered?

The king released a breath and straightened, making a move to leave. He paused at her side. "I have heard a rumour that Amitel has returned." His dark eyes were questioning, like he knew the answer, but wanted to test whether she'd lie to him. She almost considered doing so. "Am I correct?"

But she didn't. "Yes."

The king nodded, pleased. "Interesting. I might have a word with him, if he answers my call."

Celia said nothing as the king walked away. Let him call on Amitel, she decided. Because the closer Amitel was, the easier it was to watch him. Despite wanting to forgive him—for even believing—she knew deep down that in order to protect Eliza, she'd need to keep an eye on those capable of hurting her.

And that meant Amitel, too.

4

THE AETHER
ELIZA

Lessons with the Blood Witches all blurred together. Some required physical training, where Eliza learnt certain techniques to keep her blood flowing through her body in a way to maximise the magic swelling within her.

Sometimes, she learnt real spells; spells that had once taken up residence in her old, white grimoire, one Kay had gotten her. They were from another life; spells Eliza knew without knowing. Relearning them meant recognising the full potential of each one in a way she had never known before.

And on the rare occasion, Eliza learnt history. She had expected most of her training with Lennox to be found in books, impractical teachings used as punishment because she was trapped in the capital. Eliza had expected days of reading books carted down from the Labyrinth Mountains, hours of lectures and lessons about her past, her *wasted potential*.

On her first day, Eliza had asked about that. And on that first day, she'd been told the history of the Blood Witches was preserved and kept in their libraries hidden in the mountains. That outside of the mountains, no one would learn the truth. Not even about the Ecix.

So, Eliza practiced magic and glorified yoga instead, which only made her more curious about what really went on in the Labyrinth Mountains.

Eliza looked up as Lennox approached her desk. The tall, willowy woman always looked like she had a lemon pressed against her teeth. It hadn't taken Eliza long to realise the Blood Witches—besides Celia—hated being in the capital. They hated leaving their home in general.

"Today we begin your journey into the Aether," Lennox started, her gaze flicking from Eliza to the door. Eliza followed her eye and found Celia watching them from outside, but her sister disappeared before anyone could call her in.

Did Celia already know what had happened to the peddler? With Amitel? Had Thorne found the broken body of the man used by the Dark Master to deliver a message?

Something twisted in Eliza's stomach, bile rising in her throat. Her thoughts drifted back to Amitel, and a hand clamped around her throat, stealing her breath.

Eliza had been doing well pushing thoughts of her run-in with Amitel aside, but they flooded back in, as well as the informant, dead at her feet. His words floated in her mind, a reminder of what she needed to do—but couldn't, because she still had over an hour left with Lennox and her *Athir*.

Eliza blew out a breath, and found her *Athir*—the adoptive mother of the Ecix—watching her from the other side of the room. Eliza had only one memory of the woman who supposedly raised her until the age of five, and that memory was awash with the death of her *Athir's* biological daughter, who had sacrificed herself for Eliza all those years ago.

Looking away, Eliza pressed her lips together as Lennox walked to the other side of the room. She said something to *Athir*, who nodded and left the room.

"Where is she going?" Eliza asked. Her tongue felt heavy. She had barely spoken a word since her return to the palace.

Lennox raised a brow. "She is going on an errand. Nothing to worry about."

But it fed the kindling curiosity inside of Eliza. She wondered if her *Athir* even knew about the Aether, was even privy to that information.

One thing Eliza had been quick to learn: not every Blood Witch knew everything about the Ecix.

Lennox clasped her hands together and gave Eliza a bitter smile. "Today, you failed in locating a spirit." The words curdled in Eliza's stomach. "Your failure cost you information, did it not?"

Eliza didn't bother to ask how Lennox knew; the bracelet warmed, giving her the only answer she needed. So, Eliza nodded, keeping her lips pressed firmly shut.

"You entered what we consider a *passageway*. You did not quite enter the Aether proper, but you drew in enough magic to get you on the right direction. But you are not, unfortunately, strong enough on your own to travel into the land of the dead and return safely." Lennox paced the front of the room, and as much as Eliza didn't like her new teacher—she was no Davis Kindall, Keeper of the New Orleans wards, or Kay, exile of the Courts of Light—the need to know more about her power, about being the Ecix and having control over the dead, called to her.

Lennox continued, "You are rash, and do not think through the intricacies of a spell." Eliza opened her mouth to defend herself, but Lennox sent her a scathing look that shut her up. "The Aether is sacred. The passageway you entered today is about as close as any regular necromancer could get."

Except all the necromancers of Cadira are dead. Eliza didn't say it, but a sadness washed over her. Before learning the truth, Eliza had thought herself the last true necromancer of Cadira. Had thought she'd done something as a child to warrant being exiled and given to her grandfather and Kay because her birth parents didn't want her. It had been Kay who had warned her about the dangers of her power; how learning to use it would put a bullseye on her back.

But the truth had been worse.

"The Aether exists as a place for the dead to rest. All those who perish leave this world and enter the Aether through the passageways you found today."

"The only reason I could see it was because I tapped into the magic of Cadira," Eliza replied quietly. Lennox stopped and watched her for a moment, dark eyes burning. "For me, there are spirits that exist on the surface, where I can see them like I see you. The library is full of them, so is the palace. Sometimes I think they're really here and can't tell the difference. The passageway is like a hidden corridor, one I have to do a little extra work to see. I cut my hand, spill some blood, let it connect with the magic that flows through Cadira. The passageway is connected to that."

For a moment, Lennox remained quiet. But she nodded once and went back to pacing. "And do you have any... *inkling* of how you might enter the Aether from there?"

Silently, Eliza shook her head.

Lennox didn't stop, and instead made her way to one of the many stacks of books. "The exact nature of entering the Aether is unknown by many. All we have are recounts from the past Ecixes, who outlined their processes in grimoires and journals for those who came after.

"One way the High Witch found common was mediation. Many who came before you found their way into the Aether by opening their senses to that part of the world. They did not see it as a physical entrance, like you might expect, but it was a place they had to travel within their own minds."

Lennox stopped. "You are more prone to entering the Aether when you sleep, which is dangerous. You have travelled there on more than one occasion just by falling asleep. One wrong move, and you might never return."

Eliza swallowed thickly, and nodded. "Why do I go there in my dreams? Sounds like I need to be thinking about it, focusing on the Aether? Why do I just... appear there?"

"Your connection to Kay is why you find it easy to visit in your dreams. She is of the Court of Dreams, so her magic has made it... safe for you to visit in your sleep. However, without her magic to guide you—consciously or subconsciously—you are in more danger of trapping yourself with the dead."

Eliza had never thought Kay's magic would be guiding her in her dreams; what Eliza knew of Kay's past and connection to the Courts of Light was always minimal. Kay's past was always a mystery, a story she refused to tell—even though she loved spreading tales of whimsical magic and otherworldly beings.

"Your task today," Lennox said, cutting Eliza's thoughts short, "is to enter the Aether without the guidance of Kay, and while you are awake. Once you can identify the feeling of appearing there awake, I am sure you will learn how to stop yourself from travelling in your dreams."

Eliza nodded, and waited for Lennox's instruction. "Close your eyes," the Blood Witch murmured, suddenly much closer. "Free your mind of your attachments to this earth. Forget your friends, your family. Use your body as your anchor, and tether your spirit to the bones."

Closing her eyes, Eliza sucked in a deep breath and released it slowly. With each inhale, she pushed something aside; Thorne, and his strange behaviour since returning from Mesah; Celia, and her always hovering form; her grandfather, who she missed constantly; Kay, who she could only talk to through letters; Alicsar, the man she was destined to marry; and Amitel, with his betrayal and sudden return.

She let darkness surround her, and covered those thoughts in heavy weights, tying them down and locking them away. Each one went into a shoe-box, unmarked and plain, and when she put one on a shelf with the others, she released another breath.

A fog settled in her mind, and so she tethered herself to her bones, using the body she lived in as an anchor. It sank to the bottom of the sea floor, and she climbed up and up the chain towards the world of the dead, each rung a frustrated breath.

In the back of her mind, one of her little shoe boxes rattled, and before she could tuck it away again, it burst open.

Anger, sadness, relief, regret. It all swirled and dived and pushed her back down the chain. They were like sharks who had scented blood in the water, circling, keeping her from going further.

Anger attacked first, a Great White, sinking its teeth into her arm. With it came Amitel's face, the smirk that didn't meet his eyes, and his betrayal deep beneath the sand dunes. Then regret and relief gnawed on her legs, dredging up images of her friends, her family. And finally, sadness swallowed her fingers with thoughts of a life she could no longer return to, and she could no longer grip the chain. She sunk back down to her bones, and opened her eyes.

Eliza heaved a breath, head swimming. She blinked once, twice, against the bright light in their study room. Lennox watched her carefully from a desk in front of her, dark eyes searching and calculating.

"What happened?" she snapped, seizing the edge of the desk as she stood.

Eliza shook her head, rubbing her eyes. "I don't know. I was getting close, but..."

"But you let your worldly emotions stop you, didn't you?" Lennox's gaze was ice and anger. Eliza met her glare, but looked away just as quickly.

"I'm sorry," Eliza replied, closing her eyes. "I don't understand what happened."

"You will never be ready if you continue with this *attitude*," Lennox spat. "Your predecessors would be ashamed of you."

Eliza closed her eyes and tried to ignore the tears burning in the back of her throat; her head throbbed with Lennox's words, blood pounding in her ears.

Lennox tipped Eliza's chin with the tip of her pointed nail, forcing Eliza's stare back to hers. "You are *power*," she hissed, the silence of the chamber making her words echo. "You are *death*."

Eyes widening, Eliza pulled back sharply and shook her head. "I don't want to be *death*."

The Blood Witch gave her a twisted smile. "You are excused," Lennox said after a beat of silence. "I hope you do not lose your mind the next time the Aether claims your dreams."

~

Eliza's thoughts were a mess, a tangle of weeds that ruined yet another one of her training exercises. There was always something she did wrong, something that could have been done better. And with every snide remark that passed Lennox's lips about another Ecix, Eliza sunk further and further inside of herself.

Isolde did this when she surpassed her fourteenth winter.

The Ecix before her could do this as young as seven.

You cannot do this, and you are almost eighteen.

She hadn't been watching where she was going, too lost in her own thoughts to concentrate on the steps ahead of her.

The person appeared out of nowhere; a tall figure which she slammed into, who caught her before she could land on her arse in the middle of the palace hallway.

"Oh!" Eliza blinked up at the tall man. Her head cleared of all the thoughts that had distracted her. "I'm so sorry."

Henry Ivo gave her a smile and chuckled; he was one of her grandfather's oldest friends and one of the reasons why she'd been able to find the lost Cadiran prince in the first place. His silver hair was braided over one shoulder, and though he usually wore robes, he instead dressed in a fine tailored suit, similar to the ones of her world.

Ivo steadied her, patting her shoulder. "Are you alright, Miss Kindall?"

Eliza nodded. "Yes. I'm so sorry." The warmth of embarrassment flowed down her neck. "I was..."

"Lost in your own thoughts?" He raised a perfectly manicured silver brow. "It's alright. You were coming from your training, no?"

"Yes, I was." Eliza took a step back and surveyed where they were; her room was further down the corridor, beyond a bend. Along the walls were gorgeous paintings done by Cadiran artists she couldn't name, but they all depicted beautiful and ethereal landscapes that dotted the kingdom; she recognised one location as the winter palace. It had been her first stop when entering Cadira, the place she'd first met the king and Brandon Thorne.

Ivo cocked his head. "Is everything alright?"

Eliza blinked and shook her head, pushing those thoughts aside. "Yes, of course. Sorry."

"I take it your training isn't going well."

For a moment, she stayed silent. Releasing a breath, she shrugged. "The Blood Witches keep reminding me of how behind I am. The magic isn't coming easy, but I need to gain control of it."

"That is difficult," Ivo mused, "and I agree. But you struggle with it. Do you know why?"

"It might have something to do with growing up in New Orleans. I'm not sure, really. We're all learning new things about me, right?"

Ivo smiled, and it crinkled the corner of his eyes. "Yes, we are." He patted her shoulder again. It felt almost grandfatherly; she found some comfort in the Elder—a person who had once been a Keeper at one of the portals between Cadira and the mortal realm—being at the palace. It was almost like having her grandfather with her.

"I will look into your predicament," Ivo stated, pulling his hand away. Eliza opened her mouth to tell him not to worry, that she'd be fine, but he waved her away. "I promise I will find something to help you."

He left her in the corridor, his tall figure disappearing down a flight of stairs. Her thanks melted on her tongue as she turned and walked away.

~

Worry gnawed at Eliza, but she slipped into the familiar embrace of dreams. Like a mist that curled over the forest floor, it crawled into her mind and covered every inch of her consciousness.

The dagger weighed heavily in her hands, a gift and burden that could change the fate of her entire world—and could end her life. It whispered to her; its power a coil that wound around her heart. Magic like it knew her, wanted her to control it, danced over her skin.

Eliza tightened her grip on the hilt, heartbeat steady in her chest. She stared down at the long, curved blade as it caught the light of the full moons above her.

She looked up in surprise. Both moons, full. Wonder filled her at the sight. It was rare to see the twin moons full at the same time. The magnificence of it filled the sky, outshining the stars, blotting out the constellations.

A shiver raced down her spine as she looked back down at the dagger. A thick darkness worked its way from the shadows around her, slithering closer, inching towards the weapon in her hands.

The Dark Master.

His minions of darkness crept closer.

She didn't move, not out of fear. With the dagger in hand, she considered slaying them all before they could hurt her or anyone else she loved. Would it work? She didn't care, because she'd try, so that when she faced them in the waking world, she could cut them down before succumbing to fear again.

In the distance, a figure walked out of the shadows, a hood covering their face. It took little effort for her to realise who it was, who stalked her from the shadows. But standing beneath the light of Cadira's twin moons with the dagger, she felt invincible—safe. He could not touch her. Not again

He stopped at the edge of the light. It skimmed the darkness of the hood, giving her the faintest details: a strong, straight nose and jawline. It tickled at a memory of someone she knew.

Eliza took a step forward. She wanted to see beneath the hood, see who she was up against.

Another step.

The Dark Master did not back away, as if intent on letting her learn his true identity. Maybe he was tired of the lies. Maybe he wanted to be as free of his past as she did.

One more step.

The shadows seemed to darken around him. Eliza reached out with her free hand—

5

WHERE ROSES BLOOM
CELIA

Under the pale moon light, crystal roses bloomed. They reflected the milky glow of Cadira's twin moons, sparking a rainbow of light across the floor of the old greenhouse, illuminating forgotten plants that thrived in the sorrow of abandonment.

Celia traced the outline of a petal with the tip of her finger and smiled at the strange beauty. They were a creation of Wyld magic, born of the Fae lands and one of the few remnants of the strange creatures that once existed in Cadira. The roses grew no matter the season, withstanding the hottest days and coldest of nights. They bloomed no matter conditions, always beautiful, always hauntingly perfect.

Footsteps scraped against the stone of the abandoned greenhouse. Celia dropped her hand from the crystal roses and spun, clutching a hand to her chest as Lennox, her Blood Witch companion, entered the room.

The witch's dark eyes roamed the greenhouse. "What a sad, decrepit space," she murmured, hands clasped behind her back. She stopped in the centre next to a fountain. Her eyes swept over the blooming roses and found Celia's. "Why you like it is beyond me."

A hum of magic warmed Celia's blood, prickling the skin of her arms. "It has potential for beauty," Celia replied numbly, a wash of nausea ploughing into her, rocking her back a step. She sucked in a calming breath. "There is more to it than just abandonment and sadness."

Lennox cocked her head, a smile curling at the edges of her lips. "No one will find us here."

Celia wrapped her arms around herself and stepped away from the crystal roses. "You called on me, Lennox. I would very much like to know why."

The smile slipped from her superior's face. "I have strange news from our Brothers." Lennox approached, dark eyes roaming the greenhouse once more before landing on Celia. "They say the Wyld Hunt has blown their horn."

A shiver coursed down Celia's spine, eyes flashing back to the crystal roses.

Lennox continued, "It's been almost two centuries since their last hunt. The Brotherhood worry it may have something to do with the Dark Master. We reached out to our friends in the Seelie Court, but all is silent from the Fae."

Some legends said the Wyld Hunt, led by a ruthless Wylder Fae, signalled war. That the blow of their horn and the whisper of their horses meant the darkness of battle was on the horizon.

Two centuries ago, the Resurgence swept over north Cadira and destroyed everything in its path. Celia wondered if the horn had sounded before that fateful day.

She closed her eyes for a moment and sucked in a breath. The dying whisper of Isolde's voice still haunted her, creeping into her dreams. The promise Celia still hadn't fulfilled still sharp in her mind.

"Demons have been sighted, too," Lennox said. "They've even tried entering the mountains."

When Celia opened her eyes, she found Lennox shaking her head. There was no fear in her eyes, no worry over the demons or the Wyld

Hunt. Celia could not help but feel the numb hands of dread clasp around her throat.

"Are you alright, Celia?" Lennox asked, resting a hand on her shoulder.

Celia looked at the hand, then followed the length of the witch's arm, up to her unlined, unblemished face. How long had it been since they had been that close, Celia wondered numbly, as Lennox's lips parted and formed a soft *oh*.

It had been years, years where they both had chosen to lock away the soft candlelit moments in chests buried deep in their hearts.

Lennox blinked and dropped her hand. "I have something for you." She handed Celia a small, swirling vial of green liquid. It was the size of her thumb, the contents sour on her tongue, but it suppressed the remnants of her sickness. The concoction lasted only a few days, but Celia was grateful she had something to stave off the exhaustion, the vomiting and the pain that seized her.

Without a word, Celia pulled the cork from the vial and tipped it into her mouth. The taste reminded her of sour lemon and aged cheese. She winced as she swallowed and handed the vial back to Lennox.

The magic didn't work immediately; she waited for it to settle in her belly, for the sour taste to become like a whisper on her tongue. A sharp, stabbing pain made her wince and press a hand to her abdomen, but it settled into a dull ache a moment later. She sucked in a breath, and the magic worked on her, trailing through her body, healing where the dark magic had ripped holes in her body, mending the physical flesh and the weakened spirit.

"Thank you," Celia finally managed, clenching her hands into fists. She felt everything the magic touched. She had days before she would need another dose of the foul healing tonic.

"I'll have another made for you," Lennox replied, hesitating before adding, "You never told me how you were... infected."

Celia winced. "It happened during the search for Prince Alicsar."

Lennox shook her head. "You know that isn't what I meant."

Meeting her stare, Celia pressed her lips into a firm line. Rarely, did she lie to her Blood Witch sisters. Never to her superiors.

Yet the truth would not pass her lips.

Finally, Celia shook her head. "We were faced with the Dark Master's men. There is not much I remember from our journey north."

The dark eyes of the Blood Witch remained on Celia for a moment, critical... unbelieving. Lennox was easily a century older than Celia, had trained Isolde, and had known the previous Ecix—had been her sister. She had a sense for lies, and Celia waited for the witch to call her out on it.

But Lennox shook her head. "Rest. You will need it." She started for the door, chin lifted. Celia released a sigh of relief, but the Blood Witch paused by the door. "You should know... Elizabeth is greatly behind in her magic. She should be entering the Aether, connecting with her past lives, and she can do none of that."

Celia met Lennox's gaze from across the greenhouse. "She never got the same training as other Ecixes." And yet Eliza could do what others could not, something she had learnt on her own and without the help of the Blood Witches.

Lennox pursed her lips. "For that, she will need to work twice as hard, and I fear she does not appreciate the power she has been given."

"She fears it, Len," Celia murmured.

"As she should." Lennox reached for the doorhandle. "But she *must* learn how to access it, to wield it. If she does not, we are all doomed."

~

Celia returned to her room and found Brandon sitting on the edge of her bed, head in his hands, shoulders rising slowly, like he had fallen asleep waiting for her.

She paused in the doorway and cocked her head. She had never told him about the lingering illness, the aftereffect of Dorin's dark poison. Another lie Celia could not let pass her lips, out of fear that he would blame himself, like he did so many other things.

As she entered the room, Brandon looked up, tired eyes finding hers. The sleeves of his black tunic were rolled up to reveal his forearms, coiled muscle tense as he tightened his hands into fists.

Celia stopped by the small writing desk. "What are you doing here, Brandon?"

He blinked up at her and released a breath. "I haven't been able to stop thinking about Amitel. About... what he said."

"Concerning Laziroth?" she asked.

Brandon's lips formed a thin line. "Yes," he replied, voice almost a whisper, like a tired answer to a secret he'd been keeping for too long. "I have been thinking about it... a lot."

Celia waited for him to continue, but the silence was only broken by a crackling log in the small fireplace across from her. She jumped. Had she lit the fire before leaving to meet Lennox? Celia wracked her brain for a moment, but she couldn't remember. Had Brandon built the fire upon his arrival?

Her hand moved to her abdomen, where a dull ache wrapped around her, a snake that slithered from her stomach up her spine, leaving a trail of discomfort in its wake. The bitter taste of the tonic clung to her lips, sour on her tongue as she sucked in a breath.

She forced herself to move to an armchair and lowered herself slowly. "Why are you even considering his words as truth? Could he not be weaving a lie to garner sympathy? For all we know, he still works for the Dark Master and is trying to manipulate us again."

Brandon, still sitting on her bed, watched her, dark eyes swimming with uncertainty. "I don't feel as though he is," he murmured, shaking his head. "I can't explain it, Celia. But when we went to Laziroth..." As he trailed off, Celia found herself leaning forward, hoping he would tell her more. His time there had been a mystery. Over the years, he had revealed small secrets from the last oracle of Laziroth, but not too much.

To protect her, he claimed. From what though, she wasn't sure.

"When we returned the oracle to its temple, it... showed us our fates. Only neither of us were aware of what the other was shown. It was terrible at first." He closed his eyes. "Amitel took the visions away initially, so when they returned, they were... fractured. Unfinished. But when they started to make sense, Amitel was there to help me sort through them."

"And you don't think that could have been because he was trying to manipulate you, even then?" she asked quietly. "He could be telling us what we want to hear, Brandon."

Her friend shook his head. "I don't believe that to be true."

Celia released a harsh breath. "Why? Because of what happened in Laziroth?"

"What the oracle has foretold has come true." He looked up, meeting her stare. "Almost."

She frowned. "What do you mean?"

Brandon rose and ran a hand through his hair. "I'm not sure." He started for the door. "Good night, Celia."

"Goodnight," she whispered.

As he slipped from her room, Celia found herself thinking about the friend she had lost after the war. He had changed into something else after Isolde's death, and after he left the Brotherhood, she thought she would never see him again. That his grief would take over him and he would disappear like his love had.

Celia gripped her hands into fists and let her head fall back against the armchair. She had feared for him then, and that same fear spread through her like ice, settling over her heart like a cage.

"He is going to leave," she whispered to herself, closing her eyes. The words didn't taste like a lie, like something twisted had spilled from her lips. It came as a bitter truth, which was somehow worse.

How long did she have left with him, she wondered? Or would she wake up in the morning to find him gone, like centuries before?

6

GOD OF WAR
ELIZA

Words died on Eliza's tongue as she awoke. The light of Cadira's twin moons illuminated her room, the billowing curtains reminding her just how cold it was in Cadira. She pushed her blankets off and pressed her bare feet to the plush, cold carpet beneath. She breathed in the cool, night air, and started for the balcony.

Eliza rubbed tiredly at her eyes, a soft breath making her pause. She'd had no idea he'd snuck into her room, but her heart calmed itself when she spied Thorne asleep on the chaise lounge on the other side of the room. He wore no shirt or socks, didn't even have a blanket, and yet he slept like the night wasn't as cold as ice.

Eliza crept to the doors and closed them softly, latching them with trembling fingers. She hadn't noticed she was shaking. The nightmare rattled her more than she would have liked to admit.

They always did.

Her bed was already cold when she climbed beneath the heavy layers of blankets. She found herself gazing at Thorne; his chest rose and fell, one hand balled into a fist above his heart, while the other rested atop his stomach. The hand above his heart clutched something—a chain. Eliza recognised it from a memory that didn't quite belong to her.

There had been nights since Eliza had fought Dorin—the lost prince Alicsar—under the sands of Mesah, where sleep had not been kind to her or the commander.

They plagued her, the dreams. Dreams of the mountain, of the daggers soaked in her blood, of Amitel dying at her feet and using what magic he seeped to protect them. When she slept, she remembered, and when she remembered, her nightmares controlled her.

She took comfort in having Celia or Thorne with her most nights. Having someone else with her, to wake her before the dreams took control gave her a sense of security, safety. It reminded her that she wasn't alone, that she could rely on others to be there for her. It took a lot of power for her to admit she needed the help.

Eliza sighed softly and pulled the blankets close to her chest. She could just see Thorne at the end of her bed, see the lines of his body, the muscles that stiffened when his brows furrowed. He was usually a calm sleeper, but sometimes he had dreams that consumed him, too.

Thorne's eyes fluttered open, and he met her gaze with a sharp breath. "Is everything alright?" he asked. He didn't move.

She nodded and sat up. "Another nightmare, that's all."

Thorne watched her for a moment, then rolled to his feet. Her gaze followed the full length of his body, from the soft pants that hung from his hips, up his bare, sculpted chest, to his face. He was so handsome that it hurt, she thought.

She understood why her past life loved him so much.

She understood why she cared for him, too.

It was a realisation that didn't scare her. It hadn't when she'd first thought it three weeks ago, when he'd left for three days and had returned with a black eye and split lip and no explanation as to how he'd gotten either. She'd thought the words when she'd thrown her arms around his neck and breathed in his familiar, musky scent.

She just couldn't say the words aloud, not when she couldn't tell what kind of love she felt.

Did she love him because Isolde loved him? Or did she love him romantically? Maybe it was only platonic, and mutual? But she couldn't tell, because when she thought on it too long, she heard Dorin—*Alicsar's*—voice in the back of her head, laughing at her, telling her Thorne was in love with her.

Eliza swallowed thickly, cheeks hot. She forced those thoughts and feelings down, down into one of her shoe boxes, where she could hide it with the others.

Thorne padded to the bed and sat on the edge closest to her. His eyes were warm, swimming with worry. "What happened?"

She forced herself to look down at her hands. "I saw the Dark Master. I almost saw his face. And..." She shook her head.

"And what?" he asked, touching her leg. Even through the thick blankets, she could feel the warmth of his skin.

"A dagger. I was holding it. And all I could think about was killing him. Killing the Dark Master."

When she looked up, she found Thorne watching her. His gaze softened and he squeezed her leg. "It was just a dream."

Nodding, Eliza pulled her leg from his grasp and crossed them beneath her. "I never heard you come in."

"You were already asleep and I didn't want to wake you."

"I wish you would have." Eliza cocked her head. "We should talk... about Amitel."

Thorne clenched his jaw, but he nodded, pressing his hands into his lap. "I suppose we should."

"And the informant, who said... something. I just don't know if I believe it." She told him the name the informant gave her, of his sudden death and her run in with Amitel. She told him how she wasn't sure if she could trust him again, even though he sounded sincere, even though he'd tried to help.

Thorne remained silent, eyes on the floor, hands clenched in his lap. When she finished, she waited for him to say something. Every word had her tensing, waiting for some kind of reaction from the commander, but he had a way of wiping his emotions from his face.

And without looking at her, she couldn't read him.

Finally, Thorne met her stare. "When there's daylight, we'll find Celia, start looking into Alastor Verendus. I know his alias, but there isn't much about him except for stories that made it out of the Great War."

Eliza nodded. "What about Amitel?"

He hesitated a moment, running a hand through his tousled dark hair. He dropped his hand and turned fully to her. "Amitel called on us. And I wanted to kill him. Thank the Goddess Celia was there."

Eliza waited, heart racing, as Thorne continued, "Celia and I found him with the body. He tried to explain why he did what he did."

"Do you believe him?" she asked softly. Her heart thundered in her chest as she waited for his next words.

"I'm not sure." Eliza's heart skipped a beat as the silence grew long between them. "I know why Amitel did what he did. There is a time I'd like to forget, something I'm not proud of, and so I know why Amitel betrayed you." Thorne closed his eyes, as if the memories were calling to him, begging for recognition. "I don't trust him, not fully. I don't think you should either."

When he opened his eyes again, he found hers, and when she nodded, he sighed.

Standing, Thorne watched her a moment, lips parted as if he wanted to say more. Instead, he turned and walked back to the chaise. In a pile beside the legs, he'd left his shirt and shoes and sword. "Do you think you'll need me the rest of the night?" he asked, looking over his shoulder.

Silently, she shook her head and he nodded, lifting his belongings into his arms. For a moment, she considered asking him to stay. "I'll find you in the morning. Sleep well, Eliza."

She said nothing as he slipped from the room. Disappointment swelling in her chest. Sinking into the soft mattress, Eliza succumbed to the darkness of sleep, her thoughts of love a dull echo in her ears.

~

Celia's quarters were where they'd chosen to do their research. Eliza hadn't slept much the rest of the night, tossing and turning, warm and cold. Her thoughts were a mess of Thorne and Amitel and training that she hadn't noticed falling asleep until one of her maids, a sweet older woman, came knocking on her door about drawing a bath.

Refusing to take breakfast in her own room, Eliza had made her way to the guest rooms of the palace where Celia was staying, close to Lennox and Eliza's *Athir*. Their rooms were in a row, but she knew which one belonged to Celia only because the smell of food wafted from beneath the door.

Thankfully, breakfast had been sent there instead.

The door opened on quiet hinges to reveal a large chamber with a wall made of glass on the far side of the room, with glass doors leading to a balcony, which allowed a soft breeze to chill the room. Celia's bed sat on the far left wall, the canopy curtains fluttering in the wind, bed pristinely made and draped in deep red comforters and pillows. A door across from the bed lead to a bathing chamber.

There was a sitting area close to the door, which they'd converted into a research space. Books and papers were scattered across two lounges, a coffee table, and a desk they'd moved to sit behind one of the lounges.

The coffee table had been cleared for their food; scrambled eggs and thick toast, winter berries and fruits piled on a plate, syrup in a small jug, sausages and rashers of bacon in a steaming dish. Eliza breathed in the scents of breakfast, and her stomach rumbled with the reminder that she hadn't eaten dinner.

Celia looked up from the desk, a tea cup half way to her lips. She'd piled a small plate with fruit, which sat untouched by a book she'd been reading. Thorne on the other hand, ate casually on one of the lounges and didn't look at her as she entered.

"Morning," Eliza greeted, smiling over at her sister.

Celia's eyes brightened, and she smiled as she took a sip of what was likely a blueberry tea. "Good morning."

Hesitantly, Eliza took a seat on the lounge across from Thorne. She grabbed a piece of toast and bit into it. "I'm guessing Thorne already filled you in."

From the desk, Celia nodded. "Yes. I've been doing some reading and I've found... well, nothing." She shrugged helplessly and frowned. "There are barely any mentions of an Alastor Verendus who fought in the Great War."

Eliza took another slow bite of toast. "Did you look up the 'God of War'?"

Celia shook her head, ebony hair falling over her shoulder. The braid that had likely been keeping her thick hair together was now falling apart. Strands framed her soft face, making her pale skin even whiter.

"I know the reference. Heard the occasional story about a *God of War* fighting amongst the mortals of the Great War." Celia's brows furrowed, and she closed the book she'd been reading, forgetting her tea.

She stood and began a frenzied search through the new piles of books that had been stacked beside the desk. Eliza stood, and approached, just as Celia held up a small tome no larger than her hand.

The book fell onto the desk and Celia sat. Eliza walked up behind her to read over her shoulder.

"I thought I'd read *something* about the God of War earlier. Brandon and I had gathered some texts, and being so tired, I hadn't been paying much attention to what I'd been reading. I'd been looking for mentions of *Alastor*, not the alias. But..." Celia flipped through the pages. "I remember reading about what happened after the war."

Celia stopped at a page; on one side was a large block of text, and the other, an illustration of the supposed '*God of War*'. It looked almost how mortals pictured their *Ares*, hard defined muscles, a battle axe in one hand, long sword in the other, and a helmet with twist horns hiding the face. Only Eliza could feel the fear coming off the page, smell the copper scent of blood on the battlefield. Magic was imbued on the page, a warning.

"Does it say what happened to him?" Eliza asked, cocking her head. She skimmed the pages, heart pounding.

Celia pointed to a line and read it aloud: "*The God of War, who could not be killed for his crimes against Cadira, was exiled to the mortal world where he would live out his immortal life without his magic, and without his spoils of war, under the watchful eyes of the Keepers."*

Eliza and Celia looked at one another, then to Thorne, who sat back in realisation.

"It's time to pay my grandfather a visit."

7

PORTALS IN NEW ORLEANS
ELIZA

The familiar warmth of the immortal flame smothered Eliza's skin as she stepped through the barrier between Cadira and New Orleans. The biting cold of the Winter Palace and its temple disappeared, replaced with the sticky humidity of the bayou.

But she didn't care. Eliza closed her eyes and breathed in the smells of muddy water and damp leaves, rain from the last couple of days, and the sharp, citrus scent of the temple.

When she opened her eyes, she found her grandfather and Kay standing behind the podium of the eternal flame. Her grandfather hadn't bothered to wear his robes, which he only dragged out for special occasions. Instead, he wore grey slacks and a matching vest over a white button down. Which was informal and casual for him.

A smile broke out across her lips as she rushed towards her family. Davis welcomed her with open arms and clutched her tightly to him. Eliza buried her face in his chest, breathing in his familiar scent of cloves and bourbon. She let it rock her into a net of safety, his arms the cage that locked her in.

When he finally released her, she didn't have a chance to mourn his embrace, and instead was pulled into another, one she sunk into willingly, wishing it would take her away from all the things Cadira had changed.

Kay smelt like something new every time Eliza saw her. Sometimes it was floral perfume, sometimes it was earthy and rich after days spent in the gardens. When Eliza closed her eyes and breathed deeply, there were hints of cinnamon and nutmeg. Probably left over from Christmas.

Eliza hadn't been able to celebrate. Not when it fell in the middle of her missions and engagement and her nightmares. Christmas was not celebrated in Cadira, though they had a version that was similar.

Kay pulled back and cupped Eliza's cheeks. Her sad eyes swept over Eliza's face, down to the plain *passes off as mortal* clothing, back up to meet her gaze.

"I have missed you so much," Kay whispered, smiling softly.

Tears burned at the edges of her eyes, but Eliza swallowed them back with a smile. "I've missed you too."

Davis touched her shoulder, and finally, Eliza broke free of Kay. Standing close to the barrier, Celia and Thorne said nothing, quiet during the entire reunion. But Eliza beckoned them forward with a look.

They weren't in New Orleans so Eliza could cry and hug her family.

They were in New Orleans so Eliza could find a war criminal who believed he was a God.

No pressure or anything, she thought wryly.

"How long are you able to stay?" Kay asked, folding her arms over her chest as Celia and Thorne flanked either side of Eliza.

"Only a week. We have to be back before..." Eliza trailed off, unable to finish the thought.

I have to be back before my birthday. Once, she would have been excited for her eighteenth birthday. It would have marked her final stretch into adulthood, would have counted down the days before her official training into becoming a portal Keeper began. She would have started travelling the mortal world, spent time with each of the keepers so she could learn, even if it was just a little bit, of the world that exiled her.

But now she lived there more than her own home. Now, she was expected to return there to train, sleep, learn... marry.

Eliza shook her head of the thoughts and smiled up at her guardians. "We need to talk."

Her grandfather chuckled. "I had a feeling you were here for more than us." A pang of guilt shot down to the pit of Eliza's gut, but she didn't let her smile waver as her grandfather waved them outside of the temple. "Come on. Let's go home. Have a coffee. And talk."

~

Eliza, squeezed into the back of her grandfather's old BMW with Celia and Thorne, felt oddly peaceful as her grandfather drove down the familiar streets of New Orleans towards the French Quarter. With the windows rolled down, the smell of the city, of diesel fumes and pollution, should have made her stomach churn, but there was a familiarity to it that settled her nerves and made her smile.

Thorne, on the other hand, wasn't as impressed. Sometimes Eliza forgot that he hadn't spent much time in the mortal world, probably had never driven in a car before. Thorne clutched the handle above the window, and with enough force, she was sure it would snap under his grip. His other hand clutched her knee, though she wasn't sure he was even aware of his fingers digging into her skin.

Celia looked somewhat excited, though; she was almost hanging out of the open window as she took in the sites. It was early, only five in the morning, so the only people out were those working or leaving for it. A misty rain made the air thick with humidity, heavy in Eliza's lungs.

The car rumbled to a stop outside the house. Eliza looked up at the exterior; the iron balustrade that lined the outside and wrap around balcony. The windows with shutters that were constantly damaged during high winds. Ivy that hung off one side of the building that sometimes, magically, had fruit growing off it for the neighbourhood children, who were smart enough not to ask why.

Thorne wasted no time as he slid from the backseat. He rested his hand on his hip, as if he were resting his hand on the pommel of his sword, but all their gear—including his weapons—were in the trunk of the car, out of sight.

Celia got out next, though she was more excited than anything. It made Eliza wonder how they'd gotten to her house the first time they'd visited New Orleans. At the time, Eliza hadn't asked, but now she was curious.

Instead of asking, she unfolded herself from the back seat and stretched her arms over her head. "I've missed this place."

Kay smiled, and linked their arms. "This place has missed you, kid." They started for the front door, but Eliza stopped and looked back. Thorne and Celia were already with her grandfather rifling through the trunk, grabbing what they could without letting any of their neighbours see. A sword, a duffel with daggers and filled with old books stolen from the library riddled with their own unique magic.

"Let's get started on the coffee. I might have some pastries inside, too." Kay patted Eliza's hand, and when she started for the door again, Eliza didn't fight her.

The first thing one saw when they entered her home was the courtyard. A grandfather clock sat across from the doors next to two entries into the main house. To Eliza's right, there was a mismatched set of chairs around an iron table, and to her left, a row of planters filled with herbs and flowers Kay used for spells and cooking.

The scents of the courtyard were eclectic, a mix of rain and the gardens, whispers of candles and the French Quarter.

A small bell jingled and when Eliza looked down, she found their cat, Odin, a one-eyed tabby, rubbing up against her leg. He mewled softly, but before she could pick him up, he ran off, disappearing into the house.

"I promise he missed you," Kay said, chuckling. "He sleeps in your room most nights."

Eliza smiled sadly and followed Kay to the kitchen. It sat off the courtyard, and was large enough for a full wall of drying herbs and flowers.

While Kay went to work on the coffee, Eliza pulled together five mismatched chairs. Everything in their house was mismatched, mostly thrifted throughout the many years her grandfather had lived there. The table was scratched and warn, with markings of nail polish from when Eliza was eight, and chips from being moved in and out of the kitchen.

They had a cabinet close to the window with all their cups and plates. Eliza pulled it open and reached instinctively for a floral mug that was Kay's. Eliza had painted it during her first year of school, back before her guardians chose to home-school her because of her magic.

A tea cup belonging to her grandfather came next. Like the rest of their house, their collection of mugs and cups was a mix of thrifted, gifted, and downright hideous ceramics. The tea cup was one of the nicer ones they had. Nothing sentimental, just one they'd found while looking for new glass jars.

Eliza picked three more off the shelf and closed the doors. She brought them to the table as Kay set out their little coffee pot and creamer. A small plate of pastries appeared in the middle just as Davis walked in with Thorne and Celia behind him.

They all sat without a word; Thorne with his back to the wall, which Eliza had learnt was because he wanted to be able to see all possibilities of threats. Celia and Eliza sat on either side of him, while Davis had taken the chair next to Celia, and Kay between him and Eliza.

Kay poured the cups of coffee in silence.

"Is there a way we might be able to find Alastor Verendus?" Eliza asked, cupping her coffee in both hands, letting the heat warm her hands. "Apparently he's here in this world, under the watchful eye of a Keeper. I just don't know which one."

Davis considered her for a moment before shaking his head. "I cannot help you with that. The jurisdictions of other Keepers and who they may be keeping locked away is not something I can easily learn or pass on. It would be extremely dangerous."

Eliza blew out a breath. "So you can't help us?"

"If you wish to find him, I would recommend locater spells. He would have a rather unique energy." Davis lifted his cup to his lips, taking a sip. As he lowered it to the saucer, a small silver spoon lifted into the air, carrying sugar, and dipped into the black coffee, stirring itself. "Seek that out. But I cannot simply ask my fellow Keepers where he may or may not be."

"Thank you, though," Celia said, offering him a smile, "I know we ask much of you."

Davis bowed his head. "I don't mind." His bright eyes found Eliza's. "The Keeper responsible for him will have him protected using magic. He'll be hidden not far from the temple itself in case of an emergency."

Eliza nodded, biting her lip. "So, what if I went to each temple and used locater spells there?"

"It might work," Davis replied. He rubbed his chin thoughtfully. "That would be a lot of ground to cover. And you don't have much time... or magic." His gaze dropped to her wrist, to the bracelet that would never be removed.

She'd forgotten about her... limitations. Her lack of magic. She pulled her arm off the table and onto her lap, playing with the band that blocked her magic. If she could use her Blood Magic, she'd have no problem. Blood Magic didn't require a connection to Cadira in order to use it. Blood Magic was all about what dwelled within her.

"I'll figure something else out," she muttered.

Silence filled the empty spaces of the kitchen. Outside, rain fell in lazy drops, hitting the closed windows and dripping down the panes of glass.

Her thoughts drifted to the king. He wanted her back in just over seven days because her birthday was so close. Only two weeks away. It scared her. The knowledge that soon, her world would tilt and readjust in a totally different way.

"Eliza?"

She blinked, forcing herself back to the present. Everyone was watching her, gazes filled with worry. She hated that, having everyone worry about her.

"Sorry," she said. "I think I have an idea of how to find Alastor Verendus."

No one argued as she left.

~

Eliza settled into her old bedroom. There were things missing from it; photographs of her family, which now resided in her palace bedroom; pillows and throw blankets, which lived at the end of her new bed; editions of books she loved to reread, which took up space on her new nightstand. Her knickknacks were gone, too, in a box for when she returned once more.

She pursed her lips and set to work searching for what she needed. Eliza had learnt a particular tracking spell as a kid so she could find celebrities. Thinking about it, she cringed, but she'd reworked the spell so many times to give her exact locations anywhere in the world.

She pulled a world map out from her bookshelf and threw it onto her bed, rifling through her desk for a pendulum, several crystals, a small gold bowl she'd thrifted, herbs from Kay's garden that she'd stashed in her room, and an incense stick.

Now, she knew more locater spells, but she fell back on this one. It was familiar, it was *hers*. So, she spread everything out over her comforter and climbed onto the bed, crossing her legs so she could see the map in its entirety.

Its length was the size of her double bed; the bigger the map, she'd learnt, the more accurate her spell would be.

Setting up the spell was simple; she placed a mix of herbs into the gold bowl, followed by three crystals. Eliza pulled a dagger from her drawer, one she'd stolen from the palace the last time she'd returned to New Orleans, and cut into her palm. She let three drops of blood fall into the mixture in the bowl, which ignited the herbs.

The fire flickered and danced, beautiful and deadly. Eliza reached for the incense stick, swiped it through the flame, then blew it out.

The smoke from the stick swirled and twisted, but with the help of a short spell, it focused itself on the map, drew itself from the stick and down onto the paper. It moved like a snake, slithering over continents and oceans, around mountains and islands. It stopped atop Louisiana, right above New Orleans.

Two words had it dispersing over the east coast of North America, and congregating in one place.

It had been so simple, she almost didn't believe it.

Because of the Keeper's magic, she couldn't be exact in her search, but she had caught a trace of the once legendary *God of War*.

Now, she just needed to get closer.

She quickly extinguished the flame and jumped out of the bed, and hurried to the door. She pulled it open to reveal Thorne, who stared down at her with furrowed brows, one hand raised to knock.

"I was coming to check on you," he said after a moment, dropping his fist. "Are you alright?"

Nodding, Eliza grabbed his hand and pulled him into her room and over to her bed. She pointed to the map. "I know where might be."

Thorne looked between her and the map, then met her stare. "Then we should plan to leave as soon as possible."

8

DARKNESS ON THE HORIZON
CELIA

Celia watched as Eliza and Brandon disappeared through a shimmering portal, leaving her with Kay and Keeper Davis in New Orleans. It closed around their retreating figures, taking them to a city Celia only knew the name of: New York, a metropolis made of steel and glass. She had been assured the trip would be safe enough for them. Eliza had been there before, she'd been told. They would be fine.

But it didn't stop the worry eating away at her. Celia twisted a ring on her finger over and over again. It was the only thing that brought her comfort in the foreign world.

"They'll be fine," Kay said, wrapping her arms around herself. "Eliza knows what she's doing. At this point, Brandon's only there as arm candy."

Celia wanted to smile, but she couldn't. She had wanted to go with them, but the illness had stopped her from going. As much as she had been excited to see other cities in the world Eliza had grown up in, she was afraid that she'd slow them down, get in their way like she had in Mesah. Celia was surprised Brandon hadn't been more hesitant, but he was a soldier, had learnt to lock away his fears.

She was no good at that.

Keeper Davis chuckled. "I have some work I must do. Will you be alright, Celia?"

Immediately, she nodded, though she wasn't entirely sure if that was true. "Yes, of course." She watched him leave, too, entering a part of the house she'd never seen before. Shadows swallowed him, leaving her alone with Kay.

Before she could depart, Celia pressed a hand to the older woman's shoulder. "I'm worried about Eliza."

Kay lifted a thin brow. "She'll be fine. She's been to New York dozens of time." The older witch waved a hand and started for the kitchen.

Celia rushed to follow, ignoring the dull ache beginning in her spine. "It's not that. I mean, I am worried for them, but there is something else."

Kay paused in the doorway. "What do you mean?"

"Amitel has returned."

Something changed in the old woman's gaze. She beckoned Celia to follow her, and they sat across from one another at the same table as earlier, their coffee and pastries gone. Kay furrowed her brow and leaned closer. "What happened with Amitel?"

Celia swallowed. "You're aware of what happened? His... betrayal?" Kay nodded silently. "He came back to the capital a week ago. Cornered Eliza. Tried to explain to her why he did it." She stopped and shook her head. "Eliza left him, didn't want to hear any of it, and I don't blame her." Celia sucked in a sharp breath and pressed a hand to her abdomen. Warmth spread through her as she focused on the shadow illness, on submerging it in light, but the pain dimmed only slightly.

She would need to see Lennox much sooner than she expected. "He then called on Brandon and I," Celia continued, "so we went to meet him. I didn't want to truly believe he was capable of hurting anyone, especially Eliza." Celia remembered Brandon's anger when he had returned to her at the port, his own feeling of betrayal because of what Amitel had done. He'd blamed himself, most of all, for what the damage Amitel had managed, blamed himself for Eliza getting hurt. "I'm worried Amitel has returned to her hurt her further. He claims that was never his intent, that he'd been forced to betray her because of fate, and that he only wanted to protect her. But what if he is lying? I want to believe him, but I don't want to put Eliza's life at risk." Celia pressed her hands together to stop them from shaking.

Kay remained silent for several moments, but when she spoke, Celia was surprised by her words. "Amitel saved my life many years ago. He helped me when no one else would. I owe him much. I don't think he'd be so cruel."

"It has been some time since you last spoke to him," Celia replied softly. "It is possible he has changed."

Kay shook her head. "I certainly hope not," she murmured, pressing a hand to her mouth. "But I have never known him to blame *fate* for his actions."

Celia wasn't sure if she felt any better. Perhaps letting him back into their lives would give her a chance to understand what he'd done, maybe give her some kind of closure—give *Eliza* closure. Maybe she didn't need to trust him. Maybe all she needed to do was allow him to get close enough for her to decide whether he was a threat to them and their mission—if he would be a threat to Eliza once more.

"What would happen if they didn't find this *God of War*?" Kay asked, as if to fill the tense silence between them. "Are there any other leads?"

Celia shook her head, thankful for something else to discuss. "No. The informant died before Eliza could get anything else out of him. Not even his spirit remained long enough for answers."

"Eliza is determined to find him," Kay mused softly. "And she will. She's strong."

"I fear that if she doesn't, she'll lose all hope of ever finding the Dark Master."

"There are more and more beings from Cadira coming through

and seeking refuge," Kay said. "They fear war."

Celia sucked in a breath. "I sense it coming. The Dark Master is building his forces. Gathering humans to turn into unwilling soldiers, creating new demons that are getting harder to fight." She stopped and shook her head. "There have been rumours about a darkness gathering over the oceans in the north. We heard about it in Port Beewold during our search for the prince. I hadn't been worried about it then, but now, as I listen to the people filling the capital, I hear it more and more. Darkness, death, demons, Shadow Soldiers. They are no longer just a nightmare or frightening story. There are more people becoming victims of the Dark Master every day."

"It's terrifying," Kay whispered, "knowing Eliza will be caught in the middle of it all." She pressed a hand to her forehead. "And I hate how I cannot be there to help her."

"I will protect her with my life."

Kay looked up, the fear in her eyes thick. "But I raised her like she was my own. I should *be there*."

"I know," Celia replied, nodding. "I hope that they find the God of War and they get whatever information they can, so that maybe we can stop a war before it can begin."

"It'll be hard." Kay released a heavy breath. "I think I may need to lie down. Will you be okay?"

Rising from her chair, Celia nodded. "I have some work I can do while I wait for them to return."

"Don't worry about them," Kay said. "They'll be okay."

"I know." Celia offered the older woman a smile. "I just fear the Dark Master is closer than we think. I cannot explain it, but I know he is watching us." Celia paused in the doorway. "But I'm fearful most of all of the war the Shadowland might see if we do not find a way to stop the Dark Master. I fear that if he gets the war he so desperately desires, our world will come to an end."

~

Eliza appeared through the portal with a frown twisting her lips and eyes darkened by frustration.

Celia rose from an iron chair and reached for her sister, but the young Blood Witch stormed by her and entered the house without so much as a word to Celia or Brandon, who stopped beside Celia, his lips pursed. She let her hand fall to her side.

"We found nothing," he said, eyes following Eliza's retreating form.

"You were gone almost an entire day," Celia replied, returning to her seat. She reached for her cup and brought the ginger infused tea to her lips. She winced as she swallowed. "What happened?"

Brandon released a heavy breath as he claimed the chair across from her, finally dragging his eyes from the door Eliza had stormed through. It hadn't escaped Celia's notice how he looked at Eliza—at the war in his heart as the ghost of Isolde shone through the young Ecix.

"We spent most of our time in *Central Park*." He shook his head and rubbed a hand over his face. "Many creatures exiled or fleeing Cadira find themselves there. We thought *he* might have as well. Eliza found a trace of what might have once been his magic and we followed it to a museum. There were a few Exiled roaming nearby, but none that matched the trace. I think Eliza feels she's failed, that her spell didn't work."

Celia reached out and took his hand. "There's still time. We have a few more days."

"There is a chance we are searching for something that isn't real." His eyes met hers. "I'm worried that the Dark Master has sent us on a wild search for a being that never existed."

Her stomach churned with the thought. Maybe the Dark Master had sent them on a wild chase, forcing them from Cadira and into the mortal realm. But to what end? What was his plan?

Biting her lip, Celia shook her head and rose, releasing his hand. "I will speak with her."

Brandon opened his mouth, and she waited for him to speak, but after a moment he pressed his lips together and nodded. Celia sighed and picked up her skirt. The heals of her boots cracked against the uneven stonework of the courtyard, filling the heavy silence carved between them. Celia slipped into the main house and up the old stairs to the first floor, where the family cat darted out from a dark alcove and into Eliza's bedroom down the hall.

Old oil paintings and photographs lined the walls, covering faded wallpaper. Celia ran her fingers over scratches in the wood panelling and wondered what stories the marks held, what glimpse she would get into the lives of those who dwelled within the residence. What life her sister must have lived without the overbearing Blood Witches designing her every move.

Celia stopped in front of the bedroom door and winced. Agony, sharp like a knife tearing through her lower back, sliced through her. Celia sucked in a harsh breath and closed her eyes, hand hovering over her side.

A couple more days. Then Lennox should have the medicine ready for when they returned. But how much longer could Celia last without a true solution?

With the pain subsiding, Celia lifted her hand and tapped lightly on the door. From within, Eliza made a grunting sound that could have been a *come in* or *leave me alone*. Celia decided on the former, and pushed the door open, sticking her head inside.

Eliza's bedroom was an ecliptic mess of photographs and books; above the messy bed that sat against the far wall was a constellation of stars designed to mimic the Cadiran night sky, while most surfaces were covered in make-up, clothing, or jewellery—most of which Celia doubted Eliza wore.

Her sister looked up from the bed, legs crossed beneath her. A large map of the mortal realm lay before her, a vessel filled with herbs beside it. The cat eyed her from its perch on a pillow, sniffed the air, then curled into a ball, ignoring her.

"What's up?" Eliza asked, returning her gaze to the map.

Celia entered and started for the bed, taking a seat on the edge furthest from the map. "Brandon told me what happened."

Eliza huffed and stuffed her hands into her lap. "Did he tell you it was a colossal fail?"

"He told me you had the trace but couldn't track it."

"Yeah, I lost a simple trace. It should have been easy to keep hold of but I lost it." Eliza pressed her lips into a thin line and shook her head. "Again, Celia. I lost it *again*."

Celia wanted to reach out and take Eliza's hand, or pull her into a tight embrace, but she forced herself to remain still. She pulled her hands into her lap and tightened her fists into balls.

"Tell me what happened, Eliza."

Her sister met her stare; flecks of dark green swirled in her mossy eyes, darkening them with frustration. "We got to Central Park, spoke to a couple of pixies from Cadira who pointed us in the direction of the trace. They said the magic comes and goes, so Thorne and I assumed he must visit the park often."

"Perhaps you lost it because he left," Celia offered. "He might have had help disappearing. If he can sense you coming, then he will likely hide."

Eliza pursed her lips. "You're probably right," she replied, rubbing a hand over her face.

Celia rose. "Start at the museum," she said, turning to leave. "That's where you lost the trace. Pick it up there, and follow it."

As she left, her mind wandered to darker thoughts, to the tingling in her spine and the dull throb in her temples. *A couple more days,* she thought again, her hand moving to her abdomen, digging into the soft flesh around her bellybutton. The Shadow Sickness reared its ugly head and snapped at her magic.

The hall grew dim as day shifted into night. Frosted lights flickered on, but her vision swam, and she stumbled to a wooden door sitting ajar, the darkness within welcoming.

She entered the guest bedroom, and locked the door behind her. The bed, neatly made up with a white duvet and a colourful quilt, came into focus. Celia staggered to the bed and fell into the thick blankets. She sucked in calming breaths until the pain subsided. Her gaze fell to the open window, where a golden-eyed raven watched her from the railing of her terrace. The creature blinked before diving into the night, leaving her to her thoughts and worries, and the echoes of her dying promise to lull her into sleep.

9

MISSION GONE WRONG
ELIZA

Eliza made a face as another car sped past them. Muddy water sprayed from the tires, hitting her legs and soaking through her jeans. The rain had only stopped an hour ago, but water still covered the asphalt and glimmered off cars.

Thorne grabbed her arm and pulled her away from the curb, eyes shining with uncertainty. "You need to be more careful," he snapped, shaking his head.

"This is my world," she reminded him, rolling her eyes and pulling her hand away. "I know what I'm doing."

"Are you sure?" He eyed her warily, gaze dancing over her clothing. Ripped jeans, brand-new Doc Martins—courtesy of her now dwindling bank account since she hadn't been to work in months—and a black sweatshirt with a sewn middle-finger over her heart.

When Thorne had seen that particular design, he'd made her pull her hair down to cover it.

She pulled a face at the immortal commander and went back to stand on the side of the road. She was, for the most part, attempting to call for a cab. But each one that sped past ignored her flailing arms and whistles, leaving her and Brandon stranded on a quiet street somewhere off fifth avenue on the upper east side, close enough to Central Park and the Met that she knew where she was, but far from the busy park that seemed to get in the way of her locater spell.

They were too far away from the closest portal and Keeper to ask for help. Eliza was sure about that. She pulled her cell from her back pocket, the screen an infinite black, the battery drained by an irate pixie who wouldn't answer their questions.

Eliza sighed. They'd hit another dead end, her magic was spent casting locater spells, and now she needed to call her grandfather to get them back to New Orleans.

I just can't do anything right.

"We'll try again," Thorne said, as if sensing her thoughts.

Eliza shook her head. "It's not that. We can keep trying, sure, but we aren't going to find anything."

Thorne took her hand gently. Pulling her away from the road, she watched as more cars passed, oblivious to what they were doing. "Eliza, we'll find him."

"If he still exists," she muttered.

Because there was a chance that he didn't, that the Dark Master's informant was sending them on a wild goose chase while he planned something even worse.

She'd been so wrapped up in the idea of a lead that she hadn't even *thought* of it being a trap. Now, after hours of *nothing*, it was all she could think about.

"He exists," Thorne replied finally, eyes darkening.

She wondered if he was so adamant because he, too, had been so caught up in the idea of finding *something* that he hadn't considered the possibility that they had been wrong. They had once again fallen into one of the Dark Master's plans without questioning it.

"Okay," Eliza said, nodding. "But we don't know if he's even alive."

Thorne sighed. "The spells were inconclusive."

"I know." She bit her lip and looked around. The night was closing in on them, the sky too dark for the city. Rain threatened to drown the roads again and soak them to the bone.

In the distance, thunder crackled. A reminder that they had to hurry.

All Eliza needed was a cab and somewhere to charge her phone.

This time, though, she'd been so sure she'd gotten the location right.

"Let's just get out of the rain," she said, waving a hand frantically at a passing car. "After that we can figure out where we go next."

"We have time..."

Eliza shot him a look, and his words died on his lips.

Until your eighteenth birthday. The night that would mark the countdown to her marriage to Cadira's lost Prince, Alicsar. Except they'd been out searching for almost five days straight

Five days down, gone, washed away by the rain.

Five days of locater spells, of almost passing out from exhaustion and magic depletion.

Five days of returning to New Orleans with nothing.

"I know," she whispered, running a hand through her knotted hair. Thinking about it made her stomach twist, blood boil. "I know."

A tingle ran up the length of Eliza's spine. The warning didn't prepare her for the wave of dark magic that shuddered through her.

Eliza spun, heart racing. Darkness leaked from every crevice; the shadows of the alley grew thicker, tendrils slithering out, reaching for her and Thorne.

She grasped for her own dagger, a gift from Captain Jed, the captain of the king's guard. It was simple, light, and perfect for close-combat.

Weak magic danced at Eliza's fingertips. She touched the heavy gold band around her wrist.

But that didn't stop her from lifting her hand, ready to deflect the magic slithering towards them. *Like it's going to help, though.* She bit the inside of her cheek. Unfortunately, a dagger wasn't going to help her defeat the darkness before them.

A blinding light appeared in the back of the alley, stopping the darkness in its tracks. The shadows skittered off like living creatures, like demons who had been dragged from the depths of hell, rolling like tar to safety.

Eliza swallowed thickly and hesitantly stepped towards the mouth of the alley. The light dimmed, but the shadows did not return.

"Eliza—" Thorne grabbed her hand, stopping her from going any further.

In the darkness, a figure appeared, shrouded in a heavy cloak, the hood lifted so their face couldn't be seen. They held a long staff in one hand, and what looked like a knife in the other.

With only a little magic burning in her veins, she had no choice but to fight.

She hated to admit that Thorne had been right when he'd hammered the idea of physical training into their days at the palace.

The figure slammed the butt of their staff into the stone ground. Light erupted from the wood, illuminating the alley—

And the portal behind them.

Eliza sucked in a breath. The figure pulled the hood away to reveal a half-faery man with tusks and horns, dark green skin pulled tight over large bones and coiled muscles. Slitted eyes met hers, red pupils critical.

"Ecix," the man said, voice a low growl. "I have been waiting for you."

Eliza clenched her jaw, ignoring her trembling fingers as she tightened her hold on the useless dagger. Weapons of steel would be no match against half-Fae like him. "And you are?" she asked.

The man chuckled, resembling the thunder that echoed overhead. "I am the God of War."

Her breath left her in an instant.

"You have been searching for me," he continued, not moving from the portal, "I have come to find out why. It is not every day an Ecix comes searching for the man she banished."

If anything, she felt like their research should have at least revealed that.

The sky opened and rain misted around them. A terrifying shiver raced down her spine. "Are you going to kill us?" she asked, raising a brow.

Beside her, Thorne tensed, his hand moving to her wrist, like yanking her away from the imposing immortal half-Fae would protect her. But Eliza dug her heals in, squaring her shoulders. The commander's stare burnt a hole in the back of her head, the loud *thud-thud-thud* of her heart ringing in her ears, and yet she stared the God of War down.

A smile flickered across his thin, dark lips. "Why would I do that?" he growled. "I want to talk."

"Eliza," Thorne hissed, tugging her back. "This doesn't feel right."

She pressed her lips into a frown. The portal swirling behind the half-Fae didn't have the same magical signature as the ones she'd seen conjured by Keepers like her grandfather, or the ones created from Blood Magic. She reached out to it carefully, letting the weak tendrils of her own magic brush against it.

Alastor beckoned to the portal with a large, clawed hand. "Come."

"Eliza," Thorne warned again. "Don't."

"You shouldn't have access to a portal," Eliza said, stepping back. "You should be locked away." She reeled her magic back in and tensed. Beside her, Thorne reached for his sword, sliding it free of its sheath.

Alastor grinned. "Wouldn't you like to know why I have my powers?"

She shook her head. "I don't think you do," she replied, stomach sinking. "I think someone else is behind this."

In response, he growled, the sound low like thunder. Eliza raised her hand, ready to fend off an attack, but nothing happened.

Eliza frowned. All the horrors she'd heard, and... nothing. She and Thorne shared a glance as another figure appeared from the portal. As he entered the alley, a heavy powerful magic settled around them, fending off the rain and creating a barrier around their bodies. If they wanted to run, she'd have to magic her way out, something she couldn't imagine doing in her weakened state.

Thorne stepped in front of her and tightened his grip on his sword. He squared his shoulders, forcing her back a step as their visitor stopped at the God of War's side.

There is something wrong here. Eliza peaked around Thorne's shoulder and stared between the two. *What the hell is going on?*

"It's alright." The little old man chuckled and patted the arm of Alastor. "He won't hurt you."

Bright blue eyes met Eliza's. The old man had white, thinning hair and pale luminescent skin. A long-sleeved white shirt draped his small frame, while a beige knitted vest hugged his chest and belly, with white trousers and a pair of black crocks. His smile was polite, genuine even.

"Please," he said, "come in. It's raining and I would hate for you two to catch your deaths."

Eliza and Thorne shared another glance. Confusion filled her. The books—nor her grandfather and the New York Keeper—prepared her for this.

She shook her head slowly. "I'm sorry, but who are you?"

The old man smiled. "I'm the person you're *really* searching for." He stepped out from behind the half-Fae and clapped his hands. "I am Alastor Verendus. And I think I know what it is you're looking for."

10

POWER OF A GOD
ELIZA

The hairs on Eliza's arms prickled as she stepped through Alastor's portal. Thorne, at her side, kept his hand tucked into hers, even as the light of the portal died out to reveal a modern kitchen, with marble countertops and a cotton-candy maker.

Eliza frowned. Though they might have been in New York, she'd half assumed she'd find herself in a dungeon, surrounded by rats and cockroaches, chains and skeletons. Likely a few spirits warning her of her upcoming demise.

She hadn't been expecting a fifth avenue apartment overlooking Central Park.

Thorne tensed but didn't speak. His gaze met hers, and he gave her a tight-lipped shake of his head.

Surrounding the apartment was an intricate boundary spell, a woven lattice of Fae magic she'd never felt before. Her time with Faery magic was limited to a few trinkets and a half-Fae she'd met over Christmas back in Cadira, and a hint of magic her grandfather had locked away back in New Orleans.

Nothing like what she was experiencing with Alastor Verendus though.

Even in her weakened state, the magic surrounding her was powerful. She'd assumed he wouldn't have access to magic, and being in the mortal realm, she'd never expected something as potent as the spell surrounding the apartment to survive.

But with the boundary spell came a new complication: if they wanted to leave, they would have to do so by the will of their host. Escape wouldn't be possible.

They were trapped.

Alastor smiled warmly and waddled over to a kettle. He flipped the switch, grabbed four matching pastel-blue soup mugs, and added tea bags to them. "There's sugar on the table, and Xeb over there will get you two some towels. Take a seat, please."

The table he pointed to was round and had a vase of red roses in the centre.

At some point, Xeb—the half-Fae tusked man—had disappeared, only to reappear, not looking the same. The slitted eyes remained, along with the dark green skin, but the horns and tusks had vanished.

"Glamour," he explained as he met Eliza's confused stare. "It protects *him*."

Alastor chuckled from the kitchen. "He likes to scare people."

Inky red-black hair now fell over Xeb's face, and there were small horns peaking from beneath his thick hair. He wasn't as large as he'd first appeared, and now stood a head taller than Thorne, broad still, but not as imposing. He'd changed into a grey-knit sweater and slacks, no longer wearing the cloak. As he approached, he handed her and Thorne a towel each.

They weren't too wet, but Eliza smiled and thanked him anyway.

Xeb motioned to the table. "Sit."

Eliza hesitated, but Thorne tightened his grip on her hand. Their eyes met.

I'll protect you, his gaze said.

That's what I'm worried about, she wanted to reply. She offered him a tight-lipped smile instead.

Thorne started for the offered seats, claiming the one closest to their hosts, placing himself between her and them. Eliza perched on the edge of her seat, the soft leather almost too comfortable for her to feel safe on.

The commander eyed the room critically and diligently. There was a pastel blue, sage green, and white colour-scheme to the open-plan kitchen, dining, and living room; a TV was mounted to the wall, and on either side of it, the heads of faery creatures instead of hogs or deer like mortals. Large bay windows overlooked Central Park.

Eliza swallowed thickly as Alastor approached the table with cups of tea.

"Here we go," he said, setting them in front of Eliza and Thorne. Xeb had the milk and sugar and placed them down on the table. "Now, we can talk."

"We appreciate your hospitality," Thorne started, eying the cup in front of him, "but we're here for more pressing reasons."

The pair sitting across from her shared a strange look. "Yes, we've heard." Before Eliza could asked more, Alastor waved a hand. "You've been searching quite loudly for me."

"A week," she replied quietly. "We've spent a week looking for you. Not even the Keeper tasked with... *watching* you would tell us where you were."

Alastor nodded, and brought the cup to his lips. "Yes well, when you've been exiled for a thousand years for war crimes, those tasked with locking you away tend to want to keep nosy witches away from the scary criminals."

Eliza shifted uncomfortable, and shared a look with Thorne, who narrowed his eyes. "You *are* the God of War, right? The same God of War the Dark Master is searching for?" she asked.

Xeb's features darkened as a low growl left his lips. "Why are you here, witch?"

Eliza flinched. Thorne's hand found hers beneath the table, while the other inched closer to his sword. *Well, I should have expected that*, she thought, biting her lip. "To find out why the Dark Master might be seeking you out. And to find out what you might know of him." Her gaze flickered between the two.

"If the Dark Master is hunting you, then you have something he wants," Thorne said. "That means you might have something we need."

Alastor nodded slowly. He reached for Xeb and patted his arm. "It's alright, my love. They didn't know."

Eliza frowned. "I'm sorry to bring this to you."

"I had a feeling he would seek me out. After five hundred years, I thought I was safe from his wrath. A thousand, and he might have forgotten me." Alastor released a heavy breath and waved his hand; the vase of red roses disappeared, replaced by a shimmering image of war.

Great towers crumbled to the ground, where fire—purple and green, powered by dangerous magic—leapt at a blackened city. A long wall surrounded it, and beyond its gates waged a war she'd only read in history books.

Eliza pressed a hand to her mouth. The image moved like a slow movie, revealing the bloodshed of the Great War. Dragons soared through the smoke like dark omens, shooting through black clouds of ash.

Alastor's eyes were locked on the image, sadness filling the pale blue. "The Dark Master... I never knew him personally. What I know about him isn't much, so I don't know if this will truly help you, but..." The old man sighed, and the image vanished. He lowered his head. "The Dark Master came from Valonde, during the Great War. He survived, along with the few who would later form the Resurgence. The Dark Master led them, and his whole purpose was to end you—the Ecix—forever."

Eliza's heart skipped a beat. "End, as in...?"

He looked up, and their eyes met. "Kill. Destroy the power. Every death of the Ecix since the Great War of Valonde has been caused by him, and him alone. He's been hunting and killing holders of the Ecix in order to find a way to destroy the power once and for all."

Eliza sat back, heart thundering in her chest. She could barely breathe. "Is... is there a way for the power to be destroyed?"

Alastor shook his head, but something sparked in his bright eyes. "Not that I am aware of, no. If he had found a way, then you would already be dead."

"Why does he want you, then?" Thorne asked, leaning forward. "Why is he sending out soldiers for information about *you*."

"Revenge, I believe." Alastor took Xeb's hand. "I was as much responsible for the destruction of Valonde as the Ecix. Though we did not fight together, my magic is powered by destruction, and the more of it, the greater my power becomes. I revelled in the Great War. I revelled in his people's deaths."

Shame glinted in his eyes. "There is not a day that goes by where I don't regret what I did in Valonde, where I haven't thought about it." Alastor rose and padded into the kitchen. He pulled a small bottle of what looked like Faery wine from a cupboard and carried it back to the table. "If not revenge, then he wants to question me himself," he finished, pouring the wine into his tea.

Eliza turned to Thorne, who watched every movement carefully. "Question you about what?" he asked.

"Probably the same thing you'll ask me," Alastor replied, taking a sip. "I've been around a very long time, young witch. During my time as... *him*, I learnt much about our world."

Eliza stiffened. "Like what?"

"Things the Blood Witches would kill me for knowing." Their eyes met, his turning hard.

"You know of a way to kill me," she whispered.

The God of War bowed his head. "I know of something, yes."

Eliza turned to Thorne; rage swirled in the dark blue of his eyes, turning his features to stone. "What do you know?"

"Nothing I feel safe saying aloud," Alastor said, leaning back in his chair. "But I will give you something, young Ecix, that will aid you."

She frowned. "What?" A shiver of fear raced down her spice; Thorne's hand tightened around hers as the man before them waved a hand.

An image appeared mid-air, shimmering and holographic. It

looked like an illustration straight from a book, different to what he had shown them earlier.

Alastor met her eye, and said, "I am the last living being who knows about the one weapon capable of killing a god."

She looked from him to the image. It depicted a dagger, blade curved and made of stone, hilt a pale, bone-like material. It could have been anyone's dagger.

But a raven with its wings outstretched was depicted behind the dagger, talons wrapped around the handle. Eliza sucked in a breath.

"Azula's dagger," she said.

Alastor nodded. "Powerful, but it's been lost for centuries. Some say it sleeps at the bottom of the Crystal Ocean in the east where only the sirens may find it. Others will claim it's being protected by the Fae deep in the Willican forest."

Eliza swallowed thickly. "Where do you think it is?"

"I think it's been truly forgotten," Alastor replied softly. "Where it is now... well." He patted Xeb's hand. "I may be able to give you a location to start. Whether it still rests there, I do not know."

"Do you know anything else?" Thorne asked, squeezing her hand beneath the table. She hadn't noticed it shaking, but he quelled the tremor, and a sense of relief rose within her.

Alastor shook his head, and her relief wavered. "What I have revealed his dangerous enough.

Eliza gnawed the inside of her lip and turned from the pair to face Thorne. "Is this what we need to do?" she asked quietly.

The commander dragged his attention from Alastor; his storm grey eyes searched her face, torn between worry and uncertainty. "Celia promised Isolde that she'd find a way to defeat the Dark Master," he replied, running a hand through his dark hair. "I think... I think it might be, yes."

The legends of Azula had followed her on her quest to find the lost prince, and now... now she'd have to search for Azula, search for the dagger a goddess had once wielded to protect Cadira from war thousands of years ago.

"We need to kill him before he can kill you again," Thorne

murmured.

Something in her stomach churned as his eyes darkened a fraction, and he pressed his lips firmly together. A thousand memories flashed in his eyes, none that she could remember, but her past life reared its head in reminder that what Eliza had was not entirely hers.

Eliza pulled back, putting distance between herself and the commander. "The power is the reason he's doing this. If the power were gone..."

"You exist because of the power," Alastor replied, voice soft. "I do not think you could survive separating from the magic that brought you to life. He is powerful, but he isn't a God. He *thinks* he is, and he certainly has grown powerful enough to take one on. But he isn't."

"But if he's as powerful as a God..." Eliza ran a hand over her face, cheeks warm with the impossibility of the task. "It would make killing him almost impossible, right?"

Xeb shook his head. "Not if you use a weapon of the Gods."

Like that's easy. She blew out a breath and slumped back in her chair. She'd always thought of Cadira's gods as a pantheon of beings similar to the Greek or Norse Gods of the mortal realm. Stories and legends could always be explained logically. Weapons supposedly blessed by gods were just cursed by warlocks or created by the Fae, maybe from the time of the Elves, blessed with the old magic of Cadira.

But Gods? True Gods? She wasn't cut out for that.

"Are you a God?" she asked Alastor after a moment, almost afraid of his answer.

The old man laughed, winking at her. "No, though thank you for thinking that. I'm half-Fae, like Xeb. Father was a Seelie and a direct descendent of the Elves, Mother was from the Court of Light."

Eliza grimaced. "Sorry, I—"

The old man waved a hand. "It's alright. An easy mistake with a title like mine." The amusement slipped from his features. "A lot changes in a thousand years. We're Soul Bound," he continued, squeezing Xeb's hand. The way they looked at one another... Eliza's stomach clenched. "That means soul mates, if you weren't sure. I know you grew up in New Orleans. Lovely place."

Eliza shifted uncomfortably. "How did you know that?"

"You're the Ecix," Xeb said, as if that should have been answer enough. "We're both old and very powerful. We know how to recognise you."

Eliza cleared her throat and offered them an awkward smile. And yet it hadn't answered her question about New Orleans "But how did you know where I—?"

"You've been asking a lot of questions," Alastor replied. He sipped his tea, nodding. "We have friends all over the mortal realm. And we also have many friends in Central Park."

"As soon as you got close," Xeb continued, "we decided to come to you. We had to make sure it was safe, especially for Alastor. But the moment you entered this world thirteen years ago, there was a... shift in the magic. I can count the number of times an Ecix has entered this world."

Thorne shifted beside her. "What does that have to do with any of this?"

"She must learn to protect herself better, is all," Alastor said gently. "Those who came before her were at full power, but she is not, and so her magic is a little more potent without the experience."

Eliza stared down at the bracelet around her wrist. "And here I thought I was safe."

Alastor gave her a sympathetic smile. "Power like yours... Unfortunately, my dear, you will never be safe. Not until you come into your magic. And not until you've saved yourself."

Sighing, Eliza rubbed a hand over her face. "Great," she muttered.

"I've been interested in properly meeting you for a while." Alastor took another sip of his tea. "The last time we saw each other, you had a different name and I'd been a different man."

She looked up. "No hard feelings?" Eliza raised a brow, biting her lip.

Alastor laughed. "All is fine. If it weren't for you, I wouldn't have met my heart and soul." He stopped laughing. The air of the dining room changed.

A shiver raced down her spine, and a whisper in her ear said, *Run.*

He's found you.

Eliza jumped from her seat and spun to face one of the large bay windows in the living room. Magic bubbled deep below the surface, and she called upon it, dragging it to the surface.

But she didn't get the chance to do anything before the glass shattered.

The Dark Master had found them.

11

BOUND BY DEATH
ELIZA

A startled scream tore through Eliza's throat as the glass shattered around her. Four red-eyed Shadow Soldiers landed amongst the debris, their mouths covered by black cloth. They wore darkness like cloaks, while shadows twisted around their chests like armour.

Thorne shoved Eliza behind him and pulled his sword from beneath his coat. A dark look entered his eyes as he rushed the soldiers, but she couldn't move, feet glued to the hardwood floors. For a moment, she thought she could smell the dry air of Mesah, feel the sand between her blood-soaked fingers.

Alastor appeared at Eliza's side. "You must go," he said. Eliza thought she saw something like ancient anger and... fear in his eyes. "You and your friend need to leave. We can hold them off."

Wide eyed, Eliza shook her head. "No way," she said. "They're here for me. You two need to save yourselves."

Xeb and Alastor shared a glance. "This is our home," Xeb said finally, "and we'll defend it to our last breaths."

Eliza opened her mouth to protest, but the half-Fae started shedding his mortal clothing, revealing the legs of a Satyr beneath. A tail whipped out and curled, the tip igniting with a dark burgundy flame. Twin swords appeared in his hands, and fire danced along the edges of the blades to match the flame of his tail.

Eliza reached for her dagger. The magic she summoned was still weak, barely a flicker in her veins, but she would make do.

She had to.

A soldier broke off from Thorne and approached her. His eyes were dull, dead, and bored into her with such a darkness it made her pause. His spirit floated behind him, translucent and fading, a reminder of what Eliza wasn't capable of doing again.

Heart thundering in her chest, she ducked under the arm of the soldier and struck with her dagger. It barely touched him as he spun out of her grasp, dead eyes on hers, unseeing. Though dark magic wafted from him, Eliza couldn't recognise the source. It was different to under the mountain.

When she turned to take in the kitchen, she couldn't see the old god, couldn't feel his magic nearby. Eliza hoped he'd ran, prayed he escaped.

The Shadow Soldier slammed into Eliza, knocking her to the ground. The breath left her in a gasp as pain shot up her spine.

She blinked, and she was no longer in the living room.

Red walls surround her, the floor beneath her soft sand. Her back ached from the throwing-knife she'd just pulled from her spine. Standing over her wasn't a soldier. Instead, Eliza stared into the familiar green eyes of her fiancé.

Aliesar, with his charming features and windswept hair, smiled—

"Eliza!"

She blinked, and Mesah was gone. The prince, the sand, the blood. *It was nothing.*

The soldier brought his sword down, but she rolled in time to avoid the blade.

These soldiers aren't here for me. The Dark Master had never tried to kill her before, not so brazenly. All his soldiers and demons had been careful not to kill, only disable.

Not these ones.

Eliza shot to her feet and searched for Alastor and Xeb. The former was still nowhere to be seen, while the latter fought with two of the soldiers.

Thorne met her gaze from across the room. Fear flashed across his features as he ran his eyes over her body. His lips parted with another shout, but Eliza froze and turned in a slow circle.

The Shadow Soldier she'd been fighting... was gone.

"Crap," she hissed, spinning in a circle.

Where is he?

Eliza flexed her fingers and pulled at the natural magic that spread through the mortal realm. The trace of it was faint, but she could just touch it. She brushed her fingers over it and grasped onto the tendrils that snaked towards her.

The connection was weak, like a dull thrum in her veins. But it was just enough to help her. Eliza opened her eyes, and using that connection, she followed Alastor's trace through the house. Somewhere above her, glass smashed.

No.

"Eliza!" Thorne shouted, but she ignored him, heart thundering, pushing her further into the apartment, and away from the protection of the commander. Her magic was weak, but she summoned what she could, reeling it into herself, shaping it into a weapon.

She rushed up a set of wooden stairs and into a white hall. White and red roses had been placed between doors. One vase had fallen, glass scattering across wood panelling, the roses strewn across the floor.

And the door had been wedged open.

No.

With trembling fingers, Eliza pushed open the door. She swallowed a lump in her throat, vision blurry.

What have I done?

The room came into focus, revealing the soldier, crumpled on the ground, the spirit once attached to his shoulder gone. He didn't move as blood spurted from his throat, staining a white rug covering hardwood floors. But standing over him, Alastor gripped a battle axe in hand, a smile curving his lips.

"It's been many years since I've taken a life," he said, meeting her eye. His blue eyes had gone black as night.

"He wasn't technically alive," she replied, mouth dry. Her gaze dropped to the body, and she couldn't take her eyes off it. "You did him a favour."

Did he though? A shiver raced down her spine. She'd thought the same thing before...

Alastor stepped over the body; she expected him to meet her at the door, but instead he crossed the room to a wall lined with books, all hidden behind glass that shimmered like chains across a chest. He swept his hand over the spell that locked away the books, and skimmed the titles.

It was instant, the rush of power that assaulted her. Eliza took a stumbling step back, and ran into the doorframe. "What are those?" she asked, voice no more than a whisper. The onslaught of magic burned in her veins, and her ears rang from the impact.

"Oh, just some insurance," Alastor replied. He was searching for something, running his fingers over the spines of books that threatened to bite them off. Some of the books lashed out with powerful, dark magic. One even had shadows slipping from the pages, coursing over the shelves and down to the blood-soaked rug.

"Aha!" Alastor pulled a small tome from a bottom shelf and quickly dusted off the cover. He smiled to himself before relocking the library of dangerous magic.

"Here." He handed her the tome. There was no title on the cover or spine; the leather was worn, a bruised purple. The way it felt in her hands made her wonder if the leather was actually skin pulled taught over wood.

Eliza looked between Alastor and the book. When their eyes met, he patted her hand. "It's what *he* wants." He took her wrist in his pale hand and pushed the book to her chest. "It'll give you what you need to find the weapon. Protect the book. Only you can unlock it." He winked. "I did steal it from one of your pasts, after all."

She frowned, but didn't question it. Instead, she shoved it into the waist band of her jeans so it sat snuggly against her abdomen. Her sweatshirt billowed enough to hide it from view.

Something like a scream of agony sounded downstairs. Alastor's face darkened, and his hands tightened around the handle of his axe.

"Xeb." He motioned towards the door Eliza stood in, the look in his eyes concerning her more than the bloody axe.

Silently, she entered the hall. The sound of fighting below trickled up the stairs towards her. As she waited for Alastor, Eliza palmed her dagger. Her hands shook, but she waited until he was with her before speaking.

"I'm sorry," she said, staring down at the broken vase. The shattered glass glinted under the bright lights of the hallway. A chandelier that hung over the entry rattled with a force of dark magic. She took a step and hesitated.

"Don't be." He took hold of her arm, steadying her, reddened eyes moving to the stairs. "There are worse things."

Alastor made to move, but she grasped his small, cold hand. "I don't think they're here for me," she whispered. "That soldier tried to kill me. Had the chance to, but went for you. He wanted the information you have."

Alastor nodded slowly and they descended the stairs. "I had a feeling this day would come."

The words made her stomach clench. She expected to be ambushed as soon as they descended the stairs, but the clashing of swords and the grunts of battle were nowhere to be heard. Instead, a heavy silence penetrated the house, so still it scared her more. Were the soldiers dead? Or was Thorne? Fear clenched its fist around her heart and quickened her steps.

She stayed one step ahead of Alastor as they entered the living room.

Dread circled her gut. The Shadow Soldiers weren't dead. Instead, eight more had joined them, surrounding Xeb and Thorne. Their blades, tipped in darkness, were raised to her friend's throats, poised to strike and spill dark blood.

Eliza came to a stop and sucked in a breath. "If they're after you," she said, "then you need to disappear."

"I can't," Alastor replied, shaking his head.

"I don't care about your exile or what King Bastian thinks," she hissed. "Go now."

He met her stare, eyes hardening. "It isn't that simple, Ecix. You of all people should know that." Alastor placed a hand on her shoulder, and within the blink of an eye, she was inside the circle of soldiers.

As she stumbled into Thorne's arms, she couldn't help but send Alastor an incredulous look. But he paid no attention to her.

What is he doing?

He pulled Xeb's arm around his lithe shoulders and looked up into the slitted eyes of his partner. Xeb, who had just been drinking tea with them, looked close to death, a deep wound on his abdomen seeping blood and a yellow-green poison that would kill him if not treated. His blood glinted like starlight as it dripped down his side and through the tufts of fur that lined his legs. As it pooled on the rug, Eliza thought she could see the Cadiran night sky.

Why aren't they leaving?

Alastor twisted his free hand, and a portal appeared behind her. Eliza shook her head, but Alastor nodded in Thorne's direction. The commander pulled her back, as if understanding the God of War's silent command.

"No!" she shouted, writhing in his grasp, reaching out for either Alastor or Xeb.

But Alastor smiled, winking at Eliza. "We'll meet again, one day, Ecix," he said, eyes flickering up once more to his loves.

Xeb tried to smile, but blood dripped down his lips. The soldiers closed around them, poison-tipped swords angled up at their throats.

Eliza screamed again, the sound burning her throat, but the portal closed around her.

The soldiers advanced, and Alastor and Xeb disappeared behind a layer of swirling smoke and shimmering light.

12

AZULA AND HER DAGGER
ELIZA

Eliza limped several steps before collapsing against the side of a mausoleum. She emptied her stomach as tears stung her eyes and ran down her cheeks.

No. No, no, no! She slammed her hands into the stone beneath her. She should have done more. She could have.

She could have stopped Alastor from giving himself over.

She could have stopped Thorne from dragging her through the portal.

Thorne rubbed a soothing hand down her back. "There's nothing you could have done," he murmured.

She flinched, wiping a hand over her mouth. "I could have done more," she said, voice shaky in her ears. "I could have fought, helped them, Thorne. I froze with the soldier, and then..." Her stomach roiled, bile rising in her throat.

When she looked up, she found the commander kneeling beside her. His stormy-blue eyes watched her warily, lips pulled in a worried line. Blood spattered his face and clothes, all Xeb's, she thought. "No," he said, "you couldn't." His eyes flickered down to the bracelet on her wrist.

Eliza growled and slammed her wrist into the side of the mausoleum. "If it wasn't for the Blood Witches and their stupid rules, I could have helped them. They've weakened me, Thorne. If it weren't for them, maybe Xeb and Alastor would still be alive."

"We don't know that they're dead."

She shook her head, stumbling to her feet. "Of course they are. Either that, or they'll wish they were." She pressed a hand to her belly, and felt the hardness of the book, still carefully tucked out of sight. She sucked in a breath. "The Dark Master wanted Alastor because of what he knew about the dagger. I know it."

The cemetery grew colder as she started in the direction of what she hoped was the exit. She recognised some of the old plaques. Moonlight danced off of the metal.

"Eliza."

Anger burned in her veins, riddled with her guilt and fear of what she'd done. Eliza turned. "You left them."

Thorne lowered his head, sighing. "It's complicated..."

"No," she said, stepping back. "It isn't. They needed us, and you were ready to abandon them!"

"I needed to get you out." Thorne met her stare.

Eliza turned on her heel and started again for the exit. She heard Thorne behind her, his heavy boots crunching in the loose rocks and dead flowers. She even felt his eyes on her, burning holes in the back of her shirt.

She sighed and crossed her arms.

Several steps ahead of Thorne, she didn't notice that she'd stepped off her usual path. Too caught up in her own thoughts, she hadn't been paying attention to where she'd been going.

Thorne was no longer behind her.

A shiver danced down Eliza's spine. A rush of ancient power coursed over her skin. The bracelet warmed until it burned against her flesh, reacting to the magic that swept through the cemetery.

Eliza stilled as she looked up into the bright eyes of the faery knight, an immortal being she'd first encountered before receiving word from the king about her mission, in the same cemetery they stood in. Her heart thundered in her chest, and she stumbled back several steps before steadying.

The knight tucked his helmet under his arm. The raven on his shoulder watched her carefully, golden eyes luminescent in the dark.

"What?" Eliza asked.

The knight blinked, eyes wary. But he said nothing. For the first time, Eliza could take in his features. He had a strong, pointed jaw and sharp ears, bright eyes that glowed in the darkness. His moon-pale skin shone against the dark chain mail beneath his breastplate, the light of the moon reflecting off his armour. Up close, the details of his breastplate were clear: thorns and roses lined the edges, the sigil of a raven in flight outlined over his chest. But between the thorns and roses, there were small creatures, woodland pixies and nymphs peeking out through the gaps.

Her anger and frustrations didn't waver, and seeing the knight for the first time since she'd been in Mesah, she wanted to snap. Instead, she released a cooling breath. "Why do you follow me? Or are you two a figment of my imagination?"

Something in the knight changed at her words, his eyes saddening as his gaze passed from her to the raven. The raven dropped its head, before swooping from the knight's shoulders, disappearing into the darkness of the cemetery.

Within the blink of an eye, the knight was gone.

"Eliza, there you are."

She spun to face Thorne; his brows were knotted, lips pulled in a thin line. Worry etched itself into his handsome features.

"I'm still pissed at you," she said, and stormed off.

It didn't take long to get home, and when they did, Eliza wanted nothing more than to go straight to her room and lock herself away for the rest of the night.

But that didn't seem like it was going to be an option. Not with her family waiting in the courtyard.

"It's got to be midnight," Eliza said, stopping in the gateway. "Shouldn't you all be in bed?"

Her grandfather rose first. Worried lines marked his face, grey hair dishevelled and silver eyes searching. She knew she probably looked like a mess, and Thorne had blood on his clothes and face.

"Eliza..."

She shook her head and held a trembling hand up. "I really don't want to hear it. I just want to go and have a shower and crawl into bed."

No one said a word as she left.

~

Loud music drummed in her ears, drowning out the sound of her heart. Her blood thrummed as she stared down at her wrist, at the bracelet that could have prevented everything.

Eliza clenched her hand into a fist. Her nails bit into the soft skin of her palm, pressing deep enough that she wondered if it would draw blood.

She didn't hear the door open, but she looked up when her grandfather's magic brushed against hers.

"I brought you some cocoa," he said, carefully placing her mug down on her bed-side table. "And I came to talk to you."

Eliza sighed and pulled out her earbuds, turning the music off. She shoved the old iPod under one of her pillows before running a hand through her wet hair. "Thorne told you."

Her grandfather nodded. "He explained what happened." Reaching out, Davis took Eliza's hand and stared down at the half-moons her nails had left. He closed both his hands around hers before sighing. "I'm sorry."

"You aren't going to tell me there was nothing more I could have done?" she asked.

He shook his head. "No, of course not."

The door creaked open. Eliza expected Kay or Celia to enter, but their cat, Odin, pranced into the room and jumped onto the bed. His purrs filled the air as he rubbed himself against Eliza's leg. She scratched the back of his ears. The one-eyed old cat hated everything but attention.

"You aren't a little girl anymore," her grandfather said. Eliza met his stare, heart rate picking up. "There are far more dangers out in the world. I had been afraid Alastor would be one of those dangers, but I had never expected he'd be a target of the Dark Master, too."

She rubbed her eyes. "What if I never went to see them? Would they still be safe? Or would the Dark Master have found him eventually?"

Davis sighed. "You'll never know. I need you to calm yourself, now, Eliza. You cannot control everything."

She clenched her jaw and looked away. "I could have controlled this."

Her grandfather remained silent for a moment before moving closer to wrap an arm around her. "My poor girl," he murmured, kissing the top of her head, "I wish there was more I could do for you."

Eliza squeezed her eyes shut. "Night, grandpa."

Davis brushed a stray tear from her cheek before rising from the bed. It creaked as his weight disappeared.

Eliza didn't open her eyes until the door to her room clicked shut. She released a shaky breath and stared down at her mug. The faded label stared at her, reminding her of a simpler time. Back when she didn't have to worry about the Dark Master or marrying the Prince of Cadira.

Back when she wasn't the target of evil masterminds who made her question her every move.

Eliza reached under her pillow, but not for her iPod. Instead, she felt for the old tome from Alastor, hidden as soon as she'd collapsed on her bed when she'd returned.

Settling in, Eliza sipped at the cocoa. Odin cozied up beside her and fell asleep as she began flipping through the worn pages.

THE GODDESS AZULA

The Goddess of Spirits, Lifeblood, Prophecy, and Enchantments

Believed to be the sister of the twin Gods of Death. Bestowed upon her by Thrinarv, King of the Gods and Father of the Brithien Elves was a dagger forged to protect the secrets of the Gods, and slay those who dared rise against them.

Azula took mortal form to wed a mortal king, and produced no heirs to him. However, she did not love the king. She had fallen in love with a Faery. After the king's death, she joined the Gods once more amongst the stars, until that same Faery caught her attention again.

Eliza skimmed through the passages, searching for more about the dagger.

Azula's dagger was lost after she bore a child to her Fae lover. There is little known about the child, other than the possible location of where Azula had left it upon returning to the Gods.

It is believed that a powerful witch stole the dagger and hid it from the Goddess. However, the location was forgotten. Its power is only rumoured, the truth lost to time.

Now, there is no trace of its whereabouts. Not even the name of the witch is remembered. But it is said that this witch was cursed with a dark magic born not of the land. And with this magic she fled to cultivate a new practice of believers, ones who worshipped the goddess Azula in cities built around her image.

The dagger must have existed once, long ago. Eliza knew that much. And something tickled the back of her mind. *A city built around her image.* Had Eliza not found two such cities buried beneath Cadira?

Which meant she had somewhere to start. For months, she'd been searching for something, *anything*. Alastor had been taken to stop her from learning that information.

She smiled.

Eliza flipped the page to read on, but nothing stared up at her. No words, no illustrations, nothing.

The next page held much of the same.

As did the next.

Whatever else had been hidden within the pages was gone, erased somehow. Anything else she might need to know about Azula and her dagger, gone.

The smile slipped from her lips.

But I know where to start, she thought.

The Dark Master wouldn't know what hit him.

But first, she had to deal with King Bastian.

13

WARNINGS
CELIA

Brandon touched the mug, but he didn't move to pick it up. He was too busy staring at his hands, where he had scrubbed so hard to remove all the dried blood caked under his nails and around his knuckles that his skin reddened. None of it had been his own, from what Celia could tell.

A shallow cut at his side healed slowly, whatever poison that had been used on the Shadow Soldier's blades non-lethal to an extent. Whatever had entered his system would works its way out with the salve she and Kay created, so long as he drank the tea.

"The cut had been quick," he'd said as she cleaned and dressed the wound, Kay standing in the doorway with a scowl and her arms crossed. "I'd barely had a chance to register I'd been hit. Eliza hadn't noticed, and I don't want her to know." As he'd said the last part, his gaze had flickered up to Kay, who had pressed her lips into a firm line then left the room.

Celia curled her legs beneath her and watched Brandon for a

moment. His dark eyes were trained on the mug between his hands, guilt swirling in his irises like lightning in a storm.

"So, what now?" Celia asked, cocking her head. She admired her handiwork; the blood stopped welling and clotted around the red skin, which slowly knitted together. "Drink your tea. It'll help with the internal healing."

Brandon made a face, but he picked up the mug and drank. When he set the cup back down, half finished, he shook his head. "I don't know. Eliza is angry, and I don't blame her."

"You wanted to save her. It sounded like Alastor wanted to as well." Celia settled back in her chair and hugged herself; sleep clawed at the edges of her consciousness, a yawn bubbling from her lips. "But you know what to do now, right?"

He looked up and met her stare. Something unsaid lingered between them, a truth neither were ready to divulge. "Alastor said the only thing that will stop the Dark Master is a dagger." He paused and looked down at his hands. His next words almost stole her breath. "Azula's dagger."

Celia slumped in her chair. Of all the things she'd thought Brandon and Eliza would learn on their visit with Alastor, she hadn't expected them to return with Azula's dagger as the answer.

Fear for what that might mean churned in her stomach. *Goddess help them,* she thought, though she knew Azula wasn't listening.

"That's not going to be easy to find," she whispered, tightening her arms around herself as a sharp pain flared at the base of her spine. "I didn't think..."

"I don't think Eliza could handle what that will mean."

Celia released a heavy breath. "I don't think so either. There is too much tied to that dagger, and what if she learns something too soon? What if she learns the truth?"

Brandon shook his head. "I don't know."

They remained silent for a moment, lost in the mess of their own thoughts, but Celia watched her friend from the corner of her eye. She knew he would swallow his guilt over what had happened to Alastor and Xeb, and concede that he had made a decision that saved Eliza's life. He'd gotten her out. And if they had stayed to fight, she wondered if the soldiers would have taken either of them alive.

But Brandon wouldn't confide in her about any of that, though Celia couldn't understand why. She wanted to help, and he wouldn't allow her to offer it.

"We need to tell the king," he said, finally breaking the quiet. Celia met his stare, eyes widening as she pursed her lips. "We need to update him."

Celia shook her head slowly. "Eliza won't like that."

Brandon shrugged, a tired sigh slipping past his lips. "He needs to know one of his most dangerous exiles is gone. It's no longer just about Eliza. The Dark Master took a prisoner who had been in hiding. It's my duty to report it."

Celia watched him for a moment. "It'll be your head, you know that, right?"

They were working without the king's blessing, entirely of their own accord. She wasn't naïve in thinking he had no idea of their search, but since their return and the announcement of the engagement, he'd remained content with what they were doing. It didn't interfere with his plans.

Until now.

Celia chewed the inside of her cheek as Brandon pulled a piece of parchment towards him. The breakfast nook just off the kitchen had been set up as their base for their search for Alastor, a number of texts and tiny colourful pieces of paper stuck to the faded walls. An assortment of Cadiran and mortal writing implements scattered the tabletop, most shoved unceremoniously into mismatched mugs pulled from the large variety lining the room.

Brandon bowed his head over the parchment, lips tugged down into a frown. The edges of the paper shimmered with magic, and as he wrote, the ink turned dark red. The message was short, likely formal and to the point. Celia silently hoped the king was asleep in Cadira and would not receive the message.

When Brandon signed off, the parchment shuddered and curled in upon itself as invisible flame ate away at the letter. All that was left was ash.

Celia watched it float away in an invisible breeze before pressing closer to her friend. "Do you remember anything else from the attack?" she asked, curling her hands into fists. "Maybe something that might help us understand why the Dark Master wanted him?"

Brandon shook his head. "I just know Alastor is apparently the last person who knows the truth of the dagger. I think the Dark Master wants to get the dagger so he can use it on Eliza, destroy the Ecix once and for all."

Before Celia could respond, a burning letter appeared and dropped onto the table between them. Brandon snatched up the reply and read it aloud:

"When light breaks in the mortal realm, return to the barriers. We must meet immediately." Brandon watched the paper turn to ash. "Eliza won't want to leave."

Celia raised a brow. "I know." She stood, taking their cups to the sink. As she rinsed them, she said, "I warned you. She'll have your head for this. He'll make her stop now."

Brandon rose, exhaustion darkening his features. He moved sluggishly to the door, careful of the wound. "I know. But I'll deal with the repercussions in the morning."

She gave a short, startling laugh. "Oh, I hope you know what you're doing."

Sending her a look, he turned and left. Celia let the water run as she stared after him.

~

Celia looked up as Eliza slipped into the kitchen without so much as a glance in Brandon's direction. She wore loose grey pants and an oversized shirt with holes in the hem, a pair of socks the only thing on her feet. Her soft hair fell in curls down her back. As she approached her birthday, she began to resemble Isolde more and more. It sent a pang of sadness through Celia as she watched the faint memory of her sister grow stronger in Eliza.

Brandon tensed beside her as Eliza approached what Kay fondly called the *coffee machine*. Eliza went through the motions to make herself a cup, pouring in an amber liquid as well as the dark, bitter coffee, topped with steamed milk, all the while saying nothing.

Beneath the table, Celia kicked Brandon's shin in warning. He cut her a look, clenching his jaw. His eyes conveyed the message: *I know*, but he shook his head regardless.

Celia waited, hands tightening around her tea as the tension grew thick. Tired circles lined Eliza's eyes, though Celia doubted anyone slept deeply the night before. Her own dreams were filled with blood and screams and shadows that cut her to the bone.

She brought the cooled cup to her lips and took a sip, peppermint filling her nose.

"Morning, Celia," Eliza muttered, starting for the door. Celia kicked him in the shin again.

Brandon sent her look and finally cleared his throat. "We need to talk."

Eliza turned slowly, eyes narrowed. "We have to leave, don't we?"

He nodded, though her words weren't phrased like a question. "King Bastian has requested your return."

Eliza stiffened, jaw clenching. A war waged in her eyes, as she looked from him then to Celia. "I don't have much of a choice then, do I?"

Brandon hesitated, then shook his head. "We need to leave soon."

The next breath she released was shaky. "Alright. Let me change and talk to Grandpa."

"Eliza—" Celia started, but her sister disappeared around the corner.

Brandon released a heavy breath as she went. Celia rose, gazing after Eliza, torn between chasing after her and scolding her friend. She shook her head, and slipped out from behind the table, starting for the door.

"She would have been hurt if I hadn't pulled her through," he murmured, making her pause. Celia looked back and found him staring at the door, a deep sadness filling his eyes. "I can't lose her again, Celia."

"She's not Isolde, Brandon." Celia sucked in a breath.

His gaze flickered to hers. "I still see the ghost of her in Eliza. I don't mean to. I know it isn't fair." He stopped and ran a hand over his face, releasing a heavy breath. "I didn't want to have to watch her get hurt again."

"I know," she replied, and deep down she understood. Sometimes she saw Isolde in Eliza too, mistook Eliza for the sister she'd lost all those years ago.

Brandon dropped his stare. What was playing through his mind, she wondered, and would he tell her? Or would he disappear again under the cover of darkness and leave her alone to the pain and guilt for what they could not prevent?

14

A DUTY TO THE KING
ELIZA

Eliza stared down at her wrist as she, Celia, and Thorne re-entered Cadira. The portal dropped them outside of the palace, the intricate Blood Witch magic making Eliza's head spin.

At least I know how Amitel got around, she thought, frowning.

Other than the wards—which acted as the barriers between worlds—portal's born of Blood Magic were the fastest ways to travel. They definitely made it easier for her to go between the now deserted Winter Palace temple and the capital.

Portals were a new magic to her. She'd thought them only to be in sci-fi movies, but now she was learning how to create her own. Only, she was still mad Celia had never created a portal during their search for the prince. It would have gotten them to Mesah a lot faster. But Eliza knew the reason why: Celia had been forbidden to use Blood Magic in front of Eliza, at the request of the High Witch Matron, who decided all factors of Eliza's learning when it came to the Blood Witches.

Nothing surprising there. Eliza tightened the scarf around her throat. Snow had finally cast its dark shadow over the palace, turning the once vibrant gardens white. But every inch of snow glistened like glass. If she didn't know any better, it looked almost peaceful.

"What will you tell King Bastian?" Celia asked as they trudged through the snow towards a servant entrance into the palace. The last thing His Majesty wanted was for everyone to see Eliza coming and going from the palace as she pleased.

"Eliza?" Celia brought them to a stop. Her bright blue eyes were shadowed with worry.

Shaking her head, Eliza shoved her hands into the pocket of her snow-coat. "I don't know."

Celia and Thorne shared a look, one Eliza read as: *they know something I don't.*

She looked between them. "What?"

Thorne released a breath. "He already knows about Alastor and the attack and that it was the Dark Master."

Eliza took a step back and stared at him, but Thorne refused to meet her eye. "How?" She turned to Celia. "Did one of the Keepers already tell him?"

Of course, she understood why he'd have to know. Alastor Verendus was a war criminal, hidden in the mortal world because there was no stronger prison than a world with limited magic. They couldn't kill him, so they held him captive.

But there was something they weren't telling her.

Her eyes narrowed. "What?"

Thorne stepped forward. "I told him about the attack. He needed to know about Verendus, but I said nothing about the dagger."

Eliza shook her head. "You told him." She looked away and blinked back frustrated tears. She'd never be able to return to the mortal world... not with that hanging over her head. The witch who lost the God of War. The witch who potentially lost the one person who knew how to kill the *Ecix*.

"You should have told me." Finally, she looked up and met his stare. "You should have at least warned me you were going to tell the king. Now..." She stopped, all breath leaving her. "He's never going to let me go near this. He's never going to let me leave the palace."

Celia touched her arm, but Eliza stepped out of her grasp. "He might not, Eliza. He might be lenient."

But Eliza shook her head, running a hand over her stiff, cold hair. "Yes he will. He's probably been looking for an excuse to keep me under his thumb and now he has it." She closed her eyes tight and tried to calm her racing heart.

It's not that bad, she thought, but even she knew that wasn't entirely true. For weeks she'd been conducting the search right under his nose, never letting it slip, never letting it interfere with whatever ridiculous ball or party or lesson he had planned. He never asked, and she never told.

For a while, she believed it some kind of silent agreement.

But she'd screwed up. Played into some twisted scheme of the Dark Master, and now...

But why Thorne?

She opened her eyes and watched him for a moment. Thorne said nothing, made no move to defend himself. Had he done it on purpose? When she searched his eyes, there was nothing malicious in the swirling greys and blues of his irises, but since their return from Mesah, he had been different.

She didn't need to ask why. She knew what he was thinking about, what he always thought about: *Isolde.*

Eliza looked away from Celia and Thorne, instead searching the white landscape. Only guards and the occasional servant traipsed through the icy gardens, heads bowed and unbothered by the chill morning. No one looked to her or her companions—they might as well have been ghosts.

"Bastian won't let me go after the dagger if he learns of the truth," Eliza muttered, biting her lip. "Especially now because he knows of the attack. Maybe if he knew of the dagger and what it can do, he'd let me go after it. Surely he'll see how important it is."

Though Thorne was shaking his head, it was Celia who seemed more inclined to agree. "The king knows he needs the Dark Master gone in order to maintain power," Celia said quietly. "If we tell him about the dagger, that there is a chance of defeating this evil once and for all, then perhaps he might allow us to continue our search for it."

Eliza shook her head. "You."

Celia frowned, hand straying to her side. "What?"

"He will let *you* search for it," Eliza said, following the movement. "My birthday is soon, remember? Big ball to celebrate, and only a couple weeks after that is the wedding. I won't be allowed to leave."

And she wanted to. It was *her* mission, after all. The Dark Master and his minions were after her, and she'd be damned if she wasn't part of the team sent out to look for the dagger.

"I can't let you guys go out there and put yourselves in danger like that. We have no idea what the Dark Master knows," Eliza said.

"But we can assume he's also searching for the dagger now." Thorne rubbed his forehead before the sighing. "I would much rather you stay here, at the palace." His eyes, grey like the stormy skies above, met hers. "But I also don't trust anyone here with your safety."

Eliza's heart twisted. *He is only looking out for Isolde.* The thought was bitter and hard, but she had to start looking out for herself.

Turning away, Eliza swallowed thickly and ignored her thoughts. "I don't care about my safety, I care about everyone else who might be put in the path of the Dark Master. If there *is* a weapon that can defeat him, then I want to be out there searching, not *here* playing princess."

Celia reached out and took Eliza's hand. "You have to be prepared, because I doubt the king will let you go lightly."

Eliza closed her eyes and sucked in a breath. "Then I will make him."

~

King Bastian's office was exactly as Eliza remembered: dark mahogany and velvet, old tomes lining the walls while a heavy, almost reddish desk sat in the centre of the room. The hearth crackled with fire to run away the chill of winter, though it didn't do much to the ice lacing the windows overlooking the kingdom's capital. The Captain of the guard, Jed, stood at the king's left, while Eliza's Blood Witch trainer, Lennox, a graceful woman of at least three-hundred-years, stood to the side. Her dark eyes never left Eliza's.

Even with Celia and Thorne at her side, she still hated how weak the king made her feel. Before the mission, before the lost Prince and the Dark Master, she had believed she could stand a chance against him and his wishes.

But now, with the Blood Witches taking up residence in the palace, Eliza believed nothing other than the fact that she was their pawn, and she had no choice.

She bowed and kept her eyes on the king. In the end, he held the power.

"Was your *mission* successful?" King Bastian asked, leaning forward in his chair. Every movement he made was precise and calculated, something Eliza had learnt early in her stay at the palace. For the last month, she'd been watching him as he did her, and during that time she'd realised just how screwed she was.

If she lied, he would know. He already knew the truth and yet he wanted to test her. Lennox's eyes drilled into her, as if begging her to lie and find out the consequences.

But the king wouldn't let his anger show. He would reel it in and make it clear through his punishment.

Eliza rose from her bow and clutched her hand in front of her. "Unfortunately, we lost the informant, but we did come across information that can change the tide of this war."

Bastian raised a questioning brow and waved an uninterested hand. "And what might that be?"

"A weapon," she replied, heart racing. Her hands shook. "More precisely, a legendary dagger. It has the power to destroy Gods. And it should have the power to destroy *him*."

She could almost see the cogs working inside his mind as he weighed the possibilities—take the risk and send her out to find the weapon, or sit back and let the Dark Master continue his reign of terror.

Eliza wasn't as naïve as she once was; there was more to the king's plans than he ever let on. Now that he had his son back... there was no telling what he'd do next. And now that he had her...

Eliza's gaze flickered to the witch at his side, whose face was a careful mask of calm. What would she relay back to the Blood Witches about the dagger?

When the king didn't speak, Eliza continued, keeping her voice as strong as she could, "I, along with Commander Brandon Thorne and Blood Witch Celia can begin the search. It will be a journey, but with the right tools we can find evidence of the dagger, might even find the thing itself, we just need time—"

"No," Bastian said, and her gaze shot back to his. The king's dark eyes blazed with anger. "You will remain at the palace until your eighteenth birthday. And you will prepare for the wedding. I will call upon another to take over now, but you will not pursue this."

Eliza's eyes widened as the reality set in: King Bastian had chosen power over the people of Cadira, chosen to finally put an end to her search. "But—"

His eyes never left hers. "As your king, understand this: your duty is to the people now. There are plenty of soldiers who can continue this search. But you will not join them. Understood?"

She bit the inside of her cheek to stop of her from snapping. One wrong move and her family's life was ruined. He'd threatened them before, and she had no doubt that threat carried through now.

But accepting it could kill so many...

Bowing her head, Eliza sucked in a cooling breath. "Understood." The word tasted bitter on her lips, but she said it nonetheless.

But that didn't mean she'd listen.

15

IMMORTAL BETRAYAL
ELIZA

The sweet smell of winter blossoms filled Eliza's nose as she stepped into the confines of the court gardens. The exclusively royal orchard was home to the more exotic and colourful flora, with vines that crept along the walls bleeding red flowers, and strange bushes producing berries of pink and yellow. Though they smelt amazing, there was no way Eliza would dare touch the forbidden fruits.

She released a breath. Her conversation with the king echoed in the back of her mind, swirling and churning just like the sky above her. She closed her eyes, focusing on the cold breeze as it lingered on her flushed cheeks.

Things were spiralling out of control, and there was nothing she could do to stop it. Her eighteenth birthday was fast approaching and although she should have been excited, every second leading up to the day made her sick to her stomach. She hated the feeling of losing control, that she no longer *had* power over her own life.

Her life, that now belonged to the Blood Witches and King

Bastian. Had it ever been hers to begin with?

Sighing, she opened her eyes and shoved her hands into the pockets of her coat. Each day just crawled along and dragged with it questions with no answers, and thoughts that did nothing more than send her stomach churning.

Magic brushed lightly against her, sending shivers down her spine. She came to a stop inside the maze of flowers and bushes and searched the white landscape.

"Well hello, love."

Spinning, Eliza stumbled back a step as Amitel appeared in the archway of the gardens. There were no guards in sight, no royals lingering in the pavilions or walking the paths.

Eliza was alone.

Amitel had changed since their reunion in the alley; the same golden hair curled around his ears looked clean and soft, outlining his sharp features and red-flecked golden eyes. It seemed as though he had finally gotten some sun, his skin taking on a bronze colour, smooth and unblemished, as immortal as it always had been.

"What do you want?" Eliza asked, taking another step back. She cursed herself. This section of the gardens wasn't only lifeless, it was secluded, especially late in the morning.

Amitel approached slowly. "To talk."

"Really?" she asked, a bitter laugh bubbling from her lips. "Are you sure about that? Or are you here to spy on me again for the Dark Master?"

His lips pursed into a thin line. Up close, Eliza could see the beauty of his plain black dress-shirt, the gold embellishment along the cuffs and the shining buttons. Knee-high riding boots covered the black pants that seemed to cling to his thighs, making him look like a storybook prince rather than a cunning warlock.

"I've changed," he said quietly, eyes pleading with her.

Eliza's heart thundered in her chest. She should run, or scream. She should have blasted his ass into next week.

Celia and Thorne's voices in the back of her mind reminded her that they had spoken to him. That they heard him out, and wanted to believe him.

But that didn't mean she did. "I find it hard to believe you, Amitel," she said, shaking her head. "Even if *they* do, I'm not sure if I can."

"Please."

Eliza swallowed down the thickness in her throat. And she waited, because she was afraid she'd say something she'd regret.

He appeared in front of her; one strong step brought them together, an inch apart, and she was forced to look up into his molten-gold eyes, where she could read every one of his emotions. He was open to her, completely.

"You didn't tell the king about me. Why?" he asked, voice low in her ear.

"Stupidity."

He chuckled softly. "I doubt that, love."

Eliza pulled away and stepped back, crossing her arms over her chest. "Don't call me that," she snapped, her heart racing.

"Listen to me," he said. "Give me a chance to explain."

She looked at him, lips pursed, and considered it for a moment. He'd reappeared so conveniently in the alley, and thinking on it, she wondered if he had been tied to the death of the informant as well.

Guilt danced and pleaded with her to listen, so she nodded.

"Now will you hear me out?" he asked, raising a brow.

Eliza released a heavy breath. "Amitel, if you haven't noticed, I don't trust you." She tried to look anywhere but at him, unable to meet his stare, not because she was uncomfortable, but because she could see the sincerity in them. "I don't trust that you are on the same team as the rest of us. What happens when the Dark Master makes you a shiny new offer? Will you screw me over again?"

"You can trust me," he said. "You've always been able to trust me. You know that. Otherwise we never would have been in that watermill in the first place."

"The Blood Witches did that," she said quietly, catching his stare from the corner of her eye. The first time they'd met had been inside a crumbling watermill north of the Winter Palace, outside the small village of Harrenhal. Eliza had been forced to speak with him alone, Thorne barred from the mill by use of Blood Magic. "Probably to test whether or not I'd pick up on you being a spy for the Dark Master."

Amitel released a frustrated breath. "Fine. Don't trust me then, but I will be here, and I will be searching for the Dark Master too. I owe you a life debt, Eliza."

Her heart stopped in her chest. "What did you say?"

He stepped away, as if ready to walk out of the garden. Anger highlighted his handsome features, magic crackling around him. It reminded her that he was a dangerous warlock, that he was old and that he was powerful.

"The king called on me," he replied, "to take over the search for the Dark Master—and the dagger."

Bile rose in her throat. She took a stumbling step back. *No,* she thought, shaking her head. *Anyone but him.*

They watched each other for a silent heartbeat.

The dunes of Mesah, the blood and sand caked under her fingernails, the dark and suffocating tunnels beneath the desert came back to her. How naïve she had been, trusting him. How naïve they had all been.

And now she was faced with another choice: trust him, or go against her friends and turn him into the king.

But would the king give her back what was rightfully hers? Would he allow her to go after the dagger?

No, she realised, heart plummeting. She'd get herself into even more trouble. She'd risk her friends, who hadn't yet been stifled by the king and his rules.

Amitel turned on his heel and spared her a look over his shoulder. "If that's all, love, I have a meeting with King Bastian."

And what if he's telling the truth? A little voice in her head asked. *What if Amitel is here to help? What is he risking?* If he had truly turned his back on the Dark Master, what kind of danger was he putting himself--and everyone else--in.

"Why come back at all?" she asked, voice soft. Amitel's footsteps faltered, and he turned. "Why not just... disappear? You had every chance, and hell it'd be a lot safer for you and everyone if you did. But you're here, and I can't tell if that's out of stupidity, or because you haven't changed at all."

Amitel flinched, but she continued. "I could go back to the king and tell him everything. Tell him how you were working with the Dark Master, that you might have even been complicit in Alicsar's disappearance. You could kill me now or wipe my memories and no one would know." Eliza crossed her arms and cocked her head.

Before she could make a decision, footsteps sounded behind them. Eliza turned to take in Celia; her inky black hair was unbound and flowing freely down her back, milky skin flushed beneath the red hood she wore. Her striking blue eyes found Eliza's as a soft smile tipped her scarlet-painted lips.

"Eliza, Amitel." Celia stepped under the archway and into the garden. She threw her shoulders back, tense. "I'm glad to see you both."

Eliza breathed a sigh of relief and rushed to Celia's side. A shiver raced down Eliza's spine as Amitel's gaze darkened, steady on hers. "Suppose you'll have to wait for that answer, love," he murmured, bowing his head. He cut Celia glance, and nodded in her direction. "Celia."

Eliza said nothing as she watched the warlock leave, his hair gold in the light of the sun. Heat warmed her cheeks, anger flooding through her.

Celia touched her hand. "Are you alright? Did he do anything to you?"

Silently, Eliza shook her head. *What game is he playing*, she wondered, taking a step in the direction he'd left. He had fooled her once, betrayed her. He was capable of doing it again.

"The king summoned him to take over the search for the dagger," Eliza whispered. "And now everything is falling apart."

16

PRINCESS OF THE PEOPLE
ELIZA

Dreams of Azula's lost dagger and the Dark Master made it easy for Eliza to forget that it was her eighteenth birthday.

Lights created by magic lined the gardens outside Eliza's window. The sun dipped towards the horizon, casting the land in a golden hue that almost looked ethereal.

In the distance, Eliza watched as carriages rolled into the palace grounds, carrying nobility from all over Cadira. Someone outside in the snow was playing a violin as guests arrived, the sound floating up to her balcony.

Eliza supressed a shiver and crossed her arms over her chest.

Just one night, she thought, then almost laughed. She'd said that to herself before, on a night similar to this one. But she'd been in a mask, and yet now she felt more like an imposter than ever before.

"How are you feeling?"

Eliza jumped and spun to face Amitel, who took up the doorway with his tall, lean frame. He looked both messy and handsome in his black and red suit.

She narrowed her eyes. "I was doing better before you got here." Taking a hesitant step back, Eliza bumped into the railing of the balcony and rested her hands against the freezing metal. "What do you want?"

Amitel's lips twitched into a half-smile, her cheeks heating as his eyes roamed her body. "You look gorgeous, love."

Not even she could fault the gown King Bastian had bought her; rose-gold and silver flowers lined the neckline, which dipped into a V, stopping around her breasts. The sleeves were tulle and billowed out with pearl stitching, only to cuff at her wrists. The over-skirt was of the same material, rose-gold satin beneath matching the bodice. The gown itself was gorgeous—not her, though she had been pleasantly surprised by how she'd looked wearing it, like a faerie from a *Disney* movie. Less like the wicked witch half of Cadira saw her as. She'd never had her hair curled so perfectly, half pulled back in a messy plait woven with matching rose-gold and silver flowers with strands framing her face.

So artful, pretty, that she could almost forget that she would be introduced into Cadiran society, and by the end of the night, her fate would be sealed.

Unless Amitel was there to kill her, steal her magic, and report back to the Dark Master.

At least it would be a quick death, she thought sourly.

Eliza cleared her throat. "I don't want compliments from you."

Amitel released a heavy breath and shook his head. "I don't know how many times I have to apologise."

"You set me up!" She took a step forward and jabbed a finger into his chest. "*You* were working for the Dark Master, Amitel. You have a *lot* of grovelling to do before I forgive you for *anything*."

He opened his mouth to respond, but the door to her suite opened.

Celia took two steps into the room before coming to a stop, her pleasant smile shifting into one of unease. "What's wrong?" she asked, looking between Eliza and Amitel.

Eliza rolled her eyes. "Take a guess."

"Eliza." Celia glided to where Amitel stood in the doorway and looked between the two of them.

"What?" Eliza asked.

Celia shook her head in response. "We've no time for this," she muttered. "Eliza, you look beautiful. Amitel, please leave. We must finish readying her for the ball."

Amitel's golden gaze slid back to Eliza, full of unkept promises, betrayals, and even worse, sincerity. Eliza had to force herself to stop looking at him, and instead brushed past him back into the suite where Celia waited.

"I'm ready," Eliza finally said, the lie sweet on her tongue. "Let's just get this over with."

~

Eliza descended the grand staircase as the silence of the ballroom settled around her. The music was gone, the voices quiet, all attention on her, waiting for her to either fall, or take one more step towards being the future Queen of Cadira.

The last thought scared her more than tripping over her skirt.

Waiting at the foot of the stairs, her grandfather smiled warmly up at her. Several Keepers dotted the crowd, primarily standing close to the king, who sat poised on his throne, with the prince—and her fiancé—beside him. Eliza had the motions memorised thanks to weeks of practice.

At the bottom step, the crowd parted so there was a clear path to King Bastian. To Prince Alicsar.

Celia was already amongst the crowd, Amitel by her side, but Eliza couldn't see Thorne anywhere amongst the generals or nobility. Anyone of importance had appeared to see off their future Queen, but not Thorne.

Where the hell is he?

Eliza swallowed thickly. Wherever he was, she hoped he had a good reason for missing her birthday.

Clutching the skirts of her gown, Eliza dropped into a low curtsey.

The crowd watched her give her respects to the king, and watched her do the same to Lennox and Celia, the only Blood Witches in attendance. Their red robes had silver detailing around the cuffs and hems, hoods pulled back. The long sleeves covered their hands, almost long enough to trail along the floor.

Briefly, Eliza met Celia's eye. Something passed between them; a spark of awareness that Eliza couldn't shake. Like they had done this before.

Although Bastian sat only feet away, it seemed more like miles, the path between them treacherous. She was glad she hadn't eaten anything all day, because the churning in her stomach would have made her vomit—everywhere.

Straightening, Eliza took her grandfather's outstretched arm and tucked her hand in the crook of his elbow.

"You look beautiful, Lizzy."

The pet name made her heart shudder; it had been years since he'd called her that. She couldn't even remember the last time she'd heard that name, but all the same, it made her feel young again, protected.

She gave her grandfather a strained smile. "Thanks."

The wry smile on his own lips disappeared as they began their trek to the king.

In the back of her mind, Eliza could hear her tutor, a lady with an unpronounceable name and pompous wigs, muttering in the back of her head. *Back straight. Head high. Eyes lowered, dainty, Elizabeth. Do not look the king in the eye, and by the Gods, do not look at your feet. Keep that stray hand behind your back so you don't go flouncing it about, yes like that.*

From the corner of her eye, Eliza spotted her tutor with her husband and two daughters, both at least five years older than Eliza, neither wed because no man in his right mind wanted to deal with the likes of Lady Pompous.

As if sensing her stare, the tutor made a motion with her hand and tapped it beneath her chin. Eliza remembered that instruction well enough to know she had let her chin dip too much.

But she lifted her chin just as she reached the bottom of the dais, where Alicsar waited. She hadn't noticed him move from his father's side, but now she had no choice but to see him; his hair was shorter than it had been last time she'd seen him, now cut around his ears but longer in the top. The crown—silver with a sapphire at the very front, surrounded by small, reflective diamonds—sat perfectly atop his styled hair, unmoving.

Her heart leapt into her throat, palms clammy as she took the prince in. Since his return to the palace, the remnants of his time in the desert under the Dark Master's influence had slipped away. The tan that had once darkened his skin dimmed, his sun-kissed golden brown hair now the colour of burnt sand on a summer day.

But his eyes were the same, the colour of the deepest parts of the Willican forest, shadowed by lost memories and a life he, too, didn't belong to.

As they came to a stop, Eliza could feel her grandfather's arm disentangling from hers. Already engaged, Eliza would be handed off to her future husband, as per custom. Ridiculous and outdated as it was, it happened to both boys and girls coming of age. Sons were passed off to their future wives just as much as girls were.

Every movement Alicsar made was gentle, like he was aware of the way she felt around him. For the most part, she had tried tirelessly not to flinch in his presence, but there had been days—long mornings after a restless sleep, or afternoons following hours of Blood Witch training—where she forgot to hide the effects of what happened in the desert. And she knew he picked up on those moments, as tiny as they were.

It wasn't lost on her that he watched her, paid attention. It reminded her of Thorne, but unlike the commander, Prince Alicsar wasn't waiting for the ghost of his dead girlfriend to reappear.

Her grandfather nudged her, reminder of where she was and what she was supposed to be doing.

Like she'd been taught, the handoff was easy enough; after pulling her hand away from her grandfather's arm, Eliza unwillingly let the prince take her left hand.

The part Eliza knew the least about was the king's role in the ceremony. He rarely appeared at balls such as these.

Bastian's smile was not warm, nor did it reach his eyes as they swept over her and then the crowd. "I am honoured to be hosting you all today as we welcome the hero of Cadira, Blood Witch Elizabeth Kindall, into our society." The king paused for a soft round of applause. "She bravely ventured out into Cadira to locate my son, who had been kept from us for twenty long years. For that I will be forever grateful."

His gaze cut to hers. "Let us welcome Elizabeth Kindall into society, Princess of the people."

The words echoed in her ears, drowning out the thundering applause. Bastian certainly knew how to work the crowds. Because somehow even *she* believed him. A princess of the people, he called her. It was what he had wanted right from the beginning.

Her thoughts turned sour, and finally she tore her eyes away from his.

With the end of the speech came a lull of doubt. The entire night was ingrained in her mind, from the descent into the ballroom right down to the acceptable time for her to leave.

Her stomach churned with the knowledge of what was to come next.

Alicsar's hands were as gentle as his eyes as he guided her into the middle of the dancefloor. Around them, the crowd parted like the red sea. From the corner of the ballroom, the orchestra started a slow song, the notes of the violin eerily familiar. From the corner of her eye, she spotted Amitel standing beside Henry Ivo.

A shiver raced down her spine as she took the two men in, but her gaze was pulled away as Alicsar spun her in preparation for their first dance.

One thing she could be thankful of was that she hadn't been forced into the spotlight with the prince since the announcement of their engagement. Because she wasn't eighteen, and hadn't been announced to society, their dances had always been chaperoned and kept short, because both had to fill their dance cards with others.

Now, with their engagement set in stone, the king could finally show them off like he had always wanted to.

Swallowing thickly, Eliza straightened and fell into the familiar, flowing movements of the dance. Hours spent with her tutor had made it easy to follow along. It had also helped that Eliza had taken dance classes as a child, and had even joined her elderly neighbour once or twice at ballroom classes out of boredom.

Alicsar, however, wasn't a natural dancer, and despite the hours he'd spent learning alongside her, he still couldn't quite get the right steps.

As if sensing her thoughts, the prince gave her a wry smile. "Don't let me fall."

The smile—and his words—were innocent enough. But together, they brought back memories of *him*. Of kisses witnessed only by the stars and sand, where she had felt a brief moment of happiness despite the pressure of her mission.

That smile had ripped away that happiness. Words like his had made her suffer.

The music's tempo increased enough to make her concentrate on the steps. She tried to ignore Alicsar's attempt at making a joke, but with all eyes on them, she couldn't be sure how she'd respond.

A flash of sadness entered his eyes. "Happy birthday," he murmured quietly. Eliza could feel the tension of his body against hers as they danced. So far, he hadn't made a wrong step, and for that, she couldn't help but be slightly proud.

"Thanks," she replied stiffly. She couldn't ignore the awkwardness—it was so thick she could have cut it with a knife.

Alicsar's jaw clenched. "I'm sorry Bastian's making a big deal out of this. I know you don't like..." he trailed off and looked away, surprising her. "I'm sorry."

Eliza wasn't entirely sure how to respond, and couldn't quite get the words in before the end of the song.

Weeks of trying to separate herself from the prince she'd saved seemed almost useless in that moment. She was forced to remember the man he had been before, though the shadow of his betrayal could never quite disappear.

The music ended, and they were forced to part and bow to one another. Eliza and Alicsar were perhaps a foot apart, but she could feel the distance between them in the pit of her stomach.

As she rose from her curtsey, she almost missed the quick glance Alicsar sent his father, but the movements that followed her unmistakable.

Because she hadn't been eighteen yet, their engagement had never truly been legitimate in the eyes of the nobility around them. It had been more of a promise than a commitment. The ball and the birthday itself would secure it, would show to the royals and nobility gathered that the king had been serious in making his son marry the Blood Witch who saved him.

Eliza's breath hitched in her throat as the prince pulled a small box from his pocket, but her response had nothing to do with happiness. She shouldn't have been shocked, and yet her heart thundered and her palms grew clammy.

Slowly, Alicsar opened the lid and showed her the teardrop emerald stone that matched the colour of his eyes. The thin band was encrusted with small diamonds. It was beautiful, elegant, and not at all as flashy as she had been expecting.

This is it, she thought, feeling the blood rush from her face. *My fate is sealed.*

17

GUILT UNDER THE STARS
CELIA

Celia watched the first dance. Sadness built a wall around her heart as Eliza moved through the crowds, her dress drifting behind her like a golden shadow.

The ball was beautiful. Enchantingly perfect. Orbs of light floated above her head, while servants dressed like white roses glided through the crowd, carrying flutes of sparkling wine from the Courts of Light.

But Eliza wanted none of it. Celia had seen it in her eyes when she'd walked into the bedroom. Had seen it while escorting her to the ballroom. She had been like a ghost of herself, not quite there. Every move she'd made had been tense, like she was waiting for someone to attack her.

And Celia had been unable to do anything to help her.

She hadn't missed her roaming eyes, either.

In the faces of the crowd, she had searched for Brandon, but he hadn't been there. He had planned on escorting her to the ball.

Celia stepped into the shadows circulating the ballroom and

searched for her friend, reaching out with her magic for that familiar presence, but the Blood Magic that made him immortal, that flowed through the veins of all knights of the Brotherhood, was faint, a whisper in the cacophony of music.

Oh Brandon, where are you?

Glancing around her, Celia made sure no one was watching her as she slipped through the crowd towards a balcony off the ballroom. Her heart quickened as she pulled the cloak from her shoulders and rolled it into a ball in her hands, twisting the material around her fingers until the fabric was wrinkled and tangled. Before she could do anymore damage to her ceremonial cloak, it vanished from her hands, returning to her rooms.

The night was still, like it respected and understood the importance of Eliza's birthday. The sky had cleared to reveal a glittering array of stars and constellations, allowing the twin moons of Cadira to light the gardens of the palace. But there was a sadness to the stars and moons overlooking the ball, their light not as bright, subdued in their melancholy.

Celia pressed her lips into a thin line and made for the stairs, spreading her magic wide. But Brandon's presence was weakening, growing softer the longer she waited.

For weeks she'd noticed the changes, the silences and the longing gazes. Since Amitel's return, Brandon had been subtly pulling away, some notion forming in his mind that would inevitably take him away—again.

It was something she couldn't let happen. Eliza couldn't lose him, and neither could she.

Celia steeled herself and picked up the skirt of her dress. The stone balcony was icy, but magic steadied her feet as she approached the stairs.

"Darling Celia." Amitel appeared at her side, leaning against the railing of the balcony. He smiled at her like a cat; her old friend was all feline grace and arrogance, which he'd regained since their reunion in the alley. "What are you doing out here?"

Celia frowned, and spared a look in Brandon's direction. But she breathed a sigh and turned to Amitel, eyes roaming over his figure. The smell of Light Court wine wafted from his person, sweet and tangy in the air. A languid smile played at his stained lips. "Are you drunk?" she asked, taking a step back.

He raised a golden brow and pointed to his chest. "Who? *Me?*" He shook his head. "Of course not. What would make you say that?"

She exhaled and turned back to the gardens. "I don't feel like listening to your drunken complaints."

He turned and faced the gardens, too. Their shoulders brushed together; the suit he wore was exquisitely made, tailored perfectly to his lean, tall frame. The fabric was soft against her bare arm.

"Where's the commander?" the warlock drawled, bumping into her softly. "I thought he would have been at your hip—or Eliza's."

She didn't miss the bitterness that darkened his voice, but when she spared him a look, his face was deceptively blank. "He's leaving."

His gaze cut to hers. "What?" Even in the dim light, she couldn't mistake the red flecks that danced in his eyes.

She cleared her throat and looked away. "Brandon is leaving, likely because of what *you* said to him."

"That's rubbish." Amitel swore under his breath and shook his head. "He shouldn't leave Eliza. Where will he go?"

"Where do you think?" she snapped. Though she wanted to unburden herself so badly, she wondered if Amitel would let Brandon leave for the land across the sea, if he wanted Brandon to understand what really happened two hundred years ago. She couldn't help but glare at the warlock, who watched her so intently she might combust.

Did Amitel blame Brandon for what happened in the desert, if maybe he blamed *her* for Dorin manipulating Eliza when he could not step in? Had he planned on staying with the Dark Master longer? She had to wonder if perhaps he'd had plans of his own, plans that were derailed when Eliza went with Dorin willingly into the tunnels without Brandon or herself at her side.

Celia shook her head. "Brandon is following his own lead. There is nothing we can do to stop him.

Nothing I can do to stop him. The bitter thought caught her by surprise, and she straightened.

"Like hell there isn't," Amitel hissed, gripping her arm. Celia looked down at where his ringed fingers wrapped around her pale skin, then up at him. After a moment, he released her and ran his hand through his hair. "I'm sorry." He clenched his jaw. "He shouldn't have left her. Not again."

Celia's heart skipped a beat, and although she didn't want to betray her friend, she agreed. "I'm afraid nothing can stop him now."

The trace of magic, the whisper that was Brandon, faded.

"And if she gets hurt?" he asked. "He had a purpose here: protecting Eliza. I don't understand why that isn't enough anymore."

"Perhaps because he knew she was safe," she murmured, "with us."

The knuckles of Amitel's hands turned white where they gripped the railing. "I'm not entirely sure that's true, Celia." Instead of looking at her, he pulled away and disappeared into the darkness of the gardens.

For a long moment, she watched after him; a war of emotions plagued her, neither side as tempting as they once had been. And with that came a somewhat unsavoury thought: she agreed—to some extent—with Amitel. The concept made her stomach twist.

Celia closed her eyes and tightened her hands into fists. Brandon's trace was weak, but it still pulsed within the palace grounds. For how long, she wasn't sure.

Gravel and ice crunched beneath the heel of her boot as she entered the gardens, the trill of music dimming the further she went. Her fingers grew cold despite being trapped in the skirt of her dress, hiked up to keep from tripping her or dragging through the slush lining the paths.

Brandon's trace guided her through the darkness towards the palace stables, where a lone figure and horse stood against the shadows. Her heart leapt into her throat. Stumbling to a stop she watched him for a moment. A low breeze carried a soft tune from violins outside the palace entrance, guiding visitors and guests into the warmth of the ballroom. Winter blossoms and night roses bloomed under the watchful gaze of the twin moons, their wispy floral scent refreshing.

Celia swallowed the lump forming in her throat. She lifted her hand and flicked her wrist, igniting a dead lantern hanging above the stables. As the light flooded the gravel path, she stepped into its warmth.

"Won't you say goodbye?"

Brandon lowered his head, but he did not step back from the horse. "Celia—"

"You would leave us—leave *Eliza*—to see if your secrets are still in Laziroth?" she asked, harsher than intended, but hurt filled her chest and boiled her blood.

He flinched. "What Amitel said—"

"No." Celia stepped around him, forcing his eye to hers. "I don't want to hear about what *Amitel* said. For once, I agree with him. You should not—*cannot*—leave Eliza, not now."

"I cannot watch her marry him. I cannot stay here and pretend like there isn't more I can do."

"We are going to find the dagger, Brandon. *Together.* We cannot do that if you run off to another kingdom and pretend like you're on your own." She pulled his arm away from the horn of the saddle, clasping his hand between hers. "Please, Brandon."

He released a heavy breath and closed his eyes. As his had tightened around hers, she let a small smile of relief cross her lips.

"Give her this," he murmured, reaching into his back pocket, "from me." The flimsy envelope glared up at her, Eliza's name scrawled across the front. Celia swallowed hard and took it from him.

"You would not tell her yourself? Or me, for that matter?"

He gave a slight shake of his head. "I was going to send it to her, once I made it to Port Hein."

"And me?" she asked, voice trembling.

Finally, he met her stare. "I knew you would find me," he replied. "You always do."

Her heart cracked. Brandon softly slipped his hand from her grasp and replaced his hand on the saddle horn, lifting his body up to straddle the horse. With each movement, he refused to look at her, to meet her eye, and something inside her cracked with the realisation that he was going to leave, and there was nothing she could do or say to stop him.

Celia pressed her lips into a thin line to stop them from trembling as she stepped back from the horse. Brandon reached for the hood of his cloak and settled it atop his head, casting his face in darkness.

"I'm sorry," was all he said, a whisper caught in the breeze, fluttering away as he kicked the horse into motion.

Her hands fell to her sides as the horse carried him through a side entrance of the palace and out of her sight.

~

The guilt dragged her through the palace halls in a quiet daze. She almost completely walked past Lennox, and only paused when the other Blood Witch tapped her shoulder.

Celia spun and blinked at her. "What?"

Lennox narrowed her eyes. "Are you alright, Celia?"

"Yes, of course," she replied, nodding. "Why?" Nerves churned in the pit of her stomach, aided by a wave of sadness and exhaustion.

Her superior cast a glance around the hall, as if searching for wandering ears, and when she noticed no one lurking, she leaned in. "Have you heard of the attacks? In the mountains?"

Dread churned in her gut. "What?"

A sadness entered Lennox's eyes. "One of ours, and two Knights. In the western woods." She released a breath, and Celia realised it was the first time she'd seen the woman rattled. "Another girl is missing. A young one. The High Witch is unsure if it is related to the Dark Master."

A chill ran down Celia's spine. "Are we to return with Eliza?"

Lennox shook her head. "Knights are on their way to help better protect the Ecix. We still have an agreement with the king to uphold."

Mutely, Celia nodded. Lennox touched her arm softly. "They are with the Goddess now," she whispered, stepping around Celia, "May they rest with her."

Celia murmured a response, but her thoughts went back to Eliza; to what the extra protection and eyes would mean for her.

"Celia!"

Both Celia and Lennox spun to face Eliza, who clutched the heavy skirts of her dress in her gloved hands. Her chest rose and fell with heavy breaths, and as she stumbled to a halt in front of Celia, her glassy eyes flickered between them, fear swirling within the bright depths.

Celia frowned and strode to Eliza's side. "What's wrong?" she asked. "Are you hurt?"

Eliza shook her head. "No, I'm fine." She pulled away from Celia and crossed her arms. "Where's Thorne? I haven't seen him all night."

Behind them, Lennox made a sound in the back of her throat. "Is there an issue, Celia?"

Tensing, Celia shook her head. "None. I will escort Eliza back to her room. Have a nice night."

Before they could wait for Lennox's response, Celia entwined her fingers with Eliza's and pulled her down the hall. "What—?"

Celia hushed her. "I'll tell you soon."

Eliza pressed her lips into a line and followed without argument; fear twisted Celia's gut, worry pounding in her head. She wiped at her forehead and found her skin clammy and cold. The sickness was returning faster, and she wasn't ready.

The halls were quiet, a dim whisper of music carrying from the ballroom. As they walked further away, Celia became more aware of how hard her heart was pounding in her chest. The letter in her pocket grew heavier with each step.

How far was he now, she wondered? Would he return by the morning, spilling apologies?

No. She swallowed hard, and as the door to her room came into view, she quickened her pace.

Celia tugged Eliza into her bedroom and closed the door, waiting a heartbeat before releasing a breath. as she stepped back, her sister came into view, pacing back and forth behind the desk.

"What is going on?" she demanded. She stopped and threw her

arms up in the air. "What aren't you telling me? Where is Brandon?"

The letter burned in Celia's pocket, and she said nothing as she pulled it free. Her hand trembled as she handed it over.

Eliza snatched it from her grip and frowned. "*Dear Eliza, I'm sorry, but I cannot stay any longer. We may not ever find the Dark Master or the dagger if I remain at the palace with you, and my priority is your safety above all else. But in order to keep you safe, I must leave.*" She paused, tears burning in her green eyes. Celia took a step towards her, but Eliza stumbled back and continued reading. "*I intend on leaving for Laziroth while you celebrate your birthday. And when I return, I hope to deliver you the answers you seek, no matter the cost. Happy birthday. Brandon.*"

The letter fell from her hands, and Celia rushed to her side to catch Eliza before she fell with it. Tears cut lines down her cheeks, through the glitter highlighting her cheekbones and the rouge colouring her skin.

But Eliza said nothing, her eyes on the bleeding ink.

"I am so sorry," Celia whispered, hugging her sister tightly. "I wish I could have stopped him."

Eliza released a shuddering breath. "You knew he was leaving?" she asked, voice cracking.

Celia's heart skipped a beat. "I knew he was thinking about it." She wiped away a tear, and cupped Eliza's cheek. "But I didn't think he'd leave tonight. I went to him, but his mind was made up."

Closing her eyes, Eliza pressed her lips into a thin line. "I don't know why I'm so surprised. I just thought…"

That he'd say goodbye himself? Celia thought, though she couldn't brave asking the question aloud. Instead, she wiped another tear away. "We will do all we can here," Celia whispered. "I promise. I will not leave you alone."

Eliza opened her eyes finally, but something changed; a hardness entered her irises, casting the moss green in darkness. Her jaw ticked as she stepped out of Celia's grasp.

A shiver raced down her spine as Eliza used the back of her hand to wipe the tear streaks from her cheeks. Reaching down, Celia picked up the letter and held it out for Eliza to take, but her sister stared at it for a moment before shaking her head.

"I think it's time for me to go to bed," she said, voice quiet. Something twisted in Celia's stomach as Eliza clasped her hands in front of her. "Goodnight, Celia."

The shift was so quick, but it wasn't hard for Celia to miss it. Eliza had her own plans now, spurred by Brandon's departure. "Eliza, please wait—" Celia reached for her, but Eliza twisted out of her grasp and opened the door, saying nothing more as she slipped out of the room.

Heart thundering, Celia went to the door and threw it open, but her sister had already disappeared down another hall. She sighed, closing the door, and rested her forehead against the cool wood. A thousand thoughts ran through her head, but there was only one that mattered.

And she needed to be prepared.

18

WITCHING HOUR
ELIZA

Eliza stared up at the canopy of her bed, twisting the engagement ring around her finger. The heavy rock turned icy in her grip, but she hesitated in taking it off.

Her thoughts drifted to Thorne, to his departure, and a wave of sadness washed over her, waring with the anger bubbling deep in her gut. But part of her couldn't fault Thorne, not when her own mind had strayed to the idea of leaving, of disappearing without a word in search of the dagger.

She almost reached beneath her bed for her bag, already packed with clothing and food, the map of ancient cities buried beneath the Kingdom, and Alastor's book on the legendary goddess.

A soft knock at her door forced her to rise from the bed. It was still dark outside her windows, the long night unending. No one else should have been awake besides her. It was closing in on three, the palace otherwise silent.

A small part of her hoped it was Thorne, returning, ready to apologise for leaving.

Slowly, Eliza padded to the door. The handle was cold to the touch.

It opened with a creak to reveal a tired eyed Celia. Dark circles lined her eyes, skin flushed. But she wasn't wearing a sleeping gown like Eliza would have thought, but a pair of thick leggings, and a loose white tunic. What stuck out the most to Eliza, though, was the knee-high riding boots and satchel.

Eliza frowned and looked Celia over. "What are you doing?"

Celia entered the room and closed the door behind herself. "I already know you're planning on leaving."

"What?" Eliza crossed her arms and turned to face her sister. "No..."

Celia raised a brow. "So you *aren't* considering leaving to find the dagger?"

Eliza wasn't certain what to say to that, because she had been. The idea had become a ticking time bomb in the back of her mind. Leaving the palace could mean a different fate for her, one she could probably control on her own. It would give her the chance to finish what she had started all those months ago, before her destiny was larger than a Keeper position at the wards.

Taking a step back, Eliza ignored the way Celia's stare drilled into her. And she knew that it wouldn't be right to disappear, to escape into the night and leave behind everything at the palace, but it didn't stop the urges from coming.

Maybe, deep down, she understood why Thorne had to leave.

Being around Alicsar too often made her sick and brought back memories of his betrayal. She was no good at her princess lessons, though that had more to do with her disinterest and not being capable. If she were being totally honest with herself, the prospect of becoming a *princess of the people* was far more daunting than she wanted to admit.

Releasing a breath, Eliza said, "I can't *stay*. Not anymore."

Celia cocked her head in sympathy. "You cannot just... leave, Eliza. It wouldn't be right."

"Oh?" Eliza turned on Celia. "And what about Thorne? He left. He decided he couldn't be here anymore, and he just walked away to do only Gods know what! He didn't even say *goodbye*."

"Brandon had his reasons."

"If he can have his," Eliza replied, "then I can have mine. I won't *find* anything here, and the longer I stick around..."

"The closer you get to marrying Alicsar." Celia's eyes softened. "But it is not safe for you out there."

"It isn't safe for me *anywhere*, Celia. The Dark Master knows where I am, knows what I'm doing, even knows how to get inside my head. If he wanted me, he would have already gotten me. Does it matter *where* he finds me?"

Celia nodded. "Of course it does. Here, you are protected. Safe. Out there... we cannot know what will happen, what dangers might appear. At least in the palace, we know the variables."

Eliza scoffed and began to pace. "We never knew Alastor would be taken. We never knew Amitel would come back. We never knew Thorne would just leave."

"In the palace, we can protect you better."

"You're already dressed to go!" Eliza sucked in a breath, her cheeks flaming. "You clearly believed I would leave, Celia," she said quietly. "I mean what I said. I can't *do* anything here, and I can't wait around to become someone's wife. I just... can't."

"I know."

Eliza didn't break her stare. "If I leave, will you stop me?"

It took a moment for her to respond, but Celia sighed, closing her eyes. "No, I will not."

"Then you'll join me?" Eliza asked, hopeful. "You'll help me?"

"Of course." Celia reached out and took Eliza's hand. "I made you a promise. But we will need help."

"Thorne?"

Celia shook her head. "We can continue without him. What he is doing... it is something he needs to do, alone. But he has hope now, so I believe he will be alright."

Despite the hurt that still curdled in Eliza's stomach, she agreed.

Since their return from the desert, things had changed, even for him. She couldn't even begin to imagine what it was like, seeing his dead love in the face of his friend.

"Alright," Eliza said, "then who comes with us?"

"You won't like it..."

Eliza narrowed her eyes. "No."

"He is better than anyone else we know. He knows the terrain, and he knows the Dark Master. He can help us, Eliza." Celia hesitated before adding, "And we can keep an eye on him."

Biting her lip, Eliza pulled her hand from Celia's and crossed her arms. "We don't know if he's actually on our side."

"Amitel has always been on his own side. But I think he is finally choosing to do what is right. I have to believe that. And if he is with us, we can make sure others remain safe, right?"

Eliza sighed. Since he had gotten back, her gut had been screaming at her to forgive him, to find out *why* he had sided with the Dark Master in the first place.

Perhaps dragging him along on their newest mission to find the dagger would give her the answers she sought. Maybe she'd finally be able to decide if Amitel is on her side, or if he was the enemy she feared him to be.

~

Eliza covered her head with the dark hood of her cloak. The patchwork creation had been a gift from Kay, made from the cuts from whatever project Kay had been working on. It was cute, and reminded her of the home she could no longer belong to.

Best of all, it kept her warm. The frigid air was only growing colder, but adrenaline rushed through her as Eliza walked the garden paths alone; no matter what the unnamed God said, she was still going.

Because for the first time in months, *she* was taking control.

But she couldn't ignore the weight of the golden band around her wrist. Its dull reminder made her head hurt. She just hoped Celia had found a way to nullify its power long enough for Eliza to slip it off and discard it.

Another frigid breeze coasted over the gardens and circled her. Pulling the cloak around her tighter, Eliza soldiered on.

Thankfully, there were no guards roaming the grounds. With the time turning over to the witching hour, most were changing shift, or smart enough to escape the cold. Any who were brave enough to stand in the winter air were either located high in the guard's towers, or gathered around small fires close to the palace proper.

A hand circled around her wrist, warm and strong. Eliza didn't have time to yelp as she was pulled into a hedge.

Why does this seem familiar?

Amitel smirked as dim lamplight flickered across his face. Beside him, Celia had her arms crossed, her lips pursed, unamused. She wore a black cloak rather than her usual red, and with her ink black hair, she blended into the night.

"Why do you keep doing that?" Eliza asked, brushing her cloak off.

Amitel's smirk turned into a smile as he looked her over. "I just have so much fun seeing twigs and leaves in your hair, love."

Rolling her eyes, Eliza turned to Celia instead. "He knows what we're doing?"

Celia nodded. "Yes. He knows."

"This is a rather stupid plan," he said, though the smile still illuminated his face, "but I like it."

"You're only here because we apparently need your help."

Amitel pouted. "And here I thought you'd forgiven me."

Eliza rolled her eyes. "When Mesah freezes over." She returned her stare to Celia, who had let a half-smile creep upon her face. "Can you do the spell?"

The amusement disappeared, and solemnly, Celia nodded. "It'll take a lot of energy, but yes. I can remove the band."

Eliza released a breath. "Let's do this quickly, before we're caught."

Amitel took a step back from them, a look of intrigue crossing his face. Eliza couldn't help but be momentarily surprised that he didn't know how to remove the Blood Witch's magic.

And here I thought he knew everything. Eliza couldn't help but look at him and roll her eyes.

Celia made an impatient noise and motioned for Eliza's wrist.

Giving her sister a half-smile, Eliza took a quick step closer and pulled the sleeves of her cloak up to reveal the tight, golden band. It glowed with magic, the light only dim, but enough to prove how powerful the spell was.

Eliza gulped as Celia muttered a spell under her breath. Very few Blood Witches used words when performing spells, unless the spell itself required more than three witches and required a lot of Blood Magic.

The uncertainty trickled back as Eliza watched Celia work through the spell. Was there something she could do to help?

If there was, she thought bitterly, *then Celia would have asked.*

But when she looked to Amitel, his eyes were closed, and the same spell was being uttered from his lips, too.

Eliza hissed as the bracelet began to burn. The skin of her wrist heated beneath the touch of the gold, searing up her arm and in her blood.

"Stop," she gasped, looking to Celia pleadingly. "I don't think it's working."

Cool fingers wrapped around her upper arm and held her steady. "Just a little longer," Amitel murmured, his lips close to her ear. He pressed his chest into her back and held her up. His long fingers reminded her of the musician's that swarmed the streets of the French Quarter, but his strong, lean body was something else.

Eliza jabbed backwards with her elbow and hit Amitel in the gut.

Instead of grunting, he chuckled. She was tempted to do it again, but harder, to see if he'd *chuckle* at that.

But before she could, the heat disappeared, and the weight of the bracelet snapped from her wrist. Eliza snatched her hand back from Celia and inspected the pale line where the gold band had been.

"Huh," she muttered, staring at the blank skin. "You did it."

The full restoration of her magic felt more relaxing than she ever would have expected. The rush of power that flooded her veins, the tingle of Blood Magic and her connection to Cadira... it felt like a limb being reconnected, no longer the whisper of magic she had been feeling for weeks.

A sigh passed her lips. *Feels good to be back*, Eliza thought. She could even feel the dead, which felt... good.

Amitel watched her with a strange look on his face, lips parted. When their eyes met, his mouth snapped shut and he shook his head.

Celia grunted. "Now we must leave. It will not be long until Lennox learns of this." Celia looked away for a moment, panic crossing her cerulean eyes, but it disappeared. "If she has not already."

Nodding, Eliza let the sleave of her cloak slip back down her arm. She had no more time to marvel at the wonder of Celia's power. It was time to leave, and hope the king wouldn't be too mad.

"Ready?" Amitel asked, clearing his throat. He motioned the two of them closer. Eliza hesitated before taking the step, but made sure to stand closer to Celia rather than the sneaky warlock.

Eliza cast one look back at the palace. Could she really just... leave? Because leaving meant forfeiting New Orleans. It meant leaving behind her family.

She closed her eyes and bowed her head. *I'll make it right*, she promised her grandfather and Kay. *I'll see you again.*

Finally, Eliza cleared her throat at met Amitel's gold and red stare, the smile feeling more forced that amused like earlier. "Yeah. Let's go."

The smile disappeared as the hedges rustled. Eliza called upon her newly restored magic, and they waited tentatively as a body fell through the thick greenery.

Eliza eyes widened as the spy rose from the ground. He found her gaze first, cheeks flushed.

What is he doing here? she wondered, suddenly afraid for their plans.

"Prince Alicsar," Amitel said, voice stiff. "What a surprise."

19

ANCIENT DEATH
ELIZA

The prince looked somewhat uncomfortable, maybe even surprised that he had found them. His wide eyes flickered over Eliza, then between Celia and Amitel. Time seemed frozen within the hedges as the prince considered them; Eliza tried not to squirm beneath his gaze, but she crossed her arms.

Before he could speak, Eliza snapped, "What the hell are you doing?"

Alicsar blinked, then frowned. "I believe I should be asking *you* that question." He looked between the three of them inquisitively, one meticulous brow raised, like they owed him some kind of explanation.

You sort of do though, a little nagging voice in the back of her mind said. *You are is fiancé.*

She ignored that voice and instead stepped forward, lowering her voice. "You should go."

"And why is that?" he asked, mimicking her by crossed his own arms. "You're clearly leaving. Eliza, we're to be married in weeks—"

Amitel barked a laugh. "There are more important things than your engagement, Your Highness."

Eliza had almost forgotten the disdain Amitel had shown towards Alicsar when he had been known as Dorin. She'd brushed it off, but now she couldn't help but wonder if there had been more between the two men before Alicsar lost his memories.

Alicsar glanced at Amitel and looked him over once before returning his gaze to Eliza. "My priority is finding and stopping the Dark Master before another war breaks out," she said. "I don't care about your father's politics."

His jaw tightened. "I know. Which is why I'm not here to stop you."

Eliza's brows rose, but she couldn't help but wonder if his admission had anything to do with the Dark Master. Was there a chance his memories had reappeared and he was now playing them?

Or was he being sincere?

"Then why are you here?" she asked slowly, stepping back.

He hesitated briefly before releasing a breath. It clouded in front of him. "Because I want to join you."

"That would be catastrophically stupid," Amitel said before she could respond. "Do you know what would happen if you joined us? What your father—the *king*—would do if you suddenly went missing?"

"He's right," Eliza said, though agreeing with the warlock caused a bitter taste in her mouth. "If you come with us, then who knows what Bastian will do. He might think you've been kidnapped again, or worse."

Alicsar gave her a pleading look, one that resonated deep within her—one she couldn't ignore, because she had felt as desperate as he did now. It called to the part of her that wanted freedom, but also wanted to do what was right.

If he's close, she thought, looking between the prince and Amitel as Celia's words echoed in her ears, *then I can keep an eye on him.* When Eliza turned to her sister, the Blood Witch bowed her head, as if her own thoughts had returned to her early sentiment.

Eliza sighed and spared a glance towards the palace, then let her gaze settle on the prince once again. "No matter what we say, you're just going to find us, aren't you?"

Alicsar tipped his head. "I need to help, do something better than all of... *this*."

Deep down, she understood him perfectly, and she hated that. She wanted to do more than what was waiting for her in the palace.

And if he'd gotten his memories back, perhaps letting him go with her would give her a chance to watch him, make sure he wasn't under the Dark Master's influence anymore... Could she risk leaving him behind, where no one could watch him? Where no one knew the truth of his past and his capabilities?

Releasing a breath, Eliza shook her head, already regretting what she was about to do. "You can come," she said, sharing a look with Celia. "But one wrong move, Your Highness, and I will drag you back here."

The prince gave her a crooked smile. "Noted."

Behind her, Amitel cleared his throat. "If it's all sorted, then we should leave before the *both* of you are reported missing."

Eliza grimaced, but returned to her place beside Celia, as Alicsar rushed to Amitel's other side.

As the magic of the portal washed over them, Eliza couldn't help but wonder if Alicsar's intentions were anything but noble.

~

Snow so thick it muffled their footsteps and voices blanketed the southern region of Cadira. It was so unlike the capital that it made her wonder if they'd accidentally stumbled upon a new world. The ruins of the Spring Manor looked almost peaceful under the weight of winters gaze, enough so it was easy for Eliza to forget the wandering spirits that roamed the manor's grounds.

Alicsar was the first to step away from their group, his eyes wide. "This is where the Dark Master kidnapped me?"

"It is," Celia replied.

Eliza blinked in surprise as Celia slowly made her way to the prince's side.

"And this is where he killed my mother and sister." Sadness darkened his voice, the words drifting in the winter air, not a question, but a fact stated with a certainty that made her heart ache.

No one responded. Eliza held her breath as he took three hesitant steps towards the skeleton of a house. She'd forgotten that he probably had never seen the remains of what used to be his father's home, that Dorin likely hadn't seen it either. Sometimes she swore she saw flickers of familiarity in his gaze whenever they walked around the palace—it had always been small, a double take here and there, but it had been enough to tell her that somewhere deep inside his mind, Dorin was still there.

But she didn't see that as he gazed up at the ruins.

A shudder coursed down her spine as spirits rose from the remains of the manor. They drifted closer, as if drawn to the prince they died for. Mauled guards bowed while servants reached with unseen hands to wipe the tears from Alicsar's face.

Eliza wondered if the queen and princess would make an appearance, if they still walked the halls of their spring home in hopes their prince would return.

Alicsar cleared his throat and turned his back on the manor and wiped angrily at the tears that marked his face. "We should go, before the cold kills us," he muttered, unwilling to look at anyone, not even her.

Silently, Eliza nodded and met Celia's eye. The Blood Witch tried to hide her sympathy for the prince, but Eliza could see it in her eyes; the flicker of uncertainty, the untested belief that maybe he wasn't the same man he was on their initial journey.

Eliza gave a small shake of her head. *Thinking like that might get you killed*, she thought, shoving her hands into her pockets. Thinking like that would certainly set her up for betrayal, failure... probably even death. Again.

She huffed a breath and watched it cloud in front of her. The night was so still, quiet. Their footsteps crunched through the freshly lain snow, the only sound heard in the silence of the maze and surrounding forest.

The maze welcomed Eliza; she felt the magic of the entity encompass her.

'*Welcome,*' it breathed, sending shivers down her spine. '*Welcome back.*'

'*Thank you,*' Eliza responded silently. She reached out a hand and ran her fingers over the frozen leaves of the maze.

'*You found him,*' the maze said. '*You found the lost prince.*'

To that, Eliza didn't respond. Instead, the statue of Azula and her Fae lover came into sight. She couldn't help but stare at the Fae male; the familiarity and likeness was uncanny to the Fae Knight who followed her. But she saw the resemblance because of dreams—the Knight rarely showed his face. Eliza couldn't help but wonder if she had somehow given the Knight Azula's lovers face, or if it wasn't a coincidence at all.

She thought back to her last night in New Orleans, but it had been dark. She had likely imagined his likeness then, too.

Eliza said nothing as she stepped into the water. It wasn't cold like she had imagined; instead, it was warm, inviting. It didn't soak through her pants or boots, either.

Amitel stepped in after. "I never liked this," he said, frowning down at his boots. "I don't understand why it couldn't be a doorway."

"What?" Eliza asked. "Afraid to get a little wet?"

His lips twisted into a smirk, gold eyes shining. "These are my good boots, love. I'd hate to see them ruined."

She rolled her eyes and motioned for Alicsar and Celia to step into the fountain. "This is the portal that'll take us down into the city."

"Interesting..." Alicsar murmured. He said nothing else as he stepped in beside her. Celia was last.

Staring into the maze, Eliza nodded. "Take us down."

The portal's magic cascaded over them. The water rose over their bodies, wrapping around them like a current, lifting their cloaks and hair, before depositing them in the cavern beneath the Spring Manor.

Like before, Eliza was astounded by the magnificence of the underground city; the sweeping towers and statues dedicated to Azula, the stillness of a world that had long since been forgotten.

The towering statue of Azula stared down at her, the goddesses legendary dagger held in one hand, the other raised over the city. A raven perched on one shoulder, her lover stood behind the other, just as imposing as the goddess herself.

And surrounding Azula, her sprawling city, buildings made of white stone discoloured over the course of time, and temples with wide columns, some shattered and fallen, other standing as tall as the city's statue.

Bile rose in Eliza's throat as she stepped around the skeletons of those who had worshipped the Goddess of Necromancy. What had they given up, Eliza wondered, to live below ground? And what secrets did they take to their graves?

"We should give them a proper burial," Eliza said to no one in particular. Throughout her life, she had seen the torment that had lingered in spirits when not properly laid to rest; as a child she had seen the aftermath of disasters, and the spirits who still roamed the earth, waiting for their burial, and never receiving it.

"Do you see them?" Celia asked, carefully resting a hand on Eliza's arm.

Eliza shook her head. "No, but it's the right thing to do."

Stepping away from a body, she started for the centre of the city. She almost didn't catch Amitel's murmured, "Interesting."

Her first trip beneath the manor, she had noticed the silence of the dead first. Where there were bodies, she'd expected spirits, but there had been none during her and Thorne's long journey through the tunnels. Only the demon and the dead-end.

Celia caught up to her and interlocked their arms. "It is magnificent down here."

Eliza nodded, eyes drifting to the largest monument to the Goddess. There, in her hand, was a replica of the dagger they sought. "I hope it holds the answers."

"We'll find something," Celia replied. Their gazes met. "If there is a temple, we should look there first. Religious texts might reveal whether the dagger appeared in the city or if it vanished somewhere else."

There was only one place Eliza thought would hold that kind of information. She turned towards the large temple not far from Azula's statue. She hadn't paid it much attention the last time she'd been in the city, but now she took it in. The monument was perhaps as large as the Acropolis in Greece, with pillars just as high, supporting a ceiling that had engravings carved into the stone. The building was marble, beautiful and old, a structure that would have collapsed in her own world.

Starting for the structure, Eliza reached into her magic and spread it across the abandoned city. She wasn't sure what to expect; were there still shadows of spirits wandering the forgotten city, or were they all gone, having moved on years ago? Or was she not strong enough to reach them, to see them?

Blood Magic was supposed to heighten her necromancy, and yet she felt as powerless as she did when she'd been wearing the bracelet.

And being able to see those who had died in the city would have been helpful, she thought. Being able to ask them questions might have gotten more answers than books.

She sighed and reigned in her magic. There was no inkling of ghosts, no gut feeling that they weren't alone.

She should have felt peace in the silence, and yet the lack of spirits made her uneasy.

"What do you think we'll find in there?" Eliza asked Celia as they stopped outside the temple. Up close, it was even larger than expected.

Celia reached out and took Eliza's hand. "Answers, I hope."

Amitel and Alicsar bounded up the stairs; curiosity and excitement burned in the prince's eyes as he slowly touched one of the many pillars. He looked so similar to the first time they'd met: under the gaze of the golden dragon where he'd explained the history of Cadira, of the Great War. She hadn't thought much of it before, but now she knew... the Dark Master had told him of the war, of the dragon's purpose in destroying Valonde.

A shudder raced down her spine. It was hard to forget that he'd once been on the side of her enemy, that he had once been set on stealing her power away for himself.

Eliza pushed those thoughts aside and climbed the stairs. As they entered the great temple of the underground city, she veered away from the group, her mind elsewhere; partly due to her discomfort around Alicsar and partly because she wasn't sure what was going to happen and what they'd find. Her stomach churned as she approached the darkness of an alcove. With every step, her heart rate sped up until the sound of it thundered in her ears.

The darkness swarmed around three identical crates; made of dark stone, the lids were tipped on their sides. Eliza summoned just enough light to peer into the darkness.

Small vials of golden orange liquid glowed under the dim light, all topped with caps that looked so old she wondered if they would ever come off—or if they'd crumble under her touch.

Slowly, she reached into one of the crates and held up one of the vials to the light. She recognised it dimly, like the memory of it existed somewhere else in her mind.

Eliza gave it a small shake, and what looked like fire exploded from within. She almost dropped the vial, if it weren't for the memory that broke the surface.

Isolde and her death, the Resurgence, the Dark Master...

She quickly set it back into the crate and took a step back, breath rattling in her chest. The liquid fire glared up at her; after years of silence and not being touched, she didn't know how volatile the magic would be.

A hand clamped down on her shoulder and she spun, flinging a hand out. But Amitel's half-smile stopped her from diving into her magic or hitting him—though the latter option did seem rather tempting.

Eliza exhaled sharply. "What the hell?"

"I should be asking you that question," he replied, stepping around her to look in the crates. His brows knotted together. "Peculiar."

"*Peculiar?*" Eliza shook her head. "Dangerous."

"You disrupted them," he said, pulling the explosive one out. Eliza flinched. "They're so old, I'm surprised they're even viable."

"Wow." Hesitantly, though, she took another step back. "How *peculiar*."

Amitel chuckled, running a hand through his hair. "The magic in these..." He stepped back, sighing. "Someone extremely powerful created these. The crates too. They're acting as a dampener, so the vials are easier to move and won't combust within."

Intrigued, Eliza cocked her head. If they were used in wars, like the Resurgence, then why were they hidden beneath Azula's city?

Eliza pressed her lips into a thin line. She moved back another step and watched Amitel warily. "What do you want, Amitel?"

The warlock dropped the vial back into the crate and wiped his hands. "I came to talk," he said, crossing his arms.

She rolled her eyes and started down the corridor. "Don't really feel like it, Amitel."

Amitel made a sound in the back of his throat. "Eliza, wait."

"What?" She stopped and turned.

In the dim light, there was something so ethereal about Amitel, like he lived and breathed magic so much that it clung to him like a second skin. In the light of day, she hadn't noticed it as much, but in the ancient city, Amitel blended so well into the beauty of the agelessness that surrounded them.

Eliza blinked and cleared her throat, shaking her head. She started again through the temple, but with no destination in mind. The corridor she followed led out into a small, dead garden; a well in the centre had a bucket hanging from a discarded rope, while rows of planters lay dead, their flora forgotten. A gate at the other end of the garden hung off its hinges, as if one foul breath of wind would knock it completely over. There was no way for Eliza to avoid it, so she pushed it off completed and grimaced at the rust that clung to her hands.

"I need to explain to you *why* I did what I did," Amitel said, voice breathless. "Please, Eliza."

Somewhere in the distance, the echo of crumbling rocks met her ears. Eliza paused outside the temple, waited to hear something else, but shook her head.

It's probably just Celia and Alicsar. A pang of guilt shot through her. She'd left Celia alone with the prince. What if something happened? Eliza knew Celia could take care of herself, but no one suspected any danger from him now that his memories were gone.

Amitel appeared in front of her, eyes narrowed. "I cannot take the silence, or the cold shoulder, not from you."

She rolled her eyes. "You can't deal with the lack of *attention.*" Without meaning to, she met his stare. "I trusted you. Thorne trusted you."

The thought of the commander made her heart ache. Wherever he was...

"I realise that," the warlock replied, voice softening. "But it was a lot more complicated than that. Eliza—"

She turned away from Amitel as the sound of scattering rocks met her ears again. "What was that?" she asked, interrupting Amitel.

The warlock came to a stop, his bright eyes scanning the ancient city. He was silent only a moment before bringing a long finger to his lips. The muscles of his shoulders tensed.

Holding her breath, Eliza dove into her well of magic. She reached as far as she dared, never taking her eyes off the warlock.

She didn't breathe until his muscles uncoiled. The air rushed from her lungs in a sharp exhale.

Amitel turned to face her, a smirk slowly unfurling. "There is nothing—"

From the darkness of the ancient city, a creature reared its head, growl rumbling through the streets. On bowed legs, with claws as long as Eliza's forearms, it screamed into the shadows swirling around it, and attacked.

20

RISE OF THE DEMONS
ELIZA

Eliza leapt in front of Amitel and created a shield of fire around their bodies.

Amitel made a sound that reverberated deep in his chest. "So you *do* like me, love."

She grunted and pushed him back towards the garden and the temple. "We need to find Celia and Alicsar."

"No need," he replied. Eliza spared a quick glance behind them to see the prince and the Blood Witch appear, though they were thankfully still within the boundary of the gardens. "Looks like they heard all the commotion."

"We need to get to them," she replied through gritted teeth. Demons rose from the dirt in a flurry of sand and shadows. Their bodies resembled those of the creatures she had fought beneath Mesah.

Eliza swallowed thickly as her magic faltered. She felt the warm presence of Amitel at her back; the pressure was enough to remind her that she wasn't beneath the desert and facing off an army created for her to animate; that she wasn't alone with no one to help her.

A hand—Amitel's, one with gold, glinting rings lining his fingers—wrapped around her wrist. "Eliza, focus," he hissed, dragging her from the past, and back into the present.

"I'm fine," Eliza replied. Amitel had added a touch of his own magic to their small shield, just enough to stop the small swarm of demons from entering the temple garden.

Amitel was silent for a moment before grunting. "I hope so." He cast his hand out, golden light forming in the palm of his hand. It arched from his outstretched palm, bending in front of them before swinging into the approaching demons and igniting into a wall of fire.

She felt his arms wrap around her mid-section and pull her away from the floundering demons. Any creature close enough might have been destroyed in the distraction, but it would make them much angrier, that she could be sure of.

The arms released her the moment the bright light dimmed, and suddenly she was running with her hand tucked into Celia's. The cries of demons flooded the city, gruelling and almost human-like.

A shudder ran down Eliza's spine. The magic that encompassed the demons felt different and new, not unlike the magic she had felt when she'd been beneath the mountain with Dorin, facing his army.

And yet there was something strange about it, like the Dark Master had learnt new tricks since the last time they'd fought.

He was learning, and so was she.

The once tomblike silence of Azula's city exploded with sound as they ran from the expanding group of demons. From the corner of her eye, she spotted them rising from the dust in bursts of shadows and darkness. The demons were shaped like wild beasts, wolves maybe, bred to chase. To hunt.

A blast of hot air brushed past the nape of her neck and into the body of a demon poised to lunge. Her gaze cut quickly to Amitel, who winked before guiding their group into the safety of the temple. Great doors that probably hadn't closed in a thousand years slammed shut, locking them in and keeping the beasts at bay.

The historian inside of Eliza grimaced at the sound of claws grating against the marble. How much damage was about to be done in order to get her? The once peacefulness of the city was gone because she'd led the Dark Master's creatures there.

Her ex-boss, Ambrose, historian and once amateur archaeologist, would be so disappointed in her.

Eliza sucked in a sharp breath and eyed the doors. Even though they were made of the same marble that made up the temple, they shook with the impact of the demons. It reminded her of the creatures that had attacked the wards in New Orleans. That felt like a lifetime ago, a memory greyed by so many experiences it felt like someone else had lived through it.

Celia threw out a wave of magic; it tingled across Eliza's skin as it hit the doors, and like spiderwebs, it covered the marble before disappearing. The shaking dimmed, but Eliza could still hear the smack of bodies outside.

"We can't stay in here," Amitel said, head cocked. His eyes danced over the temple. There were doorways everywhere, rotten pews, and statues and murals depicting the Goddess surrounding them. But no clear exit.

Eliza turned in a slow circle. "There has to be a way out of here."

"There aren't any windows," Alicsar said. The prince met her stare, and she looked away.

"Thanks for pointing that out," she muttered. "Back door maybe?"

This time, Amitel shook his head. "One way in and out that we know of."

"Great. That means we have to either wait until they get tired, or until they break down the doors and crush us." Eliza turned to Celia. "Or we could portal out?"

Celia and Amitel shared a look. "So, love, where do you want to go?" the warlock asked.

Eliza smiled. "Outside."

~

The portal opened up behind one of the tall buildings that surrounded the temple. There were probably forty demons at the door, clambering to get inside. Their claws had made a dent; long marks marred the marble, deep enough to make Eliza shudder. It wouldn't have taken them long to break in.

"What do we do now?" Alicsar asked, taking a step back from the corner. He wrung his fingers as his gaze darted around the alley they hid in.

Although Eliza very much wanted to blame their current circumstances on him, he looked more worried and scared than a cruel mastermind. Unfortunately, neither Amitel nor Alicsar could have had a chance to give the demons access to the city.

Or at least, she hoped not.

Pursing her lips, Eliza cast one last glance around the corner. "They still think we're in there. We can take them by surprise."

"Stab them in the back." Amitel looked mildly impressed, which should have worried her more than the demons. "Enough fire could wipe them out."

Eliza turned to Celia. "What do you think?"

"Defensive magic and manoeuvres are my biggest weakness," she admitted with a small shrug. "If you believe it will be enough and stop them, then I trust you."

Biting her lip, Eliza cast Amitel a worried glance, but his face had hardened with resolve. Meeting Celia's gaze again, she released a breath and nodded. "Fine. We'll hit them from behind."

A smirk tipped Amitel's lips. Forcing her gaze away from the insufferable warlock, she turned to the prince. "Stay here," she said. "Shout if any make it past us."

The prince nodded. He met her gaze evenly, a flash of worry passing through the emerald depths of his eyes.

As she looked away, Eliza met Celia and Amitel as they started for the temple. The demons continued their attack on the doors, but they weren't as eager in their attempt, as if they were growing tired. But their growls sent goosebumps over Eliza's flesh, the hairs along her arms rising.

The three came to a stop, mere yards from the demons. One creature pulled away from the group and sniffed the air, ichor and sulphur dripping from its maws. They had maybe three seconds before the others realised their prey no longer resided within the confines of the temple.

"Now," Eliza breathed, lifting her hands.

She didn't wait to see if Celia and Amitel had followed her movements. Instead, she focused on the hellish creatures and summoned the element of flame.

It had been a while since she'd used her elemental magic; it had been even longer since she'd used it against the minions of the Dark Master. She remembered her attack on the demons of Mesah's hidden city, how the fire had washed them away, giving her—and Dorin—a chance to make it into the tunnels.

Fire leapt from her fingertips, more powerful than it had ever been. Mixed with her blood and her connection to Cadira's natural magic, she let it flow through her.

She felt the heat of the flames on either side of her. Sweat rolled off her skin as she gritted her teeth and let the magic consume her.

"Just a bit more," Amitel muttered beside her.

Eliza clenched her jaw. Demons attempted to escape the wrath of their blaze, but it was all-consuming, entangling all that got in its way. It hoped from one creature to another until they were all wrapped in its warm embrace, their wolfish-forms crackling under the heat.

They collapsed under the weight of the fire. She didn't stop, breath ragged in her ears, afraid that if she did, they might rise again. It took her a moment to lower her hands, to suck in a cooling breath.

Eliza grimaced as the demons turned to ash. Their bodies joined the dirt at their feet, until an invisible breeze cast them away. A sigh of relief built in her throat, and she turned to face Celia.

But her friend wasn't watching her; following her line of sight, Eliza's heart stopped as a row of twelve Shadow Soldiers breached the line of the city with swords dripping liquid darkness drawn. Helms made of a dark iron covered their faces; Eliza took some comfort in not being able to see their faces, because in the end, they would die at her hands, never to return to the master that created them.

As they grew closer, she tensed. Reaching out her magic, she probed the darkness that enclosed them. It felt nothing like what she'd experienced in Mesah. Like something was stopping her from connecting with the death that shrouded them. It reminded her of the soldiers she'd tracked in the capital, the ones who had led her to the informant.

Her heart stopped, and for a moment she couldn't breathe. There were no tethered spirits clinging to the flesh.

Unless they weren't the same soldiers she'd faced under Mesah...

No. She gave a sharp shake of her head. There was still a waft of death surrounding the twelve approaching figures, but she couldn't understand why she couldn't see anything.

Someone beside her grabbed her hand. When she looked down, she saw the familiar long fingers of Amitel, and frowned.

"We have to move, love, unless you think you can control all of them."

When she looked back to the soldiers, she relented, because she knew she couldn't. If she couldn't connect with their spirits, then what use was she?

"I have no weapon," Alicsar said, pulling her attention. "I don't have magic I can fight with. I need a sword."

"Why don't you just stand behind us?" Amitel offered. "We'll protect you, Your Highness."

Alicsar frowned, cheeks reddening. "I can defend myself."

Amitel rolled his eyes, just dramatic enough for everyone to notice. "You have no memories of your life, how can you know how to fight? Sure, the guards at the palace are good, but they aren't *that* good. You've been in their care all of what, two months? And I doubt dear old Dad would have liked his precious son to handle such a deadly weapon."

When Eliza stole a look at the prince, she almost blanched at the cruel lines of his lips and the darkening of his eyes. Silently, she summoned a sword—one of simple make, with a wicked edge that would at least protect him, and handed it over. "You should still stand behind us. These soldiers aren't like the ones you've trained with."

Unless you remember being in their ranks. She couldn't say that, and after sparing both Celia and Amitel a glance, she could see the unspoken words in their eyes as well.

Clearing her throat, Eliza unsheathed her dagger from her side; the blade was as long as her forearm, made of steal and dipped in iron. It would, she hoped, be enough against the soldiers. She wasn't particularly the best in combat, but her magic was spent, her access dimming. It felt like a chord being pulled, and the more she used, the tighter it became. It was slowly becoming more and more uncomfortable.

This is what I get for leaving. The Blood Witches basically want me dead. Though dramatic, the thought didn't sit right with her. It would have been easy for them to just...replace her, wouldn't it?

The dagger grew heavy in her hand, just another reminder of what she had to lose.

21

THE SHADOW SOLDIERS
ELIZA

When the soldiers were close enough, Eliza struck; fire leapt from her outstretched hand into the first two and knocked them back. She swiped with her dagger and fell into a familiar rhythm, one she'd almost perfected under Thorne's guidance.

Her heart ached, and she wished—not for the first time—to know where he was, and why he wasn't there, with her.

The Shadow Soldiers reached for shields made of darkness. Their swords, blackened like coal, swiped through the air. Fire danced off the face of a sword and arced through the air before fizzling out above the soldier's head. Before Eliza could counter the next swing of his blade, the soldier retreated, clipping the edge of her dagger, rather than moving in to kill. Unlike the attack on Xeb and Alastor, when they had tried to kill her. It seemed the Dark Master was aware of his last mistake. Though she couldn't say the same for the others. Every move her friends made were countered with harsh blows. The Shadow Soldiers had certainly been sent to kill them.

Eliza summoned magic and sent a wave of air to knock down four soldiers that stood over Alicsar. She might not have liked the prince, but the last thing she needed was his death on her hands.

The dagger was no match against the heavy swords the soldiers wielded. But she had little training with swords, the weapons too heavy for her to carry on a good day, and as it was, a Lady of the Court would never wield a sword. A dagger, yes, but swords were harder to conceal within ones dress—or so Eliza had been told.

The helm of a soldier was knocked free; Eliza paused, her breathing harsh in her ears, and took in the reddened eyes of the soldier. Even without it, she couldn't see the spirit that was surely latched onto his shoulder.

She froze. The Shadow Soldier glared down at her with unseeing eyes, the muscles in his face lax and without emotion. But there was an eery familiarity that struck a chord within her. Like she'd met him before, faced him under the mountains of Mesah.

The sound of clashing swords and the hum of magic died as the soldier prowled towards her. Head spinning, all she could do was back up until she hit the wall of a building. She pressed herself into the stone, almost like she could disappear inside of it.

Flashes of the desert made her stomach roil. She could no longer move as the solider pressed the tip of his sword into her shoulder. "The Dark Master will have you."

Tongue heavy, Eliza couldn't respond.

Before she could blink, the Shadow Soldier was ripped away from her, and thrown with a force that would have killed a mortal. He slammed into one of the pillars that held up the temple. She wondered if the force could have knocked it over, but the soldier merely slid to the ground, struggling to stand.

It took her several moments to drag her eyes from his flailing body. Standing before her, Amitel breathed heavily, the red-flecks of his eyes more prominent than they had ever been.

He cupped her cheek with one cool hand, and she flinched, squeezing her eyes shut until the churning of her stomach eased.

"What was that, love?" Amitel asked. His fingers remained

pressed against her erratic pulse. "You could have gotten yourself killed, or stolen away by the Dark Master."

Eliza finally opened her eyes. "I'm fine." She shrugged off his hand and stumbled away from the wall. When she looked for the Shadow Soldier, he was already gone.

Celia and Alicsar were cornered, still fighting, but she felt their eyes on her. Swallowing, Eliza summoned her dagger and rushed the soldiers who remained and threw herself back into the rhythm of battle.

She ignored the worried stare of Amitel, and instead focused on not letting memories of the desert catch her again. For some time, she'd tried to keep the nightmares at bay, used whatever potion she could find, any spell, to lock those memories into shoes boxes deep in her mind. Sometimes they slithered out and took her by surprise, but she refused to let them out again.

Another soldier approached, this time helm intact. The weight of his sword rocked her back, but a quick spell brought roots to the surface to trap his feet.

The spell didn't hold, the roots dying as they touched his boots. *Iron.* Natural magic was strong, but against metals like iron, it was different. Iron was unnatural, going against magic and the Fae.

Eliza swore under her breath. *Typical.*

She spun, dagger raised, but she wasn't met with the blade of a Shadow Soldier; instead, piercing dark eyes met hers. Recognition flared in his eyes as he stared down at her, and he hesitated for a moment before his gaze went over her head.

He growled, and in one swooping motion, pulled her behind him. "Watch out."

She didn't get the chance to breathe as he slammed his sword into the chest of an approaching soldier. A gasp lodged in her throat as the soldier stilled on the end of the man's blade.

Impossible. She'd been throwing out spell after spell trying to get the Shadow Soldiers to stay down, but nothing had worked.

What was so special about him?

The newcomer pulled his sword from the body and watched it

crumple. He wore armour, though something about it sparked a memory in the back of Eliza's mind. There was another in matching armour, and he too pulled his sword from a now freshly dead soldier.

The Shadow Soldiers came to a shuddering stop. There were demons approaching now to flank their sides.

A tremor ran down her spine. Eliza sought out Celia and found her beside Alicsar. The other newcomer flanked her other side. Eliza stood between Amitel and the dark eyed man.

They were surrounded by the Shadow Soldiers. But they did not attack.

Why aren't they attacking?

Eliza reached once again for the spirits that should have been latched onto the soldiers, but came up dry. Was it her or the city making her abilities suffer?

What sounded like the crackle of flames filled the cavern, causing the demons and Shadow Soldiers to disappear. Eliza breathed in sharply as smoke and darkness shrouded their forms until there was nothing but dust and sand where they once stood.

Eliza blinked and took a trembling step forward, dagger falling from her grasp. "How the hell did they know we were here?" she asked. Everyone watched her, their gazes uncertain. Had she spoken aloud or to herself? She couldn't remember. Blood pounded too loudly in her ears.

Celia rushed to her side wrapped her arms around Eliza, holding her tight for a moment before releasing her. "Are you alright?"

Nodding, Eliza stared down at her hands. There were two thin slices on both her palms. She couldn't remember how she'd gotten them. "Fine." Quickly, her gaze went to the prince. "What about you?"

His emerald-green eyes met hers sharply. "I'm not the one who was almost *killed*."

Eliza pressed her lips into a thin line. There were two possibilities running through her head: the Dark Master had been following them... or either Alicsar or Amitel had sent word to their enemy.

The former made more sense; she wasn't deluded into believing she had been safe at the palace, wasn't stupid enough to believe their exit hadn't been missed by their enemy.

But the latter made sense too... had she made a mistake in allowing Amitel and Alicsar to join her? Should it have been only her and Celia to make the journey?

The thought didn't sit well with her and made her stomach churn.

Eliza dropped the prince's stare and instead focused on the two men who had joined them; dressed in armour, they could have passed as King Bastian's ornamental knights, but with the Blood Witch emblem etched into their breast plates, Eliza knew better.

"So, you two here to drag me back to the king? Or worse, to the Labyrinth Mountains?" she asked, crossed her arms.

The two knights of the Brotherhood bowed their heads; both were attractive in the way immortals were: young, steeped in magic, and probably old enough to be her grandfather. The one closest to her was immortal in a different way, though, with the slightly pointed ears of a half-Fae.

Strange, she thought, biting the inside of her cheek as she watched him. She didn't think the Blood Witches allowed half-Fae into the ranks of the Brotherhood.

He had smooth umber skin and even darker eyes, piercing and smouldering with the fierceness of a warrior. His ink-black hair was short, curled into tight coils against his scalp. He had no facial-hair, which made him look younger, with a crooked nose and full lips. He wasn't as broad as Thorne, instead lithe and tall. He was gorgeous, like the Fae in Kay's stories.

Then there was the knight beside him. In total contrast, he was pale with caramel-coloured eyes. His hair was a vibrant orange a similar shade to Clio, the servant who had died to protect Eliza during the attack on the Winter Palace. He stood taller than the half-Fae, slim yet muscled, his age hard to determine. But when he'd joined the knights he likely would have been in his mid-twenties. His features weren't as striking as his friends, instead he looked softer. And yet a look in his eyes told her he was much older and harder than he seemed.

The half-Fae cleared his throat. "We are not here to take you back to the Blood Witches. We have been tasked with protecting you on this journey."

Eliza narrowed her eyes. There was something about him that struck a chord inside of her, like she knew him. Not in a *past-life* kind of way like she did with Celia and Thorne, but something else. "I didn't think this was the kind of *journey* they would condone."

The knights shared a look.

"What?" Celia asked, stepping up. "Caden?"

The red-head—*Caden*—looked to her sharply. Something passed in his eyes, a look Eliza couldn't read. "If we are to speak, then let it be us two. You might wish to know what will come of your actions."

Eliza stiffened at the hidden warning in his voice. "What does that mean?" she asked as Celia stepped away from their group.

Her sister shook her head. "It's alright, Eliza. I knew this might happen."

"Knew *what* might happen?" Eliza demanded. "That you'd get in serious trouble helping me?"

"Of course," Caden replied. "There are consequences in defying the High Council, Ecix."

Eliza clamped her mouth shut. *Of course*, she thought bitterly. Because the High Council and the High Witch knew *everything* and made all the final decisions regarding Eliza and her future.

She should have known better.

Celia gave her a tight-lipped smile. "It'll be fine. This isn't the first time I've been under the gaze of the council."

"I still don't like it," Eliza muttered. "If they threaten you, we'll leave. Find some other way to get the dagger."

"The High Council have not made any threats against any of you." Caden narrowed his eyes as he addressed Celia. "But we should talk about what they did say."

Eliza said nothing as Celia guided the knight away. Celia's shoulders were tense, and every step was stiff. No matter how much she tried to hide her worry, it was still evident in the way she moved.

Slowly, Eliza traced a finger around her ear and focused on the pair. The last time she'd done the spell, it had been to learn why Celia had been sick. At the time, they had believed it was the doing of the

Blood Witches. But it had been Dorin the entire time, picking at Celia's magic and her connection to the tribes. He had wanted her gone so that she couldn't protect Eliza—and so Thorne would have to choose.

Eliza swallowed thickly and listened. "What's wrong?" Celia asked. Her voice was soft, and there was a hint of familiarness in it.

Caden sighed. "The High Council is worried about their alliance with the Cadiran King now that his son and the Ecix are gone."

"Is he aware that the prince is with us?"

"Yes. Lennox confirmed his location, but it has made him question us—and her."

"Eliza is no danger to him."

"But he could be," Caden replied quietly.

Celia paused before lowering her voice enough so Eliza had to strain to hear her. "What do you know about him?"

"Enough." The knight stopped and released a sigh.

"And what does Darius know?" Celia asked.

"Enough."

Eliza swallowed thickly. What did the other knight have to do with Alicsar? And what did Celia know? There were plenty of secrets between them, though mostly hidden on Celia's part. Eliza knew little of the witch's past, and it seemed Celia was feeling less and less inclined to share anything.

It was Celia who spoke next. "Why are you really here?"

"To protect," Caden replied, "though I do not believe it is the entire truth."

"Neither do I." Eliza watched as Celia paced. "Your priority has to be Eliza. If anything happens..."

"We have orders to take her directly to the stronghold."

Celia stopped pacing. "Good."

"But our orders do not include you, Celia. If something happens, we must take the Ecix—and leave you behind."

Eliza pulled away from the conversation, her eyes drifting to where the second knight—Darius, whose identity seemed all the more interesting—built a fire in the towns centre, beneath Azula's statue. She hadn't noticed it before, but the city had grown cold.

She released a breath. The High Council wasn't mad, but they weren't pleased either. For that, she should have been relieved. But they didn't care about Celia, her life or saving her should anything happen.

Did they believe something would?

There had already been an attack, though Eliza couldn't help but wonder if the attack had even been orchestrated by the Dark Master.

Was there a chance the Blood Witches no longer needed Celia and were trying to get rid of her?

~

The smell of sulphur made Eliza's nose burn, but she managed to stop herself from gagging as she, Celia, and Amitel created a barrier around Azula's city.

Blood Magic pounded in her veins as the intricacies of the spell flowed through her. Despite her lack of knowledge about Blood Witch protections, somehow she knew the workings of the spell. Whether it was dumb luck or a deep, buried part of her past, she didn't know.

A flash of light signalled the spell coming to an end; the light speared up to the top of the cavern and flowed over the city, creating a dome around the buildings. Tendrils of protective magic spread over the ground before sinking into the dust and stone.

For now, they were protected. *But for how long?* Eliza wondered. She brought her hands to her chest and closed her eyes.

She thought about the knights, the clear threat of the Blood Witches. She wanted to gag, but it felt like sand was filling her belly, each grain a second closer to what was to come.

"We should go as close to the temple as we can, set up camp in some of the buildings," Caden said, eyes grazing over the houses that surrounded them.

Eliza started for the cities centre, and said to no one in particular, "As long as I don't have to share a house with any of you men, I'm fine. I've come to enjoy not having to listen to anyone snore."

Amitel snorted. "I don't snore."

"I don't care." Eliza flashed him a grim smile. "I like sleep. And I could use a full twelve hours right now."

The smile slipped from her face as she and Celia entered one of the first buildings deemed safe by Caden and Darius; it was large, three storeys, with open windows facing out over the cities centre. Eliza said nothing as she surveyed the accommodations.

The entrance opened up into a living area with decaying wooden chairs and stone benches. There was a kitchen, with plates lining one of the countertops, with matching bowls and cups, all coated in a thick layer of dust. Wrinkling her nose, Eliza strode over to the pile and swiped her finger over one of the ceramic plates. The dust lifted, dark and almost sooty.

There hadn't been any sign of a fire, though that didn't mean the house they'd chosen hadn't been abandoned before all the others. The way it was set out—sparse furnishing, no personal touches, with all the kitchenware spread out over the counters—Eliza couldn't help but wonder if the owners of the apartment had predicted that something bad was going to happen, and had been prepared to leave.

Eliza pressed her lips together as she wiped the layer of dust from her fingers.

"According to Caden, most of these buildings are apartments," Celia said, her voice soft, as if she were afraid to disturb the dead.

Frowning, Eliza turned to the Blood Witch. "I think they were planning to leave."

"No personal effects." Celia strode over to a fireplace in the back of the living area. "No books or portraits. It looks as if whoever was in here was already long gone before the rest of the city died."

"There must have been some kind of mass warning of danger," Eliza replied. She wandered to one of the windows that overlooked the statue and city centre, and could just make out the remains of several people reaching for the Goddess who probably never came.

She turned away from the window, frowning. "A fireplace seems a little strange for an underground city," Eliza said, taking in the cold, dry hearth.

Celia shrugged her lithe shoulders before moving away. "We need to get wood. It might grow cold."

Eliza lifted a brow. "Cold down here?"

"Well..." Celia looked pointedly at the fireplace. "It might."

Following her stare, Eliza gazed into the hardened ash. "Maybe the city wasn't always underground."

"What?" Celia met her eye.

"What if it was above ground?" Eliza asked.

Celia was silent for a moment as she spun in a slow circle to take in the room. "What in the name of the Goddess happened?" she asked, voice a whisper.

A splintering pain shot through Eliza's skull. She stumbled back a step and squeezed her eyes shut, the feeling only easing momentarily before it spread down her spine, throbbing throughout her body. A gasp pierced the silence that had blossomed between the pair, causing Celia to take a hesitant step towards Eliza's shuddering body.

She felt as though her brain was being stomped on repeatedly, leaving her skull intact, the nerves throughout her body pulsing with each kick. When she closed her eyes, she found some reprieve, but her lungs started closing up, and her breathing became harsh and laboured.

"Eliza!" Celia's voice cracked with fear that sent a shiver down Eliza's spine. "What's wrong?"

Peeling her eyes open, Eliza stared into the pit of ash as the world around her blurred together. Her tongue grew heavy and leaden in her mouth, keeping her silent as she tried to blink away the pain.

Stay away, a voice hissed. The hairs on her arms rose and a shudder made its way down into her bones.

Stay back.

The gripping pain released her. Eliza gasped for breath, falling into Celia's awaiting arms.

"What happened?" Celia asked softly. Her fingers brushed lightly as Eliza's messy hair.

Eliza pulled away, mouth dry. "Nothing, I just—" She closed her eyes and sucked in another breath. "I don't know what happened."

It took her a moment to be able to climb to her feet. She expected to feel some lingering pain, but instead there was only a slight ache in her temple. Nothing like what had struck her.

"Perhaps Amitel and I should—"

"Celia, I'm fine now." Eliza tried to smile, but it felt forced, fake on her lips. "I think I just need to lie down."

The Blood Witch sighed. "Please, Eliza—"

Without looking at Celia, Eliza walked slowly towards the entrance of the apartment, where a set of stone stairs clung to the side of the building. Quietly, she slipped up the stairs towards the second apartment, heart heavy with all that had happened that day, head thrumming and magic tired. And her friend said nothing as silence once again fell over the city of Azula.

22

SECRETS OF THE ECIX
CELIA

Blinking tiredly, Celia carefully dropped her last load of texts off into the small house she'd commandeered for her work. Four bulky wood tables were pushed together in the middle, pulled from the surrounding homes, and though Celia felt a pang of guilt over stealing from the dead, she said a prayer and hoped for their forgiveness.

She'd spent hours plundering an old library, the surrounding homes, and the temple for any text that had survived the years of abandonment. With how well the tomes and scrolls had been preserved, Celia was grateful for the city's abandonment. A majority of the books she'd found were largely religious, full of prayers and stories that Celia herself had grown up hearing about Azula.

When they'd found stashes of them, Eliza had seemed more than surprised, almost like she hadn't expected to find stories about the Goddess they were seeking. At the time, it had made Celia laugh, but now as she settled into her self-appointed research space, a pang of guilt shot through her.

There is nothing I can do about it now, she thought with a shake of her head. No matter how hard she tried, however, she couldn't shake away the guilt.

Celia settled in. More than anything, there were more mentions of her dagger within the books they'd found. Not detailed references, but interesting remarks.

Like the fact that the Goddess never wielded the dagger before her people when they were present. The dagger had always remained at the Goddesses hip, until it wasn't.

There were two recounts of times when Azula did not wear the dagger. Without dates or any additional information, Celia couldn't tell if it had escaped the writer's attention or if there was something else at play.

Celia sighed and flipped through another heavy, leather-bound tome, the book she'd found in the palace library by her side. Somewhere in the cavern, she could hear Eliza yelling at Amitel about something trivial and nonsensical. It brought a small smile to her face.

Magic rumbled throughout the room and she braced the table as Amitel appeared in front of her. Dust lined his shoulders and the tip of his nose, lips pinched together. The magic settled around him before curling around his body and disappearing.

"She is absolutely terrifying," he muttered, brushing his shoulders of the dust. "I fell two floors because of her."

Celia snorted and shook her head. "You deserve worse," she replied, pressing her chin into her hand. "What are you doing?"

"Hoping for some reprieve from that monster you call a sister." He pulled a chair from a different table and sat, spreading his legs out in front of him. "And you said you wanted to speak to me."

"Later." She rolled her eyes. "Right now, I'm busy."

"Celia." He leaned forward and mimicked her, placing his chin on his hand. "Please."

Closing her eyes, she sighed. "I need you to train Eliza in Blood Magic."

"No."

She opened her eyes and frowned. "Why not?"

"Last I checked, *you* were the Blood Witch." He rose and shook his head, laughing quietly under his breath.

Celia pressed her lips into a thin line. "I was never allowed to spend time learning the ways of an Ecix," she said, dropping her hand from her chin. "I wouldn't know where to start with her training. Rarely am I allowed to sit in with her magic lessons with Lennox. But you know more about the Ecix than most outsiders. And you can be a good teacher."

Though it pained her to admit it, from what she'd witness since meeting him, Amitel knew Blood Magic. He had far more years' experience than her, and though he was younger than the power of the Ecix, he'd spent time in its presence, in many forms.

She might not trust him yet, but she knew what he was capable of.

"There's an arena in the back of the city. It'll be perfect for Eliza. She needs help, especially after what happened during the attack." Amitel opened him mouth, but he shut it quickly, jaw clenched. "Her power is so volatile right now, and she doesn't understand it yet. But you might be able to help her with that."

The warlock looked away for a moment before sighing. "I agree that she needs to be trained," he said, meeting her stare. "But I don't believe I'm the one to do this, Celia. She doesn't trust me."

Rising from the chair, Celia stepped around the desk. "Let this serve as an opportunity for you to prove your loyalty." She offered him a tight smile. "Train Eliza, prepare her for what's to come. I fear you might be the only one capable of doing so."

Amitel searched her face for a moment, eyes narrowed, but after a heartbeat of silence, he nodded. "Alright Celia. But who gets to tell her."

Celia's smile brightened. "You can. I have faith in you."

He closed his eyes with a heavy breath. "She'll be the death of me."

"If you hurt her again," Celia replied, patting his arm, "she will."

His eyes cut to hers, but he bowed his head and said nothing else, leaving her in the makeshift office. When his footsteps disappeared, a spike of fear made her heart stutter. How much time would they have before *he* attacked again? How much time did Eliza have? Celia moved back to her chair and sat, staring down at the old books. Somewhere in the city, Eliza shouted, followed by Amitel's easy laugh. Though Celia tried to muster a smile, her stomach squeezed with panic.

The Dark Master knew where they were. It didn't matter that they had managed to form a barrier spell around the ancient city, it was too late. She just hoped they had enough time to go through the contents of the city before they were forced to move on to another.

She returned to the texts she'd gathered, her mind focused on the dagger. She flipped to the next page of *Legends*, a small hand-bound journal she'd found beneath the temple.

Azula's dagger is nothing short of legendary. The blade, born of the Goddess, is believed to kill even the undying, to rip soul from body, to rip power from the mind.

Celia read the short passage again and sat back. *Kill the undying.* If the legends were true, then there was a chance it could kill the Dark Master. Alastor, Eliza had said, believed the Dark Master nothing short of a God.

The un-killable.

That is if it's true. The bitter thought entered her mind before she could push it away. What she needed was hope, hope that they would summon the dagger and could turn it on the Dark Master.

~

The pull of sleep dragged her away from her texts.

Celia couldn't remember the last time she'd been in the old cabin out by Lake Mab. Nestled amongst the towering pines of the Labyrinth Mountain's valley, the lake had been one of the only places Celia hated to be near while she was alone.

Older Blood Witches claimed face-eating and youth-drinking sirens dwelled beneath the turquoise depths, deep down where the eye couldn't see. Once or twice, Celia thought she'd seen the sparkle of scales, or glimpse a dorsal fin when no one else was looking. But there were other legends surrounding the lake, stories all the daughters of the Blood Witches learnt in their youth. She knew they were only meant to scare her, but there was truth to those stories.

But the cabin was different. Abandoned by the Brotherhood, the inside looked more like the base of a war camp rather than a nice getaway from the coven and tribes. As girls, Celia and Isolde had found it while escaping their mother, and ever since Celia used it as a way to feel closer to her dead sister.

Pine-needles snapped underfoot several paces away. Celia spun and took in the forest-green wisp of a dress her sister had always adored, her dark hair braided like a crown around her head, the mischievous moss-green eyes, and the cruel twist of her lips, painted a crimson so dark it almost looked like blood.

Taking a step back, Celia stared wide eyed. "Isolde?"

The twist of Isolde's lips turned into a sincere smile, and tentatively, she took a step closer. "Hello, sister."

"Is it really you?" Celia asked, voice thickening with tears. She stumbled forward and hesitated before throwing her arms around Isolde's shoulders.

Her sister laughed. "Are you happy to see me?"

"Of course, I just..." Memories of Isolde's death flashed into her mind, overriding the joy she felt at seeing her long dead sister. She pulled back, brows furrowing, and took her in.

"Stop worrying." Isolde laughed and stepped up to wrap her arms around Celia, though her sisters arms felt more like a whisper of what it used to, rather than solid, warm. "I'm happy to see you."

As Isolde pulled away, Celia asked, "Is this real?"

"Does it matter?" Isolde motioned to the cabin, to the lake. "We're together. Here in the place we love."

"You know I never liked this place," Celia said with a frown, though part of her missed it dearly, if only because her sister had loved it once.

Isolde snorted and stepped to the lake's edge, kneeling to run her fingers over the still surface. "Liar."

"There's a reason you're here," Celia said, eyes searching for *some kind of answer. "I can sense it."*

Isolde gave a small nod and rose, the water rippling with her movement. *"How much do you know about my power, sister?"*

The sky above them darkened as Celia eyed Isolde. Something dark and worrisome flickered in her familiar green eyes. A small twitch started in her fingers, and when she looked up at the sky, fear darkened her eyes.

The question surprised Celia; she'd expected something about the dagger, or their mission. She'd expected a reprimanding about letting Eliza leave the safety of the palace, or maybe about how Brandon was gone, searching for some other way.

But she had expected nothing of the power.

"Only as much as you or the High Witch would tell me," Celia replied warily, taking a step back from Isolde. *"Why?"*

"The power can be weaponised," she whispered, as if someone would hear them.

"I know," Celia said with a frown. *"Before you—"*

"Yes, before me there were girls who wielded it like a weapon." Isolde rolled her eyes and started for the trees, the sound of breaking pine-needles filling Celia's ears as she rushed to follow. Every step Isolde made was jerky, sudden. It frightened Celia.

"But I am not talking about it being weaponised by the holder," Isolde continued.

Brows furrowed, Celia's eyes narrowed questioningly. *"What?"*

"How do you think the power is given?" Isolde asked, her voice startlingly loud.

What is she going on about? *Celia wondered. There was a nervous energy about Isolde, something not quite right about her. Celia wanted to chalk it up to it just being a dream, but... the Isolde she knew wouldn't be so frazzled. The questions, the jumbled responses...*

Celia did not recognise her.

Shaking her head, Celia hurried to catch her sister. "I thought..."

"Wrong again. What do they teach these days?" Isolde stopped and gazed up at the darkened sky, fear flicker across her features

once more. "As you were going to say, the holder is made. The High Witch governs that. Especially when the holder is being reborn. However, who holds the power when there is no true holder?"

Celia looked from her sister to the sky. "I assume the High Witch."

A cruel smile twisted at Isolde's lips. "Semi-correct. You're catching on, sister. Yes, the High Witch is responsible for holding on to the power while there is no holder. But only in part. The power reverts to the Original."

"The original what?" Celia asked.

"Original Ecix, of course. Aren't you listening?" Isolde snapped, fear tinging her voice.

What is she so afraid of? Isolde, who fought the Resurgence, who had no fear of dying. Who had made Celia vow to find a way to kill the shadow creature who murdered her.

Celia replied, "Start making sense, sister, and I might."

Isolde rolled her eyes. "Look who grew a backbone. I'm proud of you. Tell Eliza of the Original. It is the key to finding what you seek. Without knowing about her, you cannot wield the blade."

"Is she going to know what that even means?" Celia asked with a frown.

"She should once they start teaching her how to find me, find us. But they won't. Not yet." Isolde pressed a hand to her mouth, eyes flickering over the darkness, widening with fear. "The dagger is linked to the Original. Without that knowledge, all is lost."

"What do you mean?" Celia snapped. Celia herself had spent hours with Eliza over the last couple of months teaching her the ways of the Blood Witch. Amitel and herself were continuing her training in the ancient city. "Eliza has been training since she returned from Mesah. They have to be teaching her—"

Isolde cast Celia a doubtful look and said, "Have they?"

Celia opened her mouth to answer, but the words caught in her throat, and she couldn't form a response. She couldn't know what Lennox was teaching Eliza, because she hadn't been allowed to sit in on most lessons.

STEPHANIE ANNE

But Amitel wouldn't know the specifics of how to connect Eliza with her past lives. No one but those tasked with teaching Eliza the ways of Blood Magic did.

"Isolde, what do we do?" she asked, voice barely a whisper. "Where do we look? What—"

Within the blink of an eye, Isolde was gone.

"Isolde?" Celia spun in a slow circle as the world around her faded to black. "Isolde!"

23

THE ORIGINAL
ELIZA

Eliza rubbed tiredly at her eyes as Celia paced the length of the living room. It was near midnight in the world above—thanks to a nice big clock Amitel had created to keep them all in line—but that hadn't stopped Celia from startling Eliza awake from a sleep filled with dreams of Brendan Fraser from *The Mummy*.

Sighing, Eliza rested her cheek on her balled-up fist. "What did she say?"

Celia halted in front of the fire, which crackled with low, warm flames. "That I needed to tell you about the Original."

"Ecix?" Eliza frowned as Celia nodded, meeting her stare. "I have no idea what she's talking about. I'm pretty sure Isolde is crazy."

"She isn't crazy." Celia shook her head but she hesitated with her next words. "She was... different, though."

"She couldn't have elaborated any further? You know, maybe given us a name, or a reason *why* she was vaguely warning us about the Original?"

"I do not believe it was going to be that simple."

Eliza couldn't help but roll her eyes. "It never is with these people. Looks like I won't get a straight answer until I'm dead."

Celia scowled, but she didn't seem to disagree. "I have no way of contacting her, and I have no idea how she's getting to me."

"Let me guess." Eliza stood and crossed her arms. "I'm supposed to find her."

"Your training should have included being able to contact your past lives," Celia said, rubbing a hand over her eyes, "but Lennox wasn't teaching you any of that, was she?"

Eliza shook her head. "Can't you teach me?"

Celia released a heavy breath and dropped her hand. "I was never privy to those sessions with Isolde, and only three Witches know the rituals and lessons that go into what the Ecix must learn. Isolde was forbidden to tell me, took a blood oath, like all those before her."

"Excuse me, a *what?*" Eliza gaped at Celia before shaking her head. "This is ridiculous."

"This is why your training with Amitel is so important." Eliza looked up at Celia, who knelt in front of her. "I cannot teach you much in terms of being the Ecix, but Amitel has had many encounters with your magic. There are things he knows that not even I know."

"It's hard." Before Celia could respond, Eliza shook her head. "Not the learning part. I can learn magic. Listening to Amitel, being around him."

"But you saved him, in Mesah. Why?"

Eliza shrugged. "I can't explain it."

The smile Celia gave her was soft, but it dropped from her face a moment later, eyes going dark. *"Azula's dagger is nothing short of legendary. The blade, born of the Goddess, is believed to kill even the undying, to rip soul from body, to rip power from the mind."*

"What?" Eliza frowned.

"Something I read." Celia stood and paced the length of the living room before disappearing into one of the bedrooms. She emerged with a book. Eliza didn't recognise it. "I had assumed it might do what we needed—with the Dark Master. But perhaps that's how the Original

Ecix lost her power. The dagger was used to rip the power from her."

A memory tickled the back of Eliza's mind, blurred and shapeless, yet the feeling of fear shot through her like a bucket of ice water had been tipped over her head. Whatever the memory was, it was ripped away from her, because the sense of fear and the blurred image abruptly disappeared.

Blinking, Eliza wrung her fingers. "That could be it..."

It should have been easy for her to believe that was what happened. It made sense, though whether it was true was something else entirely. But if the dagger really did have the power to take away magic, then she could be sure the Dark Master had learnt all this already, and that was why he was seeking it as well.

If he couldn't have the person with the power, then he would take the power for himself.

As if sensing the uncertainty and fear now freely taking control inside of Eliza's mind, Celia touched her shoulder lightly. "Go back to bed. I'm sorry I woke you so early."

With a sigh, Eliza stood and started for the stairs up to her apartment, but stopped. "Do you think the Original has something to do with why the dagger is missing?"

She looked back to Celia, who shook her head. "I don't know. It's possible. Isolde said they were connected."

Eliza said nothing more as she climbed the stairs, entering the barren space where she imagined a family had once lived, hundreds of years ago, happy and alive.

There was a chance everything was connected, and yet Eliza didn't want to believe any of it. *It's too easy*, she thought entering her room.

In the distance, the clock struck the hour. *Witching Hour*. She wasn't sure if she should be amused or worried. Either way, she climbed back into bed and stared up at the ceiling. She knew one thing for certain:

Whatever it was Isolde wanted her to know, it had to wait.

~

The amphitheatre was cold and small, a damp smell seeping through the stone that surrounded them. When she had been ten, Eliza had visited Rome with her grandfather and Kay, where they had spent their days taking tours like the other tourists, and the nights with beings of the Shadowland. Eliza didn't remember the nights, not when the days had been so interesting.

Despite hating school, she'd always been fascinated with history and the past. She'd never quite grasped why, and eventually it had led her to taking a job at a local museum in the French Quarter, but now she guessed it had something to do with the hundreds of years of missing memory and past lives that resided deep inside of her.

It made studying the Roman-styled amphitheatre less fun, but she continued to examining it nonetheless.

Amitel stood at the other end of the arena, his arms folded across his chest. He'd forgone style, instead donning a pair of cotton pants and a long-sleeved pirate-styled shirt that hung off his lithe frame. The neckline was deep enough to give Eliza a view of his golden chest— which she had tried to ignore since the moment she met up with him.

She'd chosen black yoga pants—baggy enough that she looked like she was about to go back to bed—and a tank-top, both from home because the training clothes she'd been given while at the palace were too heavy to pack into her bags.

Today, though, they'd been joined by the Brotherhood and Alicsar, who scattered the arena. They'd all dressed ready to fight, which made Eliza wish she'd worn tights or track pants instead. But she wanted to be comfortable... even though she looked ridiculous.

Silence fell over them. Eliza turned in time to see Amitel stalk towards her, any hint of teasing or arrogance gone. He looked like he was about to give her one hell of a training session.

Great.

Amitel stopped and looked her over, eyes grazing down the front of her tank—and stopping. She knew immediately what had caught his attention: the scar from Isolde. It was just visible above the neckline, pink and faded. Sometimes, she felt the ache or the burning cut of shadows as it attempted to rip her apart.

Before she could comment on his stare, his eyes met hers, burning gold. Today, the flecks of red were gone, like they had never existed in the first place.

"We're going to incorporate magic with physical fighting. But this time you're going to have to fight someone *with* magic." Amitel motioned to a blank wall. One moment, it had been empty, and the next it was filled with a rack of weapons similar to the ones she'd seen in the training halls at the palace barracks.

She closed her eyes and released a sigh. It made sense as to why the knights had joined them, then. Though she couldn't be certain why Alicsar was with them, instead of being with Celia, or devouring his own texts.

"Great," she replied, opening her eyes and grimacing. "Just what I wanted."

Amitel nodded to the weapons. "Choose your poison."

"Why are we doing this again?" She walked slowly to the rack and eyed the daggers. "I thought you'd be teaching me *real* magic. Maybe some Blood Magic, or Ecix magic for beginners."

"Not today. Not after what happened with the Shadow Soldiers." He reached over her and grasped a dagger. All of a sudden, he was too close, his chest only a breath from her shoulder. She felt his eyes on her, burning into the side of her head. "You hesitated when the soldiers attacked," he said, voice a whisper. "I know why, and I understand. But you need to be more careful. I won't always be there to save you, love."

Her heart stuttered, but she pushed it down, down, *down* where it couldn't breathe. Shoving away from him, she grabbed her own blade and started for the centre of the arena. Before her eyes, a circle appeared in the dirt. *Great.* "I don't need you do save me. I can do that myself, thank you very much."

She came to a stop and spun, but he was directly behind her, pressing the tip of the blade into her abdomen. "You could have stabbed me," she said, staring down at the point, refusing to meet his eye—or acknowledge the smirk that was likely painting his lips.

Amitel pulled away and danced back two steps. "What are you going to do about it?"

"Smack you." When his brows lifted and the smirk widened into a grin, she was *almost* tempted to end his life. "Let's get this over with so I can go help Celia."

The warlock said nothing else as he circled her, dagger loose in his grip. The warmth of his magic tickled hers as she called upon what dwelled in her blood.

Unable to help it, she cut a small gash into her arm, just below her elbow. It was only the length of her fingernail, shallow enough that it wouldn't scar, but would allow her blood to flow and let her access the magic within it.

Amitel's eyes went to the cut. "Cheat."

"I'm a Blood Witch." Although she rolled her eyes, she couldn't stop the pang of embarrassment that flared in her gut.

Shaking his head, Amitel flipped the dagger in his hand. "Point to the one who *kills* the other. Three rounds, the one with the most kills wins."

"Seems a bit brutal."

He raised a brow. "Already admitting defeat, love?"

She paused and finally let the magic cover her. "You wish."

Eliza spun, the movements like a dance. Her feet knew where to go, her weapon an extension of her arms. Even her magic glided over her like a second skin, joining with the blunt steel of her blade to give it an edge.

All the training she'd done with Thorne was finally coming in handy.

His dagger met hers, but he was quick enough to jump back before her magic could tear into his shirt.

Amitel smirked. "If you wanted to see me naked so badly, all you had to do was ask."

She gritted her teeth. "Shut up."

"Did I hit a nerve?"

Pausing, Eliza contemplated how much trouble she'd get into if she threw her dagger at him. Celia's disappointed face crossed her mind, so she tossed it in the air. "I get why no one wants to be around you. *You never shut up.*"

Amitel scowled. Without another word, he struck. His movements were as quick as a viper and just a dangerous. Eliza dove, rolling to the ground before popping up behind the warlock as the blade of his dagger sunk into the earth where her feet had been.

She swore under her breath. That would have been an easy point to him.

The boys were silent on the sidelines, but at least they weren't a distraction.

Heart thundering, Eliza blocked out everything else. She only saw and heard Amitel.

He ran a hand through his thick golden hair, but he hadn't broken out in a single sweat—unlike her. She suddenly regretted the poofy yoga pants, which were becoming more of a hinderance than anything comfortable.

The steel of Amitel's practice blade sung through the air, and without hesitation, Eliza spun out of the way—

Her foot caught on Amitel's, and she went down. She hit the dirt hard enough to knock the wind out of her.

Amitel was on top of her a moment later, blade pressed to her heart. "Dead."

"I was going easy on you," she muttered, shoving him off. Ignoring the slight twist in her stomach, she jumped away and palmed her dagger once again. "I won't be nice."

"You were being nice?" His grin was teasing, and yet there was something else hidden beneath it.

This time, Eliza didn't give him the chance to strike. She gathered her swelling magic as a shield around her, protection enough from the swipe that was aimed at her abdomen. The tip of the blade scraped the shield with enough force to knock her back again, but the weapon flew from Amitel's hand.

"Smart girl." His golden eyes brightened as they met hers. "But how long will it last you?"

As if on cue, the shield around her wavered. The blood on her arm dried, which dimmed her connection to her Blood Magic.

Dammit. She sent Amitel a scathing look before quickly pressing the tip of her blade into her soft flesh again.

"Remind me to teach you how *not* to do that," Amitel muttered, something like anger flashing in his eyes.

Rolling her shoulders, Eliza raised her hands, ignoring him. The once compacted dirt rumbled beneath their feet. The amphitheatre shook. Eliza lifted her hands a little higher before slamming them down onto the earth, and watched as it knocked Amitel from his feet. He rolled but wasn't fast enough.

Pouncing, Eliza took to the ground and rolled him onto his back. As she went to straddle him, she considered the implications—well, she considered the remarks from Amitel later about something entirely sexual. But she was close enough to winning this round that she didn't care.

Holding her breath, she pressed her knees into his hands, which forced him to release his dagger. She held the knife to his throat. "Dead."

"Impressive." He grunted. She scrambled to get off him, but instead landed on her back with the warlock hovering over her with a sheepish grin. "Not fast enough."

"I would be fine," she muttered, "because you'd be dead."

Amitel chuckled and stood, offering her a hand. She slapped it aside and rose, brushing off her pants.

"One point each." Amitel danced back several steps and motioned for her to do the same. Begrudgingly, she did. "Final round, love. Who will win?"

"Careful," she replied, "your ego is getting a little too big for that head of yours."

The smile he gave her sent shivers down her spine. Whatever was going on between them... she knew it wasn't good. Safe. That if she got too close to him again, he'd only hurt her in the end.

So she bottled any feelings for him that were arising. Friendship would be hard to maintain, but she'd rather that then whatever else could happen.

Amitel moved so fast, she almost missed him. The warlock appeared beside her, but he didn't go for the kill. Instead, he ran the blades tip teasingly over her bare arm. Where it touched, fire erupted on her skin, the feeling flooding her stomach.

So much for pushing him aside.

He was too busy toying with her that he almost didn't catch the swing of her arm as she aimed her fist at his jaw. He ducked out of the way quickly enough that her fist only skimmed his cheek. But the look of shock that flashed across his eyes made her laugh.

She moved before he could retaliate, and kicked up dust to blur his vision. Behind her, he coughed, but his footsteps were heavy as he chased after her. Something flew past her head, and she looked back in time to see a rock soar past her nose.

"Hey!" She stopped. "What the hell?"

"I thought we were playing dirty." The insufferable smirk that tipped his lips almost made her reconsider killing him for real.

"So violent," he purred, circling her. She frowned. "I can see it. And feel it." He winked.

Eliza scoffed and widened her stance again. "Shut up."

Amitel shrugged, and he threw the next punch. Despite ducking out of reach, a wave of magic ploughed through the air, knocking her from the circle. She hit the ground and rolled before jumping to her feet. Gathering a ball of fire, she threw it at him.

Each throw, he ducked. Each punch, she side-stepped. It might have started out as a training session, but it quickly developed into some kind of taunting game. Eliza knew she was the prey—Amitel was older, faster, stronger. He toyed with her at every move.

She should have been seething, and yet she appreciated it. Although he held back, every time he used her own magic against her, she learnt something new. She needed to be smarter than her opponents, especially him.

They were outside of the circle now, no longer playing by the basic rules of training. The circle disappeared as they drew closer to the walls of the arena. But with each step, her muscles protested. No coffee, limited sleep, and aching muscles made it harder to keep up. Sweat coated her like a second skin, and yet Amitel looked like he'd just stepped out of a photoshoot.

Frustration curdled in her gut.

She caught her opening. It was likely an oversight by Amitel, maybe he hadn't expected her to take the chance, but she ducked under his arm, took hold of his hand, turned him and slammed him into the wall of the arena. His eyes went wide as they met hers.

Eliza pressed the dagger against Amitel's throat, breath even despite the fight. "Dead," she whispered. She hadn't meant to, and yet she could get no words out as his chest heaved against hers. They were pressed into a wall of the arena, but it should have been an alcove or a room; fire burned in the pit of Eliza's stomach as she gazed up at her opponent.

Something old burned deep within her, something she couldn't name. It made her magic sing and hide, threaten to leap from her skin, or transport her away, away, away—

Amitel's eyes changed; one moment they were a ferocious gold, but red devoured the pupil and bled into the iris, almost taking over the gold.

She gasped. "Your eyes."

The warlock blinked, and it was enough for Eliza to realise where they were—and what it must look like to the others.

Pulling back, Eliza sheathed her dagger and plastered a smirk across her face, like it would save her from the burning embarrassment of holding Amitel against a wall.

"I think I need a better opponent," she said, voice trembling just enough to make her stop. She ran a hand through her hair. What was it about the warlock that affected her so much?

Amitel matched her arrogance. "I let you win. Let's call it a learning opportunity."

She scowled. "Shut up. I won fair and square. You're dead, now act like it."

He held a hand to his heart. "You wound me, love."

Eliza rolled her eyes, but her heart still thundered from the proximity of Amitel. *Why?* He'd never had an effect on her before. What had changed? She could barely stand to be around him normally, and even though he'd been trying to explain his betrayal, she couldn't get past it—wouldn't, because she didn't want to be hurt again.

By *him*.

Instead of giving him a response, she started for the stands that overlooked the arena. There were stairs built into the sides of the amphitheatre that led up to the old seating. "I'm taking a break," she said to no one in particular.

As she passed Alicsar, Caden, and Darius, she made the mistake of meeting the princes gaze; his eyes had darkened, hardened, and there was no mistaking the pang of hurt that flickered across his face.

She swallowed hard and forced herself to look away and focus on the stairs. She took them two at a time as her stomach dropped and guilt flooded her.

Stop it, she chided herself. *You owe him nothing.* She shook her head and dropped down onto one of the benches. They were all compacted dirt and stone, smoothed over from years of use. There were even initials carved into the benches beside her, and as she ran her fingers over them lightly, she was once again consumed with questions about the people.

"All right, Your Highness, let's see what you can do."

Frowning, Eliza tore her gaze from the initials and stared out into the arena. Alicsar, shoulders tense and a death grip on his practice sword, strode towards the centre of the arena. At his side was Darius, whose broad shoulders were loose, muscles relaxed.

Oh no. She wrapped her arms around herself as they met in the middle. *What is he doing?*

Although there had been whispers in the palace about Alicsar's affection towards her, she'd done her best to block them out. If she thought on them too much, she knew she'd break, especially after what he—Dorin—had done to her in Mesah.

He only likes me because he thinks I saved him. He had no idea what really happened in Mesah, and she wanted to keep it that way.

Eliza leaned forward as they entered the circle. Alicsar swung the sword in a lazy arc, more arrogance than actual skill. *Does he want to get himself killed?* The Brotherhood were as skilled as they were immortal, and the half-Fae that Alicsar circled was no different.

Darius was light of his feet, and quicker than any mortal she'd met. He struck first—and fast, with a calmness that scared her more than anger did. But there was nothing brutal in the way he moved, almost like he was too afraid to show his true strength.

Eliza was caught in the dance between her fiancé and the knight of the Brotherhood. Two entirely different people, and yet, it seemed, forged on the same path.

Where Darius was quick and light, Alicsar was angry and confused. Every step was countered and yet he threw himself into the fight harder than she ever would have expected from him. She couldn't help but wonder where the anger was coming from, unless it was a figment of her imagination, or a shadow of the man he had once been.

She didn't want to think about either option.

Their supposed training session was less about learning manoeuvres and more about releasing testosterone, it seemed.

Despite the few training sessions that had been reserved for Alicsar by his father, he appeared to be more in tune with his past than she ever would have realised. It must have been muscle memory with the way he was keeping up with Darius.

The Fae were fast, stealthy, lethal, and yet Alicsar had no problem matching the knights blows. But, she caught Darius pulling back. It didn't look like it was out of respect for the prince's title—since he'd arrived, he'd done nothing to indicate that he cared about his status—but for something else.

Their fight turned more brutal, and within moments they were covered in sweat and dust. Eliza rose. She found Caden, stiff and unmoveable, his gaze never straying from the two sparing inside the circle. Amitel, across the arena, looked more intrigued than worried about what was going on.

She felt the power of the blood even before it hit the dirt.

Darius stopped, chest heaving. The sword dropped from his hand, the sound piercing the silence of the city. Even she could hear the harshness of his breaths.

Caden hesitated at the edge of the arena. Alicsar was no threat— at least, not yet. The prince staggered back, surprise and fear crossing his face as he did.

Something had changed in him. But whether it was his memories or something else, she didn't know.

The prince dropped his sword and left the arena through the main entrance, never once meeting her stare. Uncertainty warred within her. She stood, prepared to go after him, but her feet felt heavy, like weights had been sewn into the bottoms of her boots.

Then there was the knight, who watched the prince's every move. Eliza couldn't ignore how he'd pulled his punches, how his movements had been slower than when they'd been fighting the Shadow Soldiers. She shook her head. There was something he knew, too.

Amitel met her stare from the other side of the arena. Despite the distance, she could read it as clearly as if he were right in front of her. There was something going on with Alicsar, but she wasn't sure if she wanted to know what.

24

A FLOWER OF TRUTH
CELIA

The tangy scent of lemon verbena wafted from an untouched tea-cup sitting beside a stack of texts. Celia flipped between the pages of two books, a dull throb starting in her temples, the ache of her Shadow Sickness darkening her thoughts and souring her mood.

Her thoughts drifted to Isolde's warnings, and she wondered—not for the first time since that dream—if her sister was sending her on a wild goose chase searching for the Original. But her sisters' fear... that had been real. There was something truly terrible happening, something Celia was yet to figure out.

What had she meant about it being the key?

Of course, Celia knew there had to be a first. The first Ecix, the one who started the cycle. What she didn't understand was why it had anything to do with Azula's dagger.

She dropped her head into her hands with a groan. The longer she continued to search through useless texts, the more confused she grew, which only heightened the pain throbbing throughout her body.

A tingle of magic raced over her skin. She looked up as a message appeared, ash forming paper, which turned into a letter. The neat scrawl and perfumed parchment sent a pang of guilt through her, but she snatched it out of the air and read the short passage eagerly.

Dearest Miridi,

I took to the stacks today in search of what you asked for. Unfortunately, it is as you feared: there is no mention of the 'Original', and I searched the halls of the library for hours. Little about the Ecix is kept within these walls anymore. Since the appearance of the new Ecix, the High Witch and the council have been removing many great texts and locking them away.

If there is anything remaining of this history, it will be kept within the Temple of the Ecix.

I am sorry I could not be of more help.

I thank you for trusting me with this task.

Until you return,

Sonya

Celia sighed and crumpled up the letter. She threw it to the ground and watched it roll out of view, the little hope she had disappearing with it. Dropping her head into her hands, she released a heavy sigh. Tears of frustration burned behind her eyes, but she rubbed them with the heels of her palms, scrubbing away her doubts and fears.

She breathed in deeply, and counted to ten.

One. *We still have time.*

Two. *There are many options for us to try.*

Three. *Azula has other cities; we can always search them.*

Four. *Isolde could still return with more answers.*

Five. *Brandon might return with answers of his own.*

Six. *Eliza is still learning to enter the Aether.*

Seven. *If all else fails, we return to the Labyrinth Mountains and pray to the Goddess that the Temple reveals the truth.*

Eight. *We can still find the dagger without this knowledge, I am certain.*

Nine. *There is still time.*

Ten. *There is still hope.*

As she breathed out, Celia lowered her hands from her eyes and blinked. The room focused, and her gaze dropped onto where the letter had rolled out of view.

She scrawled a short note of thanks to Sonya and watched the ash flutter away. A kernel of guilt wedged its way into her chest, but she rose, pushing away from the table. *A walk will do me some good,* she thought.

"Clear my mind, and pray to the Goddess I'll find something useful in these texts," she muttered to herself.

There was a reason she preferred the gardens and greenhouses of the Crystal City to the giant tomb of a library hidden within the mountain. The open air meant freedom, while the library—grand and deep as it was—suffocated her.

Though Celia found some excitement of being in Azula's hidden city, it reminded her too much of her time within the stacks, forced to learn languages and histories of those long since dead.

As much as she would have loved scouring the ruins of the old manor above the city, caution made her turn down a path leading further into the city. Maybe she'd be able to find an old garden, could attempt to revive whatever might have grown there a thousand years ago. The garden attached to the temple had been ruined during the fight with the demons, but she believed there was another somewhere.

Head down, she searched the old streets. Under layers of dirt, there once was large stone pavers that marked the roads, where the indents of carts could still be seen in the rock. Not for the first time, she wondered what could have happened to the city for it to be buried beneath a new Cadira.

Turning a corner, Celia hadn't noticed anyone else approaching. A body slammed into her, and she stumbled back several paces rubbing her forehead. An explosion of pain erupted in her temples, so fast she had to catch her breath. Hands reached for her, but she swatted them away. The Shadow Sickness burned behind her eyes, pounding against her skull. Her breaths came in short, quick pants that wracked her chest.

Finally, she looked up and found the prince watching her, hands still reaching for her. She gasped. "Alicsar!"

"I'm so sorry, Celia, I didn't see you." There was a slight hitch to his voice that drove away any anger she might have felt towards him in that moment.

She grimaced and waved a hand. "No, no, it's alright." Celia gathered herself and rose, allowing his hand to help her stand. He steadied her, worried eyes roaming her body. "Are you?" she asked.

He blinked down at her for a moment, almost a head taller than she. Sweat glistened across his high cheek bones and upper lip, redness rising up from the collar of his white tunic to his cheeks. "Hm? Oh yes, about as fine as one can be."

The prince took a step back, eyes flickering to the direction of the arena. Celia turned and noticed a larger road leading to the amphitheatres entrance; two mirrored statues of Azula guided the way, a set of tall pillars behind the goddess alight with flickering flames, something Amitel had done, she thought. The gates were open, but shadows darkened the entrance.

Celia frowned and turned back to the prince. "Alicsar..."

"Truly, I am fine," he replied, shaking his head. He took another step back, something within him shutting down.

The Shadow Sickness poked at her, a dark reminder of what he'd been capable of under the Dark Masters control. But the prince before her was someone else entirely.

She reached out and grasped his forearm, bringing him to a halt. "No, I don't believe that," she said, offering him a small smile. "Please, walk with me."

The prince released a shuddering breath and bowed his head. "Alright."

Celia grasped her hands in front of her as they strolled down a path in the opposite direction of the arena. The dirt wasn't packed as tightly in the less common streets, so as they walked, they revealed the old stone paths and cart grooves of the ancient people who once thrived in the city. Celia kept one eye on the prince as they followed the natural path, and one eye out for a garden to explore.

"There is something wrong. I can see it," she said after a moment of tense silence. "If you would like to say what it is, I will not repeat it to anyone."

Alicsar sighed and looked up to the ceiling, the darkness so thick above them it almost seemed like night, rather than a cavern. "I'm not worried about you repeating it, Celia. I just don't want to burden you with my worries."

A small smile crossed her lips as she shook her head. "I offered my ear, Alicsar. You can tell me."

They turned down another road, one lined by smaller homesteads, rather than the apartment buildings surrounding the temple and city square. Celia slowed to take in the houses; squat, made of stone, they were enclosed by fences half destroyed. She frowned as they continued down the street.

"You don't call me your highness."

Celia looked up. "Would you prefer it if I did?" she asked.

"No. I... I like it. My name being used, I mean. I hate the formality of the title. I... hate it all." He paused, and she waited for him to continue. "I've been struggling with my past, trying to reconnect with it. I know there is no way to bring back my memories, Blood Witch Lennox has already said as much, but I always wonder if there might be a chance someday."

They came to a stop outside a building; she spied a garden in the front, the soil long since dead, but a twinge of hope had her feeling for a seedling of life.

"Why is that?" Celia asked. He wasn't watching her; instead, he trailed his fingers over another fallen fence, a frown darkening his lips.

"Everyone assumes something different about who I was before Mesah. I did not think I could fight until Captain Jed told me I had extraordinary swordsmanship. And when I went to train with the Brotherhood, I..." He stopped and shook his head, hand falling away from the fence.

Celia dropped her magic and approached him, hesitant to reach out. "You what, Alicsar?"

Had he remembered something about his life before? About the Dark Master? She swallowed hard and tucked her hands into the pockets of her skirt to keep from fiddling. She couldn't ignore the dull ache at the base of her spine anymore, which flared the longer Alicsar hesitated.

"I lost control in the arena. I was so angry, and I'm not entirely sure why," he finished, pursing his lips. He looked as if he did know, but if he said it aloud, it might be true.

"What happened?" she asked.

"I–" He shook his head. "I feel as though I am missing something, like there is something everybody else knows that I am not privy to. Am I wrong?"

"Alicsar–"

"Celia!" They turned and found Amitel standing at the mouth of an alley, a hand curled in his hair. "I've been searching the city for you."

She lifted a brow, breathing a sigh. "What do you want, Amitel?"

Beside her, Alicsar cleared his throat. "Excuse me, I think I might go find Eliza."

Celia opened her mouth, but the prince stormed off, hands shoved into the pockets of his trousers. She watched him a moment, as he hunched his shoulders and bowed his head, disappearing beyond a bend. The shift had been immediate, the change in his mood startling.

And it had everything to do with the warlock behind her.

A quiet sigh left her lips. Celia turned to Amitel and crossed her arms. "What did you do to the prince, Amitel?"

The warlock pressed a hand to his heart as he approached. "Me? Nothing. I thought you knew me better than that, darling Celia."

She rolled her eyes. "What did you say to him?" Her magic flared once more and she allowed it to flow through her and into the dead soil, focusing it on what had once grew within the shallow beds of dirt.

Because if she focused on the warlock *strutting* towards her, she might've tried smacking him. Her pent up anger would do nothing to help, so expending it through her magic was her only choice.

Amitel strolled to a stop at the edge of the garden, three feet from her, and eyed the soil. "Nothing. He was in a sour mood when Eliza and I started our training. He follows her around like a lost puppy and mopes around when she won't give him the time of day."

Celia didn't look at him. "You think he's in love with her?"

The thought wasn't a new one, though she found it strange that the prince had chosen to latch onto Eliza in such a way. She wondered if his affection towards her had something to do with Dorin and the relationship they had shared during the journey. It was why Eliza refused to entertain anything with the prince; those memories and feelings were still fresh, Celia could see that, despite Eliza's attempt to bury them.

Amitel snorted. "Oh, I know it. I all but proved it today."

Celia shook her head, raising her hands as her magic brushed against something deep below the surface layer of soil. "I don't think I want to know how," she muttered, narrowing her eyes.

She could hear the smirk in his voice as he said, "No, you certainly don't."

Celia didn't respond; she closed her eyes and dove deeper into her magic. Hidden beneath layers of dead earth, she searched for that seedling of life, that one memory of the past that still remained despite centuries of darkness.

The dirt churned and shifted as a green sprout broke through layers of neglect. Celia hid a smile as she entered the small garden and crouched beside it. She released the magic, and summoned a small clay pot. With a wave of her hand, the sprout, as well as a clump of soil, lifted into the air before settling into the vessel.

All the while, she felt Amitel's stare on the back of her head. As she rose, she tucked her new plant under her arm. "What do you want, Amitel?" she asked, stepping away from the garden bed.

Amitel offered her a smile. "A couple of moments of your time. To... talk."

She started back on the path she and Alicsar had walked, recounting the route they'd taken in order to return to the house and city square. "Talk about what, exactly? Because I didn't think we had anything else to discuss."

"Celia." He took her forearm and pulled her to a stop. "You must understand. I did only what I thought necessary."

"What *you* thought necessary?" She turned sharply to face him. "Amitel, what you did almost cost us our lives. Could have killed Eliza." She shook her head. "You must understand, I find it hard to forgive you for what you did."

What she didn't say was that what he did could have killed her because of the Shadow Sickness.

Amitel didn't respond, and dropped his hand. They walked without speaking another word to one another, not as they climbed the stairs to Celia's rooms, and not as they entered the dimly lit office she'd carved out for herself.

She placed her new plant onto the table beside her overwhelming stacks. At a glance, she couldn't tell what it was precisely, but the process of discovery excited her more than scouring texts.

"I want you to know that I had no idea Dorin was Alicsar," Amitel said, pausing in the doorway. "Until I saw him at the palace, I had met him twice. I had assumed him a messenger of the Dark Master. I had no idea he was more than that."

Celia nodded, dropping into a chair. Her stomach churned. "Why are you telling me this?" she asked. Amitel ran a hand through his dishevelled hair, glancing between her and the door.

After a moment, he sighed. "Because I know you still don't believe me."

"It's not that I don't believe you, Amitel." She slumped back in her chair. "Brandon does, and although I question him, I trust *his* judgement. Obviously whatever you did meant something to him. It's why he left, after all."

Amitel nodded. "You don't forgive me, then."

"I don't trust you, Amitel."

The warlock flinched. "I understand."

"Do you?" she asked, cocking her head. Their eyes met, and for a moment, she didn't recognise the man standing in front of her. Though he looked and sounded like the Amitel she had come to know, his aura shifted, usually dim, hidden beneath layers of glamour and years of expert spell work. But a deep red flared around his being, giving shape to something else.

"That's why I'm here, Celia," he said, and the aura disappeared. "You don't have to forgive me. That'll take a long time to happen, and I understand that. Trust is something I intend on earning back. But I need *you* to understand that I did what I thought I had to in order to protect everyone."

Amitel paced the space, hands behind his back, and she waited for him to continue, watching each step. "I made a mistake in trusting the oracle. I fell into that age old trap of prophecy and destiny and I let it run my life for two centuries. I let it hurt the people closest to me, and for that, I will forever be sorry. I truly thought by doing what the creature prophesied, I could stay in control."

"It still almost killed Eliza, when she was just a child. Did you have any hand in that?" she softly asked, almost afraid of his answer.

Amitel stumbled to a stop and spun to face her, eyes wide. "No, I swear upon the Goddess, I had no idea the Dark Master was going to attack the mountains. During my time with him, I was merely eyes and ears. I knew he had taken the prince so I merely led the king's trackers astray. I kept Bastian's ear and reported back to the Dark Master's messengers."

Celia shifted; the ache in her spine crept upwards to her ribcage, sending tendrils of pain through her body. She eyed her bag, but she couldn't let Amitel know the truth of her condition—not yet. "So you never saw him, never spoke to him yourself?" she asked, swallowing down the pain.

"Only through letters and messengers, never him."

"The one Eliza found in the city? Did you know him?"

"No." Amitel shook his head. "He must have been new."

Eyes narrowed, Celia let her suspicions guide her questions. "How can I believe you?"

Amitel's gaze found hers. "When Eliza... saved me, under the mountain, I disappeared. It was to seek out those connections to the

Dark Master. I'd hoped to bring at least one back. The demon you encountered in Port Hein, it was one of the Dark Masters *generals*. I found it dead not three days after Eliza was pulled from the rubble of the mountain."

Celia tensed. "How did you know...?"

"I always had my eye on you," he replied, shrugging. "Dorin, he made his reports to me. He updated me—and likely the Dark Master—of your travels. I believe he was tasked to watch me. I believe the Dark Master suspected I might leave his side."

"Why?"

Amitel hesitated and looked away. "Eliza," he said, voice so soft she almost didn't catch it. "My intention was never to hurt her."

Celia pursed her lips and gave a slight shake of her head. "I know you've held a... *disdain* towards the Ecix, Amitel," she murmured. "Don't lie to me."

"I'm not, Celia." He strode to the desk and knelt beside it. "I have a history with the Ecix, yes, and that might have swayed my decision to join the Dark Master in the first place. But..." He scrubbed a hand through his hair.

"But what?" she asked.

"I'm not entirely sure. Magic is changing, and it has something to do with Eliza. I haven't seen this since the Great War."

Celia fell back in her chair. She'd felt the change the moment they travelled north all those months ago and into the desert. The stories she'd been hearing since only solidified what he told her, what she knew to be happening. "Then you sense it too? That something is coming."

Amitel pressed his lips together. "I watched an entire civilisation get wiped out. I will not let that happen again. If war is coming, then I intend on making sure the destruction I saw a thousand years ago never has to happen again."

"So that's it?" she asked, anger flaring in her chest. "You want to influence Eliza?"

"I had the Ecix's ear during the war and it did nothing." Amitel looked down at his hands before closing his eyes. "I have made many mistakes, Celia. I thought the Resurgence was the darkness, the change. So I stayed out of it. I remained hidden in my palace, and I did not step foot on the battlefield. I will next time, so long as the Ecix is fighting for what is right, and not what the Blood Witches want."

The anger dimmed, but it did not subside. "Those are dangerous words, Amitel," she said quietly.

He watched her from the corner of his eye as he stood and brushed the knees of his trousers. "And yet they are true. I'm here because *they* will try to influence her in ways that could destroy everything. That is Eliza's power, and I have no doubts the High Witch will work harder to be in Eliza's ear. The Great War cannot be repeated."

Celia chewed on those words, on the treasonous thoughts that plagued her mind. Isolde once had warned her of a darkness in the mountains. Isolde had warned her something was wrong with the council. It had been why she'd accepted King Oron's cry for help all those years ago, why she had fought during the Resurgence in the first place.

The High Witch opposed, and Isolde had left anyway.

Bile rose in her throat, but she swallowed it and sucked in a breath. "I think we have an understanding then, Amitel. You must speak to Eliza soon, about all of this. Tell her what you told me. She needs to understand." Celia met his stare, narrowing her eyes. "But know this: if I find you manipulating her in any way for your own gain, if I find you on the doorstep of the Dark Master again, I will kill you."

The warlock dipped his head. "I understand." his golden eyes flickered up and met hers. "I will let you get back to your reading then."

Celia watched him turn towards the door. Her heart crashed against her ribcage as his words settled around her, the implication a dagger in the gut. She pressed a hand to her eyes and shook her head.

And yet, she still had no clue as to how the Original and the dagger are connected, and still no path to take in finding the dagger.

"Amitel," she called, lowering her hand. He paused in the doorway. "What do you know of the Original Ecix?"

The warlock turned to face her with a frown. "Why do you ask?"

She hesitated, pursing her lips. "Something Eliza and I learnt put us on the track of the Original. And her connection to the dagger."

Amitel bit his bottom lip as he thought. "I don't know anything that'll be of help. Honestly, there's nothing I know about her other than possible rumours and stories." He took a step and lowered his head. "But I will tell you this: the Dark Master asked the same question of me some years ago, and I gave him the same answer."

Heart thundering, all Celia could do was nod as the warlock slipped from her room. *The Dark Master...* a pit of fear opened in her gut. The dull ache in her spine intensified, as if brought on by his name.

She knew for certain that they had no other choice than to dig deeper into the Original. If the Dark Master knew there was a connection, and Isolde was warning them...

Celia waited until she could no longer hear Amitel's footsteps before reaching into her bag. Nestled within a small leather pouch the length of her hand were three vials of swirling green elixir. She pulled one of the corked vials free of its binds and held it lightly in her hands.

She was meant to wait, give it a few more days. She had no idea how long they would be away from the palace and Lennox.

But the pain was growing too much for her.

Celia uncorked the elixir and tipped her head back. She couldn't taste the sour lemon or aged cheese. She waited for it to begin its healing of her body, placing the vial back into the pouch. The remaining two glared up at her.

I'll make them last, she promised herself, carefully packing them away.

But she knew—the longer she was away, the worse it would get.

She needed to understand what Isolde's riddle meant.

Celia needed the dagger.

25

A MARRIAGE OF DEATH
ELIZA

Eliza dropped a collection of books on a table across from her cot. The old wood creaked from the impact, but she whispered a reinforcement spell under her breath to give the old legs a fighting chance against the weight of all her reading material. The old tables had lasted centuries inside the ancient city, and there was no way she'd be responsible for their demise.

A heavy breath fell from her lips as she stumbled to the cot and dropped, resting her elbows on her knees. Her gaze landed on her satchel, which sat untouched, all her previous research into the dagger forgotten. The top of Alastor's book poked out of the bag, the blank pages a constant taunt at her inability to understand why he'd given it to her in the first place.

Footsteps approached, dragging Eliza's attention away from the book. Celia knocked on the door, poking her head through the crack. "I heard training went well," she said, entering slowly.

Eliza looked up and sighed, rubbing her eyes. "It was... something. I wouldn't say it went well, though." For the most part of the day, she'd been able to ignore the ache in her joints from her spar with Amitel. But since arriving back at her room, she'd begun to feel it again deep in her bones.

Celia offered her a half-smile, and approached the bed slowly, hands clasped in front of her. "I spoke to Amitel. And Alicsar."

"Please tell me it wasn't at the same time," Eliza muttered, shaking her head. "I don't know what it is with those two, but I don't think they should ever be left alone in a room together."

The sparring session between Alicsar and Darius played through her mind; Alicsar's anger, which certainly hadn't been pointed towards the knight, and the brutality to his swings.

Celia chuckled, and reached for a book from the stack. Eliza watched as Celia flipped through the pages with furrowed brows. "I spoke to Alicsar first. He seemed... odd. And yes, I noticed the tension." Celia looked up and met Eliza's stare. "We discussed his training, but nothing more. I do expect he knows something is wrong, that there's more that we aren't telling him."

"You feel sorry for him now?"

Celia lifted a brow. "Don't you?"

Eliza bit her lip, but didn't respond. She supposed she did, deep down, but with it came fear; fear that he might be lying, that he'll turn on them and report all their secrets to the Dark Master.

"So, what did you and Amitel talk about then?" Eliza asked, changing the subject.

Celia released a heavy breath, but she didn't say anything more about Alicsar. "We spoke about his time with the Dark Master."

Eliza's gaze snapped to Celia's. "What?"

Her sister refused to look at her, and instead she stared down at the book in her hands. "It was strange, and almost too hard to believe. But there is a part of me that wants to believe him. Maybe even forgive him."

"Have you?" Eliza asked quietly. "Forgiven him?"

"I don't think that is my place, not entirely. We have a complicated relationship, and I believe it will always be complicated. He betrayed everyone, especially you, with what he did." Celia shrugged and bit the inside of her cheek. "So no, I haven't quite forgiven him. I understand him better, though. And perhaps that is the first step."

Eliza pursed her lips. "I don't think I'll ever understand him."

Celia reached out and placed a hand over hers. "You don't have to, not yet. But don't do it for him. Do it for yourself."

Was she capable of doing that? Eliza wasn't entirely sure if that was something she could do. Not yet, not when the wounds were so fresh, and he was trying too hard to win her over.

"What else happened today?" Eliza asked, shifting from the topic of Amitel. "Did you get in contact with anyone who might be able to tell us about the Original?"

Celia dropped the book onto the pile. "Yes and no." She ran a hand over her face. "I wrote to another Blood Witch, who said they'd search the archives for me. But she said she could not access anything to do with the Original, and said those records would likely be kept in the Temple of the Ecix." Celia met Eliza's stare. "I'm sorry."

Sighing, Eliza shook her head. "It's alright. Suppose we should have expected that from the Blood Witches."

Celia nodded. "I suppose we should have..." Her voice trailed off. Eliza looked over and found her sister staring off, a sadness filling her cerulean eyes.

"Thank you for asking, though," Eliza offered, giving her a smile.

Celia blinked once and reciprocated the smile. "It was worth looking into. We may have more luck searching through the contents of the city." Rising, Celia reached out and tucked a strand of Eliza's hair behind her ear. "Get some rest. We have much more work to do."

Eliza said nothing as Celia slipped out of the room, closing the door behind her. The room fell silent, eerie, and she found herself looking towards Alastor's book once more. The blank pages had her almost giving up on the text, but a flicker of hope—brought on by the heavy weight of need—had her reaching for it.

The book slid free of her satchel, falling into her lap. Eliza cocked her head as she ran her fingers over the leather cover. Magic still pulsed from between the pages, dancing over her fingers as she flipped it open to the first chapter. The passage was exactly the same as when she'd first read it, but as she flipped through the pages, she hoped that maybe something new would appear, that maybe she would find something she had missed before.

But all was the same with the book.

She sighed and threw it down on the bed beside her. Burning frustration made her almost throw it out the window at the stupid clock Amitel had created, but instead she pushed off the cot and prepared for bed. Her limbs ached from training, and her mind was a frazzled mess from Amitel.

Stupid warlock. Stupid games. She wanted to believe what Celia had said about him, but she would rather cut out her own tongue than give Amitel the satisfaction of her *understanding*.

And then there was Alicsar. *Stupid prince.* She supposed she did feel sorry for him in some capacity; he, at least, did not remember tricking her into starlit kisses and trapping her beneath the mountain. She could muster some kind of understanding for him; she was, after all, lying to him, much like he had her.

At least I don't plan on stabbing him in the back.

She huffed and fell onto the bed, a chill working its way into her bones. The leggings she wore from home had paint stains on the knees, and her socks a hole in the toe from one of Odin's unprecedented attacks. She wiggled her feet and couldn't help but smile, heart aching for the family she had been forced to leave behind.

Once I have the dagger, she thought, *I'll be able to protect them. And myself.* She'd be able to stop the Dark Master if he attacked her again, and maybe she'd be able to return home once and for all.

Doubt, however, nagged at her, and she looked back over at the damned book.

Eliza slipped beneath her blanket and pulled Alastor's book to her chest. He had been determined to give it to her, but why? He surely would have known about the spell on the book. Had he been the one to put it there? Was he responsible for the blank pages?

A frown twisted her lips as she opened it up to the first blank page.

She ran her fingers lightly over the textured paper, wishing to understand why he had wanted her to have it so badly.

It has been him to send her on the path of the dagger, after all.

He had said it would help her defeat the Dark Master.

Eliza slid her index finger along the edge of the page and hissed, pulling back. "You have got to be kidding me," she muttered, staring down at the blood beading along the tip of her finger.

A paper cut. She almost laughed at how mundane the injury was. How many times, she wondered, over the years had she gotten paper cuts from her grandfather's old books?

She brought her finger to her lips but hesitated, gaze flickering from the blood to the blank page.

What's the worst that could happen?

Eliza squeezed several drops of blood from her finger and watched as it fell to the paper. Almost immediately, it disappeared, the page rippling like water as it swallowed her blood.

She sat up, cradling the book in her lap, and waited. *Son of a bitch.* The words appeared, new passages coming to light before her eyes. They shifted and moved, becoming clear and stark and *real*. The magic behind the book grew heavy in her hands, warming with each new word it revealed, each new passage it gave her.

Blood Magic. It should have been obvious. But he'd known she would figure it out... eventually.

Eliza grinned and almost screamed from joy. Instead, she brought the now healed finger to her lips and sucked away the rest of the blood. Her heart raced, slamming against her ribcage as she flipped to the new pages, chapters and paintings appearing as she skimmed the passages. She came to a new set of blank pages, disappointment wedging itself inside her mind, but perhaps she needed to give it more blood, or she would need Alastor to reveal the rest.

But for now, she decided, she would read on from where she left off.

THE GODS OF OLD
Thrinarv, King of the Gods, and father of the Brithien Elves, God of

War and Wisdom, considered the Old Gods his children, much like the Elves, who descended from the Isle of Evigheden.

Thrinarv, betrothed to the God of Wrath and Sin, Titan, descended into the Shadowland, alongside his children and the Gods of Old. Life had no place in the Shadowland, until the God of Light and Life, Amadeus, gave existence to the sun. Zoroya, Goddess of Dreams and Night, and her sister Kaia, Goddess of Nightmares and Darkness, gave the elves night and the stars.

A thousand years passed, and new creatures, some born of the darkness of the Shadowland, and others created by the new light and life of the land, populated the continents. Beasts took to the sky, while the Elves transcended into a new species: the Fae.

Gateways opened into the land of mortals. Magic bled from the Shadowland into the barren realm and created doorways between the two.

Eliza pursed her lips. Some of what she read, she could understand. The Shadowland referred to Cadira, while the realm of mortals was her home. It was a creation story, one that differed depending on who was asked.

She'd learnt, from her grandfather, that Cadira had already been alive with magic before Thrinarv and his gods walked the land, that Fae were the ruling deities long before.

But if she asked Kay, she would get an entirely different answer, a story designed by the Courts of Light.

The stories varied so much, she doubted it mattered if she skipped over another form of the tale. Eliza rubbed her eyes tiredly as she searched for any reference of Azula or the dagger. It seemed, however, that Azula wasn't prominent in the creation of Cadira—or at least, there was little said about her presence with the other gods.

Several pages in, she found a breakdown of the major and minor deities. The names blurred as she squinted, running her finger down the page in search of Azula. Eliza skimmed over the gods previously mentioned, but found no sign of her Goddess.

A breath escaped her lips. Rubbing her eyes tiredly, Eliza considered turning in for the night, to sleep off Amitel's cruel training and stupid games. But a pang of fear made her flip the page, like she might lose her only chance at answers if she closed the book now.

Two more pages of faceless gods, all of whom made no impression on her memory. Some had names she could understand, others were nothing more than smudges on a page that meant nothing to her.

Finally, she found Azula, her summary much like the one from the first passages she'd been able to read. Goddess of Magic and Spirits. Gifted the dagger in order to protect the secrets of Thrinarv and the elves.

But why? Eliza wondered, chewing her lip as she flipped to the next page.

A new image, one Eliza had never seen before appeared, a mixture of red and gold depicting a scene that made her pause.

Eliza recognised Azula, with spirits surrounding her like a veil, but there were other gods filling the page. Thrinarv, the King, and his betrothed, Titan, standing at an altar behind Azula. Beside her, a man wearing nothing more than a dazzling gold headdress.

A series of passages covered the page across from the image.

Eliza settled back into the bed and with a snap of her finger, the candle's light grew brighter, bathing the room in a warm glow.

A MARRIAGE OF LIFE AND DEATH

The Goddess Azula, before her marriage to the mortal King, was betrothed to another. Although she spent little time with the Gods, preferring to ferry souls from the land of the living and into the Aether, she was expected to give herself to the God of Light, Amadeus, Thrinarv's favourite son.

Eliza paused, a shiver running down her spine. The name was familiar, yet it brought on a spasm of fear in her heart. She'd read it earlier in the book, but there was something different about it there, alongside the image.

A chill made her fingers pause on the line, eyes flicker between the words and the depiction. *A marriage of life and death*, the heading read. *A marriage between Azula and Amadeus*, she realised.

The God of Light fought for the Goddess of Spirits attention, alongside other suitors who basked in her dark beauty. It is said she saw none as her Soul Bound, the missing half of her heart, and would not settle for any of the Gods or Elves who begged for her hand.

Amadeus, however, would not take her rejection, and instead begged the King of Gods for his help. Thrinarv, convinced the union would strengthen their rule over the Shadowland, forced the betrothal upon Azula.

Closing her eyes, Eliza sucked in a breath. She pushed down bubbling sadness, and instead turned the page, forcing the image of Azula, forced to marry one she didn't love, out of her mind.

Upon their wedding day, Azula vanished with her dagger, a gift from the Elves and Thrinarv for her betrothal. She hid from Amadeus by taking mortal form and marrying a king, and there she remained until his death, upon which she was forced to join the Gods once more.

Her heart, however, remained in the Shadowland, with a Fae.

That much Eliza knew, though she found little comfort with this variation of the story. Azula would return to her love, and would bear a half-Fae child, lose the dagger, and disappear. The story, which she had read earlier in the book, did not change as she skimmed through the rest.

Eliza was coming to the end of the new pages, and still she had found nothing new to answer her questions. Where had the dagger gone? Why was Alastor so certain the key to the dagger lived within the pages of the book?

Why give it to her at all, if it was going to give her nothing more than stories she already knew?

Eliza closed it, the clock in the courtyard chiming the late hour. Her eyes flickered shut, a wave of exhaustion turning her limbs to liquid. Finally–though with much frustration–she set the book down on the table beside her and drew her blankets closer to her body. For the first time in weeks, she didn't fight the darkness, and let it lull her to sleep.

~

The gauzy curtains leading to Eliza's balcony billowed in the chilling wind, sending shivers down her spine. Icy winter air blew off the lake, fog lining the streets of the city. Cadira's twin moons were full in the twinkling night sky, unburdened by clouds.

Sad, blood-chilling music drifted through the night air, catching on the breeze and slowly making its way to Eliza. It almost brought a tear to her eye. But the familiarity of the tune haunted her more than the song itself.

Eliza lifted a hand in front of her face and frowned. Her skin, iridescent in the moonlight, tingled as she moved, as if she were stepping through thick magic rather than cold, winter air. The strange feeling grew as voices joined the haunting music. The chanting started low, deep in her ears, muffled by the walls of her bedroom. Eliza searched for the sounds, but she was alone in the darkness.

A figure on her balcony caught her attention. Draped in shadows and armour, Eliza recognised the pointed ears and the dark, flowing hair of the faery Knight. Hands pressed against the railing, he looked different to how she usually saw him; lean, stoic, always wary, especially when in her presence.

But there was a calmness to him as he stood in the pools of moonlight. The tenseness of his shoulders was gone, though paper— the same paper she'd seen before—was clutched in his hand.

Eliza stepped towards the open glass door, hand raised. Her skin glowed white in the darkness, the ring on her left hand heavy. Even in dreams her impending marriage struck her silent.

At least this is a dream, she thought, thankful for the reprieve. She didn't think she could handle more bone-chilling memories that left her gasping for breath and wishing she were dead.

Eliza stepped onto the balcony and stopped. The knight had disappeared, leaving nothing but a lingering impression of where he'd been standing. She spun in a slow circle, taking in the view of the city, the same view she tried to memorise every night before settling into a bed that didn't feel like her own, in a room that was as foreign as always was when she was away from New Orleans and her family.

But he was gone.

She scrubbed at her eyes and blinked heavily, mind whirling.

Eliza dragged herself back into the bedroom and frowned at the neatly made bed. Her knitted quilts and crocheted pillows were gone, leaving only white sheets and white pillows, adorned only by a blood red rose in the centre of the bed.

Stepping up to it, she hesitated. She couldn't remember if she'd seen it before.

Eliza cocked her head, reaching a hand out hesitantly. Soft to touch, the petals of the rose shivered beneath her fingertips. As she snatched her hand back, her index finger caught on the edge of a silver thorn, pricked by the sharp point. Eliza drew her finger to her chest with a gasp and watched as the rose melted into the white covers, the stench of copper filled her nose.

Blood replaced the petals, bubbling and thick, the puddle growing in size as Eliza stepped away. She watched it with wide eyes, stumbling until she collided with the balcony doors.

Darkness washed over Eliza for a split moment before all she could feel was pain. It drilled into her bones. Her blood was like acid running through her veins, burning until it could escape the confines of her skin. Her throat, raw from screaming, gave her no voice to call out.

Now, she wasn't too sure if she was stuck in a dream or not. The *pain of the shackles binding her wrists and ankles felt too familiar to her, too real. In one of her past lives, she must have been tortured.*

"Please," a woman begged, voice hoarse, "let her go."

Eliza peeled her eyes open despite the wash of agony that swept through her.

Standing at her feet, a woman shrouded in black shadows stood with her arms pinned by shackles above her head. Blood dripped from open wounds around her body, staining a dark, billowing dress and skin marred by darkness. Veins of gold wound over the woman's arms and legs.

Anguish flared in the woman's bright eyes as they found Eliza.

A chuckle sounded somewhere in the shadows. Eliza flinched away from the dark sound, pulling uselessly at her chains.

"You know what I want," the harsh voice said. It came from all around Eliza. She recognised it; the voice of her nightmares.

The woman made a sound in the back of her throat. "Please."

"The girl will die if you do not do as I ask."

Eliza recoiled from the voice again. Fear made her tremble, made the chains that held her down rattle, a wail that stung her ears.

"This has gone on long enough," the woman whispered. "You have gone too far."

The voice sounded behind Eliza's head. "I will stop once all you love is dead."

"No." The woman's voice cracked, and a scream tore through her. A light around her flared blindingly, searing into Eliza's eyes. She squeezed her eyes shut against the sudden brightness, until a raven's caw made her eyes snap open.

Standing where the woman had been hanging, the faery knight—young, sharp featured and tense with anger—stood poised to attack, the raven swooping over his head.

Darkness brushed Eliza's vision, and a sword made of bone lifted over her head.

She didn't have time to scream as the blade came down, killing her before the knight could free her from her bonds.

26

AMITEL'S TRUTH
ELIZA

Eliza awoke with a start and leaned over the side of her cot to empty her stomach. The feeling of cuffs around her wrists didn't disappear, and neither did the cries of the woman, the dark laugh of the monster that hunted her, the scream burning her throat as the knife came down. Eliza shuddered.

The puddle of vomit disappeared before she could blink.

"Are you okay?"

Embarrassment coloured Eliza's cheeks as she slowly turned in the cot to face the now open door to her room. Standing in the frame, Amitel wore no shirt, his golden skin exposed in the artificial light of the underground city.

Groaning, Eliza fell back and covered her eyes with her arm. "I'm fine."

"The vomit says otherwise," he replied.

She couldn't hear any amusement in his voice, but she had no doubt he was internally making fun of her. Why wouldn't he? It wasn't the first time a nightmare had made her throw everything but her intestines up.

Closing her eyes, she released a heavy breath. "What are you doing here?"

"I heard you scream."

The way he said it... Eliza peeled her eyes open and met his stare. Worry flickered within the gold irises. It looked like he'd been asleep himself, which meant she'd woken him, and probably everyone else, too.

Her cheeks heated again. "Sorry."

Amitel frowned and entered the room hesitantly, before stopping. "Why are you sorry?"

She shrugged. "For waking you. For screaming..." she trailed off and released a heavy breath.

"Don't ever be sorry for that." He ran a hand through his dishevelled hair, giving her a good look at the planes of his stomach. He was more chiselled than she'd imagined; his broad chest was golden like the rest of him, accented by abs that would have otherwise made her drool—if it weren't for the man they were attached to—and from his belly-button down, a sculpted v dipped beneath the hem of his pants...

Eliza dragged her eyes away from his bare chest and sucked in even breaths. She rose, knees trembling. The room around her spun, blurring at the edges of her vision, and she stumbled.

In the blink of an eye, Amitel was no longer in the doorway. One arm went around her waist, secure and warm, while the other gripped her elbow. Slowly, he lowered her back onto the bed, sitting beside her as he did. It took him a moment to remove his arm, but the one behind her he planted on the bed, forearm brushing her spine—and the scar left from Dorin's throwing knives.

A shiver raced through her.

"Are you okay? Really?" Amitel asked.

She shook her head, afraid to close her eyes. Because if she did, she would see the knife, over and over again, feel the sharp pain of it piercing her skin, stabbing her through the heart.

Eliza wrapped her arms around herself. "Yes. I'm fine."

But he didn't leave. Eliza watched him from the corner of her eye as he stared at her; the concern wasn't masked like she'd expected, but instead danced across his eyes, turning the burning gold a shade of red that made shivers course down her spine. Seeing the colours war for dominance was both terrifying and beautiful, something she wasn't sure Amitel wanted her to see. It felt almost intimate, seeing the colours swirl together until the gold won out.

"Maybe we can talk," he replied finally, looking away. "If you're feeling up to it."

She shrugged. "Are you finally going to tell me why you were working with the Dark Master and lying to me?"

"And then some, if you let me." He gave her a half smile before a mask of seriousness slipped over his face. "I'm not sure if Brandon ever told you about our time in Laziroth."

Eliza stiffened at the mention of Thorne's name. She shook her head and waited for Amitel to continue.

"He and I... it was the first time we'd ever met, and it had been after the Resurgence, after he lost..."

"Isolde." Eliza no longer felt the same kind of bitterness when she thought of the past life that existed only in her mind and blood.

Amitel ran a hand down the length of his pants. "We were sent to Laziroth to find a... *unique* item. It turned out to be an Oracle. And it warned us of the future."

"About what, exactly?" she asked, biting back fear.

"About *your* future. About Alicsar. And it told me, that in order to protect you, I would first have to betray you." His eyes sought hers. "I didn't do it because I didn't want to. I fought to protect you; did what was within my power to make sure you remained *safe*."

Something burned inside of her at his words. Nothing about her world was simple, nor were her circumstances. Everything was complicated and convoluted, hidden in shadows or shining in the light of day. She couldn't expect him to be perfect or good straight away— that wasn't right of her. Some people had to grow.

"What did you do for the Dark Master, Amitel? Were you close with him? Did you kill for him? Worse?"

The warlock shook his head. "No, nothing like that."

"Then what *did* you do, Amitel?" she asked, crossing her arms.

Amitel stared out into the distance, looking over the city. He masked his expressions and emotions as he spoke. "I was never part of the Dark Masters plot. Not until *after* the Resurgence. He never sought me out, and I never looked for him." He closed his eyes and inhaled sharply. Eliza remined silent and still as he spoke. "But I knew about what he'd been doing to the line of Ecix's. I knew he was forcing the cycle to happen quicker, killing them sooner and sooner, hoping that the younger they—*you*—were, it might stop the rebirth entirely. I knew he was experimenting with different magic in hopes you wouldn't be brought back."

A small gasp escaped her lips, eyes wide. Beside her, Amitel nodded. "That's why he attacked when you were five."

"How do you know all this?" she whispered, stilling as his golden eyes, ringed with crimson, found hers.

"I knew because of my connections to the Blood Witches. The High Council and the High Witch believed as much, and I agreed with them. It was only confirmed after the Resurgence, when I sought the Dark Master out—after what I'd learnt in Laziroth with Brandon."

"Did Thorne know?" she asked brows furrowed. "That you were... were *working* with—"

"No." He shook his head, golden hair tumbling over his forehead. He combed his fingers through it, pushing it out of his face. The muscles in his arm coiled as he did. "I should have told him, but I knew how he'd react. That he'd call me an idiot for doing something so risky. But..."

"But what?"

His eyes found hers again, and he hesitated. She watched the words form on his lips, but what he said next wasn't what he'd been thinking about, that she was certain of. "But I know the Ecix and the power is all part of Cadira's natural balance. Despite what you might think, this power isn't any less natural than being able to summon flame from nothing."

"Doesn't seem very natural," she muttered, ignoring the obvious half-truth.

Amitel smirked. "There always has to be balance, love. Otherwise our world could crumble." His stare intensified. "That's why the power can't be destroyed."

The words made her stomach tighten. She didn't respond.

"I don't know why I decided to help *you*, specifically. Maybe it was out of fear thanks to that Oracle. It could have been because Isolde was the youngest Ecix to die yet, and it meant time was running out." He looked at her earnestly, features softening. "I never wanted to know who you were. I never expected to meet you in this lifetime. I'd hoped to remain in the shadows.

"But then you made Brandon call on me, and I had no excuses to hide. So I tried to scare you away, hoping maybe you'd realise I was a dead-end with information. But I didn't know what to expect; you were so different to the other Ecixes I'd known, which should have been obvious since you were raised by Kay." He shook his head and chuckled, but Eliza frowned.

"You know Kay?" Her heart fluttered with sadness. She missed her guardian, missed their trips to the gardens where they'd people watch and drink coffee.

Amitel nodded. "How do you think she wound up with Davis?"

"I... I don't know. She never talks about it."

"Then I won't say anything."

She huffed and crossed her arms. "So, *you* got her to New Orleans?" she guessed.

Amitel's eyes twinkled as he winked. "Yes. One of my more reckless moves, since I'm now banned from the Courts of Light."

Eliza choked on her breath, half caught between a laugh and a cough as she stare at him. "Seriously?"

He shrugged. "That's what happens when you help a fugitive like Kay."

"I'm surprised you weren't exiled."

His half-smile returned. "So am I. But I'm much older than all of them, and I happen to be pretty powerful." He winked again, but she rolled her eyes, unable to stop the flutter of her heart. "I made a deal with them. I'll never enter the Courts, if they spare Kay. She was exiled—so I introduced her to your grandfather—and I'm magically banned until they get sick of not having me around."

Eliza shook her head. "How am I not surprised?"

"I'm a man of many mysteries, Elizabeth Kindall," he murmured. Suddenly, he was closer than before, his burning eyes flashing to her lips. Eliza sucked in a breath as he inched closer. She couldn't move; wasn't sure if she wanted to, not when her heart betrayed her head.

Amitel blinked and pulled away. Clearing his throat, he continued, "After our first meeting, I'd hoped I wouldn't have to see you again. But I felt guilty."

"Why?" Eliza ignored the disappointment that sparked in her check when he'd pulled away.

He said nothing as he reached over and touched her temple. A spark of light flashed from his skin to hers, racing through her, magic she vaguely remembered. It left a bitter taste in her mouth.

Something *snapped* inside her mind; as the fog cleared, memories came rushing back—Russia, her sixteenth birthday, an attack in the temple that had resulted Keeper Inessa's death. There had been two men there to help... *no.* It had been Thorne and Amitel, and they had told her grandfather to wipe her memories of them.

Eliza pulled away sharply and locked eyes with Amitel. "You knew me—*me*, Eliza—and you and Thorne never said anything?"

"I'm sorry."

She looked away, unsure of what to say. Blood boiled in her veins, but she wasn't sure if she was angry at him for never saying anything, or if she was angry because something else had been taken from her without her knowledge, because it was something else she'd never had control over in her life.

Closing her eyes, Eliza dredged up the memory; the Russian temple and the wards, the man—*Shadow Soldier*, she knew now—and Kay telling her to let Thorne and Amitel in. They couldn't get the sword out of the soldier's hands, so Eliza did it for them. And then they had told her grandfather to take away her memories of them.

There was something else about the memory, but it was fleeting and she couldn't catch hold of it quick enough.

A breath shuddered from her lips. "Why?"

"We wanted to spare you of this fate just a little longer."

She squeezed her eyes shut against the burning tears that threatened to slip down her cheeks. "Were you with the Dark Master back then?"

"Yes." It was barely a whisper, but she felt it slide over her skin. "After the Resurgence, I started getting close to him. I want to say I was doing it to be noble—to protect you from dying, to help save more from a useless war. But it was selfish, because I was protecting myself."

Eliza opened her eyes and stared down at her hands. "It's all about self-preservation."

She felt him flinch beside her. Guilt clawed at her, but it was too late for her to take back her words.

"It wasn't just that," he replied. After a moment, he sighed, almost like he wasn't sure what to say.

From the corner of her eye, she watched him. The darkness of her room cast shadows over his angular face, but whatever light still flickered outside from the lanterns they'd lit around the city square, almost chased away the shadows, casting a halo of dim light around him. But the shadows of his face weren't caused by any light; guilt and shame contorted his features and made the gold of his irises dim.

Before she could stop herself, Eliza reached out and took his hand. Surprise crossed his face as he met her stare.

"Fate is tricky, especially when you hear about your own from an Oracle. I don't mean that as an excuse, but even those of us old enough to remember the Great War fall subject to these... habits." He ran a hand through his hair, balling his fist into the strands brushing the nape of his neck. "I don't fully understand why I let the oracle's prophecy control me, Eliza. The war had just ended, and maybe it was because I sat back and let it happen, I thought maybe if I could get close enough, maybe I could stop it from happening again."

His gaze found hers before dropping to their joined hands. "I hated the Ecix for many years, and that fuelled my decision. I let my emotions guide me."

Eliza swallowed the lump forming in her throat. "Why did you hate the Ecix?"

He looked away from their hands and stared down at the floor. "A long time ago, I went to war with the Ecix and I watched her destroy an entire civilisation." He paused and looked up, eyes shining. "I vowed I would never let that happen again, Eliza."

"I get it. I don't agree with it, but I get it," she murmured. "You did what you thought would save you, and maybe even help me. You put aside a thousand years of hatred for me, and tried to keep me alive."

"I never hated you."

She shrugged, pulling her hand away from his and ignored the sudden chill of being away. "I hope you know I can't just... *trust* you again, Amitel. Not straight away."

He released a breath. "I know." He looked down at the hand she'd been holding and clenched his fist. "And I understand that. I have a lot of work to do in order to gain your trust again, don't I?" he said, cracking a smile.

Eliza didn't stop the little smile that formed on her lips. "That you do." She let a moment of silence pass between them, before asking, "You're totally out from the Dark Master?"

Amitel nodded. "I let the prince stab me in the gut with a knife imbued with magic so powerful it would have killed me, because I needed to protect you." She swallowed hard, heart hammering in her chest. "Even if I wanted to, the Dark Master won't take me back. I've protected you in front of his soldiers one too many times."

"Thank you for that," she said, and she meant it. If it wasn't for him, she probably never would have survived being taken by the Dark Master or Dorin. It all would have ended before she could even begin to understand what was at stake.

Amitel stood, a strange look passing over his face. "Goodnight, Elizabeth Kindall."

27

FOLLOWING THE GODS
CELIA

"How does a city that hasn't been touched in probably a thousand years *not* have any books on Azula herself?" Eliza muttered, more to herself than to Celia or Alicsar, though Celia couldn't help but look up at her sister and smile at the frustrated frown pulling at her lips. "Seriously. How can we not find *anything* useful?"

From the other side of the piles, Celia huffed as dust rose into the air. "I really have no idea." The smile slipped from her face as she took in the aftermath of their pillaging.

After hours spent pouring over books, they'd come to a simple conclusion: either the people of the underground city never *wrote* about Azula, or any texts dedicated to her had been destroyed or lost. But whichever it was, meant they weren't finding anything practical.

There were some religious texts, but they'd concluded that they sounded more like hear-say, like whoever wrote them was only writing down what they'd heard from someone else.

But there was nothing about the dagger.

"Maybe we should move on," Eliza said, slamming her book closed. "Maybe one of the other cities has something."

"There are others?" Alicsar asked, looking up from his texts for the first time since they'd sat down.

Celia nodded, rising from her desk. Every bone in her body ached from sitting for so long, a dull throb behind her eyes the only reminder she needed for fresh air, water, and to stretch. "There are. When Eliza... *retrieved* you from Mesah, you travelled through one of these cities. That one had been destroyed, though. But there are others."

Eliza cleared her throat and stood, wincing. "We have a map," she said. "Of other potential cities. But we don't even know if they still exist or not." Reaching for her bag, Eliza pulled the folded map from one of the pockets. They'd requested it from the Elders, a community of retired Keepers who held much of Cadira's history and keep many of its secrets, for the map. It had led them to Mesah and the fountain that acted as the portal into the underground city.

Celia watched as Eliza spread the map over the table, and leaned over to take it in. Marked were portals, though whether cities lay beneath them was something they were unsure of. Port Hein, the largest port of Cadira that has roads leading directly to the capital, had a portal that connected to a tunnel, but at the end was nothing but a wall.

Two were in the desert, which Celia was sure connected to the city beneath Mesah that had been destroyed. Aside from the three Mesah ones; there was the one in Port Hein; the Spring Manor; one wedged between the Labyrinth Mountains and the ocean; another just north of the mountains, but in the east along the coast; there was one just east of the capital, along the river; and one west of the capital, on the coast. Nine portals marked, but she knew for sure they didn't all have cities beneath them. Tunnels, perhaps, that wove beneath Cadira, but what other secrets were they hiding?

Alicsar pointed to a smudge north of the troll bridge, nestled in the trees marked as the Willican Forest, which bordered Cadira and the Fae Territories. "What's that?"

Frowning, Eliza squinted to look at it better. "A... *smudge*."

Alicsar rolled his eyes. "But is something supposed to *be there*?"

Celia, head cocked, ran her fingers over it. "Potentially. But..." She bit her lip. Something in her gut told her to question it, but there was too great a chance if they pursued it, there would be nothing there. A smudge could be just that. And yet...

"It's not too far from one of the portals. If there is anything there..." Eliza trailed off, pursing her lips, and Celia looked up with a frown.

"A smudge could be a smudge," Celia muttered, sitting once more, though her heart sped up at the possibility.

The prince looked over, hope glinting in his eyes. "Or it could be an answer to all our questions."

~

Celia paced the length of her make-shift office, thoughts overrun by the smudge. *What could it be?* She wondered, hopelessly glancing at a map of Cadira, one unmarked by portals and lost cities. A coin sat over where she believed the smudge was.

"Tell me, Goddess," she whispered, looking up to the ceiling, "tell me if this is worth looking into. Tell me if this is a sign." Closing her eyes, she came to a stop in front of the map and rested her hands against the frayed corners. Head bowed, she breathed evenly, shoulders relaxing.

Magic pulsed through her veins as she focused on the coin. Her words to the Goddess echoed in her ears as the pounding of her blood became a steady melody, the song of Blood Magic weaving through each beat.

Is this what I am meant to do?

A pulse of warmth spread from her heart through the rest of her body. The tips of her fingers grew hot. Celia opened her eyes, and reached for the coin, the metal cool beneath her touch. But the paper beneath burned, a blackened hole from the coin signifying the smudge.

Thank you. The warmth disappeared, leaving her body buzzing.

She reached for her pack and checked the contents, eyes falling onto the original map of the cities.

A knock sounded at the door, and she looked up as Caden slipped through, his head lowered.

"Is something the matter?" she asked, frowning. She discarded her bag and stepped around the table.

Caden shook his head, copper curls bouncing against his forehead. "No, not really." He looked up, uncertainty playing in his dark eyes. "But do you have a moment to talk?"

Celia pursed her lips, but nodded. "Of course, please." She motioned to a chair and lowered herself slowly into her own. Heart thumping against her ribs, Celia cleared her throat. "What did you want to talk about?"

"It's about Eliza." He shifted in his seat, and released a sigh. "And the Blood Witches."

"What about them?" Celia asked, frowning. In the back of her head, she heard Isolde's warning about the Original and the Blood Witches, dark and foreboding. Something in her stomach twisted with the thought.

Caden hesitated a moment, a battle in his eyes Celia knew all too well. He was loyal to the Brotherhood—the Blood Witches. What he was going to reveal went against his oath. For as long as she'd known him, he'd been steadfast in his loyalty.

So what made him change his mind?

"There's talk amongst the witches and knights about what is happening with Eliza in the capital. About her marriage to the prince and what that could mean for the tribes." Caden leaned back in his chair, placing a hand on the table. "The council could have known about Eliza's attempt at escape a lot sooner than she did."

Celia curled her hands into fists, nails biting into the beds of her palms. "What do you mean?"

"They knew she might try and run. It's why the council sent Darius and I out when they did. It was under the guise of wanting Knights present at the palace before the wedding in order to protect the Ecix, but I was warned to prepare for her escape."

"By who?" Celia asked. "Who warned you?"

He shook his head. "In order to protect them, I cannot say." Caden scrubbed a hand over his face. "There's... more."

Celia waited, each beat of her heart a loud thud in her ears. It would mean Lennox knew Eliza was going to leave, that Celia would follow. *But why?* The Blood Witches had no reason to let Eliza go.

Unless...

"They want the marriage arrangement to end," he said finally, releasing a breath. "Of course they do. They want it to fail. Letting Eliza go, keeping her magic weak; it was meant to make King Bastian look incompetent. They had hoped because she was performing poorly with her magic training at the palace, he would release her from the contract."

"The Blood Witches want her to fail?" Celia asked, frowning. "Why? How do you know this?"

Caden closed his hand into a fist, staring down at the soft orange freckles that lined the skin of his knuckles. "I overheard Murtagh and Rosaline talking about it. Have you heard of the attacks? In the Labyrinth forests?"

Hesitantly, she nodded. "Lennox said they've killed at least three so far."

"Apparently the council has been... *advocating* to bring the Ecix back for the *Idrindis*. The witches need more girls, and the knights need soldiers."

Celia sat back, bile rising in her throat. Her gaze wandered to Eliza, whose chin was perched in her palm, books scattered around her, brows furrowed in concentration. "She has to succeed, then," Celia murmured.

"The witches know she won't." Celia's eyes snapped back to his. "They know this is a fool's errand and they know something is going to take *her* back to the mountains," Caden finished with a shake of his head.

Celia fell back into her chair as Caden rose. "I thought you needed to know. For whatever reason, they don't want Eliza finding this weapon. And they'll make sure she returns to the mountains, where she belongs."

Then I must leave, Celia thought, as Caden moved to the door. Her eyes fell to her bag, then to the burnt map. The Goddess had given her a sign, and perhaps a warning. There was something at the smudge they would need—and if what Caden said was true, she would need to leave sooner to protect Eliza.

Caden paused in the doorway, his back to her. "The witches are looking for any excuse to take Eliza back to the mountains," Caden warned. "You are running out of time you never had."

~

The eerie silence of the city was almost thick enough to muffle the crackling fire, but as soon as the meat Darius and Caden had been set atop the flames to cook, the dusty smell had vanished, and the sizzling flesh echoed through the town square.

Sitting across the fire, Eliza watched the flames, elbows resting atop her knees. Celia paused outside the ring and watched her for a moment, Isolde and Caden's warnings replaying in her head. A war raged in her heart; leave Eliza alone with the prince who almost killed her, the warlock who betrayed them all, the knights sent to retrieve her, or stay and hope they all can make it to the smudge together.

Celia steeled herself and rolled her shoulders. Heat from the fire warmed her body as she approached her sister. Eliza still hadn't looked up, but her eyes, bright under the flickering fire, shot between the suckling pig and the knights.

Celia dropped onto the bench beside Eliza, heart racing. "I would like to talk to you about something," she said, staring into the fire.

"Me?" Eliza asked, frowning. "Or the dinner?"

Celia laughed softly. "You." When Eliza didn't respond, Celia continued, "I've been thinking. About that *smudge*, and I'm... curious."

Eliza turned from the fire, brows pursed. "It could just be nothing."

Celia stared down at her hands. "Do you really want to take that risk?"

Silently, Eliza shook her head. "When would you leave?"

"Soon. I want to be useful, and I know if I leave for it now, I will find something," Celia finally said. "We are going around in circles, and we haven't much time. I fear what Isolde has told us."

Eliza's throat bobbed as she swallowed, and she nodded. "Yeah, I understand."

Celia's sharp blue eyes met hers. "You do?"

"Thorne couldn't stick around because he felt like he wasn't doing anything." Eliza shrugged, her gaze drifting back to the fire as Alicsar and Amitel took the benches across from one another, neither looking at the other, silence falling over their little camp. "I don't blame you, and I agree. Seems like there's a time limit, a deadline we don't know about."

Celia reached for Eliza's hand, and gave it a squeeze. "I'm sorry."

"Don't be." Eliza forced a smile, but hidden behind her green eyes, sadness swirled, and the guilt already rising within Celia grew stronger. "We need answers."

Celia hesitated before turning to Amitel, who sat to Eliza's right on the next bench. "I have decided to leave and travel to a location, one we found on the map of portals."

Amitel frowned. "Alone?"

Celia nodded as everyone turned to her. "Eliza, Alicsar and I were looking at it earlier. It looks like it could be the location of something, but the symbol had been erased. There is a portal nearby, too. It could just be a mistake, but I can go ahead discretely and find out if there is something there."

The warlocks golden eyes went to Eliza, and he watched her as he spoke. "It would be better if I went, or someone else. You should stay here."

"No." Celia squeezed Eliza's hand again. "I will go, and in one week, if you find nothing more here, meet me at the nearest portal. If I find something, I will send word to you all."

"Then that's what we'll do," Amitel replied, eyes still on Eliza. "If that's what *you* want?"

The way Amitel watched her sister made her stomach clench.

Eliza pulled her hand from Celia's and nodded. "Yeah, of course. One week. We'll keep looking here, and you get a head start up there. If we find nothing, we keep moving."

Celia tried not to feel the absence of Eliza's hand, but she knew her sister was lost to her own thoughts concerning the smudge—and Celia's decision to leave.

They spent the rest of the night eating and discussing Celia's travel to the *smudge*. It was risky to use the roads, but Celia couldn't portal, not without alerting the Blood Witches of her whereabouts, and if what Caden had warned her about was true, then Celia knew she needed to remain hidden from her coven for as long as possible.

The two knights had horses, ones hidden in the stables above, cloaked in magic to protect them from thieves. They'd been riding the horses to get supplies, but Caden happily gave his mare to her to ride up to the *smudge*.

When the clock finally chimed *five*, everyone rose. They hadn't planned on spending the entire night talking, but there had been too much to discuss, too many possibilities consider. What happened if Celia was caught by King Bastian's soldiers? What if the Dark Master attacked again?

Celia reached for Eliza's hand before they could reach the portal and tugged her aside, falling behind the group of men. "While I'm gone, try and break whatever spell Alastor put on that book. He gave it to you for a reason. It's time to find out why."

Eliza swallowed thickly. "I'm a little afraid."

"Don't be." Celia stopped and cupped Eliza's cheek. "He gave us this much. Perhaps there's more, and if I don't find anything at the smudge, then this rests on you."

Slowly, Eliza nodded. "Alright." She released a heavy breath. "I'll start reading it."

Celia dropped her hand. "Good. And when we meet next, you will tell me what you find."

Eliza hesitated before releasing a breath. "Alright."

Celia pressed her lips into a thin line. From the portal, Amitel called for her, and when she looked back, she found the four men watching her and Eliza.

"I won't say goodbye," Celia whispered, pulling Eliza in for a tight hug, "but I will see you again soon, little sister."

Eliza made a sound in the back of her throat.

Before she could change her mind, Celia released Eliza and rushed to the portal. Her sister remained behind, head lowered; something in Celia's heart cracked as she stepped beneath the fountain.

"Are you sure about this?" Amitel asked again, handing her a bag.

"Of course," she replied, nodding. "Look after her."

The warlock bowed his head. "Of course, darling Celia."

She shook her head. *Take me up.* She sent a wave of magic towards the ancient maze, which awoke with her call. The power danced over her skin, and the feeling of water coursed over her, like being submerged in a pool with no way of knowing which way was up.

Celia entered the clear, crisp winter air of Cadira with a heavy sigh. Days spent below ground left her feeling nauseous and unsteady, claustrophobic despite the expanse of the city beneath her feet. She welcomed the quiet cold of the morning though, and sucked in cooling breaths to calm her racing heart.

The pressure to find the dagger weighed heavily on her shoulders as she trekked to the crumbling stables behind the manor, where Caden and Darius had left their steeds. They were large, beautiful creatures born and bred in the Labyrinth Mountains, both a sleek black that blended well into the night. The same ones grazed the pasture by her cottage, though the ones she cared for were older, slower.

Celia untied one and guided it from the stables before placing a protective barrier around the old structure. She only had a vague idea of where to look, but it was enough to get her moving and out of the tunnels. There was only so much she could do there; sitting around was doing them no good.

Running a hand down the steed's neck, Celia bit her lip.

Eliza will be fine. She has Amitel and Alicsar. Darius and Caden will protect her.

Celia couldn't help but question that. Two of the men down there had been working with the Dark Master, and the other two had been sent to drag her back to the High Council of the Blood Witches.

She would go, she reasoned, and she would find something, some way to help Eliza and defeat the Dark Master, and she would trust that her sister was safe, and could take care of herself.

28

THE WYLD HUNT
CELIA

The horn of the Fae Hunt echoed through the air, bringing Celia to a stop on the road outside of the Willican Forest. Her heart thundered in her chest as she eyed the forest beyond the ravine, taking in the wild foliage and the dense forestry that belonged to the Fae.

Every colour within looked heightened by the strong, powerful magic that stemmed from the land. Standing beside it, Celia's skin prickled with the waves of raw energy that radiated from the forest. Everything within the Fae Territory was alive and imbued with magic. Sometimes that flowed into Cadira, but not with the same force as it did throughout the Fae Territory.

As a girl, Celia had wanted to enter the eerie world of the Fae. So much of her heritage, the history of the Blood Witches, came from the ancient creatures. It fascinated her, but the Witches forbade interacting with the Fae.

Blood Witches were the cousins of Fae, though barely. In truth, the Witches were born from the blood of Elves, creatures that no longer roamed the earth. Enemies of the Fae, or so she had been told.

Trees rustled and groaned with the force of the Hunt. Their magic steeds could clear the trees with wings made of air, but on the ground, the trees moved for them.

The Hunt is far away, Celia thought with a frown. *I will not see them.*

A spark of anticipation flared in her chest. How many other Blood Witches—even mortals—could say they'd spotted the Wyld Hunt? Isolde had wanted the Wyld Hunt to join the fight against the Resurgence, had even petitioned their aid.

The thought of her sister brought on a sobering effect.

Move on, Celia thought, tugging the reigns of her horse. *Clear the bridge and make for the forests.*

But she was glued to the road, unable to move.

The sound of the horn grew louder and pierced through her.

She sucked in a breath as she caught sight of the Hunt through the trees. She could see horses of the inkiest black adorned with silver like they'd been drawn from the night sky with riders made from forest and bathed in the light of dawn.

They were an eclectic group, ranging from the regular looking Fae, who had almost human features save for their ethereal beauty and infinite power, to creatures shaped by vines and wreathed in flowers, with wings of gossamer and powerful antlers shaped like crowns.

What they were chasing, Celia couldn't be sure. There was a flash of white between the trees, dark skin, but nothing more.

Whoever it was, they cleared the thick of the trees as the horn of the Hunt sounded again. Celia's horse startled, rising on its hind legs as the full force of the Hunt came into view.

There were perhaps twenty riders towering over a woman in white. She looked Seelie, doused in the colours of Summer, the court of gold and ocean breezes.

The young woman paused at the edge of the forest, her eyes finding Celia. Fear marked her movements as hurried, sloppy. It looked strange on a being as perfectly sculpted as a Faery.

What is she going to do? The Hunt had her surrounded.

Celia's eyes widened as the girl backed up and cleared the ravine, stumbling onto the road. Thin pointed ears poked through the mass of dark hair atop her head, gold bands covering her upper arms and wrists. Rings of the same shining gold glimmered on her ears and fingers, catching the light as she straightened in the middle of the road.

The Fae girl was gorgeous, with dark brown skin that shined with gold powder, and a white dress that hugged her figure. Small daggers, ceremonial in style, hung from her waist, and as she took Celia in, her hands reached for those same small weapons like they would protect her from a witch.

"I will not hurt you," Celia said, holding a hand up in defence. Something about her made Celia's heart race with anticipation and longing.

From the other side of the ravine, at the forests edge, the Wyld Hunt blew their horn.

From Celia's knowledge of the truce between the monarchs of Cadira and the Fae courts, the Wyld Hunt was not permitted to enter Cadira without permission from the ruling monarch. Celia doubted King Bastian would permit their entry, but with the bloodthirsty way the sharp toothed men and women of the Hunt watched their prey, Celia wondered if they'd break the truce to capture her.

The woman lowered her hands from her weapons, though her defensive stance did not falter.

Turning back to the Hunt, Celia almost flinched from their ferocious stares. "You cannot cross into these lands. For as long as she is here, she is free from your wrath," Celia said, loud enough for their Fae hearing. She did not have to yell over the crashing water of the ravine, for even it quietened under the pressure of the Hunt

The leader of the Hunt stepped forward. Great antlers protruded from his head, decorated with small skulls dangling from vines and thorns leaking a silver substance from their points.

"And who are you to speak on behalf of the mortal king?" His voice reminded Celia of trees crashing in a forest after a lightning strike.

"I am the Blood Witch Celia of the High Council, Coven of Mab,

Sister of the Ecix."

Their laugher rattled like crashing waves and the buzz of insects. Celia squared her shoulders at the insult.

Once, the Fae had looked to the Blood Witches as potential enemies. It was the Elves who had given the Blood Witches their power, their immortality. The Blood Witches were the grandchildren of the Gods.

Blood Witches were some of the most deadly creatures in all the lands. And their magic could rival that of any Fae.

But something had happened with the Fae. It had come before Celia's time, but there had been a shift in power. Blood Witches and Fae lost communication. Darius was half-Fae and high in the ranks of the Brotherhood, but Celia's own interaction with the Fae remained partially with the Resurgence, but even then she had not interacted personally with those who had fought—she had only seen what they could do.

"Blood Witch," he said, like the words were dirty in his mouth. "You stray far from your magical mountains, no?"

Celia clenched her jaw and remained quiet. There was no point reasoning with a brute like Arawn, the leader of the Hunt, a legend Isolde once met before her death. He was warped by years of ancient tradition, of brute force before reason.

All she could do was stand her ground. "As I have said. You cannot cross."

"And what of the fugitive you stand with?" Arawn asked. "What of her and the crimes she committed?"

"You ought to have thought about that before cornering her by the boarder," Celia snapped. "If her crimes are so horrible, then why not consider that possibility? Or were you just too caught up in your little hunt to even think of the consequences of *your* actions."

Arawn's dark eyes narrowed. "Then I hold you accountable, Blood Witch." A clawed hand dipped in silver rose from the reigns of his horse, held out to Celia and the woman. "I curse thee to her. Life-force to life-force, you will be bound to remain together until the Wyld Hunt finds you. And you *will* suffer the same fate as her, should you be caught by the Hunt."

Celia had only heard rumours about the strength of a binding spell such as the one that now linked her to the Fae criminal. She hadn't even had the time to create a protection spell around herself to ward off the powerful magic.

But it was too late.

Pain flared around her wrist, searing like someone had wrapped lightning around her forearm. Celia gasped and wrapped her fingers around her wrist to clamp down on the burning sensation, to even cool it with her own magic, but the fierce scorching sensation only intensified.

"Know that we will be back for her," Arawn continued, a bitter smile on his face. "And for you, too, pretty Blood Witch."

Celia gritted her teeth, tears stinging her eyes as the pain began to ease. "You will have to fight the Ecix for me, Arawn. She does not give up easily."

Fear flickered across his handsome face. Not even the Fae would cross an Ecix; they knew the power, what it could do. "I will see you soon, Blood Witch," he replied stiffly. He did not look to his now released prey. Growls of anger followed the Hunt as they entered the forest, disappearing from sight.

"You did not have to help me," the young woman said, voice low. Gratitude sparked in her dark eyes despite her protests.

Celia swallowed, touching the faint scar that now circled her wrist. *A curse.* How many stories had she heard within the mountains?

Do not interfere with the Wyld Hunt. They are more animal than man, than Fae. Fae trick and spell truths with lies and lies with truths. But the Wyld Hunt will do worse to those who stand in the way of their prey.

Celia should have known better than anyone not to interfere. She should have walked away.

But what kind of person would she have been if she had? The mere thought ate at her. Eliza would have remained, and so would Brandon. Perhaps even Amitel on a good day, though she had no doubt her old friend would berate her once he learned of what happened.

Though she doubted they would have let themselves be cursed by the Wyld Hunt.

"Do you have a name?" Celia asked, looking back to the dark-skinned beauty.

Dark brown, almost black hair fell over her shoulders in thick box braids, warm under Cadira's winter sun. "Soh," she said, a smirk playing at her lips. "You can call me Soh."

29

ATTACK OF THE GODS
CELIA

Celia and the Fae woman deviated from the main road and into the hidden oasis of a pixie circle. Tall trees surrounded the crystalised mushrooms that created the barrier of safety. It was smaller than ones Celia had found before, but it would do for the time being.

"We'll be safe here," Celia said, dismounting. The ebony horse whinnied, throwing its head in irritation. Celia ran her hand down its neck to sooth it, grimacing.

The Fae woman looked around the circle as Celia led the horse towards the centre of the clearing, where a small, bubbling brook cut through the grove. From the corner of her eye, Celia could see the blank expression the woman wore, hiding her feelings for Celia well enough that Celia couldn't find it within her to ask how she was.

Heat warmed her belly when the woman—*Soh*—met her stare. Fire flickered within them, a kind of power that sent shivers down Celia's spine. From the moment Celia had lain eyes on her, she'd been able to feel the power that radiated from her, and something within her called to that magic, sang when it was near.

Celia cleared her throat. "We need to find a way to unbind ourselves," Celia said, frowning once again at the thin scar around her wrist. She covered it quickly with the sleeve of her riding cloak, like it would be enough to remove the mark.

Soh looked down at Celia's wrist, then at her own. Celia followed the movement as Soh said, "I have lived many years, and I know of no way to undo a spell as complex as the one Arawn put upon us."

Celia sighed, defeated, and sat down on a fallen log. "You don't understand. I have a mission I need to complete. There are too many people relying on me to get answers, and I fear that I may not be able to do that while bound to you."

Soh took a seat beside her, her movements hesitant yet graceful. Celia watched her from the corner of her eye, watched as the light hit her smooth dark skin and the gold powder that dusted her cheekbones.

"What is it that you need to do?" Soh asked quietly. Dark eyes found Celia's.

Shaking her head, Celia looked away. She needed to quench whatever was spreading through her. There was something about Soh that called out to Celia, more so now than before.

But that did not mean she could trust the Fae woman. She had still been prey of the Hunt. Her crimes, whatever they were, were great. And Celia knew she couldn't trust her with the mission of finding Azula's dagger.

As if seeing those thoughts reflected in her blue eyes, Soh said, "You cannot tell me."

"Trust me when I say that it is for your protection, and also my own," Celia replied.

Questions danced in Soh's dark eyes. "Then why did you save me? Why do it when you know it might put you at risk?"

"It was the right thing to do." Celia shrugged and took in the clearing again, from the filtered light through the canopy of tall trees, the running brook and the horse waiting happily in a patch of tall grass. Peaceful, quiet, safe. If she could, she would have left Soh there.

Arawn and the Hunt couldn't enter pixie circles. They were strong enough to keep even the most powerful demons out.

But the binding would make it difficult. What little she knew about the Fae magic warranted serious concern from her.

"Look," Celia started with a sigh, "I don't have the time to go over this curse and how to break it. I cannot put this mission on hold, especially when those I love are in danger. Because of that, you will need to come with me."

Soh bristled as Celia stood. "And if I don't want to?" Soh asked, meeting her stare.

"I'm afraid you will have to." Celia strode to the horse, heart thundering with every step. "This mission could mean stopping a war before it even starts."

As Celia turned to face the Fae woman, something flashed in her dark eyes. Like hope. Were the Fae aware of the looming war with the Dark Master? They had fought in both the Great War and the Resurgence... would they stand again and fight should the war break?

Celia waited for Soh to laugh and refuse, but the Fae woman rose slowly.

"Then I will go with you," Soh replied. "It would be better to be with you, than being chased by Arawn and the Hunt by myself."

"I don't think we can be separated anyway," Celia muttered.

A smile flickered on Soh's lips. "Where do you need to go?"

Celia pulled a map from the saddle bag and took it to Soh. Spreading it across the log, Celia pointed to a marked area within the Cadiran forest where they had decided the *smudge* would be on a regular map.

"There is a location I must seek out hidden somewhere in these forests," Celia said, gesturing to the wide expanse of forest sitting behind the Cadiran capital, north of the Willican forest and south of the Labyrinth mountains. "It is ancient, from the time of the Goddess Azula, I believe."

"Alright." Soh nodded and stood. "Then we should go before we lose sunlight. Travelling through the forests at night, especially now, is dangerous. The Hunt reported strange sightings of demons, both inside and outside of the Fae lands."

Celia rose with furrowed brows. "Demons are always roaming."

"These were packs." Before Celia could respond, Soh picked up the map and folded it, handing it to her. "Wafting dark magic. I spotted something similar before I ran."

Lennox's warning echoed in her ears, about the Wyld Hunt's horn and demons appearing in the mountains. Celia turned from the Fae and rubbed a hand over her face.

Celia watched Soh from the corner of her eye, unease trapping her where she stood. The Goddess, Celia realised, might have guided her to more than just the smudge.

~

Darkness descended over the forest as Celia and Soh cleared the underbrush and entered the clearing holding an old temple. It had taken them only a couple hours of continuous travel, but they had made good time—enough so that they hadn't run into any of the wayward demons Soh had mentioned.

The temple looked mostly intact, with its ceiling raised by pillars. What used to be white stone was now discoloured and grey, green vines climbing the sides. The overgrown path leading up to the stone doors was littered with perfectly round stones, leftover perhaps from a beautiful path.

"Fascinating," Soh said, dismounting. She played with the rings on her fingers as she gazed up at the exterior. Hidden behind vines and grime on one of the pillars was a symbol—for necromancy.

Celia jumped down beside her and gazed up at the temple. Barely discernible was a raven carved into the door.

Alicsar had been correct in his assumption: there *had* been something within the smudge. Something that didn't want to be found.

"We're definitely in the right place," Celia replied quietly. "I hope."

Soh stepped towards the temple, lips parted. "I did not think Azula was such an influence on the mortals here."

"I didn't think so either." Celia led the horse over to a tree and wrapped the reigns around a branch, securing it, before pulling a small dagger from her saddlebag. "From what I understand, Azula is a Goddess of the Blood Witches. But she's been everywhere. So much so that I wonder what the Goddess truly stands for."

"Why is that?" Soh asked. She hadn't touched the knives at her hips since facing Arawn, but now her fingers itched towards them.

Celia replied, "In the mortal mythology, she is not real. She is a myth, a legend, a story you tell your children. A Goddess Queen who saved the land from a terrible enemy." Celia pointed the tip of her dagger to the raven, a symbol of the Blood Witches. "But she is not that to the Blood Witches. She is our founder, our Mother. She created us, and she is our patron."

Soh touched the beak of the raven, head cocked. "Can she not be both?"

"I suppose she can," Celia replied. "But she is more than just that."

Soh raised a questioning brow.

Shaking her head, Celia stepped away, sheathing her dagger in a scabbard on her leg. "I cannot tell you. It is forbidden."

Soh shook her head, releasing a breath. "Suit yourself. Are we going in or not?"

Celia bit her lip. "We don't have much of a choice."

Rustling behind them caught Celia's attention. Blood thrummed in her ears, singing the familiar song of magic. She turned to face the darkness, spearing fingers of magic into it, searching for a threat.

Nothing but the natural creatures of the forest. There were no pixies this far into the forest, though Celia didn't blame them. There was an air of wrongness about the temple that set her magic on edge.

"Alright," Celia said, nodding, turning to face Soh once again. "We go in."

Surrounding the raven was a layer of thick vines. Celia pulled at them with her bare hands, feeling thorns bite into the soft flesh of her palms, but the pain was minimal compared to the way her heart raced with anticipation. The archway was carved with unfamiliar symbols, the scenery behind the raven a strange forest Celia didn't recognise.

"What are we looking for?" Soh asked as she helped Celia removed the vines.

Celia hesitated. "A mention of the Goddesses dagger."

Soh made a small noise in the back of her throat, but didn't comment any further.

The heavy stone door gave way under Celia's touch. Pushing it open, the musty smell of the temple hit her, dust motes rising into the air. No light penetrated the darkness within, making her hesitate before stepping beyond the threshold.

Stone shifted around her. Celia held up a hand to stop Soh from entering further and waited with bated breath as a fire flickered on in a large metal dish in the centre of the temple, illuminating the resting creatures that surrounded it.

Wide, red eyes blinked open and regarded Celia with mirth. The closest one growled, low in its throat.

"We must run," Soh whispered, taking hold of Celia's hand.

"Not yet." As she spoke, the first demon rose, and attacked.

30

MEMORIES OF THE PAST
ELIZA

Eliza paced the length of the hallway outside Amitel's rooms, wringing her hands as she did. She tried to think rationally, but fear made her mind race. She closed her eyes and attempted to suck in calming breaths, but the darkness only made her fearful thoughts fester.

When was the last time she'd heard from Thorne? Or Celia? When would she hear from either of them? Would she at all?

A warm, strong hand stopped her, and she halted in her tracks. "Good morning, love."

Eliza frowned and brushed his hand off. "Just because I listened to what you had to say, doesn't mean you get to call me *love*."

As she pushed past him and into the rooms he'd claimed for himself, the warlock gave a dark chuckle. "If you say so, *love*."

Eliza swore under her breath and considered turning him into a toad for a couple of hours, if only to get some peace. But she needed the training; her magic felt strained and being cooped up in the underground city was making her head fuzzy. She hated to admit it, but she was missing the palace; the open air of the gardens, Lennox's erratic lessons across the grounds, even her luxurious bed and the ladies' maids who loved to play with her hair.

There was no running water in the underground city, though there was evidence within the walls of the old buildings that showed there might have been a thousand years ago. But whatever pipes had filtered water throughout the city were backed up or decayed. A hot shower, or even a bath would have been enough to satiate her for a couple more days below. But she was clean through magic—and magic left a residue.

Shuddering, Eliza crossed her arms and turned in a slow circle to take in the room. Amitel had pushed his cot against the far wall, the blankets neatly folded at the foot, accompanied by a stack of books. Anything personal was sitting on a small table beside the bed, though it was hidden beneath a discarded shirt—the only mess in the room.

A table had been set up in the centre, accompanied by two chairs. Another table by the door held bowls and jars filled with strange herbs, flowers, and stones, all neatly compiled and lined up.

"So why can you teach *me* how to enter the Aether?" she asked, letting her arms fall to her sides as she turned her stare on the warlock. "Why not Celia? Or anyone else?"

He chuckled, entering behind her. The door clicked shut, locking her within. "An Ecix taught me, though the Blood Witches would likely kill me if they knew."

Eliza's eyes widened, following Amitel as he passed her, crossing to the table filled with items. "What? Why?"

"The Aether and anything to do with the Ecix is sacred, love. None outside of the tribes and mountains can—or should—know how it all works." He didn't look at her as he rifled through the contents, head bowed over the workstation.

"But Celia knows about you." Eliza frowned. "She could have had you killed for that."

"Celia has no proof, unfortunately. But yes, she definitely could have set Lennox on me. I know that witch would like my head." His shoulders moved as if he were laughing to himself over a joke only he knew. Eliza could only raise a brow as she turned away from his huddled form.

"That makes two of us," she muttered, striding to the centre table.

"Cute." His eyes cut to hers, golden hair falling over his brows. "Sit."

Eliza perched on the edge of a chair and narrowed her eyes. "Why would an Ecix teach you?"

"I think she was in love with me." He winked in Eliza's direction, to which she rolled her eyes. "We had a mutual fascination with all magic," he continued, "not just what we each could muster. Your ability to create illusions? The monsters your imagination conjured under Mesah? Your past life learnt that from a travelling witch from a far off land. And you carry that ability in your blood, where your past lives and memories live. I think that's why you also draw blood when trying to access your Blood Magic. You subconsciously try to access those lives in order to aid your magic."

She gnawed on that for a moment, considering his words carefully while he continued to work. He didn't seem to be paying close attention to her, so it made it easier for her to watch him instead; the delicate movements of his fingers as he worked through flowers and herbs while flipping through a grimoire she hadn't noticed before; the slight downturn of his lips as he concentrated on his task; the furrow of his brow and the intensity of his golden eyes.

Reading people wasn't part of her repertoire, but it didn't seem as though he was hiding anything from her. His assessment, although somewhat outlandish, made some sort of sense to her. He at least explained it better than Lennox could.

There was little, she was slowly learning, that he hid from her—at least, not anymore. A lie by omission was still a lie, Kay always warned her, but sometimes lies were better than the truth.

He knew more than he was telling her, of that Eliza was certain. If there was one thing she could read, it was his eyes: the gold was a facade for what hid beneath, the truth of his emotions and words, and that unravelled to reveal his true intentions: the dark, crimson of his irises were the words he could not say, and rarely could he hide that from her.

Eliza swallowed hard and let her gaze fall from him. She focused instead on her nails, on the bitten down quicks and almost gone nail polish. "So, what does that mean for me entering the Aether?" she asked. A small spot remained on her left thumb, and while she waited, she picked at it.

"Lennox doesn't let you draw blood, does she?"

Eliza shook her head, refusing to look up from her fingers. "I think she assumes I should be able to do it all *without* hurting myself."

"Well, she's right, if only for that," Amitel replied. Her head snapped up, eyes narrowing as he gathered a bowl and several herbs, as well as a small dagger. "You shouldn't have to hurt yourself to access your magic. You should be able to dive into what's within, not just what happens to appear on the surface."

"I've only ever known natural magic," she said, dropping her hands into her lap. "Blood Magic is different."

"Consider it the same way, then." He settled the bowl and herbs in front of her. "You draw on natural magic by taking from what's around you, yes?" She nodded. "You only use what you can access, what threads are made present to you. Natural magic is bound to the land. Blood magic is similar. It is bound to your blood. There will never be a time where you won't be able to access that magic, because it is always under the surface. You just need to listen to that magic, and learn what threads you can access."

"You make it sound easy."

He smiled, and the gold of his iris swirled and shifted to reveal a hint of red. "Because it is."

"It's *not*. Blood Magic is dangerous." Those were words that made her stiffen, because not even she was sure of the truth of them. All magic was dangerous, depending on whose hands it was in. Blood Magic was the same, she hoped.

"Only to those who are not Blood Witches," he replied, the smile softening, like he was teaching a child. "You are a Blood Witch, Eliza.

The Blood Witch. The Ecix. It is quite literally in your blood."

She huffed. "Okay, so what do I need to do to cross over into the Aether then?"

"You need to let go of all the assumptions you have about Blood Magic and natural magic. Neither exist. You've been at a disadvantage your whole life, but that'll make you stronger in the end."

"Okay."

"Close your eyes. Rest your hands atop the table, palms facing up."

Eliza did what she was told. She placed her hands on the worn surface of the table and flipped her hands, palms up. Closing her eyes, she released a soft breath and waited.

"I am placing the bowl between your hands. Within, I am adding Velesate, a herb found only in the Labyrinth mountains. It's common to burn the bodies of Knights with this plant, as it is meant to carry them right to the Aether for their service." It reminded her of darkness and night; spiced like cinnamon, it tickled her nose as Amitel placed it in front of her. "Next, I am going to add Induilas, a rare flower found only in a greenhouse at the Crystal City of the Labyrinth Mountains."

Eliza opened an eye and watched him dangle three maroon petals above the bowl. "That sounds far-fetched," she said as the petals dropped.

"Eyes closed." Her eye snapped shut, but her lips pursed. "The flower first arrived on this continent by way of the Brithien Elves. It grows by use of Blood Magic, passed down through the Elves bloodlines. Through Blood Witches, like you."

"So how do you have it?" she asked, a little more curious than she had been earlier.

"Celia steals some for me every once in a while, for a collection of potions and salves. A fair trade if you ask me." She could almost imagine him shrugging in that moment, a half-smile dimpling his lips.

Internally, she rolled her eyes. "What do you need with a flower like this? What does it even do?"

"I never expected you to be much of a botanist, love."

She huffed, reopening her eyes. "I'm not. It just doesn't seem like something you should necessarily have."

"If you're wondering if I was giving it to the Dark Master, I would never," he said, voice tender. "I use it for myself, and that is all I will say on the matter."

Eliza pursed her lips, ready to voice her doubts and uncertainty, but paused. She'd have to ask Celia to be sure on whether that part of his tale was true, but she wasn't entirely certain he was lying about the Dark Master.

"I will find out the truth someday," she replied, quirking a brow. "You might as well just tell me."

"Maybe one day, love. But not today." He gave her a half-smile that tipped into a smirk as she rolled her eyes. "Today, we need to have you enter the Aether. You need to learn how to do so on your own, without crutches. And you need to learn how to do so safely. Now tell me, how did Lennox explain it to you."

"She said I wasn't strong enough on my own to travel into the Aether and return safely. She said I don't think through the *intricacies* of the spell because I'm *rash*." Eliza shook her head, but part of her believed Lennox's words. "She recommended meditation, because I tend to enter the Aether when I sleep."

"Then she does have reason to worry, but I wouldn't say that's your fault. You do what you know. Kay and her magic have influenced you for such a long time, that of course you're going to adapt your magic to suit hers. You've done so with Davis as well." Amitel rested his hands on the surface of the table, palms down, and leaned forward. "The Ecixes before you had two things in common: the Blood Witches, and their access to the past. They have all, by default, had relatively the same experience with their magic and their training. That's why you are so different. You don't have that, and while Lennox and the other witches may see it as a disadvantage, I see it more as a curve. It'll take you longer to get to the Aether, and that is fine. You are still finding your way there, regardless, which is something the others before you have not been able to do."

"I see the past through my dreams, too." She shuddered; the words had fallen from her lips without much thought, something she hadn't entirely been planning to reveal right away. "Like Isolde's death. It comes to me in dreams. And so do others. I can see Isolde there, too. When I accidentally go into the Aether. I think it's the only way she can see me, too."

Amitel nodded. "You let your guard down in your sleep. You don't have all your normal barriers in place, ones that protect you here. And with that, your magic is stronger. Your connection to the Aether is stronger."

"How do I replicate that then?" she asked, leaning in.

Amitel leaned back and produced a small blade from his pocket. He used the sharp point to prick his finger. "Close your eyes." He pressed a finger to her open palm, leaving a warm residue as he did the same to the other hand. "I've given you some of my blood. What this will do is give you access to my magic, like under Mesah. The purpose of this is to give you access to your past, which should make the transition into the Aether easier."

Her lips twisted down, and her thoughts drifted back to Mesah, when Dorin had stabbed Amitel in the gut. The warm blood coating her hands as she tried to slow the bleeding. Taking his blood—and his magic—into herself as she found the lost prince and his demons.

Eliza shuddered. "Okay," she murmured. "What next?"

"The bowl in front of you. I want you to use my blood to feel that magic. Feel for the essence of not only the natural magic, but the Blood Magic that resides in those plants. From the flower, and its past with the elves. The herbs, and their connection to the mountains. Both have been touched by Blood Magic in some way. I want you to feel it. Deep breath, and focus."

She sucked in a breath, letting it fill her lungs. The smell of blood, coated in the spice of the Velesate, and the sweet tangy Induilas filled her senses. She focused on the blood first, on the distinct magic and the warlock it belonged to. It felt like the sun after rain, warm and soothing on her cold skin. It was familiar and tangible, a breath of fresh air and the smell of fire crackling in the hearth. Eliza loosened her shoulders, and before her eyes, a thread of gold unravelled, thread slipping and dancing around her body.

A tinge of confidence had her turning to the bowl. The flower and herb, Blood Magic, a red thread that unspooled in her hands. It was the thing that grew from the very essence of her own power, a tangible creation of her past, present, and future.

Eliza focused on the red thread, and envisioned entering a memory from her past, using Amitel's blood as her guide. She thought about the Ecix who had taught him about the Aether, the one who he claimed was in love with him.

But the thread in her hands fell apart, disintegrating into the darkness. She fumbled and tried to picture it again, but the loss of focus cost her the gold thread, too.

Alone in the darkness, she wanted to scream in frustration, to throw her hands up and shout to the Blood Witches that they should have done better to prepare her. But a harsh laugh sounded somewhere behind her, sending chills down her spine.

No. She recognised it immediately from the nightmare.

It flashed across the darkness like photographs: the woman, chained to watch Eliza's death, the knight appearing to save her but being too late as the being behind her stabbed her through the heart with a blade made of bone.

Eliza's eyes snapped open, her harsh breaths filling her ears. "Amitel, I can't do it."

"You can, love. You just need—"

"I can't. I'm afraid." She looked up, and found his worried stare across the table. "I'm afraid to fall asleep because I'm afraid of dying, over and over again, at the hands of someone I can't see. I'm afraid of the shadows and the darkness because I feel like *he's* there and he knows exactly what's going on inside my head. I can't—"

"Eliza, stop." Amitel stalked from behind the table to her side. He pulled her away from the bowl and knelt in front of her, hands on her upper arms. Her eyes widened. "You are safe here. He cannot hurt you. You will not die. I am here, and I will not let anything happen to you."

"How can I trust you?" she whispered.

"Because I am real. I am here. I will not hurt you, never again."

The gold swirled and danced within his irises, revealing hints of red, mesmerising and soothing enough to calm the racing of her heart. Eliza focused on that, on the colour of his eyes, because it was all she could see in front of her, because looking back meant staring into the darkness of her own mind, her past, one that always remains at the tips of her fingers. She allowed, if only for a moment, for Amitel to be her calm, to be her anchor.

He didn't move, did not bend or fade away. He remained in front of her, on his knees, hands holding her in the present. He could have helped her with magic, could have calmed her within a moment, but he just waited.

He is here. He won't hurt me. But he had, once, not too long ago.

Eliza sucked in a breath and pulled away. "I'm okay now."

Amitel watched her for a moment, eyes searching hers. But he pressed his lips into a firm line and let his hands fall from her arms. As he stood, he tucked his hands into the pockets of his pants and stepped away. "Let's try once more, please."

"Alright." She shifted in her seat and faced the bowl. Tightening her hands into fists, she hesitated. The tips of her fingers bit into her palm, over the blood Amitel had pressed into her skin.

"Eliza."

She looked up from the bowl, and found the warlock standing in front of the table once more. Carefully, she opened her hands and let them rest, palms up, on the worn wooden surface. Amitel motioned for her to close her eyes, and as she did, he pricked his finger with the point of the small blade.

He wiped the blood against her palms. "Focus on the magic in front of you. And when you're ready, let everything else fall away. Enter your dreams, and seek out the past."

Eliza settled into her seat and let her breathing even out. The blood on her palms ignited a fire in her veins that raced through her body towards her belly, where the well of power she tried to avoid stirred and came to life.

The connection to Blood Magic formed almost instantly, a thread of deep red twisting behind her eyes. The gold of Amitel's magic danced with the Blood Magic, and she focused on that, on his blood being the connection to her past. She dove into it, into what it would reveal. A memory, something tangible for her to grasp onto.

But the threads shuddered before she could reach for them. Her breath quickened. The darkness shifted, moving against the strands she tried to hold onto. The darkness pulsed like a living creature, taking the form of a beast.

Eliza scrambled for the threads and wrapped her fingers within them. They tangled around her hands, her body, trapping her within the darkness. She fought with the web, spinning uselessly in circles, reaching for links within the strands that might be a memory for her to enter.

But the threads shuddered and disappeared, and deep within the darkness, something growled her name.

She didn't think. She ran. Fear coursed through her as she sprinted through the darkness in search of a path, something that would guide her to the Aether, or out of the dream.

The pounding of feet made her heart squeeze, but she didn't stop. The darkness pursued her, and there was nothing she could do to stop it.

In the darkness, there was nothing. She could not smell the flowers and herbs in front of her, could no longer feel the warmth of Amitel's blood against her palms. The table and chair, the room, and the underground city were gone.

She was alone in the darkness, and she had no idea what to do.

Lennox was right, she thought. *Lennox knew I couldn't do this.*

Eliza wanted to scream, but her fear of the beast chasing her stopped her.

It roared, shaking the darkness around her. Eliza stumbled and fell, but didn't crash into the darkness. It swallowed her instead, and she fell through it, shadows rippling as she passed. She let the scream tear from her lips, but she heard none of it.

A sharp prick threw her from the darkness.

Eliza fell from her chair, uneven breaths shuddering through her body. Her heart crashed against her chest, and she pressed her hands into the floor, digging her blunt nails into the wood.

Amitel appeared at her side, pressing a hand to her cheek. "Eliza? Are you alright?"

Slowly, she peeled her eyes off the ceiling and let them rest on the warlock hovering over her. His golden hair flopped over his brow, casting shadows over the red tingeing his irises. The sharp angles of his face seemed harsher somehow, but when she blinked, it was gone.

"I'm not doing that again," she whispered, unsure if she said it loud enough for him to hear.

Amitel opened his mouth, but after a moment, pressed his lips together and gave her a single nod.

His hand fell from her cheek, and gently he tugged at her hands. The tips of her fingers were bleeding, but she hadn't felt it. Amitel said nothing as he helped her to her feet, guiding her to the bed in the corner of the room. They did not speak, not as he carefully wiped her hands of his blood and cleaned her fingers, the wounds already healed like they'd never happened.

When he seemed happy with his work, Eliza stood. "From now on, we'll stick to our usual training," she said, staring at the bowl and the table.

Amitel didn't respond as she walked out. She pulled out an empty chest in her mind, and shoved the lesson within. *It will not hurt me,* she thought, letting the fear fall within. *It will not kill me.* The chest locked, and it was pushed into a place she wouldn't touch again.

31

THE TEMPLE
CELIA

Magic snapped from Celia's fingertips. Fire erupted in an arc before them, a crackling barrier between the pair and the demons stalking from the darkness within the temple. Celia stepped closer to Soh, hands outstretched, power thrumming in her veins.

Sulphur dripped from the creature's jaws, burning the tall grass around them. They gnashed their teeth as they surrounded the wall of fire, growling deep in their chests. The beasts dragged their taloned hands behind them, walking on hind legs like men.

Behind Celia, her horse whinnied, and a demon snapped its teeth.

"I have never seen a demon like this up close," Soh murmured.

From the corner of Celia's eye, she watched as Soh brandished a golden sword. It glowed with a powerful magic that called to something in Celia's blood. The feeling tugged at a memory of a war she wanted to forget.

"Blood Witch," Soh snapped, eyes darting from the demons to

hers, then back again.

Celia shook her head and returned her attention to the creatures. They prowled closer, forcing them back several steps, until the creatures were between them and the temple.

Tall as men and just as broad, there were ten in total. Odds Celia would have been fine to fight once were it not for the strange, ancient magic that rolled off of them. The magic seemed reminiscent of the beast that had attacked her in the palace, but it was not the same.

"They aren't normal demons," Celia murmured as she began delving into her magic. "These are... I don't know what they are."

"By chance are they minions of this *Dark Master* King Bastian is searching for?" Soh asked.

"I don't think so." Celia didn't bother asking how Soh knew about the Dark Master. The Fae probably had spies all throughout Cadira listening in on everything, especially related to potential enemies. The trees lining the palace grounds probably listened and reported back to their ancient masters in the Fae Territory. "These creatures are not young. They are something else."

"That makes them harder to kill," Soh hissed. The blade in her hand glowed golden as she swept it in an arch towards the first demon. Flesh hissed beneath the searing blade, turning the leering demon to mist.

Celia's eyes widened as Soh turned to the next demon and cut into it with the same ferociousness as the last. Each time the blade touched the black flesh of the demons, they turned to mist.

Fire burned at Celia's fingertips as she spun to face her own demons. They bared sharpened teeth and circled her, lifting their clawed hands, ready to strike.

Celia whipped a string of fire out and wrapped it around the throat of the first demon. Flesh burned beneath her fire, smoking at the wound. Yanking, its leathery-black head fell from its shoulders, the rest of its body slipping into mist as the head fell.

"These aren't real demons," Soh breathed, cutting down two more.

Celia gritted her teeth and called on the magic around her. The earth shook as tree roots rose from the ground, clumps of soil dropping to the burning grass. The roots snaked over the ground and struck the demons, dragging them into the dirt.

"What do you mean they aren't real?" Celia asked through gritted teeth. Another beast bounded towards them, but Soh cut through it with her burning sword, dissolving the creature into shadows and mist.

Soh strode to Celia's side. "I believe they guard the temple. They must have been created—"

The Faery stopped short, eyes widening, and pushed Celia aside. The Blood Witch stumbled as Soh raised her blade, but the demon crashed down upon her, heavy clawed hands slashing at her head. Though the sword cut through the demon, Soh fell to the ground, eyes fluttering shut, blood trickling from a wound on her temple.

Celia crawled to the woman's side. "Soh?"

A strangled sound passed Soh's lips, but she didn't move. Fear threatened to tear Celia's heart from her chest as she stared between the woman in her arms and the temple they were attempting to enter.

The demons that remained let out a cry. Celia raised a hand and summoned the roots, pushing magic and desperation into the snaking forms. She willed them to become chains and trap the demons.

As the creatures fought against their prisons, Celia returned to the Fae, cupping her cheek. "Wake up, Soh," she whispered. The magic binding them burned her wrist.

A demon ripped through the roots holding it down and started for them, its snarl echoing through the forest. Celia flinched, still cradling Soh. From the corner of her eye, Celia spotted the shine of Soh's blade. The magic imbued in the weapon had to be more than just Fae, something older than the ethereal being lying at Celia's feet.

Hand outstretched, Celia ignored the warnings of the Blood Witches in her head and summoned the wall of fire once more, the power a dim tingle on her fingertips. The demon cried out as the flames sputtered, catching on the tufts of fur lining its hind legs.

Celia swallowed and stared down at the Fae woman. Her eye lids fluttered, full lips parted, but she did not stir. Gold powder highlighted her cheekbones and the bridge of her nose, though it looked almost real, part of her skin, because not even the dark blood running down her temple smudged the colour.

The beast let out another cry as the flames surrounding her dimmed. Heart pounding, Celia spied the sword, its golden light intensifying.

The Faery stirred in her lap, and the demon shook the ground with its roar.

"Forgive me," Celia whispered, lowering Soh to the ground. The Blood Witch dove for the sword as the demon broke through the barrier of fire.

The pommel of the sword was warm in her grip, made of a silky, smooth, silver metal woven around gold. It was lighter than anything else she'd carried, the power wielded within the blade rippling through her.

The last of the temple demons—two, almost double the size of those they'd fought earlier—stalked closer to Soh's fallen body, but Celia rushed towards them, summoning her magic as she cut through the first beast's thick neck. It crumbled and disappeared, the second rearing on its hind legs with a roar that froze her blood.

Celia stumbled back, the sword growing heavy in her hands. She swung it in an arc and circled the demon.

It struck out with a clawed paw, and she ducked, rolling to the ground. She brought the sword up into the beast's abdomen and twisted until it was mist and ash in her hand.

Celia heaved a breath and stared down at the blade still in her hand as familiarity trickled through her. If Soh was who Celia believed her to be, then the power wielded within the sword was something older than Cadira. The Fae Courts were nothing short of legendary, and if Celia was right, then Soh belonged to the Seelie Court of Summer.

A daughter of the Summer Court meant a girl with a lot of power.

And it would likely explain the sword of golden light.

Another memory itched at the back of her mind from the Resurgence. There had been a Summer Knight at the Resurgence of

Valonde. Celia had seen a similar sword all those years ago.

"Blood Witch." Soh touched Celia's arm.

Celia blinked and turned in a slow circle; nothing but smoke and ash remained where the demons once stood.

Celia's hand trembled as she returned the sword, meeting Soh's stare. "Are you alright?" Celia let her gaze flicker over the woman's face, taking in the healed wound on the side of her head.

Soh wiped the blood with the back of her hand, grimacing. "I'll be fine," she muttered. She opened her mouth as if to say more, then shook her head, brows furrowing.

Stomach clenching, Celia swallowed the lump forming in her throat. "We need to go in." Celia stepped around Soh and focused on the temple.

"Are we not going to discuss these creatures?" Soh asked, rushing to catch her.

Celia entered the temple and stopped, taking in the pillars and discoloured frescos that lined the walls. In the dimness of the evening, she couldn't completely tell what was engraved along the walls. But there were no demons waiting in the shadows or lurking behind the pillars.

Celia didn't release the hold on her magic, but she could no longer sense the ancient power that had surrounded the creatures.

Towards the back of the temple, candles flickered on to reveal a small pile of offerings. They approached it hesitantly, their steps light.

A shrine? Celia knelt before it and touched the freshly dried flowers and stale offerings. *Someone has been in here. Recently.*

But who?

Who else was able to find this place? Or would even leave an offering to a Goddess not primarily worshipped?

Who was Azula really?

Despite everything Celia had been taught, she was finding herself questioning it more and more.

"She still has followers," Celia said. "Mortal ones."

Soh touched a stone carving of Azula. "Perhaps there are half-Fae in one of the towns who worship her as an Old God. She belongs to us, too."

The comment made Celia pause. *She belongs to us too.* Sometimes she forgot they—Blood Witches and Fae—shared Gods, shared stories and legends. Sometimes they differed, but they had been born of the same blood once, eons ago.

Celia shook her head. "It still doesn't make sense as to why she has so many monuments."

Rising, Celia circled the shrine and pushed aside thoughts of worshippers and long dead Gods. She paused behind an alter and frowned. "Soh."

Kneeling, Celia brushed her hands over the uneven surface of a raised block of stone. She slipped her fingers beneath it and tugged. Stone grinded against stone but didn't budge.

The Fae woman rounded the shrine and dropped to her knees. "What do you think this is?"

"I don't know," Celia said, jaw clenched. "But I want to find out."

She grunted as they removed the stone slab, pushing it to the side. Dust rose from the darkness, so thick she could see nothing beyond.

Covering her face, Celia rocked back on the balls of her feet. "Are those stairs?"

Barely distinguishable beyond the darkness, Celia could see the faint outline of stairs cutting into the side of the tight space. Where they led, she couldn't be sure. There was nothing to indicate sconces further down.

Soh dipped her glowing sword into the darkness. Shadows lapped like waves against the stone, edging closer despite the light of the Fae's sword. Thick and almost tangible, it reminded Celia of the ocean, deep and unfathomable.

"I say we go down, see what is there," Soh said. Rising, she sheathed her sword and waved a hand, sending a stream of light into the stairwell. "We might find what it is you are looking for."

Hesitation made Celia pause and reconsider. She'd already led Soh into a dangerous temple guarded by creatures as old as Gods. What would be waiting for them in the darkness below? Something far worse?

Celia cast a wary glance to her companion. There was no fear or apprehension lingering in the Fae woman's gaze. Despite the danger, she did not seem opposed to diving into the unknown.

Celia released a breath and rose, taking the first step down. "Down we go."

Darkness spread throughout the small room like death. Dust moats rose as Celia stepped into the unlit room, marking her entrance into the unknown. The light of Soh's magic illuminated the room in a golden glow, revealing rows of empty shelves surrounding a decayed desk.

A skeleton in the corner caught Celia's eye. Black robes, half decayed, slipped from the bones and pooled on the ground. It sat there, forgotten and alone, like it had been trapped with whatever secrets had been hidden within the tomb, guarding them even in death.

Slowly, Celia made her way towards the body, wishing Eliza was with her. If the spirit lingered, it could have told them more about the temple, its secrets.

Celia knelt before the body and spied a gold ring. She reached for it without thinking. It weighed heavily in her hand, engraved with the same strange symbol as outside the temple.

"What about this?" Soh asked, motioning towards a glass case towards the back of the room.

Rising, Celia followed, slipping the ring into the pocket of her riding pants. Her eyes followed the Fae, who circled the case, the arches of her dark brows drawn in a frown. Celia paused beyond the scope of Soh's light and watched her for a moment, breath caught in her throat.

The back of her neck warmed, as if the Goddess herself was with them in the room, urging Celia forward.

The Blood Witch took a step, then another, and re-entered the Fae's light.

Within the glass case, someone had put an unrolled scroll on display. "The ink is mostly faded," Celia said, clearing her throat, "but I think this might be a spell or history."

Her eyes scanned the page, noticing the small gold detailing and a sketch of the same dagger at the bottom the page. She couldn't quite understand the language, but she knew who would.

"I think this is what I need," Celia whispered. She smiled as she lifted the case. The glass came off easily under her fingers.

Even with the fading ink, Celia held onto the hope that it was what Eliza would need in order to summon Azula's dagger.

32

SECRETS
ELIZA

Sleep was a futile endeavour that only made Eliza miss the comforts of her New Orleans home more and more. Her back ached and her muscles were sore from hours spent training with Amitel and the knights, neck stiff from pouring over books that had no more answers than they did the day before.

And she missed having someone in the room with her. Thorne and Celia brought a kind of comfort she wasn't sure she could sleep without, and now with neither of them close by, she felt the lack of their presence even more.

She released a breath and dressed, donning breeches and a tunic, before pulling on knee-high boots. They almost reminded her of the kind she'd wear when she dressed for her *ghost and vampire* tours, though the ones she owned had two inch soles and were so shiny they reflect moonlight on good nights.

With her satchel thrown over her shoulder, Eliza left her

apartment and descended into the rooms Celia had claimed, that were now empty and cold without the Blood Witch. All the books Celia had taken for her own research were gone, having joined the piles they'd created in their would-be study hall and library.

The city remined quiet, their grandfather clock ticking, the hour soon to sound, but in the quiet morning, Eliza relished the silence and feeling of being alone. Caden and Darius were either asleep or on patrol in another part of the city, Amitel likely in the apartment he'd chosen, same with the prince, who had been quiet since his outburst in the arena.

Eliza sat before the cold firepit and rested her elbows on her knees. She watched the blackened wood like it would somehow reveal all the answers to her pent-up questions.

A tingle ran down the back of her neck, the whisper of magic only a moment behind it. Eliza sat up straight as ash appeared in front of her, singed paper floating through the air. She held out her hands, and watched the paper drop into her palms, rebuilding itself into a letter.

Eliza,

I found it. Something that might very well summon the dagger. I will remain at the temple for another day, until I can determine if it is the only useful artefact, but I will return.

It is in a language I cannot read, but I believe you will be able to. The temple itself is one of Azula's, and there is someone leaving offerings still. It is marked by necromancy.

I unfortunately ran into trouble on my journey here. The Wyld Hunt. They were hunting a Faery of the Seelie Court. I intervened, and Arawn, the Hunt's leader, bound us to one another as punishment. I do not know why she was being hunted, but we are now cursed. We cannot leave one another.

At the temple, demons attacked, ones guarding the temple. The Faery and I defeated them, but I do not believe they were agents of the Dark Master.

Below the temple is where we found the spell. I promise you I will bring it to you. We will leave here come first light with our findings.

Please be careful,
Celia.

Eliza made quick work of her response, heart racing. A smile formed on her lips. Celia had finally found something. Eliza wanted to laugh and cry as relief crashed into her.

The letter Eliza finished turned to ash, disappearing in a blink of an eye. There was more Eliza wanted to ask, but she'd kept it simple: they would wait at the Spring Manor for Celia and this Faery, that they'd figure it all out once they were all together again.

"Something has happened," Amitel said, startling her. The warlock appeared in the seat across from her, long legs stretched out in front of him, hands braced on the back of the bench as he leaned back. "Why are you smiling so much?"

"Celia found it," Eliza replied, keeping her voice quiet. "Something that might help us summon the dagger."

Amitel perked up, and slowly, he drew his legs in and sat up straight. "That's great." There was an edge of relief in his tone, one that surprised her. "Is she returning?"

Eliza nodded. "Yeah. But she's bringing someone with her..."

At this, the warlock frowned, but he shook his head. "Only Celia..." A half-smile twisted his lips. "Someone in need of help, I assume."

"You assume correctly." Celia's letter burned in her pocket. "A Faery being hunted by the Wyld Hunt. Celia tried helping her, and they got *bound* to one another."

A choked laugh broke from Amitel's lips as he shook his head. "Of course. Those spells are mighty difficult to break."

"I take it you've tried?"

He shrugged. "Once or twice. Usually a half-Fae or stupid mortal who got in the way of Arawn. You need a specific kind of Fae to undo that."

"Celia is going to love hearing that."

"Oh, she will." Amitel smirked. "Either the Wyld Hunt are going to break it, or they're going to have to go into the Fae Territories to do it. Neither would bode well."

Eliza sighed. "Great."

"But what Celia found... that's good news. It's a step in the right direction." All amusement disappeared from his face. "We'll be leaving here soon in search of the daggers resting place, I take it."

Eliza didn't comment, not on his words or the way his voice had changed. Part of her felt unease, but another felt... *disappointment*, like there was something she was going to miss about being in the city.

She shook her head. *It's nothing*, she thought, content with not knowing the underlying truth.

Amitel watched her and finally, she smiled, though the movement felt stiff. "Right."

The warlock stood, his eyes never straying from hers. She mimicked his movements and they stood across from one another in silence, neither speaking until Amitel bowed his head.

"I have some things I'd like to go over before we leave this place," he murmured, gold eyes bright. Finally, the grandfather clock ticked over, signing the time, six long rings echoing throughout the chamber. "We only have a couple of days left here, after all."

Eliza nodded silently as Amitel turned and walked away.

A moment later, she felt a hand brush hers, and when she turned, she found the prince standing beside her.

"Alicsar!" Eliza jumped in surprise and held a hand to her racing heart. He said nothing as they both watched Amitel walk away, the warlock disappearing into the temple.

The prince gave her an apologetic look. "I'm sorry for startling you."

Quickly, Eliza shook her head. "It's fine. I'm just a little jumpy."

Alicsar pursed his lips and said nothing, his hesitation palpable. With all her excitement about the spell and finding the dagger, she'd almost forgotten about the prince who had joined them in their journey to find the dagger.

After another moment of silence, Alicsar stepped around her and turned, facing her with a look of earnest that almost made her step back. He motioned towards the city. "Walk with me?"

She nodded, heart thundering. There was a part of her that told her she should have said no. But she was curious to find out what he wanted.

They walked in silence, taking one of the many roads that flowed through the city. Eliza grappled with her thoughts, all muddled and swampy, nothing clear except for the fact that she felt like Alicsar wanted to ask her something. About their marriage? She'd almost forgotten about that, had almost willed it from her mind. Though, she wondered if the king would still want them to marry after everything she'd put him through.

Swallowing, they rounded a corner before Alicsar finally spoke. "There is something that has been on my mind for some time, since the announcement of our engagement." He stopped, eyes caught on one of the buildings. "I have to wonder... do you feel anything towards me? Do you want to marry me at all, Eliza?"

Surprise at his questions stopped her heart, and she took a step back before she realised what she was doing. "I—" She pursed her lips.

There was a part of her that knew the answers, that could just reveal everything she'd ever felt and thought of him up until this very moment. But there was also another part of her that enjoyed being caught up in the illusion that *everything was fine*, that she could pretend for a little longer that her life wasn't revolving around the dagger and the Dark Master, that she was the one in control and no one else was.

When she looked to the prince, she found his eyes on her. There was no judgement or harshness in the emerald depths, just a deep need to understand, and maybe just a little bit of hope.

Eliza sighed. "I did feel something for you, before."

He frowned, crossed his arms. "Before what?"

"Before you lost your memories."

"We knew each other?" he asked, voice soft. Eliza couldn't bring herself to look away, not when that spark of hope seemed to ignite in his eyes.

She nodded slowly. "It was..." She bit her lip. "It wasn't easy."

"What do you mean?" he asked, but she shook her head. "Please, Eliza. I want to understand." His eyes bored into hers until guilt and shame gnawed at her.

After a moment she nodded, relenting. "You won't like it," she warned, but the prince waited. "When we met the first time, you were working with—for—the Dark Master."

Something darkened in his eyes, but he said nothing. After a moment, she continued, "We met at the palace; you were pretending to be a servant, and you'd been sent to join Thorne, Celia, and I on our mission to find the prince—you. It was strange, how quickly I felt like I knew you, but in the end it had all been lies. You had used some kind of compliance spell on me, so I thought I had feelings for you." She swallowed down the burn of tears. "You joined us on our journey to Mesah, because you said you knew the desert. It turned out, that's where the Dark Master took you after you'd been kidnapped. You'd been raised there.

"You and I went under the desert, into tunnels like the ones here. I was convinced we would be fine, you and I, that we'd find the prince together and save him. By that point, Celia had fallen ill, and Thorne had left with her..." With every word, her heart grew lighter, like the weight of her omission was finally lifting. "Amitel found us, and he knew exactly who you were, because he'd been working with the Dark Master—and you—too. And I walked into your trap."

"I attacked you," Alicsar said breathlessly. He didn't look at her. "I hurt you."

A pit yawned in her stomach as she nodded. "We fought. Amitel almost died to protect me. I almost killed you... And the cavern caved in. I thought you died, but soldiers found you, and then your memories disappeared. I don't know why; if it had something to do with the cave-in or because of the Dark Master. But you lost all your memories, and I... I made myself hate you."

Alicsar said nothing, eyes glazed over. But she pursed her lips, stopped herself from saying anything more. What more was there to say? She'd finally told him the truth, and admitted that she basically hated him.

Finally, the prince nodded, but before she could stop him, he walked away.

~

Eliza gasped awake, the pull of the dream slipping away. There was a pressure, a warmth, on her shoulder that pulled away a moment later.

Peeling her eyes open, she blinked against the bleary darkness around her, but she found a figure sitting on the edge of her bed. Fear hammered in her chest as she sat up and crawled to the other side of the cot, away from the figure.

The person stood and backed away several steps. "I'm so sorry."

The voice rang familiar in her ears. *Alicsar*. The prince. She closed her eyes and sucked in a breath, willing her heart rate to settle in her chest.

When she opened her eyes again, she could see him perfectly in the darkness; he wore dark breeches and a collared tunic tucked in at the hem, sleeves rolled up to reveal his forearms and the coiled muscle beneath. At his side, a bag, like he planned to go somewhere. She frowned, and met his stare.

"I didn't mean to scare you," he rushed, "I just wanted to talk to you before... I left."

Eliza's brows rose and slowly she climbed out of the bed. "Where are you going?" she asked.

"Home. Or well—" He stopped and shook his head. "Back to the palace, to Bastian."

"Why?"

"I hurt you." Before she could respond, he held up a hand, his eyes meeting hers. "I hurt you badly, Eliza. Back before... before I lost my memories, and that's no excuse."

He stepped forward, his eyes still on her. "I am sorry for what I did, then and now. I'm sorry for what I have done to hurt you, and I never wished to trap you in this life, a life you clearly do not want."

Alicsar stopped in front of her, only a breath away. Suddenly, she couldn't breathe, caught in his eyes, in the emotion that swirled in the bright depths.

He lowered his head, and she felt his breath on her cheek. "I wish things were different," he whispered. His lips touched her flustered skin, and though the touch was soft, it burned as he pulled away. "Amitel will take me back to the palace, and I will deal with Bastian. And when you return with the dagger, everything will be different."

He stepped back abruptly, eyes searching hers. Then he left, entering the soft darkness of the apartment.

Eliza rushed after him, down to the first floor of the building, where Amitel waited, his eyes clouded over, lost to his own thoughts. For a moment, she couldn't breathe.

"You don't have to go," she whispered, staring up into Alicsar's eyes.

The prince shook his head. "I do. And I promise, I will make this right." He held her stare, and part of her believed him, and for a moment, she wondered if he would do more, despite the watchful eyes of Amitel and the knights, despite what she'd reveal to him. "I will tell Bastian I no longer wish to go through with the engagement. I will tell him I will leave again if he forces this. I will make some kind of bargain. *I will make this right.*"

Her breath caught in her throat as the lost prince joined the warlock, and left her in the ancient city.

33

SPIRITS LIE
ELIZA

The absence of Amitel and Alicsar made the silence of the city less bearable, like it was slowly closing in on her, surrounding her on all sides until it would suffocate her. She'd been left with Caden and Darius, who were as unenthused as she was about Amitel taking Alicsar back to the palace.

"It will help, for when we leave," Darius mused, voice deep and melodic. "The king will be focused on his son once more, and it should give us time to find the weapon. It will aid in Celia's return, too."

Though the knight had a point, Eliza couldn't help but feel uncertain at his observation.

Caden nodded, his eyes flickering to her momentarily before flickering away. "We don't know how long that'll last though. Bastian might set his sights on securing Eliza next, to make sure he can protect the union."

Her heart dropped in to the pit of her stomach as she listened.

Despite what Alicsar had promised her, she wasn't sure if the king would give up on her so easily. It seemed like he'd done much to secure an alliance with the Blood Witches.

Maybe he knew there was another war coming, and that he'd need the help of the Blood Witches if he—and his people—wanted to survive.

A chill spread over her at the thought.

The conversation between Darius and Caden turned quiet, and she returned to her thoughts. Amitel had only left an hour ago; she'd expected him back sooner, thought that he'd only be dropping Alicsar off at the palace and returning as soon as it was over.

Worry ate at her, a gnawing feeling that rose from her stomach and into her heart. But she knew he would be okay.

I hope.

Darius and Caden grew louder, breaking her from her thoughts, halting the worry before it could spread.

"We could easily leave," Darius said, "there is no one here to stop us. We take the Ecix and return to the mountains."

Caden started shaking his head, but Eliza shot to her feet. "Like hell you will." She crossed her arms to stop her hands from trembling. "The only way you're taking me to the Blood Witches is if I'm dead. Which I doubt is something they'd appreciate."

Both knights scowled, but it was Darius who stood. "It would be much safer for *everyone*—"

"No." Eliza shook her head. "It would be *easier* for you, so you don't have to babysit me while I look for a way to keep *everyone* alive and stop a war before it starts."

Heart thundering in her chest, Eliza didn't give either knight the chance to respond before storming off. She took different turns and alleys and streets, determined to get lost so neither could catch up to her or find her. The streets of Azula's city were a maze, which suited her fine, until she found herself at the edge of the city and staring into the mouth of a small tunnel.

Eliza entered the darkness, the burn of tears and the ache of pressure forcing her to her knees. The shadows wrapped around her like a cocoon, protective and safe, swaddling her as she let the tears break free and the sobs pierce the silence.

No matter how much she didn't want to admit it, she was losing control, and she didn't know what to do.

~

Time in the tunnel passed, though she had no concept of how long she'd spent curled up in the darkness. She couldn't bring herself to care if Darius and Caden were worried, or if Amitel had finally returned.

She was just so *tired*.

Silence pressed down on her, and for a while, she bathed in the peacefulness. For the first time in a long time, she didn't resent the darkness that surrounded her.

Eliza pushed off of the ground and rested her head back against the stone wall. At some point she'd slipped down in a foetal position, almost like she would fall asleep, but she never did. She sucked in a breath and released it slowly, closing her eyes. Though the darkness brought peace, it also reminded her of what was left to do, what she still needed to accomplish before Celia's return, before they went in search of the dagger.

With that thought in mind, she opened her mind up to the Aether, the world only she could touch and see. She steadied her breathing until her heart slowed enough that it didn't distract her or echo in her ears. The weight of a small knife, blade no longer than the length of her palm, appeared in her hand. With it, she pressed the tip over the inside of her wrist. She made a small incision, felt the blood and magic flow through her.

She imagined her body as an anchor, and she used it to pull herself up to the surface, a place only she could reach.

Everything Amitel taught her, Lennox's lessons on leaving her worldly problems behind, fell away as she pulled at the threads surrounding her, life and death a woven structure that co-existed and lived peacefully beside one another.

Eliza released the world of the living, the thread of gold, and reached for the red tether that bound her to the world of the dead.

Finally, the spirit world opened up to her.

The Aether was like everything Eliza could have imagined; dark mist curled around her ankles, though when she took a step, grass crunched beneath her feet. There was a forest, though she only saw the outline of the trees. Thick trunks with gnarled roots lifted from the earth.

The sky above her was a dark grey, though not because of the clouds; everything around her held the same grey hue. There were no stars, no twin moons. Just a blank slate that glared down at her.

Eliza shivered and wrapped her arms around herself as she took another step.

What do I do now? In her training with Lennox, she'd never gotten this far. Fear and uncertainty over her abilities had weakened her, but now she knew—knew she had to let go and stop hesitating.

After I find Isolde, of course, she thought.

As if sensing Eliza, the past Ecix appeared; dressed in long red robes, hair bound in a crown a top her head, it was hard for Eliza to imagine they looked similar—the same, even. Isolde held herself in a confidently, her back straight, shoulders loose. She knew exactly what she was capable of, what she was and what she'd done in the past.

Eliza swallowed. "Hey."

The Blood Witch lifted a brow, though amusement flickered in her identical moss-green eyes. "Hello, Elizabeth. It took you long enough to find this place."

Should have expected nothing less, Eliza thought, though she nodded. "Yeah. I've had some trouble getting here, but I'm done being afraid."

Isolde glanced over her appraisingly before letting a smile flicker on her lips. "Well done."

"We need to talk."

Another brow shot up. "I suppose we do. Come." She motioned to the trees. It took Eliza a moment to realise there were other spirits surrounding them, keeping their distance, but always watching. "Let's walk."

Eliza matched the ghosts pace. "Did you know much about the

Dark Master, before you died?"

From the corner of her eye, Isolde shook her head. "No. I knew nothing about him, except for whispers about a shadow creature that was leading the Resurgence."

"If you had known, would you have still fought?"

Isolde stopped and pursed her lips. "Yes." She met Eliza's stare. "I don't think knowing my fate would have stopped me."

"Even if you could have lived?" Eliza pressed, frowning.

The witch shrugged. "I still would have died, one way or another, as fate commands it—as the Dark Master commands it." She stopped walking. "There is more you wish to know, isn't there?"

It was Eliza's turn to shrug. "Of course there is. My whole life has been a series of half-truths and lies that have lead me to this point. I don't know anything about being a Blood Witch. I barely know anything about the Dark Master, and I can't find *anything* about Azula or the dagger or the Original." Eliza released a heavy breath. "I'm so confused. Celia found a spell, but what if it doesn't work? What if the dagger is already gone, and the Dark Master is planning to use it against me? What if he actually *succeeds* in getting rid of me—of *us*—and the power?"

"Many of those questions are ones I cannot answer," Isolde said, voice tight. "So if you have questions for *me*, then I would very much like to hear them."

The urge to throw something at the spirit shot through Eliza, but she tampered down on her frustration, expelling a breath. "I need your help, Isolde. You're the only one on this side we can trust."

"You make it sound like there are nefarious forces working against you here in the Aether."

Eliza quirked a brow, almost mimicking her doppelganger. "Are there?"

The spirits eyes sparked with something Eliza couldn't read. "Perhaps."

As she began walking again, Eliza hesitated and glanced around the forest. The trees were gradually getting thicker, though there was still no noticeable light to illuminate the space, only the grey hue that made it just visible enough for Eliza to see and not trip over the exposed roots.

After a moment, Eliza rushed to catch up with the spirit and matched the girls pace. They walked in silence for what felt like eternity, with no other sound filtering throughout the forest. Although Eliza felt the stares of the dead, she couldn't hear them, couldn't see them through the grotesque bending of the tree limbs and underbrush.

"What about Azula's dagger?" Eliza asked.

The spirit shrugged. "A myth, to my understanding." Something in her voice told Eliza that wasn't the entire truth, but Isolde continued, "Azula exists as a connection between many peoples. Her story is one that constantly changes, and many have different ideas of who—or what—she was. But she and her dagger always remain the same; a Goddess of Death wielding a dagger strong enough to destroy the indestructible."

"Magic," Eliza whispered.

Isolde nodded. "I know why you seek it out. And I believe it might be the key to the Dark Master's defeat, but if you do not get to it first..."

"Then it could destroy me."

"I do not wish to see our end just yet," Isolde murmured. "Not when there is still so much for us to learn."

Eliza didn't comment on that. She agreed, and yet the idea of having such a destructive power taken from her almost sounded appealing. Alastor had warned her against such thoughts. Would she survive without the magic of the Ecix?

Was she prepared to find out?

Thoughts of Alastor and Xeb dragged up another memory. "Valonde," Eliza murmured. "What can you tell me about that?"

"Very little." Isolde cast a quick look around before slowing her pace. "Like with the Dark Master, I knew little about Valonde. I did not spend time researching our pasts, believing I would have all the time in the world to do so. I knew Valonde had been the enemy in the Great War, but Blood Witches spoke little about our deals with the mortals."

"So, in the dark just like me, then."

Isolde nodded. "So it seems. The High Council were very...

protective over the information about our pasts."

"Why?" Eliza asked quietly, a shiver dancing down her spine. "What are they hiding?"

The spirit shrugged, the movement elegant. "I am not sure. I've had no one to ask."

"None of our past lives?" Something dropped into the pit of Eliza's stomach, with it a rising sour feeling, a feeling like something was wrong.

Isolde's gaze found Eliza's, and she shook her head. "For the last two hundred years, I've been searching for them. When I was alive I struggled to meet them, talk to them. And even in death I cannot reach them. My—*our*—tether to the past is weak, the link almost non-existent." She paused and dragged a hand over her face, eyes suddenly weary. "I do not know why this is happening." A dark, humourless smile fractured across her lips. "Perhaps if I'd had one to talk to, I would have addressed the war differently. Perhaps you would have been able to live in peace with the witches."

Eliza looked away and stared into the darkness. "So what you're saying is you know about as much as I do."

"You have struggled to reach me, which means you cannot reach them, either."

"Yeah, you're not wrong," Eliza replied. "But I've been training with Lennox. I've been doing all the exercises, learning all the basic meditation tools so I *can* get to you. So I don't understand why I can't."

Something in Isolde's gaze changed, but she shook her head instead of voicing her thoughts. She said nothing, and they walked for longer, until they stopped in the clearing where Eliza had first appeared. There were more spirits now, all watching.

"You've been here too long now." Isolde spared Eliza one last look. "Always be afraid. Of your power, of the threats around you. Fear makes you cautious, makes you think. Do not let it *overcome* you, Elizabeth. It is then you are weak, and it is then our enemies will take control of us."

Before Eliza could respond, the Aether disintegrated, falling away until there was only darkness.

A flash of light streaked across Eliza's eyelids. Slowly, she peeled her eyes open, only to find Amitel kneeling in front of her, his face twisted with worry. One of his hands were pressed against her cheek, though when she found his stare, he quickly pulled away, rocking back on his heels.

A smirk played at his pink lips, the worry giving way to the arrogance she knew and appreciated. "Well, well, well. What brought you all the way out here?"

Eliza groaned and pushed herself up. She hadn't realised there would be any physical effects from being within the Aether, but her muscles felt like jelly, tongue like sand paper in her mouth.

Her knees buckled, but before she could hit the ground, Amitel was by her side, one hand on her elbow, the other at her waist. She leaned into him for support, head spinning.

"I've got you, love," he murmured, pressing closer. He said something else in a language she didn't understand.

She hated it, but a feeling of safety washed over her with his touch. It felt like a warmth she never wanted to leave.

There was a familiar touch of magic, which made the warmth grow stronger, until it encompassed her. Eliza rested her head against his chest, listened to the steady beat of his heart. The net around her grew tighter until she thought she might fall asleep in his arms.

The trance broke, and suddenly strength rushed through her. She opened her eyes. "You healed me?" she asked, lifting her head just enough to meet his stare.

Amitel watched her with wary eyes, and he nodded, pulling away. "You didn't look so good."

She felt the lack of warmth, of his steadying presence, almost immediately. Part of her regretted speaking. "Thanks," she replied, stepping back.

The warlock cocked his head. "So, what *were* you doing here?"

"I wanted to get away from Darius and Caden." She sighed and rubbed her eyes, which she had no doubt were red and puffy. "I just don't know what I'm doing anymore. And I needed some space and silence."

Amitel frowned. "Well, those two idiots are besides themselves, still looking for you."

Guilt pierced her heart. "I'm sorry."

The warlock shook his head. "Don't be. They'll be fine. But what about you? Are you going to be okay?"

Was she? Just like the last time she'd left Isolde, Eliza had more questions than she did answers, which made every inch of her buzz with irritation. And yet... it seemed like Isolde was as much in the dark as she was, that the witch knew little about their shared past lives, which struck Eliza as odd.

"I went into the Aether and found Isolde," Eliza said quietly. "We talked about the Dark Master, Azula's dagger... but we also talked about our past lives. I wanted to talk to the Ecix who started all this. I wanted to know what was going through her head when she thought it would be smart to start a war like that." Eliza stopped and shook her head. "But Isolde doesn't know how to find them."

"What?" Amitel asked, the shock in his voice almost similar to her own.

She nodded. "Isolde is as clueless as I am." Releasing a breath, Eliza pushed off the wall and started for the tunnels entrance. First thing she needed to do was to apologise to the two knights, though she couldn't help but feel just a smidge of satisfaction that they were worried about her.

Amitel stopped her, his hand enveloping hers. She almost missed a step as she turned to face him once more. "You need to be even more careful now, with your magic and with what you know."

"Why?" Eliza asked, tugging her hand free.

The warlocks eyes flashed red. "Because if you *and* Isolde are struggling with contacting your past lives, then that has *everything* to do with the Blood Witches."

Her breath caught in her throat, heart stuttering. She shouldn't have been surprised, and yet...

Yet it seemed like there was one more thing the Blood Witches were determined to keep from her.

34

MYSTERIES
CELIA

Celia rubbed her eyes tiredly as the words in front of her blurred together. She'd been staring at the scroll and a number of texts from the basement collection for hours trying to decipher the language, but neither made any more sense than they had hours before.

She released a breath, her frustration gnawing at her. "I don't know if I can do this," she whispered, more to herself than anyone else.

From across the room, Soh, looked up. "If you cannot decipher it, then we should take it to someone who can."

Celia's gaze went from the scroll to the woman. There was a softness to her dark eyes, the slant of her brows and lips. Celia caught herself and shook her head. "The woman who raised me worked in the catacombs of the Labyrinth Mountains. She was a scholar." She shook her head. "I should have some idea of what I'm doing, but I don't."

Soh rose in one fluid motion, her dress rustling as she did. Long, lean legs were exposed for a moment, revealing more rings of gold against her dark skin. Celia swallowed thickly, cheeks warming as she looked away.

The Fae woman approached, and slowly knelt beside her. Celia watched as she reached for the scroll and the book and removed them from her lap. Every move she made was like a dance, elegant and beautiful. Her limbs were as fluid as silk, gliding through air gracefully. Celia sucked in a sharp breath.

Soh paused once the book and scroll were secure in Celia's satchel. They were a breath apart, their noses almost touching.

Celia hadn't felt the urge to kiss someone in years. And yet, within a day of meeting her, she wanted to kiss Soh, the mysterious Fae who she was bound to.

The curse. Perhaps it was playing with her feelings, making her think things she wouldn't normally consider. Celia blinked and finally broke Soh's stare, fracturing the moment between them.

Soh rocked back on her heels and stood. She hesitated a moment before moving to stand in front of Celia, and the Fae sat in one quick movement, tucking her hands into her lap.

Guilt churned in Celia's gut. She hoped she hadn't offended her, because if it weren't for the mission... perhaps she would have allowed herself the small pleasure of the faeries lips.

Shaking her head, Celia crossed her arms, bringing her knees to her chest. "I will ask my sister for help," Celia says finally. "She might have a better understanding."

"You are here for her, then?" Soh asked.

"Yes." Celia smiled, and rested her chin atop her knees. "She is why I do everything."

A moment of silence passed between them, then, "That sounds awfully sad."

Celia looked up, frowning. "I lost her once to a terrible fate. I do not want to go through that again." Isolde dying in her arms had stayed with her for years, and she never wanted to have to watch another die like that, especially not Eliza.

The thought of her sister sent a pang of guilt through her; outside the temple, the sky would be bleeding purple, the song of birds calling for the new day. Exhaustion played in the back of her mind, but adrenaline—*hope*—made her heart race, and the promise of answers kept her awake.

Was Eliza worrying for her, hidden below the skeleton of the Spring Manor? Celia itched to return with the scroll; her gaze flickered around the basement of the temple, passing over the stacks of crumbling books and statues almost reminiscent to the ones scattering Azula's forgotten city.

Celia sat up, the realisation hitting her. "Only the Ecix can read the scroll."

"What?" Soh frowned, cocking her head.

Celia blinked. "The scroll. It's protected by a language we don't recognise, one harboured by a temple of Azula. I think only the Ecix can read it."

Something dark crossed Soh's eyes, but finally, she nodded. "It would make sense. But why are you searching for lost artefacts of Azula? I thought all regarding the Goddess resided with the Blood Witches? Are you searching for others, pillaging old temples to keep the Dark Master from learning the truth?"

Celia stiffened. "I have a mission, one the Blood Witches aren't accepting of, but I will do anything to keep the Dark Master away from the dagger."

She realised her words too late; Celia snapped her lips shut as understanding crossed Soh's eyes. The Fae woman sat back, face going blank. "You never said you were searching for Azula's dagger."

"You never needed to know," Celia replied as something heavy dropped into the pit of her stomach.

"That seems like a very dangerous endeavour, Celia," Soh continued, jaw ticking as her eyes flickered over Celia then the satchel. "Do you know what you are doing?"

"Yes, I do."

Dark eyes found Celia's, judging. "I do not believe you, Blood Witch."

Bristling, Celia clenched her hands into fists, nails biting into the soft flesh of her palms. "Well I don't have a choice. This will help save my sisters life. I cannot lose her again."

"You speak of the Ecix then, I assume." Soh's fingers twisted the white material of her dress into knots. Her knuckles whitened, and there was a flush of red high on her cheek bones, barely discernible in the flickering light of the candles.

"Yes," Celia replied tersely.

"She is not your sister," Soh snapped, golden light flickering in her inky eyes. "She is darkness and death. The Ecix is not natural."

Blood pounded in Celia's ears. "Blood Witches aren't natural, according to your people."

Soh shook her head. "This is the *Ecix*. Her power is something else entirely, not of the natural world. She should not live."

Calmness washed over Celia and she sat back, heart racing. "Say that again, and I will kill you, curse and binding be damned. She is my sister. She did not ask for this power."

"They never do." Soh laughed humourlessly. "And yet they are more than happy to use it in order to destroy entire lands."

Celia slammed her hands down and stood, blood boiling. She couldn't hear anything over the pounding of her heart. "Do not speak on what you do not know or understand. The Ecix and her power is sacred. My sister does not destroy."

"And how do you know that?" Soh asked, voice sharp. "There is a large history of the Ecix being the cause to so much destruction in this world. Your sister is not exempt from this cycle."

Barely able to hide the shaking of her hands, Celia replied, "I don't have time for this. I need Azula's dagger. And we need to meet with her. We have learnt all we can from this place." Celia shoved the satchel over her shoulder.

Soh watched her with dark, hooded eyes, cheeks flushed in anger. "What will you do? Run away from the truth?"

"I will do what I have to in order to stop the Dark Master and help my sister. That means getting hold of Azula's dagger." Celia stepped up to Soh, lowering her voice. "Do not speak of what you do not know. She is different from those who came before her."

Soh shook her head and stood. "That does not excuse the effects of the power. The truth is, magic like that wielded by the Ecix is unnatural, and it is a danger to us all. Denying that makes you blind to what else is out there," she said, stepping around Celia, her back to her. "If you truly want to help your sister, then I suggest finding a way to destroy that power and release her from that terrible curse."

Celia pushed the Faery aside and stormed up the dimly lit stairs, the words a haunting whisper she could not escape.

~

Cold, sharp rain thundered from the sky, soaking through Celia's riding leathers and chilling her to the bone. Behind her, Soh shivered as they rode through the empty landscape and up to the blackened shell of the Spring Manor.

Against the dreary grey sky, the skeleton of the manor stood out sharply, disguised in darkness and sharp with pointed beams reaching for the sky. The snow looked like fog in darkness, a shroud so thick she doubted it could be penetrated.

Soh released a breath. Celia felt it against the cold skin of her neck and shivered.

"What happened here?" Soh asked, her voice almost breathless, quiet enough so not to disturb the dead. Her arms tightened around Celia's waist.

"The Dark Master," Celia replied just as quietly. "This is where he took the prince twenty years ago and killed the Cadiran Queen and Princess. After that, it fell into disarray, and burned to the ground, killing everyone within."

Soh shuddered and fell silent. Celia felt it deep in her bones as they crossed onto the estate.

The horse whinnied as Celia guided it through the maze. Whispers of the ancient magic reached for her before recoiling. She sought out Amitel or Eliza's magic, but their familiar hum was nowhere, hidden beneath the many layers of power concealing the ancient city beneath their feet.

They approached the fountain, and Celia guided the horse to a stop. Snow dusted the hedges surrounding them, not as thick, almost like the ancient magic of the maze protected what lay within.

Azula and her Fae lover stared down at them, icy tears slipping down stone cheeks. Celia closed her eyes and bowed her head a moment.

Soh pressed a hand against Celia's hip, forcing Celia to open her eyes. "What is this?" the Fae asked, lips close to Celia's ear.

Celia supressed a shudder and dismounted, pulling away from Soh as she did. But she felt the warm stare of Soh on her, watching her every move.

"The fountain acts as the portal into Azula's city," Celia replied stiffly, tugging her satchel from the saddle and slipping it over her head. "It's how we return to my sister."

Celia spared Soh a quick, uncertain glance, expecting a frown or another remark about Eliza, but instead Soh dismounted in one fluid motion and stepped up to the lip of the fountain, running her fingers along the iced over stone.

"There is no magic like this left in Cadira," Soh whispered, "at least, that is what we are taught. This is magic from Before."

Lips pressed together, Celia wrapped the reins of the horse around her cold hands, and as she guided it back through the snow covered maze, Soh's words played through her mind, worry swirling in her gut.

35

HIDDEN MAPS
ELIZA

Magic rippled throughout the city, causing the hairs on Eliza's arms and neck to rise. Climbing to her feet, Eliza left the seclusion of the temple and rushed into the square, where Amitel, Darius, and Caden waited, weapons drawn.

"What's going on?" Eliza asked, rushing to the warlocks side.

His eyes found hers, but flickered away quickly. "Someone used the portal."

Her heart crept into her throat. "Could it be Celia?"

"Maybe," he replied softly, "but she would have alerted us by now."

With bated breath, Eliza watched, heart hammering. The magic of the portal shuddered through the city and disappeared, leaving Eliza cold and uncertain. Her heart hammered against her ribcage. The taste of fear was sour on her tongue as they waited, focused on the path leading directly to the portal.

And then...

Eliza saw her, raven hair bound in two braids down her back, riding leathers wet from either rain or snow. With her was a woman who looked no older than twenty-five, yet powerful immortality wafted from her in waves that surprised Eliza.

Fae.

But Celia started for their group, step quickening as she noticed them.

Eliza couldn't help but break free and run towards the witch, relief shuddering through her. Only a couple of days had passed and yet it'd felt like a lifetime of not knowing what might happen next. It'd been painfully lonely, a constant ache that had arisen even before Celia's departure, perhaps even before Thorne had left.

When Celia reached them, Eliza threw her arms around her and breathed in her scent of lavender and berries. The fear Eliza had been feeling quickly disappeared as Celia's arms wrapped around her, holding her tight.

"Is everything alright?" Celia murmured. Slowly, she pulled away and held Eliza at arm's length. "Did something happen?"

Eliza shook her head. "No, nothing. Not really. I was just worried."

Celia smiled, bright eyes still worried. "Are you sure?"

"I need to talk to you," Eliza whispered, "about Isolde."

The Faery beside Celia cleared her throat. Finally, Eliza stepped away, letting Celia's arms drop to her side.

Eliza took the woman in, breath catching in her throat. There was only one way to describe her, and that was ethereal; dark brown, almost black skin was highlighted with a gold shimmer that almost made it look like she was glowing. She wore a torn white dress, and gold jewellery on her hands and arms. Her hair was long and dark, braided away from her face, revealing thin pointed ears decorated with similar gold rings to the ones on her fingers.

Like the Fae Eliza had read about growing up, she was beautiful, immortal, deadly.

Eliza blinked and took another step back as a flush rose from her neck and onto her cheeks. "Hi. I'm Eliza."

"Soh." The Fae cocked her head. "You are the Ecix."

Eliza bit her lip and nodded. "In the flesh." She spared Celia a glance, who took a protective step towards Eliza. "Let me introduce you to the others."

The Fae let her stare drift over Eliza towards the three men who approached. "Two immortal knights and a warlock. Interesting."

"Where's Alicsar?" Celia asked, frowning.

"Gone." Eliza swallowed thickly. "Amitel took him back to the palace."

Celia's brows furrowed, but she didn't question it any further. She made introductions, explained what had happened. Amitel looked more intrigued than worried over the binding, but made no comment on it, which surprised Eliza.

"What exactly did you find?" Amitel asked, arms crossed.

The Blood Witch reached into her bag. She pulled out a scroll, perfectly preserved with magic, the thick paper golden with age. "The temple had an underground storage room. I suspect one of its Priests or Priestesses locked themselves within to protect the magic, but died." Celia handed the scroll to Amitel, who took it carefully. "We found something linked to Azula, but I believe it's written in a language only the Ecix can understand." Celia turned to Eliza. "We need to you to look at it."

Eliza frowned, and took the scroll from Amitel's outstretched hand. Her eyes grazed over the strange words. She didn't know what she was looking at exactly, but...

A symbol at the bottom of the page sparked a strange sense of déjà vu. Eliza ran her finger over it, wracked her brain for the memory of where she'd seen it before...

"Sorry," she said, interrupting whatever conversation had been happening around her. "I need to go."

No one said a word as she left the circle and strode to the stairs leading to her apartment. She took them two at a time, her mind a whirling mess of thoughts, heart thundering with each step. She entered the apartment. Her satchel was already waiting for her on the old table in her room.

She dropped into the chair and spread the scroll out in front of her. The language was beginning to form in her mind, a puzzle being put together as the spell work protecting her memories unravelled.

Alastor's book was heavy in her hands. There were several colourful tabs sticking out of the sides, and she flipped to a yellow one. The page held only one thing: a scribbled drawing, messy with thick black lines, overlapping words scrawled in red pen. She hadn't been paying attention to what she'd been drawing. And now it glared at her from the corner of the scroll.

She skimmed the old parchment found the strange symbols lining the bottom.

The words unjumbled themselves, forming coherent sentences in front of her eyes. The sensation made her head spin, but Eliza followed the list; she lit the wick of a candle and waited for the flame to burn bright, nearly an inch high. She lifted the scroll up to the light and watched as the words faded to reveal what looked like part of a map.

Not a spell, but not another story, either. "Instructions," Eliza whispered, bringing a hand to her mouth.

Adrenaline pumped through her veins. She'd stared at a map much similar to the one now forming on the paper. It sat rolled up in her satchel.

The old map she'd taken from King Bastian unfurled before her eyes. Eliza compared it to the new one; the marking of the Spring Manor sitting within the Willican forest near the ravine that split the Fae Territory from the rest of Cadira.

Marked along the new map was a tunnel leading below the ravine and into the Fae Territory, stopping somewhere amongst dense forest and unchartered territory.

The only marking visible was a raven.

A shiver danced down Eliza's spine as she rolled both maps up. The chair fell as she ran out of her apartment and down the old stairs. It felt like she was flying.

"I know what this is!" she said, sucking in a sharp breath as the group looked up from the camp fire. Eliza held out the maps to Celia. "Hold the scroll up to the fire."

Celia held up the page to the light. A small gasp slipped past her lips. "It's a map?"

Eliza nodded and showed her the old map. She watched as Celia compared the two, as she ran her finger over the corresponding paths.

The two maps were passed around. Eliza clamped her mouth shut as she looked between Celia, Amitel, and Soh; the warlock's eyes were wide, yet he hid his emotion well as he stared at the revealed map, the only other indication that he might be wary being the fist resting on the table. Celia and Soh shared a look.

"You two can't come with us," Eliza said finally, heart dropping into her stomach as she turned back to Celia, the warning from her sister's letter echoing in her head. "I mean, your bind, and the Wyld Hunt—"

"Of course I will go," Celia said, cutting Eliza off. "I will not let you go in there without me."

Eliza looked to Soh, for some kind of help, but the Fae woman merely shook her head. "You know nothing of the Faerie realm. It would be unsafe for you to venture in there without a guide."

"But what about *your* safety?" Eliza asked.

Celia shook her head. "We need the dagger."

Releasing a heavy breath, Eliza sat back and crossed her arms. A war raged inside her mind about what to do; the idea of waiting didn't sit right with her, though neither did having Celia and Soh join them in the Fae Territory. But Eliza knew nothing about Faerie, and she doubted either Caden or Darius knew the lands, where they would need to go or do to survive there. Amitel... she couldn't be sure about him, though when he didn't brag about his abilities, she knew deep down he would be as lost as she was.

"When do we need to leave?" Eliza finally asked, looking to each of the people around her.

Celia looked down at the map, then sighed. "We should leave tonight. The sooner we get the dagger, the safer you will be."

~

The magic of the portal disappeared, leaving them in a small fountain surrounded by white-capped forest. If Eliza couldn't feel the ancient magic, she would have suspected she were in Cadira still, and not the Fae Territory.

But in the land of Fae, everything was different. From the corner of her eye, she watched as the trees moved, their roots free of the earth as they danced with one another across the snow, uncaring of those who watched.

There were creatures—ones she saw normally in her world and Cadira—with magic that changed them into strange yet mythical beasts; a great, black bear stopped to watch them some distance away, but his eyes were silver, and he had antlers sprouting from his black fur. Perched on his shoulder was a blue bird that had the head of a snake, its wings—metallic, silver maybe—tucked into its small body.

Beautiful and deadly was the world of Faerie.

Eliza swallowed and stepped out of the fountain. A path had been cleared from the portal, leading through the forest, to where, she wasn't sure. The path was lined with decorative stone that reminded her of brambles.

"We must be careful," Soh murmured, her eyes dancing over the trees. "The Wyld Hunt can sense us now that we've entered the Wylderfae's territory."

"Wylderfae?" Eliza asked, brows furrowed.

The Seelie nodded. "The land you know as the Willican Forest. It borders the Seelie and Unseelie courts and separates us from the mortal lands. Here, it is most dangerous. The Fae who do not fit into the Courts reside here."

Eliza swallowed thickly as they began walking, following the path. "Are they dangerous?" she asked quietly.

"Not usually," Soh replied. "But the Wyld Hunt also resides here. They are the ones we must be wary of."

Eliza nodded, her stomach twisting. The land was filled with magic, so thick that she wondered if she could touch it if she ran her fingers through the air.

They walked in silence; Soh in the front with Celia at her side, their curse a clear band around each of their wrists, visible even under the dim light of the forest; at Eliza's side, she had Amitel, his eyes coasting over the forest until they landed on her. He gave her a wink and half-smile that she rolled her eyes at. On her other side, Darius walked with one hand on the pommel of his sword, the other clenched in a fist at his other side. Caden brought up the rear.

Eliza shivered and wrapped her arms around herself. The cold in the forest was damp and icy, digging through her layered cloak and into her skin, burrowing into her bones until her blood felt like sludge in her veins. No one else seemed to notice the way the air turned frigid—or if they did, they had a better way of hiding it.

Amitel brushed his hand against her side; warmth shot up from where his fingers touched her, and suddenly she was smothered by it. His magic wrapped around her, settling around her shoulders like a cloak.

She gave him a silent *thank you*, too afraid to speak. The small smile that played on his lips told her he knew.

The path wound around trees who stopped their dances, maybe to watch—Eliza doubted they were suddenly shy. Though she knew she should fear the land of the Fae, there was something so whimsically amazing about the realm, about the way its magic coiled around her in a familiar kind of way.

At the end of the path, the trees opened up to reveal a clearing with a wall of thorns surrounding it. A small pond iced over sat to one side with an old wisteria hanging over the water, a stone bench beneath the branches and hanging lilac flowers. On the other side of the clearing was a building, the roof covered in snow.

A woman with dark skin and even darker eyes appeared on the path. Pointed ears stuck out from her hair. The Faery had her hands clasped in front of her over her black robes. Rings of silver lined her long fingers—save one, her ring finger, which was only a nub on her hand. The sleeves of the robe had silver detailing's that ran up her arms to where it clasped at her throat, then down the front all the way to the hem that dragged along the frozen ground.

A shiver of anticipation made its way up Eliza's spine as the woman smiled. "Hello, Ecix and friends."

Eliza frowned. "How do you—"

"I know much. I have spent centuries learning how to identify your power, should you ever learn of this temple." She motioned to the building behind her; it reminded Eliza of a large, ornately designed mausoleum, with intricate designs etched into the stone exterior, depicting what she thought was a scene from a fairy tale. The columns looked like trees with roots that lined a path to the entrance.

"And who are you, exactly?" Eliza asked.

The Fae bowed, revealing a circlet of silver half covered by long locs. "I am Kyanya, the last Priestess of Azula."

36

THE SPELL
ELIZA

Eliza froze, her hands trembling as the dark-skinned Fae smiled. Behind her, Soh swore, but Eliza couldn't move as she took the priestess in.

Kyanya stepped forward, but before Eliza could stop them, she heard the *hiss* of blades being pulled free from their sheaths. Quickly, Eliza held up her hands. "Stop," she said, eyes flickering between Kyanya and her friends. "It's alright."

It was Soh that stepped forward into Eliza's line of sight; the Seelie had her weapon drawn, her attention on Kyanya. "She is Unseelie. She cannot be trusted."

Eliza had almost forgotten there was conflict between the main two Courts of Faerie: the Seelie and Unseelie. Broken up by seasonal courts, there was a war between the Fae older than Cadira itself, one Eliza couldn't begin to understand.

"Maybe we can?" Eliza asked. She turned to Kyanya. "You said you are the last Priestess of Azula? How? Why?"

Kyanya bowed her head, sadness filling her beautiful features. "We used to be many. Fae, half-Fae, mortals. The Goddess of Death had many followers before the Great War. We, her daughters, spread her word, and those who followed her would be protected in death.

"But everything changed once the Great War ended. Massacres of our temples saw the disappearance of our Goddess and our ways. Not long after, the Necromancers who once practiced under Azula's watchful eye were hunted into near extinction. Temples were purged and the Goddess of Death became something to fear in the eyes of mortals. Her children chose to join her rather than be tortured by angry men who did not understand our ways.

"Most of us chose death, which would have been much, much wiser than remaining, but those of us who stayed made the decision to carry on our work quietly, so that one day, when the Goddess decided to return to our world, we would be here to greet her."

Eliza swallowed thickly, glancing quickly to Soh, who looked unaffected by the Unseelie's words. "What do you know about Azula's dagger?" Eliza asked. "We found something—a map—that led us here. We need to summon it."

Kyanya cocked her head. "The dagger has not been summoned in centuries."

"But can we do it?" Celia asked, stepping forward. "Is it possible?"

Bowing her head, the priestess looked inclined to say no. Eliza watched her for a moment, saw the war waging behind her dark eyes. Fear and duty, Eliza realised, something she understood all too well.

"We need the weapon," Eliza said finally, drawing the attention of the priestess back to her. "The Dark Master is probably behind all the deaths, because he wants revenge for what the Ecix did to Valonde. We can end all of this, so that maybe you can worship peacefully." Eliza took a step forward. "Please. Let us finally end this."

The priestess watched her for a moment without response, her eyes narrowed. The friendliness from earlier slipped to reveal the Faerie within.

Fae were not humans, no matter how much they looked and spoke like them. Fae were otherworldly, the first creatures to have ever walked the lands of Cadira with the Elves. Their natures were different, not built on the same ideas of morality like mortals.

"Please," Eliza whispered. "We're so close now. I just need the dagger, and everything can end."

Something in the Unseelie's eyes changed then as strong wind filled the clearing. It picked up the loose strands of Eliza's hair and whipped it around her face. As it died down, the Unseelie finally relented.

"If you have the map, we will enter the temple," she said, voice soft.

Something in Eliza's gut told her the wind wasn't *just* a normal breeze, but she didn't want to consider it as anything other than natural.

Definitely not a Goddess giving her opinion on the matter.

Eliza shook her head. Beside her, Celia pulled the preserved map from her satchel. With it, a small gold ring fell into the snow, glinting in the mid-day sun.

Kyanya gasped. "Where did you find that?"

Celia bent and picked it up. "The temple in Cadira. Where we found the map. The owner—a Priestess or Priest, I assume—died in the catacombs beneath." Slowly, the raven-haired witch held out her hand for the Unseelie, who took the ring. It slid onto the nub of her finger, before disappearing with magic.

Sadness etched into her features. "Thank you for returning this."

Kyanya took the map and led them towards the temple. Up close, Eliza could finally see the details of the carvings; like the book she'd found in her room all those months ago, the scene depicted Azula as the Queen, who stood with dagger in hand, spirits rising around her. But in this depiction, she had her Fae Lover not far from her side, and her mortal husband at her feet.

Eliza swallowed thickly and looked away. Though, from the corner of her eye, she could have sworn the image moved.

The scent of incense and smoke wafted through the dark interior of the temple. Rows of relics and ceremonial weapons lined the intricately painted walls. Scenes of Azula, of her lover and the Fae jumped out at them as they walked, the colours vivid in the flickering light of the candles and torches.

A stone slab towards the back of the temple caught Eliza's eye. It was low enough to the ground that one could sit behind it on their knees and look out over the rest of the temple. Bare of any embellishments or relics, the slab looked strange compared to the rest of the temple. Out of place.

Their group stopped at the base of the stairs and watched in silence as the dark skinned Unseelie ascended, robes a whisper against the stone. An eerie silence permeated the temple, a sudden cold chilling to the bone. It lingered, a harsh reminder that they hadn't much time.

Eliza made a move to step up but someone's hand caught hers. When she looked back, she found Celia shaking her head. "No."

Frowning, Eliza turned to her fully. "It has to be me, Celia."

"No, it doesn't." Celia's bright eyes found that of the Unseelie, something passing between them. "I should do it. Eliza, it would be safer it was me."

"Though I agree the Ecix should be the one to search for the dagger, as it will likely call to her," the Unseelie mused, "you may try, Blood Witch."

"See?" Eliza hissed. "I should do it."

But Celia squeezed her hand, something like pain flashing in her eyes. "Please, Eliza."

Unsure of what to do, Eliza nodded, but as she watched Celia drop her supplies, unease rippled through her. Like something was going to go wrong.

Eliza couldn't shake the feeling, not when it tightened the muscles in her stomach or lifted the hairs on her arms.

"Here," Kyanya said, motioning to the stone. "Sit."

Celia nodded and climbed three steps to reach it. Chills raced up Eliza's spine as the Blood Witch settled in and the Fae moved to set up a ring of candles around her.

When they were set up, the Fae said, "Light them."

With flick of her wrist, Celia lit the candles. Eliza was mesmerised as they flickered against the dark stone interior. The room suddenly felt much smaller as the light reached the ceiling, casting dangerously strange shadows across the stone.

"Are you sure you want to do this?" Soh asked, rounding the stone slab. "This is dangerous."

Celia looked up from the flames, and took in their companion. Even in the dim light, with the ruined white gown, the gold embellishment, the gold dust that highlighted her, Eliza thought she looked ethereal.

A pang of frustration bit deep into the worry that already spread throughout Eliza. Without realising it, she'd taken Amitel's hand. The warmth was stable, familiar, a steady reminder that nothing was going to go wrong with the spell, not with all of them there, watching.

But what if something happens when she's inside the spell? Eliza supressed a shudder and squeezed Amitel's hand, focused on Celia and the Unseelie Fae.

The Blood Witch nodded and settled in, resting her hands atop her knees, palms facing up. "I know it is, but I don't care. I need to get the dagger, for Eliza."

A pang of guilt sliced through Eliza's heart as she met Celia's eye. But her friend revealed no fear or hesitation.

"These crystals will help you focus," Kyanya said, placing two jagged silver crystals on Celia's palms. "Focus your energy on them. They will allow you access into the spirit world."

Celia's brows furrowed. "How? No one but the Ecix should be able to do such a thing."

"These are conduits, a gateway almost. Use these to break through the natural barrier that separates mere mortals from the spirits. Once you are in, a spirit will guide you to what you seek."

Could have used a couple of them during my training, Eliza thought, frowning. She and Celia spared one another a lingering glance.

Celia closed her eyes, and Eliza watched as her breath evened out as her magic stroked eagerly at the flames surrounding her. It reached out to their group and ran over them lovingly, almost as if to say it was aware they were there, and was happy for them to be so close.

37

THE DEATH OF LAKE MAB
CELIA

Celia let the magic wash over her, the smell of incense and burning wax cloying her senses. The power of the two stones in her hands radiated through her body, igniting a magic in her blood she had never felt before. It reminded her of the warmth of the moon, its ever-present figure in the sky as it rotated through cycles much like mortals and witches, a powerful source of magic she bathed in. She clung to that feeling as it prickled over her skin, warming the power in her blood.

At the edge of her consciousness, a different kind of warmth settled over her skin, creating a barrier between herself and a darkness that crept towards her. This warmth made her heart skip a beat and soar, the magic winding with hers, like vines along a wall, strengthening and blooming along the foundations of her being.

But in the background, the darkness deepened, its roots digging deeper within her. The sickness inched up her spine towards her skull, a weed in the field of blossoming light, threatening, cold seeping into her bones.

Celia suppressed a shiver as she tightened her fists around the stones. The sharp edges drew blood, but she ignored the dim pain.

The blood will help. It had been a while since she'd drawn blood to aid in her spell work. But there was no connection to her Blood Witch sisters in the temple, no other strength to draw on but her own. Not even Soh or Eliza could help her now.

Darkness spread around her and settled into a mist that clung to her ankles and feet. She edged out of the bank of low fog and into a familiar clearing, pausing beyond the tree line to stare in horror at the once dark depths of Lake Mab, now barren save for the skeletons of those who had once dwelled within.

Sirens long since de-fleshed crawled from the lake's edge, much like those from Azula's secret city, though these dark creatures were escaping something terrible within the lake's depths. Celia crept closer, stepping around the spear of a siren, moss growing over the shaft, like gloves over the creature's fingers.

Where the water had once lapped at the grass, there was nothing but stone and the remnants of a great war fought beneath the water. As a child she had speculated about how deep the lake ran, where it went within the mountain, whether it existed elsewhere around her home.

Now, she could see within, the curtain of water no longer masking her view. She toed the edge, fear prickling her skin, and glanced down at what remained.

A sea beast, one of legend, lay at the bottom, curled around itself, like it had released itself from the battle and succumbed to wounds long since washed away. More bodies of sirens and small creatures lay around it, weapons of steel and stone covered by mud and debris, treasure once protected now uncovered, ready to be plucked like apples from a tree.

Celia stumbled back and covered her mouth with her hand. Her stomach churned, but not from what lay around her. The Shadow Sickness had followed her into the land of the dead, creeping through her bones like a serpent prepared to strike. She had wondered if she would be offered some reprise from it.

"You should not be here, sister."

Celia spun and searched the tree line for Isolde. The darkness was thicker between the trees, the fog billowing out from between thin trunks. Not even the forest was the same. What had once been a beautiful grove lay dead and forgotten, an illness much like her own creeping through the dead branches.

"Isolde?" Celia called, crossing her arms over her chest. A shiver wracked her body and she closed her eyes. She imagined the warmth she'd felt before entering the clearing; she let it sweep over her flesh and settle deep in her bones, repairing the damage her illness had left behind. It took her a moment to regain her ability to speak, but she opened her eyes and took in the darkness that lay around her once more. "Where are you?" she asked.

"I'm right here," her sister whispered in her ear.

Celia stumbled away, turning towards Lake Mab, but no one stood at its edge.

She was still alone.

"Isolde!" Her voice echoed through the clearing. "I don't have time for your games!"

From the tree line, her sister appeared, dressed in the red of the Blood Witches. Her dark hair billowed out around her, a diadem of silver crossing her forehead, a ruby dripping like blood in the centre. Her sister floated above the fog, over the bodies of the sirens, over the dead land that had once created safety for the two of them, where they could forego responsibilities and titles and merely be sisters.

Isolde stopped a foot away from Celia. Up close, her sister's skin was translucent, almost like crystal. It was unlike the dreams, where Isolde had appeared to her as if she was still alive. No, the woman before her was something else.

"I am not playing games." Her sister glanced around the clearing, dull-green eyes flickering over the corpses and the dried up lake. "You should not be here, Celia."

"I'm here for the dagger." Celia lifted her chin, mustering confidence that she did not feel. "Please, give it to me."

Isolde cocked her head. "What makes you think I possess the weapon?" She lifted a hand, motioning to the land, the death that lay around them. "We are not in the Aether, Celia. And I am no spirit guide. I am not capable of doing such a thing. If I could, I would have given Eliza the dagger months ago. I would have taken it for myself before my death."

Celia's heart skipped a beat, stumbling in her chest against her ribcage. "But–"

"The Aether will not open to you, my sister. You are not the Ecix. You may be touched by death, but until it consumes you, you will not see beyond this dark hell."

"What are you talking about, Isolde? We did the spell, we found the clues–*I* found what we needed to get here. I do not understand why I cannot take the dagger." Tears burned in the corners of her eyes, but Celia refused to let them fall. She sucked in a sharp breath and steadied herself.

I have not failed. I cannot fail. She repeated the words over and over in her mind, the mantra growing less confident the longer she stared at her sister.

"Only the Ecix may possess Azula's dagger." Isolde floated past her and to the lake's edge. "You know that, Celia, and yet you are here. And you have brought your Shadow Sickness with you."

"How do you know that?" Celia asked quietly.

Isolde looked over her shoulder and met Celia's stare. "I might be dead, sister. But I am not as gullible as Eliza and your other friends." A wistful smile carved itself across her lips. "I can sense the darkness that is slowly killing you. It killed me. It consumed me. I thought I might never see beyond it, see the Aether, but it did not work the way it was intended. Like it is with you."

"What do you mean?"

Isolde floated back to Celia and reached out a faded hand. "It will kill you, Celia. No matter how many potions and elixirs Lennox makes you, you will die. And I may never see you again."

"Isolde–" Celia swallowed hard, tears burning her eyes. She had feared as much, long ago, when it had first struck her. That she would die sooner, than she was meant to. But she resisted its dark embrace, for Eliza, because she still had her mission to guide her through the pain, the fear.

Celia squared her shoulders. "Then you must help me now. You must help me retrieve the dagger. I will search this lake if I must. The forest. I will find a spirit guide. I will enter the Aether by force if I must. But please, let me do this."

"Why are you so desperate, Celia? Why not allow Eliza to complete the spell—like she should?"

"It has to be me." Celia shook her head, Isolde's dying words echoing in her ears. "I made you a promise the day you died. Remember? I promised to stop the darkness. I promised to avenge you. I must stop the Dark Master. I cannot let him take you again. I cannot let him take Eliza."

Isolde approached, tears of blood streaking her luminescent skin. "You are free of your promise," she whispered. "You are free from me, from my war." Isolde brushed a hand—cold like ice, like death—over Celia's own tear-streaked skin. "You must live for yourself now, sister. You have devoted too much to me, to this mission. You and Brandon both. *Live*, for me, and for yourself. Find a cure for this sickness, fall in love, be there for Eliza when she needs it. But persist."

Celia released a breath, and a weight lifted from her shoulders and her heart, one she had ignored for almost two hundred years. The tears fell faster, harder, until she was sobbing in her hands, falling to her knees. "Thank you," she whispered through the harsh, gasping breaths. She lifted her head to take Isolde in.

Her sister seemed lighter since she first entered the clearing, the darkness around her almost brighter. Like a weight had been lifted off her own shoulders, much like it had Celia's.

She rose on shaky knees. A dull throb started in her temple, the ache so familiar she found it easy to ignore. "Isolde—"

Around them, the clearing shook, stone and debris crashing around them. Celia swayed and almost fell upon one of the skeletons, but she righted herself as the fog around her ankles shifted from mist to sand. Her head snapped up, and she found Isolde's fearful eyes on her.

"What's happening?" Celia asked. The ground shook again, but the fog held her in place, weighing her down. A tree behind Isolde snapped at the trunk and crashed into its brother, the sound rumbling through the clearing like thunder. "Isolde, what's going on?"

Her sister flickered in and out, like sunlight on a cloudy day. Celia reached for her, like she could steady Isolde, but her hand fell through the red of her sisters dress. "The Aether is trying to expel you. The Shadow Sickness—"

A low rumble followed by a crack rocked Celia back several feet. She crashed into the bank of the lake, wincing as her hand caught the edge of a siren's blade. A stone from within the caves beneath the lake crumbled and fell.

But Celia wasn't concentrating on what was falling apart behind her. Instead, her gaze fell on the thick fog, which shifted again, no longer like sand and no longer like mist. It darkened and twisted, growing larger, inching up her calves and thighs. Where this darkness touched, it burned her skin, even beneath the pants and stockings she wore, beneath her heavy boots.

Celia scrambled to her feet, but the darkness continued to climb up her body. The pain from the Shadow Sickness intensified, tightening around her stomach like barbed wire, reaching up her spine and taking hold of her heart with sharp, callous hands.

"Isolde," she whispered, staring up at her frightened sister, clutching at her chest like she could relieve the pressure surrounding her.

Isolde shook her head. "You have been here too long, Celia. Go. Go now and save yourself."

Her sister flickered out for a final time, disappearing within the darkness, returning to the land of the dead.

Celia released the magic. The pain flickered out, and so did the clearing. The death of Lake Mab fell away, and she entered the warm embrace of life once more.

38

THE BARRIER
ELIZA

Eliza kept her stare on Celia as the smell of incense became overwhelming, cloying as she breathed it in. Somewhere in the distance, the Unseelie Fae chanted. The words of the spell washed over Eliza, warming her from the chill of winter, and the fear that crashed into her as she watched.

A slow ache began in Eliza's temple. She shifted slightly at the discomfort, but the pressure only grew the longer the spell went on. *It's the spell.* Eliza closed her eyes and gritted her teeth. Celia was trying to break *into* Eliza's realm of death, but for whatever reason, Eliza knew she couldn't allow that.

The pressure split open and flowed throughout her entire body. Her knees buckled as a scream tore from her throat. An excruciating pain crashed into her, like an attack she couldn't see, couldn't protect herself from. Her ears rang from the impact, and through it she could barely hear voices.

Warm hands, cool hands. She felt them all over her body, as if trying to assess where the damage was. Her tongue was dry and heavy, making it hard to form words. But the pain wouldn't subside despite the warm, healing magic that surrounded her.

And then it was gone.

Eliza felt it pull back and recede, leaving only an echo of the agony that had befallen her. She opened her eyes to find her friends surrounding her, their expressions a mix of worry and confusion. Amitel hovered closer, and she realised then her head rest in his lap, one of his hands pressed to her chest, where her heart thundered out of control, the other on her forehead. Soh was on her other side, the Fae's hands alight with warm, golden light that quickly dimmed when their eyes met. And at her feet, the two knights, both as confused as everyone else, knelt, their hands raised with uncertainty.

"I'm fine," Eliza rasped, biting down on her lip as she attempted to sit up. Her muscles groaned in protest, but she managed to stand, her eyes snagging on Celia.

Blood dripped from her sisters nose and ears, face contorted in pain. Kyanya's eyes were white, unseeing, lips still moving, though even she looked in pain.

Eliza reached Celia before the others, felt the pain recede as soon as the stones were in her hands, as soon as Celia was released from the spell. Eliza pocketed the strange crystals as Celia opened her eyes.

"What happened?" Eliza asked.

The Blood Witch shook her head. "I failed. I couldn't... It wouldn't let me go any further."

There was a hush as the flames around them extinguished, leaving the temple dark and cold, unwelcoming.

"It isn't your fault," Eliza replied, helping Celia from the slab, despite the protest from her own body. "It's meant to be me. I felt it."

Eliza waited for an objection, but it didn't come. Amitel and Caden stepped up to the platform and helped Celia from the stone slab. They carried her limp form down, lowering her to the ground so the Seelie could heal any wounds from the spell.

Eliza could only watch for a moment before the pressure returned, though not from the spell itself—the pressure to find the dagger, of the impending deadline weighing heavily on her shoulders once more. She knew, deep down, there was no time to waste, not when the Dark Master could be close to learning what they already knew.

Before she could reach the dais, Amitel grabbed her arm. "You're too weak to do this," he hissed, red-flecked eyes searching hers. "You need to rest. Whatever Celia did in there is effecting you."

"I'm fine." Eliza pulled her hand away and was surprised when he let her go. "I can do this."

His eyes continued to search hers, so when he finally took a step back, she knew he understood. "Be careful."

She nodded and climbed the stairs to where the Unseelie Priestess waited, her eyes finally clear. She bowed her head in Eliza's direction.

Pulling the crystals from her pocket, Eliza sat on the slab. Around her, the candles erupted, the flames growing in twice their size until it looked like the bars of a cell. The crystals turned cold and burning in her hands.

And the spell consumed her.

39

PRINCESS OF RIDDLES
ELIZA

Broken glass and paper scattered the floor of the destroyed study. *What am I doing here?* Eliza wondered as she picked her way through the debris carefully.

Moonlight carved silver rays of light through the smashed window, illuminating the darkened room. The desk in the centre of the office had been tipped on its side; the six drawers that had ran down either side of the mahogany desk were strewn across the floor, contents spilling about the carpet. Eliza saw pretty silver and crystal pens and inkwells now shattered, the ink dry and staining the heavy rug that covered the stone floor. Jewellery that had been hidden away now peaked out from beneath paper and heavy shards of glass.

In the corner of the room, someone wept; Eliza could just hear them over the howling wind.

Eliza took a hesitant step towards them, heart racing. Dressed in a yellow night-gown and white feet bloody, the little girl looked up at her with silver tears in her wide, dark eyes.

"How are you here?" she asked. Hair the same colour as her brother's hung heavily in her eyes, obscuring her face. "How can you see me?"

My spirit guide, Eliza thought. Just like when she'd entered the Aether last time. Isolde had been there to guide her, and now another had appeared to take that duty.

The little girl... Eliza recognised her and the room. The study had once been the late Queen's, and was now boarded up and left to be forgotten by the passages of time. Eliza herself had stumbled upon it once, felt the strong pull of death from within, and had left it alone. She'd never thought on it again, only because it had never felt right to.

But the little girl... She had the same dark eyes as her father, the hair of her brother. She was as pretty as Eliza remembered from her visions of the Spring Manor.

The princess.

Why they were in the late Queen's study, Eliza wasn't sure.

The princess continued to weep as the study fell away, revealing a misty grey room, fog wrapping itself around Eliza's jean-clad legs. Somehow, she'd changed from breeches into something comfortable, casual. It felt wrong in a way.

"Princess?" Eliza called into the fog, turning in a slow circle to take it all in. She was almost alone, save for the figures walking through the mist and the outline of trees. Now she was in the Aether proper.

More spirits. They didn't seem to be paying any attention to Eliza, so she remained where she was, careful not to disturb any. She couldn't help but wonder if Isolde was somewhere, wandering alone.

"You are the Ecix," a small voice said, floating from behind her. "The new one."

Eliza spun quickly and paused as the princess reappeared, her feet no longer bloody. She didn't look dead, but the tint of death covered her dark eyes.

Slowly, Eliza nodded. "Yes."

"Why are you here?" the princess demanded, her head cocked.

"I need Azula's dagger," Eliza replied. "Do you think you can take me to it?"

The princess swept a hand through the mist, conjuring up the dagger as an illusion. "The dagger will not go with just anyone. You might be the Ecix, its true holder, but a weapon carved from death will not be wielded by another."

"Another what?" Eliza asked, heart thumping loudly in her chest.

"Another weapon carved from death." The princess blinked her wide eyes. She didn't look thirteen, but somehow older, wiser. Different. Not entirely right. "You and it were created in the same way, forged by the same hands. It is yours, but it isn't. Do you understand?"

Suddenly, the illusion disappeared, and in the princess's hands was the real dagger, exactly how Eliza had imagined it. The hilt was carved from bone, a stark white with ornamental engravings, while the blade itself was something else; not quite metal, more like stone, yet it shined like steel.

Eliza took a step back, her wide eyes on the dagger. Everything she needed... *Right in front of me*. If she could just figure out what the princess wanted...

Swallowing thickly, Eliza dragged her eyes from the dagger. "What do I need to understand?"

The princess did not reply straight away, her eyes glued to Eliza. Her small hands only gripped the hilt lightly, giving Eliza the idea of snatching it from her hands.

"Why the riddle?" Eliza asked, eyes still focused on the dagger.

The princess, noticing her gaze, removed the dagger entirely. "Because you are not ready. You don't know enough yet. To let you take the dagger would mean the death of us all."

No. No. Eliza shook her head. She had to be ready, she *needed* to be ready. The Dark Master was out there, and he wanted her dead— wanted her friends and family dead for helping her. No one else was more ready than she was. So long as he was allowed to roam Cadira, *he* would bring war.

She trained, she worked with the Blood Witches, she studied. She *found* the lost prince. She risked everything to go searching for the dagger.

She had died, over and over again, without the dagger.

The dagger was her only hope.

"Not ready?" Eliza asked. Anger rushed through her, warming her cheeks. "I need the dagger. I need to defeat the Dark Master before he hurts anyone else!"

"The dagger is not to be used for revenge," the girl replied, voice even.

Eliza scoffed. "The Dark Master killed you, remember? Took your little brother and hid him, brainwashed him! I found him! I found your brother and he is safe. Now I need the dagger to finally defeat the monster hunting me."

The princess shook her head again, a sadness entering her eyes. "It is not to be used to take revenge, even on murderers. Until you learn the truth, until you understand what really needs to be done, then you will have the weapon you seek. Head the warnings of your past. Do you understand?"

"Understand?" Eliza asked. "Understand what? He's a killer."

"And so are you."

Eliza stumbled back a step, and the princess continued, "You feel guilt for what has been taken, yes. But your past does not."

"My past does not define me, Princess," Eliza hissed. "My past will not dictate my future." The anger rose inside of her until it was all she could feel.

In the back of her mind, she felt the familiar touch of Celia, the sensual trace of Amitel, even the frigid bite on Kyanya, telling her to remain calm.

Sucking in a breath, Eliza looked to the princess again. "My future, the future of everyone I love is on the line. The Dark Master will not stop until he either has my power or sees it destroyed. But he will hurt everyone in his path to do it."

The princess circled her, each step slow, calculating. "Until you understand why, you cannot wield the weapon of death. Until you know what truly happened in Valonde, until you know about the Original wielder, you will not be ready."

She stopped in front of Eliza, head cocked. The fog rose up to the little princesses knees, consuming her legs, torso. "When you are ready," the princess repeated, voice now soft, distant, "you will know."

The princess disappeared, leaving Eliza alone in the darkness.

"Princess?" Eliza called, spinning. Panic rose in her.

"Princess!"

And then the Aether disappeared.

~

Eliza opened her eyes and screamed in frustration as burning tears fell from her eyes. The candles extinguished, and the crystals in her hands turned to dust.

In an instant, Celia was at her side, concerned eyes searching her face, body. "What happened?" the Blood Witch asked, pressing a cool hand to Eliza's cheek, wiping away a falling tear.

Standing, Eliza walked on wobbly knees, jumping from the stone slab and onto the dais. She descended, pushing through her friends and out of the temple, where a sharp wind cut through the clearing, stinging her warm cheeks. Overhead, the sky darkened with storm clouds, lightning cutting through the darkness.

A shiver worked down her spine as she sucked in three cooling breaths. Anger so pure burned like a white light inside her.

"Eliza!" Amitel appeared beside her, hands wrapped around her upper arms. "What happened? Where's the dagger?"

"Gone," Eliza said through gritted teeth. "I failed."

She pushed Amitel aside and followed the path back to the fountain, where she escaped into the tunnels, guilt and shame marking her every breath.

40

EXPECTATIONS
CELIA

Her silence was deafening.

Celia walked behind Eliza, watched her tense back as they followed the tunnels back to the great city of Azula. She'd been mute since they'd started their trek over an hour ago; Celia had found her after her escape from the temple standing with her back to the portal, and she'd said nothing once they were ready to return to the underground city.

No one tried to speak to her, either. Every step made Celia's stomach churn with worry and fear; she opened her mouth several times to ask Eliza how she was, to see if she needed something, but each time Celia was unable to form the words.

She released a heavy breath as the city came into view.

At her side, Soh made a sound, but she didn't say anything. The silence had sobered everyone; the knights were sombre as they took up the rear of their party, hands resting on the pommels of their swords, heads bowed.

Soh remained at her side from the moment she'd come out of the spell. Had healed her of the spells damage. Celia appreciated it, more than the faery might have known. Watching Eliza had brought back memories she otherwise would have kept hidden away. But having Soh at her side gave her a kind of calm stability she didn't realise she needed.

Amitel was on her other side, eyes focused on Eliza's back as she guided them back to the city. He'd shoved his hands into the pockets of his pants; Celia knew him well enough to know there was something on the tip of his tongue, but he bit down on his words.

For that, she wasn't sure if she was glad or not.

At the mouth of the tunnel, Amitel rested a hand on her forearm, stopping her. Soh walked several paces ahead and only stopped when the knights passed her. The barrier around the city shimmered, but it held as they stepped through.

For a moment, she and Amitel watched as Eliza disappeared down one of the many streets, while Caden and Darius each took a different route around the edge of the city. Soh hesitated at the barrier, but when Celia nodded, the Fae woman stepped into the safety of the city, and waited.

"We need to give her space," he said finally, gaze trained on the street Eliza had disappeared down.

Celia tensed. "She needs me, she needs—"

"No," he replied, voice soft. "She needs to breathe. Too much is expected of her, and going to her now might very well break her. She doesn't need any more pressure."

"She's my sister," she snapped, immediately regretting it when his eyes found hers. "I know what she needs."

For a moment, he was quiet. He regarded her darkly, eyes narrowed, but then he shook his head. "She just lost the one thing that might have saved her life. She doesn't need some sappy pep talk about finding it later. She doesn't think there's any time left. The only way to get it was ripped from her." He paused and released a breath. "She needs a friend. Not an ally."

Deep down, Celia knew he had a point, but she couldn't believe it was *Amitel* telling her how she should approach her sister. Amitel, who had worked with the Dark Master, who had spent years on the sidelines because of what the Ecix had done.

The same Amitel who knew how much Eliza didn't trust him.

Celia shook her head, and left Amitel standing in the mouth of the tunnel, his words ringing her ears despite the distance she put between them.

~

Eliza threw her belongings into her bags with a force that worried Celia. She knocked quietly on the doorframe of the small bedroom.

Eliza tensed and paused, hand clutching a rumpled tunic. She didn't turn as she said, "What?"

Celia's lips thinned. "Are you alright?"

For a moment, Eliza was silent. It happened slowly, and Celia watched every second of it; the bowing of Eliza's head and shoulders, the dropping of the tunic, the curl of her body as she dropped to her knees beside the cot, and the soft cries that almost broke her.

"I failed," she whispered, voice breaking on the final word. "I wasn't strong enough."

Tears burned in Celia's eyes. She approached Eliza and knelt beside her, touching her shoulder so she knew Celia was there, and opened her arms when her sister fell into her chest.

"It isn't your fault," Celia murmured, resting her chin against the top of Eliza's head. "None of this is your fault."

"But it is." Eliza sobbed into her chest and fisted her hands into Celia's cloak. "Maybe if I'd trained *harder*, if I knew more about the Ecix, I could have gotten it. I just don't *understand—*" She stopped, the words dying on her lips.

Celia closed her eyes and tightened her arms around her sister. "The only ones at fault here are the Blood Witches. If they had actually *prepared you*, you might have had a chance. But there have been forces working against you since the very start, Eliza." She pulled back.

"None of this is your fault."

Eliza's eyes were closed as she sucked in a breath. She tensed at the sound of footsteps, dropped her head into her hands.

Celia looked up and found Amitel watching them... watching *Eliza*. Red swirled within the gold of his irises. After years of friendship, she'd realised it happened only when his emotions were getting out of control.

Rising, Celia kept one hand on Eliza's shoulder. Her sister looked up from her hands, took in Amitel.

The warlock looked from Eliza to Celia. The look in his eyes was enough for her to purse her lips. She didn't want to admit it, but he had been right.

The pressure was too much for her.

"Everyone is ready," he said finally, crossing his arms. "They're waiting at the portal."

Eliza released a heavy breath. "Alright." She stood, finished gathering her belongings. Celia silently took on of Eliza's bags and passed it off to the waiting warlock, who accepted it without a word.

Shouldering her satchel, Eliza paused, standing between them. The tears had dried on her cheeks, but her eyes were red and puffy, skin red and raw. Celia didn't have to say anything; Eliza composed herself with a few, steadying breaths.

"Are you ready, love?" Amitel asked, voice soft.

Eliza blinked up at him; Celia watched as something passed in her sisters eyes. "Yeah."

Celia said nothing as they left the apartment and started for the portal. Standing below it, Soh, Darius, and Caden waited. Soh had changed her looks, donning glamour to appear more human, though the beauty and ancient power that clung to her remained. She had changed into something more appropriate, too; dark brown breeches tucked into ankle-high boots, a white tunic with the sleeves rolled up to her elbows, revealing her gold bands and rings. The clothes she'd chosen had all been Celia's, from the bags at her feet.

Eliza clutched Celia's hand, and as a group, the power of the portal washed over them. It dropped them in the fountain, water and snow lapping at their legs, but Celia didn't feel the icy bite of the cold. A cool wind drifted over them, ruffling their hair.

The maze shifted, opening up to reveal the path out to the Spring Manor. Celia and Soh stepped out of the fountain first, followed by the knights who left for their horses. Celia turned to say something to Eliza, but she found her sister standing several feet away, her arms crossed tightly over her chest, a faraway look in her eyes.

Amitel approached Eliza, his brows drawn in worry. It hadn't escaped her how protective he'd become, but she'd thought it only because he was trying to make up for his betrayal.

Celia's eyes narrowed as his hand brushed Eliza's. No words passed between them.

He walked away, joining the knights at the mouth of the maze, the reins of their steeds in hand, and soon after Eliza followed. For a moment, Celia could only stand there as the snow drifted down, like the world hadn't just shifted.

Soh, at her side, touched her arm. "Are you alright?"

Celia nodded. "Yes. Of course."

But even as she joined her friends, she couldn't ignore the strangeness of what she'd witnessed, and what it could possibly mean.

The portal appeared, and they stepped through as one.

It was time to face the king.

41

CONSEQUENCES
ELIZA

King Bastian waited, amusement glinting in his eyes as their party approached him in the grand, ornate throne room. Eliza didn't have it in her to marvel at how beautiful it was, with its vaulted ceilings and wide, open windows that overlooked the palace gardens on either side.

Every step was muffled by the thick rug running the centre of the room. There were only twelve guards spread throughout the throne room, all so silent she wondered if they were actually fake, just suits of armour set up to scare potential threats.

Sitting on his throne, Bastian looked no different, maybe a little more high-spirited than when she'd last seen him. He didn't seem all that surprised to see them, either.

Standing at his side, Alicsar met Eliza's eye. The tension in his arms and shoulders was enough to tell her that what was about to happen wasn't going to be good.

Three feet from the base of the throne, they stopped and dropped into bows. Eliza remained at the front of their party, Celia and Amitel on either side of her, while Soh, Darius, and Caden remained behind them. Upon their arrival, the king had demanded to see them—all of them—in his throne room. That should have given Eliza enough of an idea of the consequences she'd face. Public settings would leave no argument. She'd lost her right to private meetings with the king, because he no longer trusted that they shared the same goals.

And that is fine by me, she thought, rising.

"Your Majesty," she started, voice flat.

He gave her a half smile, eyes roaming her body. "I see you are without something."

She didn't mean to flinch, but the reminder of how badly she'd failed made her react more than she would have liked. It told him that she'd failed, that her escape had been for nothing.

Eliza cleared her throat and looked up at the king. "We found what we needed to get the dagger, but it would not be handed over."

The king raised a brow. "Would not be *handed over?*" he questioned. "Could you not take it?"

She shook her head. "No. Magic prevented it." She didn't want to mention that his dead daughter was her spirit guide in the Aether, or that it was her who had stopped Eliza from getting the dagger in the end.

"We got close, your Majesty," Celia said from behind her. "We found a way to summon it. We just could not attain it."

The king's dark eyes fell on Celia, who merely straightened her shoulders and lifted her chin in some sort of defiance, her way of telling him that she was not afraid.

Eliza wanted to emulate that, but all she felt was exhaustion.

The king's disdainful gaze returned to her. "You are no longer permitted to leave the palace without a chaperone or guards," the king said. "Your training will continue with the Blood Witches, and you will spend your afternoons with Lennox. You will be with Lady Cordelia in the mornings, for dress fittings and basic lessons in preparation for the wedding."

So I won't have time to look for the Dark Master. She should have expected it.

"Time spent with anyone else will be limited and monitored. You will not be given the chance to leave again, and if you so much as try, we will know. You will also continue courting Alicsar in front of the court to maintain expectations and your images—they think you went with the Blood Witches to be blessed for the union." The king shook his head. "Now is the time to show that we are a united front. There will be no more discussion about this."

Lennox appeared behind the throne, her face a neutral expression, eyes revealing nothing. Instinctively, Eliza stepped in front of Celia protectively, remembering full well that Darius and Caden had been sent to protect Eliza—and let Celia die if they were attacked.

Eliza swallowed as Lennox stopped in front of her. Their eyes met, but one glance down made Eliza's stomach turn, her heart twisting. The shine of the golden bracelet, the one to mute Eliza's powers, glinted in the pale light of the throne room.

Not again...

She should have known, and yet she still felt a pang of betrayal as it vanished from Lennox's hands and reappeared on her left wrist. The weight was familiar and yet foreign, heavier than it had been before.

"You will wear it for the remainder of basic training," King Bastian said as the Blood Witch stepped away from Eliza. "It'll also keep you at the palace."

"So I can't leave again," she breathed. Tears burned in her eyes and down her throat as she struggled with her composure. "Majesty, I—"

He held up a hand, silencing her. "You made me a promise the last time and you broke it. Forgive me for not trusting your word, Miss Kindall."

Eliza clamped her lips shut, but her gaze went to Alicsar, who looked as upset as she felt. She couldn't find it within herself to blame him for what was happening—it was her fault anyway.

"None of you will continue your search for the Dark Master. I trusted Amitel to take this mission and he failed." The king's eyes roamed over their party. "I do not even know where Commander Thorne is. But no problem. I will find others to do the job. We have other matters more important."

"King Bastian, please," Eliza said. "The Dark Master is more dangerous than ever. If we don't find a way to defeat him, there's no point in going through with a wedding that might not happen if I *die* three weeks in!"

The king's eyes hardened, the colour of his iris turning black. The room fell into a silence so thick she could have cut it with a knife. And then he gave her a tight lipped smile. "You have one week, Elizabeth Kindall. Then you marry my son."

~

Eliza collapsed onto her bed and released a heavy breath. Every muscle in her body ached, every breath a chore for her lungs. Her heart thumped evenly, hard against her ribs.

I failed, and nothing has changed.

She should have been relieved that the worst to happen was her continued engagement to Alicsar, that nothing had happened to her grandfather or Kay.

Yet now she felt more trapped than ever.

The bracelet burned where she twisted it on her wrist, another painful reminder that she wasn't free at all, and still remained a pawn in the king's game for power. He didn't care that they were all still in danger, that the Dark Master would be hunting her more now after her attempt to get the dagger. He wouldn't care if innocents got in his way, because though the king fought for power, the Dark Master cared only for revenge, and she feared that might be more of a powerful motivation.

His need for vengeance had started another war, one that the people of Cadira and the rest of their world were still coming back from. It had taken him almost eight hundred years to seek his revenge—would he be so quick to start another war?

She didn't want to underestimate him, but hoped he wouldn't.

The busy murmur of the palace made her ears ring; after so many days underground, where the only constant sound was the ticking clock, she found herself suddenly uncomfortable by the hum of palace life.

Well we don't have a choice now, she thought, frowning. She'd enjoyed the silence, but now it was time for her to get used to the liveliness of the palace once more.

But that didn't mean she wanted to *participate* in it.

Eliza tried to ignore the sudden knock at her door. Exhaustion pulled at her from every direction, but she needed to bathe and eat. She knew sleep would have to wait, but it would wait longer if she answered the door.

The knock came again, this time more persistent. Heaving a breath, Eliza climbed from the bed and strode to the door, flinging it open without so much as a care as to who might be behind it.

Tears burned in her eyes as her grandfather stood there, a pink and green tote bag slung over his shoulder.

"Grandpa?" she whispered. She didn't stop the tears from rolling down her cheeks as she threw herself into his arms. For several moments, they stood there, Eliza sobbing into his chest, his arms wrapped tightly and securely around her.

"I failed," she finally whispered, once the tears stopped falling and she could catch her breath. "I didn't get it."

Davis rubbed his hand in slow circles on her back. "You won't always win, my girl. Sometimes you lose battles."

She sniffed. "I needed to win this one."

"And you will." He pulled back and wiped away a stray tear. "Not every battle will be as easy as the one before. You found the prince, and I am still so, so proud of you. You did what no other could."

"I only did that because the Dark Master wanted me to find him," she muttered under her breath. "But I almost had it. I almost had the dagger."

Davis pursed his lips. "And I am proud of you for getting that far," he said. "Once again, you did what no one else could do. And that had nothing to do with the Dark Master and his plans."

She shrugged. "It could have. How do I know he didn't just make me think the dagger was my only way? How do I know he didn't plan all of that?" As she pulled away, she couldn't help but wrap her arms around herself as a shiver coursed over her body. "He could already have the dagger. And he could be planning on using it on *me*. And grandpa, I might not come back again. I don't think even the Ecix can withstand the power of that blade and what it can do."

"Your fear is not unfounded, Eliza," he murmured. "Kay and I are already looking for alternatives. But you are safer here, where we can all protect you, until there is a way to stop the Dark Master once and for all."

Another shiver, this one dark and cold, ran down her spine. The promise in his eyes made the weight on her shoulders lift, if only a little bit, which did more for her than he would ever know.

Eliza released a breath as an attendant appeared behind Davis; the young man was tall and lanky, with dark eyes that looked anywhere but at her.

"Can I help you?" she asked, tone sharp. She immediately regretted it as her grandfather pressed his lips into a thin line, as the attendant took a small step back.

In his hands he held a letter, the handwriting familiar. Eliza took it from him and watched, an apology on the tip of her tongue, as he escaped from her rooms and down the hall.

Eliza released a breath and broke the red-wax seal. Celia's handwriting decorated the parchment, though her note was only short.

Eliza,
We are meeting in Alicsar's suite to discuss what we do next. You should be there.
Celia

She bit her lip. "Celia wants to meet." When she looked up, she found her grandfather nodding, his smile soft.

He pressed a hand to Eliza's cheek. "Your friends await," he murmured before kissing the top of her head. "Go and see them. I will come visit as soon as I can." He handed her the tote bag, one Eliza had gotten at a market years ago. It usually lived in a cupboard of reusable bags they took to the grocery store.

Swallowing, Eliza rifled through the contents and laughed softly. Instant coffee, a brand-new mug, bags of chocolate and gummy bears—all things she immediately needed and wished to consume, even though the note in her hand was urgent.

Eliza closed the bag and set it down beside the door. She looked back to her grandfather, who was already stepping away—already prepared to say good-bye.

Could she do it again? Keep doing it? A frustrated breath left her lips, but she nodded and met his stare—likely for the last time until her wedding. "I miss you and Kay and Odin."

He smiled. "We miss you too. Now, go, you don't want to keep them waiting."

Part of her wanted to, but she knew she couldn't. They needed to talk about the king, about their mission and what they needed to do next.

Her heart ached as she pulled away from her grandfather and said goodbye to him once more.

42

NIGHTMARES
ELIZA

Eliza entered Alicsar's suite hesitantly, her heart hammering loudly in her chest. The guards surrounding his chambers watched her silently, their helms locked in place, with only darkness and shadows visible beneath the bars of steel.

She couldn't help but wonder what, exactly, would be reported back to the king, though part of her didn't care. Let him think what he wanted, she decided. Perhaps he'd be glad to know she was spending time with her future husband.

Alicsar's suite wasn't far from her own, though it was twice as large, with a receiving room, office, bathing chamber, and bedroom, situated in a tower with even more space above them. She wondered if she would have to live in his suites once they were married, or if they'd both have to move to the royal wing, where the rooms were designed for couples to have separate beds.

She shook her head. The thought made her stomach churn.

The office door was propped open, revealing a small room with a large oak desk, a wall of bookshelves, and a round window that overlooked the city. Eliza slid into the warm room and found her friends already waiting; Celia stood by the window, her long hair left unbound. She wore a dress of deep green, simple with white sleeves that covered her arms. At the desk, Amitel and Alicsar, both men who had betrayed her—one because an oracle told him he would, the other because he'd been raised to do so. Amitel looked somewhat regal in his white long-sleeved shirt and black vest, knee high boots polished to shine, while Alicsar looked comfortable in a loose tunic and breeches.

Even the knights of the Brotherhood had joined the party; both wore simple guards clothing, which looked somewhat strange on their tall frames. Darius looked the most uncomfortable, though the light from the fire highlighted the fine structure of his bones, which only further reminded her that he was half-Fae, while Caden looked surprisingly normal, mortal even, standing by the mantle.

Then there was the Faery, Soh, who had changed her appearance to look more human back at the manor. Her ears had softened out and so had the sharpness of her features, though there was still no doubt that she was beautiful. The etherealness of her did not disappear, no matter how much she tried to change. Even wearing a pair of Celia's pants and a shirt Eliza was sure used to belong to Thorne, nowhere near as regal as those made by the Fae, she still stuck out with her striking eyes and the unnatural way she held herself.

Suddenly, Eliza wished she'd changed, but her leggings and sweater would do.

From the window, Celia smiled, "Is everything okay?"

"Yeah, everything is fine," Eliza replied, crossing her arms. "What do we do now?"

"We bide our time." Amitel picked up something from the desk and toyed with it. "We keep looking."

"We need to understand *why* you weren't given the dagger," Soh continued, "and see if we can change that."

"Once we're married, Eliza and I will have no time to help—my father will make sure of that." Alicsar stepped towards Eliza, though he hesitated and stepped back. "He's going to make it difficult on all of us."

Eliza released a heavy breath. "What if the Dark Master got the dagger first?" she asked, biting her lip. "What if we were too late?"

Celia shook her head, but it was Soh who answered, "What happened inside the spell, exactly?"

She hadn't been able to tell them what had happened within the Aether. The shock of being unable to take the dagger had left her speechless, and the guilt for not being strong enough to get it had ate at her every step back to Azula's city. She hadn't even been able to tell Celia, though it wasn't like she'd had time to recount everything. She'd wanted to escape her failure as quickly as possible.

But she sucked in a breath and released it slowly as the memory of her time in the spirit realm. "I was met by my spirit guide."

"Who?" Soh asked, voice hard.

Eliza swallowed met Alicsar's stare. "The princess. Your sister."

His eyes widened and he averted his gaze, jaw tightening. But he said nothing.

"She said I wasn't ready for it." Eliza closed her eyes, and the image of the young girl came back, the dagger in her hands. "She said the dagger and I were forged from the same material. That it was mine. But I couldn't have it. Not without understanding. She said it wasn't to be wielded for revenge."

When she opened her eyes, she found all eyes on her, their stares burning holes into her. Eliza shifted uncomfortably and looked away from them. "I don't understand what she wants," she finished, shaking her head.

"Where would we find information about Eliza's connection to the dagger?" Alicsar asked. "The Ecix's connection, even? If we can understand how the power was created, we can get the dagger, right? Could that be what the spirit guide meant?"

Eliza looked to Celia, who bit her lip. "It's entirely possible, but..." She sighed loudly and crossed her arms. "Most of that information is kept under lock and key in the Labyrinth Mountains. You have to be of a certain rank to know even the smallest detail about the Ecix, and if the Blood Witches are willing to let me die, then I assume I cannot access any of it."

"What about me?" Eliza asked. "Can I know any of it?"

"Not here, you can't. The Blood Witches would need you in the Mountains, where they can control what you learn and don't learn. Here, there are too many ears."

Eliza rubbed her eyes. "So, there's nothing we can do?"

"What about those other cities you mentioned? Like the one beneath the ruins of King Bastian's manor?" Caden asked, pressing forward. His bright eyes went to Celia, then drifted to Eliza. "They're hidden all over this land, right? Could they have information that the Blood Witches have?"

Eliza hesitated and bit her lip. Her gaze cut to Celia, who watched both knights carefully. During their time together, Eliza hadn't asked whether they could be trusted. The knights could have been tasked with keeping an eye on Eliza, reporting back what she learnt. The thought made her stomach churn.

"It's possible," Eliza replied hesitantly, as Celia found her stare. "There are at least five more that we know of because of the map, but if there are more, they aren't listed. Any one of them could hold the secrets of the dagger."

Celia cocked her head. "There may also be more temples, like the one hidden in the Willican forest. Ones that might still hold information on Azula, on her Priestesses."

"Then that is where we will go," Soh replied, though her eyes were on Celia. "We must break this bind, but you were right about stopping a war. The Dark Master is changing the very magic of our land, even in the Fae Territory. I do not think our world is prepared for another war."

Eliza swallowed thickly. "What do you mean? What do the Fae know?"

Soh met her gaze. "The Seelie have been in contact with the Courts of Light. They believe there will be a war unlike any we've seen, one greater than even the Great War, with a death toll much higher. It could destroy our land."

"Why in the name of the Goddess did you not mention this earlier?" Caden asked, pushing away from the wall. "This might have been information better received *before* we failed in locating the dagger."

The Seelie Fae rose sharply from her chair, lips pulled back in a snarl. "This is not something I would have trusted you with *earlier*, Knight of the Brotherhood. Knowledge of a brewing war could send this world into a panic, could destroy us before the Dark Master's forces even *touch* us."

Eliza swallowed down panic that bubbled in her chest. But Soh had a point; if the rest of Cadira knew there was a serious threat of war, they wouldn't know what to do with themselves. The last war they'd seen was two-hundred years prior, and since then the land has known stability and peace.

A war that could end the land. All because of her, what her past self had done, what her *power* had done.

Chest tightening, Eliza struggled to breathe through the fear and panic that rolled through her. More, now than ever, she wished she was going to the Labyrinth Mountains to train, to learn more about herself—about what she had done and what she could do.

She needed to know how to stop the war.

"She right," Eliza finally bit out, shaking her head. "We don't need to cause a panic about a war we can try and stop. But King Bastian should know."

"I'm sure he's already aware," Celia murmured, touching Eliza's arm, worry colouring her eyes. "Are you alright?"

Eliza nodded. "Fine." Her eyes went back to Soh. "How much do the Courts know?"

"I do not know. That is all I learnt before..."

She didn't need to finish. *Before the Wyld Hunt blew their horn.*

"Then we need someone to go to the Courts," Eliza said. "We need to know what they know. And the Fae. If they have any inclinations to *when* the war—"

Celia squeezed Eliza's arm, stopping her. "We have time."

"How can you be so sure?" Eliza asked.

The Blood Witch gave her a soft smile. "Do not pressure yourself with all these responsibilities. Let us take one step at a time. Otherwise we will cause panic within ourselves, which will do us absolutely no good. We have only just returned, so let us all take a breath, and then we will decide where to go from there. Alright?"

Eliza closed her eyes and nodded. *I wish Thorne was here*, she thought, pressing her lips into a thin line.

Celia pulled away from her, and as if sensing Eliza's thoughts, she said, "We need to send a message to Brandon. Tell him what we found."

Eliza nodded. She didn't want to argue with that—despite how much it had hurt for him to walk away, she wanted him back, wanted to talk to him about everything. She wanted and needed his guidance, like before.

She felt eyes on her as she walked to the desk. Someone handed her a quill and parchment and she scribbled a quick letter, one with a brief explanation. If he wanted to know more, she decided, he would have to return and ask her himself.

When the letter was finished, she checked over it one last time before scrunching it up. The paper ignited in her hands, turning to ash, remnants of the letter floating into the air before disappearing. The ash, too, vanished from her hands, off to find Thorne where ever he was.

Eliza closed her eyes and curled her hands into fists, and hoped it would find him well, and soon, he would return.

43

THE TRUTH
CELIA

Celia perched carefully on the edge of her bed as Soh wandered around the suite. The book stacks and research were gone, likely cleared from her room once the king and Lennox had realised Celia had run off with Eliza and Amitel, and taken Alicsar with them.

The only research she had now was what she'd thought to take with her. She wouldn't be surprised if Bastian or Lennox had destroyed everything else; her written notes, the pages and pages of theories and half-drawn maps leading through the mortal world and Cadira during their search for Alastor and the dagger.

A heaviness settled on her shoulders as she took in the room that had once been the centre of all her research after finding Alicsar. Now it held nothing but her clothing and a deep, unwavering sorrow.

"What do we do now?" Soh asked finally, stopping at Celia's desk. She rested a hand on the dark, glossy wood, fingers splayed across the hard surface.

Celia's gaze ran up Soh's arm, over the white circle that bound them, past the gold bands and the rolled sleeves of Celia's shirt, to finally meet the Fae's eye. "We look for a way to break the bind," Celia replied. Her stomach fluttered, and she looked away, willing her cheeks not to burn.

Soh pursed her lips, quiet for a moment before saying, "Perhaps it is not the most... *crucial* of missions."

"I thought you would want to be free of me," Celia replied, looking up.

"I—" Soh stopped and looked down at the binding charm and frowned. "I see why you and your friends are so dedicated to finding and stopping the Dark Master. I remember when word came to the Seelie Court about the Resurgence, of the horrors surfacing about what the enemy was doing to any who were caught in their path. There were too many unwilling to fight. I do not wish to stand by as another terrible war threatens to destroy everything." She shook her head and pulled her hand away from the desk. "The Seelie and Unseelie believe the war will not touch our land. They believe we are safe behind the Willican Forest and our oceans. But we are not. I fear if the Dark Master succeeds in destroying Cadira, he will come for us, for how we chose to delegate the Great War."

Staring down at her hands, Celia hesitated, unsure of how to answer. She thought about Eliza, thought about how the marriage to Alicsar meant she'd have no chance to search for a way to destroy the Dark Master. Eliza needed *her* to go out and look for another way.

If Brandon hasn't found anything, however. She curled her hands into fists. What Eliza needed was another way, and Celia hoped Brandon had been the one to find it. Because if he had failed...

Then she wasn't sure what to do.

Celia found Soh's gaze, and those worries started to slip away. "You would wait until after we found a way to destroy the Dark Master to break the bind?" Celia asked quietly.

Soh took a step forward, then another, until she was crossing the room to Celia's bed. She knelt beside the Blood Witch, never taking her eyes off her. "There are worse fates."

Celia's heart stuttered in her chest, and for a moment, as Soh's dark eyes bored into hers, she couldn't breathe.

She couldn't describe the sensation that filled her. It was strange, the way it boiled in the pit of her stomach, stemming from somewhere deep within her chest, a flower cursed under a harsh sun threatening to bloom, an ember of warmth in the darkness of winter. It spread fire through her veins and ice down her spine, beautiful and terrifying, and something else that called to her magic.

She'd felt a whisper of it once, years ago, but had blamed it on fear.

Was it still only that? A fear of what feelings for Soh might mean? Might cost her?

Would it distract her from what she needed to do to save her sister?

Celia rose at the thought, if only to put space between herself and the beautiful Faery who made her heart beat faster, whose magic sung for hers. "You would help me save my sister? An Ecix?"

Soh looked away for a moment and released a heavy breath. "I would do whatever is necessary to stop another war," she replied, turning back to Celia. "I fought in the Resurgence with six other Fae across the Seelie Court. I am lucky to be alive."

Celia frowned, taking a hesitant step forward. "What do you mean?"

"Those who defied the Courts were executed. We were told we should not interfere, but there were some of us who chose to leave and fight anyway." Soh's hands trembled as she clutched them in her lap. "I fought with them and was then forced to watch them die by the hands of those I bow to."

Pushing aside her thoughts of Eliza and distractions, Celia dropped to her knees in front of Soh and reached for her hand. "I'm sorry."

The Faery shook her head, and as their hands met, tingles spread from Celia's fingers up her arm. "I have spent two hundred years paying for my decision, and I would do it again."

A lump formed in Celia's throat. She knew she should pull away, should create distance between them, but whatever force drew her to Soh had her glued to the Fae's side.

"Is that why they hunt you?" Celia asked.

Soh nodded. "My journey into the Courts of Light called for my head. I confirmed what none of them wanted to believe. There is a war coming, and it will consume all of us. The Dark Master has amassed power that may rival any god. We do not stand a chance without Eliza and her magic."

Celia closed her eyes. War was the last thing Eliza wanted, and now, without the dagger, Celia realised it was going to be their only option to stop the Dark Master.

A darker thought crossed her mind.

Perhaps Eliza was going to have to become the weapon they needed to stop the Dark Master.

~

The cry of a raven startled Celia awake.

Moonlight slithered over the heavy comforters twisted around her legs, starlight peeking through brush strokes of cloud gliding across the night sky.

Celia blinked and pulled herself to her elbows. Sitting on the balcony railings, the golden-eyed raven watched her, head cocked. The magic of the *Changed One* washed over her, soft and familiar.

"In my many years, I have come across two *Changed Ones,* but none this powerful," Soh whispered, awe filling her voice. Celia's head snapped in the Fae's direction; her eyes were wide and fixed on the raven, full lips parted in a smile. A candle on the table flickered beside her, highlighting the gold clinging to her dark skin.

The raven gave one last cry and took off into the night. Celia pulled her eyes from the Fae and watched after the fleeing dark form of the creature, one so steeped in magic it both frightened and ignited the power dwelling in her blood.

"You're still awake," Celia said, letting Soh's words of *Changed One's* drift away like the raven. "Have you slept at all?"

Soh shook her head. "Sleep is hard in a new place."

Celia's lips formed a thin line. "Would you like me to stay up with you?"

Soh dragged her eyes from the window, meeting Celia's stare. "I think I would like that."

Heart stuttering, Celia shifted in the bed and threw off the blankets; the cold winter air stung the exposed skin of her shins but she found a dressing gown and wrapped it around herself. Padding over to the sitting area where Soh continued to watch the night, Celia curled up on the lounge across from the Fae, taking a knitted blanket from one of the arm rests and layering it over her legs.

"What have you been doing?" Celia asked quietly.

Soh shifted so they were facing one another, a heavy blanket draped over her languid form. In her lap lay a book. "Reading," she replied, holding it up. "Enjoying the simple stories of mortals."

A smile tugged at Celia's lips. "It seems too dark to read. The candle is dim."

"I have a better light to read by," Soh said, and held up a hand. Her eyes, glued to Celia's, burned gold as her finger lit up with a bright yellow light. "Reading in the dark is much easier with this."

Celia leaned forward, eyes widening. The light glowed from the tip of Soh's finger, veins of gold running the length of her index finger down to the palm of her hand, but only illuminated a small amount of space. Celia had seen light magic at work before, from Amitel and other witches, even from half-Fae. But there was a delicate beauty in the way Soh performed it that stole her breath.

The light extinguished; Celia blinked and cleared her throat, pulling back. "It was wonderful," Celia said quietly, wrapping her arms around herself.

A heavy silence danced between them. It toyed with Celia, pulling for words she buried deep within, tugging at conversations better left unsaid. There wasn't much she could say, not with the Blood Witches inside the palace, not when she wasn't sure what needed to happen next.

"How soon do you wish to leave?" Soh asked after a moment of silence, head propped on her hand. The gold strands that wove through her dark hair glinted in the flickering candle light.

Celia released a heavy breath, and hesitated. Leaving was one of those things she had yet to decide upon. She knew it would be better for both of them if they disappeared, and yet Celia faltered in saying it aloud. "After the wedding. I don't think I can leave Eliza alone for that."

Soh nodded, hand falling from her chin, shoulders tensing. "I suppose I won't be invited to that," she said, voice stiff. "Though I doubt your king would want a Faery sitting amongst the Blood Witches."

"It's best you don't go." Celia watched the Fae for a moment, unsure of how to respond. There was a bitterness in her voice that reminded her of how Amitel regarded the whole situation. "It'll be safer for you here, at the palace, and in any case, you might prefer mapping our journey." Celia averted her gaze and twisted her fingers in her lap, chest growing tight.

Could she even leave, after all that had happened, with Soh? Eliza was trapped within the confines of the palace now, but could Celia leave her alone without knowing where Brandon was—if he'd even return?

Conflicted feelings warred in her chest. Leaving could mean breaking the bind, finding more about the dagger and the Original Ecix. The Ecix was a force older than the Blood Witches, so there were places that preceded even the Labyrinth Mountains. The other cities may have more secrets hidden within, secrets Celia and Soh could uncover.

"You are unsure," Soh said, her voice cutting through the turmoil of Celia's thoughts. "You regret wanting to leave."

Celia forced her gaze to the Fae's and nodded. "It's hard to leave her without knowing she'll be okay."

"She will be safe, and I am sure she will be alright with the knights and that warlock." Soh's gaze softened, and she moved like she intended on crossing to Celia and joining her, but she stopped and settled in further.

A hint of disappointment ignited in Celia's stomach, but she brushed it aside. "Brandon, our...*friend*, he left on his own mission and merely wrote her a letter the night of her birthday. We haven't heard from him, since he left, and I'm afraid if I disappear, she'll think of me like she does him." Celia looked down at her hands. "I can't do that to her, Soh."

"You won't," Soh replied, offering her a soft smile. "But we cannot stay here."

Something fluttered in the pit of Celia's stomach, and she swallowed hard. "I know. Once the wedding is over, I'll talk to her about it."

Hidden within the fear and guilt, a sliver of excitement burned like embers. But could she nurture it? Or would she let it extinguish, like she'd done so many times before?

Isolde's last words to her played in her mind as she settled into the corner of the couch, as the silence danced between them once more, and let it lull her to sleep.

44

BLOOD RITES
ELIZA

If Lennox was mad at Eliza for disappearing and failing at finding the dagger, she didn't voice it. Instead, she made Eliza work twice as hard. In the days leading up to the wedding, they'd spent hours together in preparation—though for what, Eliza wasn't sure. Lennox didn't answer that question, the one that burned alongside her failure: *why does it matter if I know all of this when I'm stuck at the palace?*

But she was glad for the distraction; she liked the aching muscles for once, the sapped magic, the sore brain from the lessons on spells. Because once she entered her rooms at the palace, she could sleep— and no longer was her sleep accompanied by dreams.

Preparations for the wedding were well underway, to the point where Eliza was no longer needed. She went to all of two dress fittings, both of which she hadn't been required to utter a single word, so her obligations to the most expensive and important wedding of Cadira were minimal.

Now, two days before she was supposed to marry the prince, all she had to worry about was not tripping down the aisle on her way to the alter.

Standing at the head of their small table, Lennox glowered down at her, lips pursed into an impossible line. Already Eliza's brain was beginning to fog over with all the information that was being thrown at her; about Blood Magic, and the important role the Brotherhood played in the safety of the tribes. All things she knew, or at least had an inkling of, none of which answered any of the burning questions she was forced to burry.

A knock sounded, the rap against the wood loud and jarring. Lennox stopped mid-sentence to glare at the door, but neither made a move to see who was there.

The knock sounded again and this time Eliza stood, striding to the door without looking at her trainer. A servant bowed and presented her a crisp white envelope, unadorned except for her name scrawled messily across the front.

Eliza hesitated before taking the message and sent the servant away, never once taking her eye off the letter. Behind her, Lennox said nothing.

She recognised the handwriting. *Alicsar*. There hadn't been much time to speak with him except for their *meeting* after the king flaunted her failure around like a prize.

As a lump formed in her throat, Eliza opened the envelope and slid the parchment out. The message was short, but it sent a shiver down her spine.

Please meet me at sunset in the old temple behind the palace. Come alone. I'll be waiting there.
-Alicsar

She released a breath. They hadn't spoken alone to one another since he'd left the city of Azula.

Eliza pocketed the note and told Lennox briefly that is was a summons from the prince. But her trainer didn't care, and for the rest of their allotted time, continued Eliza's lesson on the history of Blood Witch's association with Cadira and its monarchy—something mildly useful, though it didn't give much of the Blood Witch secrets away.

The time slipped by slowly, until through the small window above Lennox's head, the sun finally gave way to dusk, the sky going from blue to yellow and orange. When it came time for their lesson to be over, Eliza hesitated in the doorway to the library. Behind her, Lennox huffed.

"Do not forget to be outside in the park by dawn," Lennox said. "We must complete the Blood Rites before the wedding."

Eliza nodded as the Blood Witch sidestepped her and out of the library, disappearing down one of the many corridors.

Maybe that's why Alicsar wants to talk. As far as she knew, he was also aware of what they had to do before the wedding—the Blood Rites, an old tradition that few Blood Witches partook in because it was usually reserved for the *Idrindis*.

Not even she knew what it would entail—another thing Lennox refused to discuss. Eliza hadn't had a chance to question Celia about it, who would have done the rite when she'd been of age.

Releasing a breath, Eliza stopped at the doors leading out into the gardens. The sky was changing drastically, a clear sign that if she were to meet Alicsar, she needed to hurry.

But fear stopped her from taking another step. The desire to go back to her room and sleep away her bad thoughts almost won out.

And yet...

Eliza found the ruined temple after dusk, as the purples and reds of the Cadiran sky gave way to deep indigo and black. The stars broke through the darkness to illuminate the sky, guiding her way until the twin moons could finally make their appearance.

Seeing Alicsar standing against the broken stone walls sent her heart racing. She took a fumbling step before stopping outside the temples walls.

Her gaze drifted over the old structure. It reminded her of the temples dedicated to Azula, but there were no motifs of death left on the stone; instead there were symbols of stars and moons.

"What are we doing out here?" Eliza asked, stepping into the broken walls of the temple. Around her, the stars brightened the darkened ruins, outlining a basket and large blanket that had been placed on the grassy ground.

Alicsar bit his lip. "I wanted to explain to you how *I* felt about this."

Her heart skipped a beat as worry gnawed at her. "Why here? Why now?"

"It felt right," Alicsar replied. He hesitated; she saw it flash across his eyes as he finally met her at the temple's entrance. "It felt... meaningful."

She sucked in a breath and shook her head. "Don't."

"I'm sorry," he breathed, face inches from hers. The feelings she had tried so hard to lock away resurfaced; the pain of betrayal and the brief moments of happiness, the feel of his lips and the heat of his touch, coming together to form an experience she so wanted to ignore, to forget. She had stupidly fallen for the façade of Dorin; the easy smiles and the stolen touches, the jokes and the easiness of being with him.

But Alicsar—the lost prince, the boy she had fought so hard to find, the one without the memories, who had done her no harm other than not *remembering* their times together. He'd returned to the life he hated for *her*, so that he could help her get out of an engagement she so desperately despised.

Part of her believed deep down he did remember her. That maybe the façade hadn't been just that, that maybe there had been feelings there.

Why else would he have dragged her out to the crumbling temple with a basket and a blanket, to watch the stars?

She wanted to cry at the near perfection of it, and to laugh at the feelings that washed over her. The stress of the last month, of failing to get the dagger, of their marriage only two days away, threatened to break her.

And yet she felt like that silly little girl again, the one who had set out to find a prince and win her freedom, who had met a boy so excited over the history of his kingdom that he had barely contained it.

She thought she'd managed to forget about the way *he* had made her feel, but here she was, standing beneath the canopy of stars on a red blanket with the boy who broke her heart and didn't even remember it.

Eliza took him in; he'd broadened out since they'd met, his shoulders wide, muscular. The grey long-sleeved shirt he wore was tight over his shoulders and arms. His hips were narrow, legs stronger. Someone had cut his hair since his return to the palace, but it still curled around his ears, no longer sun-bleached, the colour of darkened sand in the midst of summer. Even his eyes were different, shadowed, forgetting.

But she wasn't naïve enough to think it would be different. She refused to let those sparks of hope burn any more than they actually were. Nothing about their situation was hopeful.

"I never thought I'd be this happy," he murmured. "When I woke up on that ship, and the healer hold me I was going home, I was confused. But then I saw you on the deck. I saw the hope and relief and pain in your eyes. And something in me told me *you* would be my home."

Eliza swallowed thickly, unable to answer.

Alicsar continued, "But that pain, I caused that, even if I don't remember it. I made you fear me. And every time I looked at you, I knew I had to repent." He looked up to the stars, then, silver glistening in his eyes. "I think I fell in love with you on the deck of that ship. Seeing you standing there, outlined by the stars... You looked like a living goddess. I saw you and thought: *this is the girl who will change my life*. And then I found out that you were the one who saved me. And I wanted to thank you. But every time you looked at me, all I saw was pain, distrust, and... fear. I hated making you feel like that.

"Then Bastian announced we would be married. I thought that maybe I could make things up to you, but I saw the fear and dread in your face, and I knew you wouldn't be happy. I knew he had taken something from you.

"I talked to him after, asked him why. He said it was part of the deal; if you found me, he would give you everything you desired. But I'd seen it in your face that day: you didn't want to be Queen."

Eliza tried to crack a smile, but it felt broken on her lips. "You never thought that maybe I was only doing this for the crown?"

He gave a soft shake of his head and looked down at her. "If that were the case you wouldn't have run away, would you?"

She stiffened. "I didn't *technically* run away. The Dark Master is still out there and it's my job to find him." She shook her head. "Anyway, you ran away too."

Alicsar looked down at his hands, then hers. "I know. And I knew the marriage wasn't something you wanted, either. I thought maybe I could convince him otherwise, that if I proved I could be enough for his bid for power, he might release you. But I failed you."

A bitter laugh escaped her lips as she stepped away. "He told me I would become a symbol for hope," she murmured. "I'm not surprised he would give that up. But... I'm still surprised you would ask him to end it. Especially..."

His gentle smile made her heart skip a beat. "I wanted to make sure you were happy. I saw how you were with the others, the relief on your face whenever you left Cadira, and the peace you felt when you were in Azula's city. I—I knew I could never give you that. I owed it to you to give you your freedom. It wasn't fair that you had to be shackled to a man you hated."

Her breath caught in her throat. "I don't hate you," she said, voice thick. "I don't think I ever did." She swallowed back tears of frustration, of gratitude. "I thought the king would grant me freedom, when he told me to find you. I thought he wouldn't execute me for my magic. I never... I never expected to become Queen. And although I resented him—and you—for this marriage, I don't think I could have ever hated you. Not even after what had happened under the desert. There was always a part of me that missed you, because..."

Alicsar frowned, cocking his head. "Had we ever...?"

Eliza flushed red. "When you went by Dorin, we kissed, once or twice."

Alicsar's eyes darkened as he looked her over. "Why didn't you tell me before?"

"Because I was hurt and afraid," she whispered, looking away. "I confronted him—you and asked if any of it had been real. And you—he had laughed in my face." She shuddered at the memory; the cavern, his revelation. But she didn't see either of them as the same person, not anymore. When she looked at Alicsar, she no longer saw the steel eyes of Dorin or felt the bite of his blade in her spine. Instead she felt kinship, understanding.

"I promise you now, that I will *never* laugh at you like that again," he said, and she believed him. Conviction burned in his eyes so deeply that she had to take a step back. "I will never be that man again. So long as I know you are here, that I—that I have a chance with you, then I don't think I could ever go back to that person. The person who hurt you and took joy in it."

Eliza swallowed the lump that had formed in her throat, tears glazing her eyes. Outlined by the stars, Alicsar himself looked like a god, reaching down to pull her into the night sky itself. She had always thought he was beautiful in a classical way.

She couldn't reply. Instead, she motioned to the forgotten basket and blanket. "So, Your Highness, what exactly did you have planned?"

Alicsar, thankfully, didn't comment on her change of subject. Instead, he led her to the red blanket and sat, patting the space across from him. "Sit."

Slowly, she did as instructed and eyed him warily.

"I never got to give you your present," he said carefully. "I will admit, it's partially my fault. It wasn't done for the ball, and then I was in such a rush to go with you to the city, that I forgot about it. When I returned, I found it finished, so I planned on giving it to you as a farewell present. Instead..." His throat bobbed, heat rising to his cheeks.

"Instead it's an engagement present," she finished.

The basket was pushed over to her. Sitting across from each other, Eliza was able to take Alicsar in; the soft curl of his hair, mussed from the soft breeze that broke through the temple, the way his shirt hugged his chest, and the way his trousers hung low on his hips.

The prince smiled and motioned towards it. "Open it."

"Is it food?" She was hungry, she realised. Spending hours with Lennox without any reprise usually left her too exhausted to eat.

He laughed. "Just open it."

With a crooked smile, Eliza peeled open the top of the basket and stared down into the contents. Nestled inside were several small boxes surrounded by rose petals. In one box, chocolates—Eliza shoved several in her mouth as Alicsar laughed—in another she found a twin set of daggers.

"They're customary," he said as she pulled them from the basket and looked at them in the dim light of the moon.

"Aren't these just in case I want to kill you on our wedding night?" she asked with a cocked brow. "And aren't they supposed to be given by family members?"

He laughed again. "No. I read that the Fae—Brithien Elves, to be exact—used to give their wives daggers before their wedding as an engagement gift." Before she could speak, he waved his hand and hurriedly said, "I know you aren't technically Fae. But the Blood Witches stem from the Brithien Elves, so..."

Something twisted inside of Eliza as she gazed down at the gift. He had gone to the trouble of learning about her heritage, her people, so that he could honour it and keep to tradition. Eliza herself hadn't even thought about this, but was touched because *he* had.

She looked up, a tear sliding down her cheek. "Thank you."

Reaching over the basket, Alicsar wiped the tear away. "Do you like them?"

The handles of the daggers were carved bone, almost like Azula's dagger from the Aether; strange symbols had been carved onto the bone, while the blades curved around like crescents, made from simple silver steel. "They're beautiful," she said, looking up to meet his stare.

His smile truly transformed his face, she thought.

"Open the others."

Placing the daggers in her lap, Eliza picked up another box and brushed a rose petal off the top. The lid came off easily; inside, Eliza found a pair of diamond earrings, paired with a simple tear-drop diamond necklace.

"These look expensive," she murmured, touching them lightly with her fingertips.

Alicsar shrugged and looked into the box, too. "Honestly, Bastian's advisor got those and told me I should gift them to you. I contemplated handing them over to my tutor, because I know you don't like jewellery, but then I thought Bastian might get angry, and no one wants to deal with an angry monarch, so..."

"So you threw them in with the other presents?" she asked, grinning. The easiness of laughing, of pretending made her heart swell.

"They have no meaning to me, to you." He looked up and met her stare. "Every gift—including the chocolates you annihilated—mean something to you. Diamonds don't."

"Well," she drawled, "I could always sell them off. Fund my escape."

"Do what you will with them so long as I can escape with you."

Eliza sobered, looked down at the gifts, at the food she could see at the bottom of the basket and the bottle of wine. "I want you to know that I appreciate this—all of this. I can see this isn't King Bastian. But my freedom has been taken from me again, and I feel like I'm giving that up." She looked up and met his eye. "I can't give that up anymore, Alicsar."

"Do you think I'll keep you from doing things?"

She shook her head. "Of course not. But the king will. And the Blood Witches have already expressed how they think this is disrespectful to their traditions. So I can't help but feel that this marriage has more to do with keeping an eye on me and my power more than giving hope to the people."

Alicsar sighed. "I cannot say that I understand, but I do. I have to. But I *love* you, Eliza. I have since the moment I saw you. If I could do anything to make this easier for you, then I would."

Smiling sadly, Eliza tucked the daggers back into their box, as well as the diamonds. She placed them back into the basket. "I know," she said softly, "and for that I'm grateful. Even if I think you're crazy because we barely know each other and you're already professing your feelings for me." She gave him a crooked smile as his cheeks flushed even darker.

Alicsar ducked his head. "Yes." He cleared his throat loudly. "What I meant was—"

"I consider you my friend," she said. She meant it, felt deep in her heart, her soul. "Maybe... maybe it could be more than that. But I am thankful for you, for the understanding you've given me. I'm grateful that you tried, even though you probably went against what you believe." She swallowed thickly. "But I can't—"

His eyes found hers and he nodded. "I know."

For the rest of the night, they watched the stars.

~

As the twin moons of Cadira dipped below the horizon, Eliza stepped up to Celia and Lennox. The blood-red robes they sported were embroidered with golden thread that caught the flickering light of torches circling them.

For the Blood Rites and the following wedding ceremony, at least ten more Blood Witches had appeared, none of them looking any happier than Lennox during Eliza's last training session.

They walked from the games park and into the forest that sat behind the palace. As they passed the ruined temple, Eliza couldn't help but think about what it would be like to be free of the burdens currently weighing her down.

Their party stopped in a small clearing in the forest. Around them, unlit torches made a circle around the cleared grass, untouched by the woes of winter. In the centre, a short pillar with a metal bowl, like the ones kept in the Keepers temples.

Standing with her, Alicsar's eyes glinted nervously in the moonlight. A cape of inky-black covered his shoulders. Swirls of silver thread danced along the hem and over the back, detailing a scene from the Brotherhood; a winding road, a man on horseback, a mountain scape on one side of him and on the other, an abyss. The road to the Brotherhood and to the Blood Witches, forged by sacrifice.

Eliza swallowed the lump that rose in her throat as Lennox motioned for Eliza to hold out her hand.

Alicsar followed Eliza's movement, face serious and unreadable. They'd barely spoken since his confession, though she'd found comfort in the silence between them. Instead he'd pointed out constellations, and they'd talked about the twin moons that looked over Cadira.

As soon as their hands touched, the torches erupted, reminding her of Azula's temple. In the bowl, a flame of lavender and crimson sparked to life.

Does he feel cheated now? She cast him a quick glance. He'd confessed something to her and she'd all but thrown it back in his face. Shame gnawed at her belly for her response, but it was too late now.

As if sensing her doubt, Alicsar looked over and smiled warmly at her. Eliza's heart skipped a beat at the look in his eye, the pureness of his expression. He wasn't faking his happiness in that moment. He wanted to marry her.

Guilt for questioning him washed over her as the circle of Blood Witches began chanting. The torches flames grew brighter and higher until it created a net of fire over their heads.

And we will be blessed and cleansed by fire.

45

TO MARRY A PRINCE
ELIZA

It became hard for Eliza to ignore the churning of her stomach as she sat with her back to a team of seamstresses, hair dressers, and a number of other people all set on preparing her for the wedding.

Wedding. She swallowed thickly, cold all over. The night before, she'd been attacked by nightmares; about Valonde, the Original Ecix, the dagger... The bathing chamber floors had been cold enough to chill her feverish skin as she'd vomited her dinner, lunch, whatever she'd managed to keep down in the hours leading up to her awaking from the pain of failure.

The women who crowded around her did a stunning job hiding the gauntness of Eliza's cheeks and the dark circles around her eyes. The makeup didn't even feel heavy on her skin, likely some kind of magic she could get behind, especially when she'd spent years plastering on face paint for work.

Eliza closed her eyes and sighed. Another pin scraped against her scalp to keep her pretty curls in place.

"You're done!" Lady Pompous clapped her hands together, and when Eliza met her stare through the mirror of her vanity, she couldn't help but appreciate the silver haired woman. She'd managed to complete every task necessary without making Eliza think about it once. For it, Eliza was grateful. She doubted she'd have the energy to think about what was next on the endless to-do list of preparations for the wedding.

It took Eliza a moment to finally see herself in the mirror; her dark hair had been curled and was pinned to her head in an elaborate updo that looked simple yet sophisticated, beautiful as strands of chocolate-brown hair framed her face. Red, the shade of blood, coloured her lips, so bright against the paleness of her skin.

Lady Pompous motioned for everyone to leave. "We'll be back soon to dress you."

Without giving Eliza the chance to reply, she drifted from the room, closing Eliza within.

Alone.

Being left with her thoughts made her stomach curdle. Being left alone gave her too much silence.

Not even the dead graced her with their presence.

As the silence ticked on, Eliza found herself cursing and pushing away from the vanity. *What am I doing?* She was Eliza Kindall, the Ecix, a Blood Witch and necromancer. She's lived a hundred lives over the span of over two thousand years. And she was about to be married to a prince.

Eliza stiffened as a wave of portal magic shuddered through her room. Light flickered in the corner of her vision as the portal opened, the heat of it warming her back.

Her eyes widened, and before she could move, the light dimmed to reveal Kay, her silver hair bound in a knot atop her head, with several strands framing her angular face. A yellow shawl covered her lithe shoulders, a plethora of bangles lining her wrists. And she'd worn a dress—Eliza couldn't remember the last time she'd seen her guardian in anything other than jeans and a knitted sweater.

Kay gave her a small wave, lilac eyes sparkling as she walked over to a table laden with tea and small cakes. She sat and poured two mugs, totally casual, which made Eliza's heart warm a little.

Eliza sucked in a shuddering breath and walked slowly to the table. "What are you doing here?" she asked, sitting slowly across from her guardian.

"What does it look like I'm doing?" Kay asked, snorting. "I'm having tea, with you, on your wedding day."

Kay smiled from the other side of the tea table, totally relaxed despite the fact that she technically wasn't *allowed* in Cadira.

"What if the courts find out?" Eliza asked, unable to even touch her tea, let alone sip at it casually like Kay was. "What if they *execute you* for being here?"

Kay waved a hand dismissively. "I'm sure everything will be fine, kid. I wouldn't be here if it weren't for the king."

Frowning, Eliza touched the rim of her tea cup, though she made no move to pick it up and take a sip. Her stomach churned too much for her to eat or drink anything. Not like she could, not when her make-up was done to perfection and she was told not to ruin it.

I'm getting married in a three hours. She still couldn't believe it. Months before, she had believed she would find a way out of the arrangement. But to be sitting in the living room of her suite just waiting...

Eliza shifted and pressed her hands into her lap. Too many emotions swirled in her mind, more confusing than anything. Most importantly, she questioned whether she could actually go through with it, or if she'd try and disappear.

It's normal, she thought. *It's normal for me to be second guessing everything.*

"How are you feeling?" Kay asked, shattering the silence. She sipped at her tea, brow lifted. "And don't lie to me, kid. I know you well."

"If you know me so well," Eliza muttered, "then you tell me how I feel." Rising, Eliza strode to the fireplace that crackled with a warmth that couldn't melt the ice that was turning her blood to slush.

Kay sighed from the couch. "Well, I think nerves are a given," she said, sitting her cup down on the table. "But this is a lot, Eliza. You're marrying the prince of Cadira."

"It's not that, Kay..." Eliza sighed and shook her head. "None of this feels right."

Kay stood and made her way to where Eliza stood. "Not getting the dagger... that isn't your fault."

Tears burned behind her eyes, but Eliza blinked them away. She'd cried enough over her failure already. And she didn't need to ruin her makeup.

"If I had found it, I would be free."

Kay touched her shoulder lightly. "Eliza..."

Turning to her guardian, Eliza bit her lip in hesitation. But before she could say anything, the door opened to reveal her grandfather's smiling face.

"Am I allowed in?" he asked, eyes crinkling as his smile broadened.

Relief washed over Eliza as she rushed to his side, forgetting what she'd revealed to Kay. She threw her arms around his neck—careful of her makeup and hair, of course—but that didn't stop the tears from burning behind her eyes once more.

"You're always allowed in here," she murmured. She didn't want to let him go.

Davis patted her back fondly, rubbing his hand up and down her shoulder. "You look beautiful."

Tears threatened to overflow, but she sucked in a breath and blinked them away. "Thanks."

"Are you excited?"

"Not at all."

He chuckled, and slowly, she unwrapped herself from his embrace. "I'm so glad you came."

"I wouldn't miss it for the world, and I wouldn't miss seeing *you* before the whole event."

Eliza smiled, but it was Kay who spoke next. "Come and sit down. We're just having tea before Eliza has to get dressed. Let's try and alleviate some of her nerves so she doesn't puke walking down the aisle."

Eliza grimaced, but it was the thought that counted—not her guardian's weird way of talking about it. "Thanks, Kay."

The older woman cracked a grin. "Anything for you, kid."

They sat and talked for what felt like hours; Eliza used the time to explain what she *actually* wanted to be doing instead of the wedding, how she wished she could have seen the Labyrinth Mountains, that she wanted to explore more of the ancient cities that dotted Cadira. Her guardians, for the most part, sat and listened, and held her hand any time she was tempted to break down and cry. Davis told her about home, about how everyone missed her, which only made her heart ache more. Her old boss wished she'd return from her *travels* so she could work the night shifts again at the museum. Their elderly neighbour missed their morning walks.

An entire life she was leaving behind, because of a deal made when she'd been a child.

"Are you having second thoughts about the wedding?" Kay asked quietly, touching her hand.

Eliza blinked, her throat tightening. She looked down at her hand, at the ring weighing heavily on her finger. "Of course I'm having second thoughts about the wedding," she said sadly. "I don't want to be married yet. I want to live my life."

Her grandfather covered the ring. "I know," he said quietly, "but maybe..."

Eliza looked up. The door opened to reveal Lady Pompous holding the ball gown of a wedding dress; it had a heart-shaped neckline and was floor length, with short sleeves. The bodice was satin that hugged her chest and waist before billowing out into a full figure skirt to the floor. It was elegant and basic, a gorgeous gown that looked nothing like the ones she'd tried on during her fittings.

"But nothing," Eliza replied quietly, finally taking her eyes off the gown. "Once I'm married, that's it. I won't have a life. I'll be chained here and nothing will be done about it. The Dark Master is still out there, and the King has made it perfectly clear that my involvement is no longer necessary."

~

Eliza remembered the first time she'd spied the large temple on her first trip into the capital; spires reaching for the clouds, white and silver and reflecting rays of blinding light, arches held up by faceless gods and ceilings supported by columns depicting the wilds of the Fae Territory.

She'd never had the chance to see it up close before, but standing there before her wedding, she couldn't appreciate the beauty when her stomach twisted into knots.

"Eliza." Turning, Eliza faced Celia, who approached wearing a crimson cloak, her hair unbound and blue eyes wide with nerves. "How are you feeling?"

"Like I'm going to throw up," Eliza replied, biting her lip. "But I guess nerves are normal on a day like this."

Celia touched Eliza's hair fondly; captured by about a thousand pearl pins, Lady Pompous' hair stylist had managed to pin Eliza's hair into a chiffon with curls that framed her face. The stylist had even touched her dark brown hair with glitter until it sparkled in the light. A veil covered her face, reminding her too much of the mortal traditions back home. Only, this veil had more to do with standing before the Goddess of Marriage and the Hearth, Chara, and some archaic symbol of purity and truth.

Had she ever thought about marriage before Cadira? Of meeting someone and planning her own wedding? It had been brought up— only by older women and men asking silly questions around Thanksgiving—but it had rarely been something she'd thought about. She was too young to.

"Think about this as only a formality," Celia said. "Even though you will be legally married, it does not mean you can't take everything at your own pace."

Eliza swallowed. "Right. Own pace."

"You will be okay."

Sparing her sister a nervous glance, Eliza shifted her attention back to the temple, where most of the city already waited. Somewhere in there, Kay and Davis would already be sitting proudly near the front, with Amitel, Soh, and the Brotherhood at their sides. A row of Blood Witches would be close by, watching everything unfold, while the king likely plotted his next step to keep his power.

And waiting for her, at the doors, Alicsar. Her prince.

Heart racing, Eliza took a step forward as the doors opened to reveal Jed. The old captain of the guard smiled slightly. "We're ready for you."

Celia grabbed for Eliza's hand and stopped her before she could climb the steps. "I have something for you."

Holding out her other hand, Celia handed her a blackened crystal. Veins of silver and gold ran through it. It had been tied to a small metal chain, the only charm on the necklace.

"It's beautiful," Eliza murmured. It was no bigger than her thumb nail, but it was a gorgeous rock.

Celia smiled. "It belonged to the Ecix before Isolde. My sister never received it, and it was handed down to me. Now, I am giving it to you."

Eliza's breath caught in her throat as Celia carefully clasped it around Eliza's throat. As soon as it rested against her hammering heart, something shuddered through her, like a surge of power. Eliza gasped and touched her cold fingers to the stone.

"What is it?" Eliza asked.

"It came from Valonde," Celia said. "It is a reminder of what was taken."

Frowning down at the stone, Eliza didn't believe that was all it was a reminder of.

46

A ROYAL WEDDING
ELIZA

The hairs on the back of Eliza's neck rose as music drifted through the temple. It was a low and haunting tune that was accompanied by a Keeper who bellowed an old verse about the Goddess Chara, who he prayed would bless the union.

A shudder wracked Eliza's body as Captain Jed motioned for her to enter. The sound of people moving, of them rising to watch her made her heart drop into the pit of her stomach.

Just breathe, she thought, keeping her head lowered as she took her first step into the temple. *Don't worry about them, just try not to fall.*

Easier said than done.

Eliza stepped across the threshold and found Alicsar waiting for her. He wore white, like her, with gold detailing around the cuffs of his jacket which billowed out like a cape. The crown atop his head was gold with emeralds and diamonds, the twisted metal like thorny vines around his dark blonde hair.

Unlike mortal traditions, fiancés were expected to walk their bride down the aisle. It alluded to the Goddess Chara that there was no forceful handoff in the marriage—that they entered the union as equals.

With the eyes of every noble, dignitary and important person in Cadira on them, Eliza was glad to have Alicsar there to save her from her own clumsiness should she trip, or worse, stumble into the crowd of guests.

She swallowed thickly. Beneath the veil, she could barely see beyond a couple of steps, but a long train of black cut between the sea of people, guiding her to the front of the temple, where her future waited.

The pounding of her heart grew louder in her ears at the thought.

Alicsar smiled at her, his own nerves alight in his eyes. He offered her his arm, which she took gratefully.

She spared her groom a quick glance. He watched her like he meant what he'd said during their night of star-gazing. A soft smile broke across his face.

His happiness made it all the more real.

Together, they started their march down the aisle.

Like they'd been instructed, they took slow steps so that everyone in attendance could take them in.

The song of the Keeper continued to play as they approached the temple dais, a guiding melody that sounded more like a death march than a wedding march. The low baritone of the Keeper, mixed with the haunting melody coming from above the crowd in the orchestra's booth, made for a melancholy mood.

As she grew closer to the front of the hall, she spotted her Grandfather and Kay, both standing amongst the other guests, their faces almost lost to the crowd of bright gowns and solemn faces.

If she knew any better, Eliza would have thought she was walking towards her own funeral, not her wedding. There were more than a few faces darkened with displeasure or uncertainty—over the union or something else, she wasn't sure. Many were still opposed to the wedding; they hadn't kept that a secret, but she'd hoped they wouldn't go to the ceremony. Seeing them made her want to turn around and run even more.

Eliza sucked in a breath and released it slowly as she climbed the dais with Alicsar. The Keeper's song came to an end as the congregation lowered to their seats. From the corner of her eye, Eliza searched the rest of the temple for her friends; Celia wore a robe the colour of blood towards the front of the crowd with Lennox and several other Blood Witches. Towards the back, half hidden by shadows, Eliza spotted Amitel.

Her chest tightened at the sight of him.

"Under the ever loving gaze of the Goddess Chara, we join two souls as one," the Keeper said, voice ringing out through the temple. "Blood to blood, heart to heart, we let Her hand guide these two into a harmonious union."

A low murmur broke out across the crowd. Eliza pursed her lips, but she faced Alicsar with a kind of calm that was hard for her to muster.

"Everything is going to be fine," he whispered as the Keeper took their left hands and joined them. The skin of Alicsar's palms were soft and warm around her icy fingers. A comforting sensation filled her as his gaze softened, and the Keeper continued in the ancient language of the Keepers, only occasionally switching back to English so Eliza and Alicsar could follow a series of movements that would eventually bind them.

The Keeper produced a ceremonial knife and reached for their joined hands. Eliza hesitated before allowing the older man to take her hand from Alicsar's, but a reassuring smile from the prince calmed her.

"With this knife," the Keeper started, "I draw the lifeblood of the couple." With a careful hand, the tip of the blade cut along a line of her palm, then Alicsar's. Pocketing the knife, the Keeper brought their hands together, mixing their blood.

Eliza tried not to make a face.

"With this cloth, I bind them in the eyes of the Goddess Chara."

The Keeper held up a red silk cloth before winding it around their joined hands.

When he released their hands, leaving the cloth, the Keeper dipped his head and began another chant. A tingle raced up Eliza's spine.

She took a moment to cast her gaze around the temple once more. The high vaulted ceiling made the ceremony echo. There were balcony's above her head filled with more people; more nobility, representatives of the Courts of Light. The balcony usually reserved for the royal family was empty; Eliza found the king sitting in the very front, chin raised. He wanted to be as close as possible to see his power at work.

Another tingle danced down her spine, but something twisted in her gut.

The cloth disappeared from her hands. Eliza pulled her hands out of the prince's and stared down at the cut on her palm, at the mix of blood.

Something's wrong.

Before she could think on it more, Alicsar took her hand again, this time softly. He pressed a gold band—a ring—into her palm. In his other hand he revealed a ring with an emerald the size of her pinkie-nail in the centre. The band was made up of three twisted pieces that reminded her of vines, which carefully held the gem.

Eliza met Alicsar's gaze. Every inch of his was steady, patient, as he slid the ring onto her finger. The temple remained silent as the exchange of rings continued, only the voice of the Keeper marrying them filling the empty air. The mix of mortal and Cadiran customs caught Eliza off guard, but she tried her best to keep the surprise to herself.

Alicsar's words were like a hum in her ears, words she could no longer focus on. She concentrated on her breathing instead as her vision blurred around the edges.

With trembling fingers, Eliza slid the wedding band onto Alicsar's finger and repeated after the Keeper.

It's done.

Eliza looked up. Alicsar wore a grin that should have eased her wariness, but it didn't. When she looked out into the crowd, she noticed Kay and Celia who shared similar worry on their faces.

The Keeper said something, and suddenly Alicsar's hands were on her cheeks and his face was close to hers.

"May I kiss you?" he asked. It seemed as if everyone in the temple was watching with bated breaths.

Eliza nodded, and felt his lips against hers, though only for a moment. That was enough for the crowd to applaud.

He pulled away. "It's okay," he murmured. "It's over now."

But she shook her head. "I don't think it is."

Every window shattered, glass raining down on the congregation. Screams erupted from those unprotected; magic whipped out to stop large shards from killing those not fast enough to seek shelter.

Alicsar covered Eliza's body with his own, throwing himself over her as the stained glass directly above their heads exploded in. Over his shoulder, Eliza watched as Shadow Soldiers—the same ones who had attacked them in Alastor's apartment, who had found them in the underground city—descended upon the temple.

There were too many for her to count, all dressed in the same black leathers, weapons strapped to their hips and chests. Masks covered their faces, though their eyes were visible, the red of the irises glowing with magic Eliza couldn't recognise.

"Get up," Alicsar hissed, "and run."

"What?" Eliza gasped as gloved hands grabbed at his arms and pulled him off her. "No!"

More hands reached for her, ripping her from the ground.

There was nothing she could do as the blade touched the supple skin of the princes throat, and all hell broke loose in the temple.

47

TILL DEATH DO US PART
ELIZA

Eliza felt the brush of Lennox's magic, as familiar now as Celia's. The Witch loosened the bracelet on Eliza's wrist, and it disappeared, releasing her from the binds of her tutors Blood Magic and the restrictions that had come with it.

With the freedom from her binds and the rush of power that coursed through her blood, Eliza didn't think. She reached for a shard of broken glass and swiped her palm. Without waiting for the blood, she burrowed into her magic, and unleashed it on the Shadow Soldiers who held the prince.

Eliza searched through the dark magic that surrounded the soldiers for the tethers that anchored their souls to their flesh. These creatures were similar to the ones she'd faced in Azula's city, except the Dark Master's hold on them was stronger, and one she struggled to break.

But she'd manage.

Alicsar's eyes met hers, but there was no fear in them. Around them, the world slowed; the king's guards moved through the air like they were trekking through mud; her grandfather and Kay rose from their chairs, magic crackling at their fingertips; Blood Witches released a power unlike anything Eliza had ever felt, and it swept through the temple, devouring darkness and consuming Shadow Soldiers before they could make a move.

There was another brush of magic, this time from Amitel, which brought the world back into focus.

Eliza drew from the swelling of her blood and cast a net around the soldiers who held the prince. They released Alicsar, the knife dropping from gloved hands, but not before another dagger cut through the prince's expensive jacket and into his abdomen.

Alicsar dropped, and so did the soldiers.

She scrambled towards the prince and dragged him back behind a fallen pew. Shock lined his features. "You'll be fine," she murmured.

"I was *stabbed*," he replied, reaching for the wound, "on my *wedding day*."

Eliza couldn't help but smile. "You think this is an omen for how the rest of this marriage will go?"

His eyes hardened into resolve. "No." He shook his head, and with his free hand, he brushed away a flyaway hair that had escaped the pins tumbling from her hair. "This will not determine the rest of our lives. We are going to be more than this day, Eliza."

She swallowed. "I hope you're right." Reaching over to the wound on his side, Eliza focused on the blood and flesh, on the magic that lingered in his veins. She used it to stitch the tissue back together, in a similar way to when he'd stabbed her under the mountain.

The doors to the temple slammed open. Eliza looked up in time to see at least two dozen more Shadow Soldiers, with darkness so thick surrounding them Eliza would have mistook it for a shield. But the darkness flickered away, leaving the soldiers standing against the bright light of the capital.

A portal. It did not resemble the ones she'd used in the past. No, the one that brought the soldiers to the temple was something else, made entirely of dark magic.

Eliza struggled to her feet. "Stay here." The last thing she needed was Alicsar getting in her way—or getting hurt again. She looked down at the prince, who watched her with amazement and something else.

She entered the fight in a wedding dress, with no weapon, and a prince who needed saving.

~

As more soldiers poured into the temple, the remaining Keepers worked to the evacuate anyone who couldn't fight. The man who had married Eliza and Alicsar was dead, throat slit from ear to ear in a grim smile.

She turned away from the fallen Keeper and instead focused on three approaching soldiers. The magic that claimed them erupted; Eliza pushed at the dark magic that was thrown towards her, letting her Blood Magic reclaim the power that should only be hers.

Darkness snapped at her in retaliation.

And so did demons.

The creatures of Hell rose from the earth, made of ash and shadows, baring teeth sharp enough to score bone. Crimson eyes glowed like neon lights, and their growls shook the floor.

Crap.

Eliza looked between the soldiers and the demons. There were too many for her—for the king's men and the Keepers and witches present.

She took a moment to search the crowd for her family, but over the sea of darkness that ravaged the temple, she couldn't make anyone out clearly. There were shadows so thick attacking from all directions that she wondered if night had fallen over Cadira, but she knew well enough that wasn't the case.

Dark magic swarmed her; Eliza cut deeper into her flesh and called upon her own magic, let it slide over her like a second skin. The Blood Magic heightened everything; the visibility of spirits became more clear, their outlines hardening; the threads of magic that ran through the lands of Cadira became discernible, a tangle of light and dark magic, all at once converging in the temple.

Eliza dodged a swing from one of the Shadow Soldiers, but a blade made of darkness cut through the bodice of her wedding dress, slicing through the soft flesh of her abdomen. A hiss escaped her lips as she stumbled back, clutching one hand to her side as the skin struggled to knit back together.

What the...

The shadow-blade sung as it arced towards her once again, this time barely missing the exposed skin of her throat. But she jumped back and slammed into a fallen pillar. The sword scratched the surface of the stone, leaving a trail of her blood against the white.

Eliza spun away. The wound on her side throbbed, but she pushed the pain into the back of her mind.

Her attention went to the soldier who had attacked her first. The spirit attached to his flesh came into focus, a patchwork of greys and blues, dim compared to the spirits she usually saw in vivid colour. The Dark Master had changed something else about the dead, drawing from their spirits to hold them under his control.

Eliza clenched her jaw. She let her Blood Magic ebb and flow from her, connecting with the spirit-bound soldier before her. The strings that joined the spirit to the flesh became visible, grew taut, snapping as if cut by imaginary scissors.

The soldier fell, as did the others that circled her.

A small smile twitched at the corner of her lips. The demons that rose from the ashes attacked, rushing towards her, their claws grinding against the temples marble floors. She jumped away before the first demon could sink its teeth into her leg, but it caught the skirt of her dress and tore, shredding the hem.

"Assholes," Eliza muttered, staring down at the destroyed gown. A demon growled, but she swung out her bloodied hand, a ball of fire building in the palm. The flame leapt from her outstretched hand and consumed the creatures, returning them to ash and dirt.

Eliza backed away from the destroyed demons as fleeing guests rushed past her. But half of the temple was engulfed in dark flames; Keepers held it off from consuming the remainder of the wedding party, while Shadow Soldiers guarded the exits, keeping those within the temple trapped. Smoke plumed at the roof of the temple, its suffocating scent making its way down to where she stood. Eliza hadn't realised just how bad the situation had gotten.

From the corner of her eye, she watched as soldiers approached the prince. Fear made her stomach clench, but before she could take a step towards him, soldiers appeared before her, their red eyes the colour of blood, their faces twisted in pain, like unwitting marionettes.

Eliza backed up a step, keeping one eye on the prince. Their gazes met; something shifted in the way he looked at her, in the way he stood. A resolve seemed to settle over his features.

A low growl drew her attention from Alicsar; a demon with fangs the length of her forearm and four eyes on its wolf-shaped head. Ichor dripped from its open maw, sizzling when it hits the marble. Two more demons stepped up behind it, resembling the ones she'd fought beneath the Spring Manor.

But unlike the ones in Azula's city, these were almost three times the size, with just as much power flowing through them.

She cast a quick protection spell around herself and others as more of the large demons appeared.

Before she could cast a shield around Alicsar, the soldiers charged him, taking both his arms, wrenching them behind his back.

And she could do nothing but watch.

48

CHOICES
ALICSAR

Alicsar knew what was nothing he could do.

"Come willingly," a soldier breathed, "and she won't die."

The choice was simple then, he thought.

He would do anything to keep her safe. To protect her, like she had done for him.

He looked down at the ruined temple. There were bodies of guests littering the floor, perhaps a dozen of the Dark Master's soldiers filling the gaps. Black fire leapt at the ceiling, threatening to consume the temple.

He wondered if perhaps she'd been right; that this would be the basis of the rest of their lives.

Alicsar let the soldiers wrench him back, did not flinch as a blade tore through his white suit.

He tried not to look away from Eliza, who was screaming for him, fighting to reach him.

Alicsar found his father's eye. Had no one gotten the king out? His guards were gone.

Why was his father still in the temple?

A Keeper rushed to aid his father, tried to keep him away from the gnashing jaws of a demon.

He'll be safe, Alicsar thought. *He'll be okay.*

When he turned back to Eliza, his stomach dropped. She was reaching for him, shaking her head.

Did she know what he was planning on doing?

Did she know that he was hoping she'd be free?

The prince ripped his hand away from the soldier and held out his palm; blood and ash coated his fingers, and the wedding band glinted gold. But he did not want her help.

He did not struggle against the soldier as his hand was twisted behind his back.

He stopped struggling entirely.

Alicsar smiled at his wife one last time, a sort of peace encasing his heart.

He would go with the Dark Master.

For her.

She would be free.

49

TEAR THE WORLD APART
ELIZA

He didn't fight them. He didn't move or push them.

Eliza's eyes widened as he mouthed, *I love you.*

And there was nothing she could do as a dark portal appeared and swallowed the Shadow Soldiers—and her prince.

No.

Eliza forgot the demons and the soldiers who surrounded her. She rushed to the closing portal, Alicsar's name on the tip of her tongue, but it was if her voice had disappeared, her warning caught in her throat.

"No!" she shouted.

The portal closed around his hand just as she reached him; their fingers touched, but he was gone before she could hold him.

It was a diversion. The attack was meant to take the prince back.

But why?

Why did the Dark Master need Alicsar again?

Why?

A blade grazed her ribcage, startling her from her thoughts. Eliza jumped and spun in time to catch the next one aimed for her heart. The shadow-made dagger stopped in the air in front of her, then dropped, clattering on the marble before disappearing like smoke.

The moment of distraction almost cost her; another soldier appeared in front of her and swung. Eliza danced away and summoned her own weapon, a blade no longer than her forearm. A red flame erupted from the tip and burned its way down to the hilt. The warmth of the fire heated her hand and face, fuelled by Blood Magic, wielded by rage.

Anger made her powerful, dangerous.

Blood Magic gave her the tools to fight back.

Eliza channelled her emotions into the fight; the motions were like a long forgotten memory, ingrained in her body more than her mind. The commotion, the smell of smoke, all disappeared as she fought.

Swing. Parry. Dodge. Strike. Drop.

The dress was growing cumbersome; the silk and satin of her skirt dragged her down, carrying soot and blood, twisting around her legs so much she was surprised she hadn't fallen over yet.

Another Shadow Soldier appeared; he circled her with a demon at his heels. The beast growled, jumped forward with bared teeth, but it never attacked.

Eliza looked from it to the soldier, and smiled. "Tell me where you took Prince Alicsar. And I promise I won't kill you."

The Shadow Soldier said nothing, instead reaching behind him for a pair of twin blades.

Like her flaming dagger, shadow leapt at his, dancing down the steel and forming a layer of darkness over the deadly points. A shiver danced down her spine.

She recognised the magic.

It was the same kind that had killed Isolde, that had left the scar across her chest.

Jaw clenched, Eliza dove deeper into her magic. The well was emptying. She hadn't realised it before, but now she was burning through her own magic. Eliza grasped at the natural magic of Cadira, but it did not touch the temple.

Lennox hadn't taught her how to dip into the shared magic of the Blood Witches.

She wasn't supposed to learn how until after the wedding.

Crap.

Her grasp tightened on her dagger, and the soldier attacked.

The fight in the temple continued on around her; guests were gone, with Keepers and the kings men retreating. Eliza looked around herself as she danced out of the demons way. It had moved to corner her from behind, jaw unhinged as it nipped at her.

Demons converged on a point in the back of the temple. She spied golden hair, a wave of light that incinerated the beasts around him.

Amitel's chest heaved as he searched the temple. His eyes found hers, the gold gone, replaced by a dark red that almost seemed black. He looked like he could be one of the Shadow Soldiers, but...

She ducked beneath the arcing blade of the soldier she'd almost forgotten about and broke Amitel's stare. Eliza swung up with her dagger and slammed it into the gut of the Shadow Soldier. Twisting it, she forced a wave of magic through the dagger and into the soldier.

The sickness of death rose in her throat, but she swallowed it down as she pulled the blade free. The soldier dropped to his knees before sliding to the ground.

Before the demon could attack, a burst of light buried itself in the creatures chest. When Eliza spun, she found Soh, her glamour gone, wielding a sword of light.

The Faery bowed her head, and Eliza did the same.

Eliza wiped her blade of the soldiers thick, blackened blood and coughed. The Keepers had managed to control the fire, while her friends fought against dozens of soldiers still spilling into the temple.

They had the prince, so what more did they want?

Her death?

The blade grew heavy in her hand. Did the Dark Master know something she didn't?

Kay and her grandfather were close. Relief shuddered through her. They should have left already, she thought. They should have escaped with the other guests.

But they wouldn't leave her.

A cry from the pews made her turn. Celia and Soh had been backed into a corner, five Shadow Soldiers with darkened swords following them, a hoard of wolf-shaped demons nipping at their legs. Soh's sword had disappeared, and blood dripped from beneath Celia's cloak. Eliza felt the magic burning into the ground.

Eliza needed her family, but her sister needed her more. Sparing her grandfather and Kay one last look, Eliza started for Celia. The stairs beneath her feet were slippery with blood and soot; her feet were drenched in both. Her beautiful gown was destroyed.

She almost missed the wave of dark magic behind her. Eliza stopped in her tracks, and turned with the shout of her name. But it was too late.

She watched as her grandfather leapt in front of her, taking the blow of a Shadow Soldiers dark-infused blade. The metal sang as it cut through Davis's chest, piercing his heart before erupting through the back of his ribcage.

Blood dripped from the swords tip, ripped out before she could take a step, releasing her grandfather into the waiting arms of death.

And he fell, and she watched him do so.

She ran to him, ran to his fallen body. Blood soaked the holy ground of the temple. His blood.

The silver in his eyes dimmed as they found hers.

The smile that softened his lips should have given her hope.

But then he stopped seeing, his head rolling to the side, the smile fading.

Dead.

She touched his hand, but he had no pulse.

Dead.

Eliza reeled in her magic and focused on his wound, focused on his heart mending and pumping blood through his body.

Dead.

But it was no use. She was too weak and he did not move. She whispered his name but it fell on deaf ears.

Slowly, she pulled her grandfather closer, onto her lap. Somewhere behind them, her name was being called, but she couldn't hear them properly, couldn't respond because her mouth was dry.

Dead. Dead. Dead.

The scream tore through her throat, and before she could stop herself, Blood Magic and something deeper, something more powerful swelled in retaliation. It took hold of her like a ferocious beast, and she let it.

Around her, Shadow Soldiers stopped at her call, weapons dropping from dead hands. The creatures born of dark magic fell to their knees. Demons cried and sunk into the earth.

Eliza stood.

Magic unlike anything she'd ever felt flowed through her and she latched onto the closest soldier.

The power ripped him in two, tearing apart the dark magic that held the spirit and body together. One after another, soldiers collapsed as their spirits were torn from them, finally released from their servitude to the Dark Master.

The wave of magic shuddered through the temple, knocking humans and magical folk down as her anger and grief shot out of her in a powerful swell. It was nothing she could contain, nothing she could ever imagine holding within herself, and yet as tears dripped down her feverish cheeks, the magic continued to pour from her, a never-ending tidal-wave of ancient power.

If she did not reign it in, it would destroy everything.

She almost let it.

She was deaf to the cries and screams around her; Blood Witches and Keepers herded the remaining people out of the temple. Eliza could only close her eyes against the onslaught of magic that tried to tame her, but it was no use.

Over the ringing in her ears, of the sound of her grandfather's body breaking in front of her, she heard her sister call for her.

But that didn't cut through the haze shrouding her mind.

A gasp broke past her lips; she choked on her breath as her heart stuttered erratically in her chest. And there was nothing else she could do to stop it, to stop that anguish that flooded her.

Another sound, broken and strangled, passed her lips as she took in the damage she'd wrought; the broken pews, wood dusting the ground; stained glass from the windows scattering the floor like rose petals. The bodies of the Shadow Soldiers, mangled beyond repair. Nothing survived her grief and anger.

There was no movement as she trembled, blood-stained hands rising before her eyes.

In the distance, someone else called her name, shattering the silence. There was no-one but her now, alone in the temple, save for the dead at her feet.

Collapsing to her knees, Eliza looked around the temple, but she saw nothing more than destruction as darkness blanketed her vision, as she hit the ground.

50

KEEPER DAVIS
ELIZA

Eliza could shed no more tears, not as she stood over her grandfather's funeral pyre and stared down at his white-wrapped body. The stillness made chills wrack her body, made the blood in her veins turn to ice. There was nothing *alive* about the way her grandfather lay there, nothing remotely familiar.

Henry Ivo spoke in the ancient tongue known only by Keepers and Elders. Eliza knew some, thanks to Davis teaching her as a child, but the memory of those lessons made her heart ache. Every part of her ached at the loss.

"And into the darkness they go," Henry said, eyes falling onto Eliza, "with the light of those they love to guide them."

For the first time since she'd met the Elder, there was a heartbreaking quiver to his voice. Like regret. He'd been one of her grandfather's closest friends. Perhaps he wished they'd seen more of each other, before...

A Keeper to Eliza's right handed her a torch. The fire flickered hot, engulfing her, though she felt none of it as she laid it down on the wood beside her grandfather. She didn't blink, not as the wood caught, consumed by the fire. It licked at her face invitingly. To feel something—

"You shouldn't need to watch this," Celia murmured, her hand lightly touching hers.

Eliza stiffened, the cloying smell of wood filling her senses. *I should*, she thought, though said nothing as the Keepers' around her each laid their own torches down on the wood. Her eyes burned from the heat. She took a step towards it. Maybe more tears would be shed if she got closer. The wood crackled under the heat, climbing towards him. Eliza swallowed down bile as the flames finally touched him. And then the smell of burnt flesh hit her, knocking the air from her lungs, and everything around her broke.

I can't. At the last moment, Eliza turned and shielded her face in Celia's chest as the fire hissed and crackled. She wanted to scream.

A sob rose in her throat.

"It's going to be okay," Celia murmured, running a hand over Eliza's hair. "It's all going to be okay."

~

The world around her continued to move, as though they hadn't just burned her grandfather's body, as if they hadn't just collected the ashes and placed him in the sacred temple of the Elder's to be laid to rest.

I'll never see him again, she'd thought at the end of the ceremony, when Henry Ivo had finished reciting the ancient texts.

Since her grandfather's death, Eliza hadn't seen his spirit, either. There had been no trace of him at the ceremony. And she would never see it, not when his spirit would likely be bound to where his ashes rested.

Kay had redecorated the courtyard of their New Orleans home, having rearranged her flower-beds, moving the great grandfather clock further into the centre, where it could be viewed all those who came for the wake. But its familiar tick was gone, the sound as still as her heart.

Eliza looked up at it as Kay approached. "It doesn't work. It died with him."

"Yeah," Kay said quietly, taking Eliza's hand. Her fingers were icy cold. "I think it was linked to his life force, you know? Davis had that thing made hundreds of years ago." Kay's eyes took on a glimmer of sadness as she stared at Eliza. But she said nothing about it, merely patting Eliza's hand affectionately, like it would be enough.

It has to be enough, she thought.

Keepers wearing illusions to look human, and humans dressed in mourning white filled the courtyard, their footsteps steady, reminding her that she couldn't weep again, couldn't scream at the Dark Master or even mention him in front of the mortals. Elderly people Eliza had grown up with offered their condolences, their eyes dark with sadness.

An unforgettable anger almost knocked her over. The Dark Master had taken one more thing from her, after centuries of murdering her for the power that he could not steal. A power that she never asked for.

An old blues band played quietly in the corner. Eliza recognised some of the songs, but the memories hurt too much; they were filled with dancing in the streets with Davis and Kay, spending hours on his lap in a bar swaying to the music, or in the corner with the band after a set as they explained to her the different instruments.

When she'd gotten older, her grandfather had danced around the courtyard with her in his arms, those same songs playing in the background. Kay had always had a glass of Faery wine in one hand and the cat in the other, bobbing along while Eliza had laughed until her belly hurt.

That was when she had no memories of what her life had been before. *Purgatory.* Her life in New Orleans had always been just a bridge between her lives, her grandfather a guide.

Now that he was gone, what did that mean for her?

She spotted glaring silver in the shadows of the house, the beady golden eyes of the raven watching her from the darkness. There was no one inside, Kay having managed to keep everyone outside for the afternoon.

Kay moved on to talk to the guests, her demeanour soft, so different to her usual outspoken nature. No one was watching Eliza as she slipped out of the courtyard and into the stuffy halls of the house.

The knight went rigid as she approached. She eyed him and the raven perched on his shoulder. She wanted to yell, to scream, to beg for answers. The knight and the raven were always there, were always watching. They were as much involved in her life as the Dark Master was.

"What are you doing here?" she asked, voice unfamiliar in her own ears.

The knight blinked down at her, silver eyes illuminated under the strands of dark hair that fell over his face.

"Are you ever going to speak to me?" No answer. "Why?"

The knight bowed his head. "I am sorry for your loss."

Eliza hadn't expected that. The deep tenor of his voice sent a shiver down her spine. She wanted to hear his voice again; there had been something painfully familiar about it that she couldn't recognise.

She blinked, and he was gone.

~

"There you are."

Eliza blinked up at Amitel. After seeing the knight, she had stumbled up to her bedroom and collapsed on the floor in the corner of her room. At some point, the sky had gone from blue to pink, signalling dusk. Silence had enveloped her, thick and heavy, an embrace she hadn't wanted to leave.

No one had gone looking for her, probably thanks to Kay.

Eliza wasn't sure if she wanted to be left alone, but admired Amitel all the same for looking for her.

The warlock carefully sat down beside her, his brows set in worry. "Are you okay?"

She looked away and shook her head, bitter tears rising in her throat. "No," she said, voice thick, "I'm not. He's dead, and there was nothing I could do to save him."

"It isn't your fault, love."

Eliza spared him a look. "Except it *is*. If it wasn't for the Ecix, *none* of this would be happening."

He sighed, and reached for her hand. His fingers entwined with hers, warm and calloused, yet soft in the way he held on to her. He didn't look up from their joined hands as he said, "*That* is out of your control. You never had the choice in when you would come back. You never had the choice in *who* you would be given to."

"I could have refused." Eliza shook her head as pain gripped her temples, bile rising in her throat. "I—I could have—"

"Done nothing." His hand tightened around hers. "You were a *child*. You were being groomed for this *power*, and when it became a threat, you were handed over. You probably were never supposed to get this close to Davis, to Kay."

She swallowed thickly. He continued, finally meeting her stare, eyes soft, "You have a terrifying responsibility. One that you shouldn't have been burdened with. And this—" He stopped, eyes darkening. Red touched the iris. "This is *not* your fault."

Eliza tore her gaze from his and sucked in a ragged breath. "I don't know what to do."

"You survive." Her eyes cut to his. "You survive, and you be better. Davis would be so, so proud of you."

The intensity of his gaze cut through her, warm and comforting. But his words, they brought a warmth to her heart that had been frozen since she'd watched her grandfather fall.

It was only a spark, but it crackled, igniting a strength within her she thought she'd lost. She couldn't help the smile that softly tipped her lips.

Amitel's eyes widened slightly in surprise.

"What?" she asked, frowning.

He shook his head. "Nothing. I just..." He stopped and gave her a half-smile. "I like it when you smile."

A short, soft laugh bubbled from her lips before she could stop herself.

"I'm proud of you too, for what it's worth," he said softly, standing as Kay's voice filled the hallway.

Eliza wasn't sure how to reply as he strode over to her bedroom door. Part of her should have been mortified having him in her childhood bedroom; the posters and photographs, the stuffed animals, the old make-up and random hats that lined her desk, but she didn't.

Before he could escape, she finally found her voice. "Thank you."

He bowed his head and left without another word.

~

A cool spring breeze carried with it the promise of summer. Eliza sucked in a deep breath, relishing in the last breaths of winter before the humidity of summer kicked in.

Shade blanketed the cemetery, offering a reprieve from the sun. The skeletal trees were already beginning to flesh out, leaves and buds slowly releasing themselves from the hold winter had on them.

Miranda came into focus at the gates of the cemetery, her face set in sadness. "I heard whispers of your loss."

Eliza stiffened, throat tightening. "Have you seen him? My grandfather?"

The spirit shook her head. "Not here. I suspect he's moved on." Eliza pushed passed her and into the maze of mausoleums. "You did not want him to, Elizabeth?"

"Of course I did," Eliza said, shaking her head. "I just... I wanted to see him one last time."

Miranda floated at her side. After a moment of silence, she said, "I am sure you will, somehow."

Eliza walked with no particular destination in sight. She let her connection to the cemetery guide her through the maze of mausoleums, until she found herself standing before a row of crypts. The familiar stone and withering flowers gave her a sense of nostalgia.

Without realising, Eliza dipped into her Blood Magic. Her sight grew clearer, giving her a better view of the spirits who surrounded her. She hadn't even needed to draw blood.

An older man Eliza vaguely recognised tipped his hat. "What's got you down, little ghost girl?"

Eliza's lips quirked in amusement. "I'm not the ghost."

The man shrugged, grinning. "No, but you hang around here enough that you're almost one of us."

"Sounds about right," Eliza said. She dropped to the ground, bringing her knees to her chest and leaned her head back against the mausoleum behind her.

Spirits gathered around her; Eliza felt their energies like extensions of her own. Blood Magic—and the power of the Ecix—drew them closer, made them stronger. There were some familiar faces amongst the crowd—an old woman who had once guided Eliza through the cemetery as a child, having once been a governess to a wealthy family in New Orleans; a child who liked to hear stories and play pranks on the living—and it was those faces that brought a sense of relief to her.

Since the wedding, something had changed within her. Eliza felt it, deep within the ancient well of power that belonged only to her. It churned with a new fervour, like it had been touched for the very first time.

It brought her closer to death.

"There you are."

Eliza didn't bother to look up from her hands. "Hi, Kay."

"I shouldn't be surprised," Kay said, amusement lifting her voice. "When you were a girl, you used to sneak out whenever you were upset and come to the cemetery." The older woman groaned as she took a seat beside Eliza. "I have something for you. From your grandfather. You were supposed to get it after the wedding, for that tour you and Alicsar were supposed to take."

Eliza swallowed back tears as Kay handed her the brightly coloured birthday bag. Inside, Eliza pulled away the tissue paper and stared down at the baby-blue polaroid camera. Boxes of film were stocked at the bottom, enough to last her months if she made sure to keep track of it.

"He knew you'd need some for Cadira," Kay murmured. "Whenever he got the chance, he would stock up on the stuff. He wished he'd had it in time for the first mission, since he thought you might have liked to take photos while travelling."

A laugh bubbled from Eliza's lips, and she held her hand to her mouth to stop a sob from breaking free. "I didn't even think of this." She stared down at the gift.

"Well," Kay said with a smile, "you can have it now for whatever happens next. Capture new memories, just like he would have wanted."

"I don't know how I can do that, Kay." Eliza set the bag down and rubbed a hand over her face, wiping away stray tears. "How can I keep going while he isn't here? He's dead because of me."

Kay shook her head and took Eliza's hand, squeezing it. "This is not on you. It never was, and it never should be."

"But it is," Eliza said helplessly. "It's because of this power that the Dark Master is after me and everyone I love."

"Eliza, you are *not* this power. This power doesn't define you." Kay hesitantly touched Eliza's cheek. "Your grandfather wouldn't have wanted you to stop living life, kid."

Another tear rolled down Eliza's cheek. "It's not fair."

"Sometimes, life isn't fair. But what we make out of the worst situations is what matters. Your grandfather would have wanted you to take this and keep moving. It's what I would want too," Kay said.

Eliza shot her guardian a look. "Don't tell me you're going to die too," she said half-jokingly. But she couldn't lose Kay too.

"I've lived a very long and very happy life. But I'll stick around as long as I can." Kay winked, her half-smile bringing a smile to Eliza's face.

Eliza wrapped her arms around Kay's thin frame. "Thank you, Kay."

"That's what I'm here for, kid." Kay wrapped an arm around Eliza's shoulders and began leading her out of the cemetery. "Now, are you going to go back to Cadira and deal with that king? Or..."

"I think I might spend a couple more days here, for grandpa.

Then... then I'll go back to it all. I'll figure out what needs to happen next."

Kay nodded, and pressed a kiss to the top of Eliza's head. "I understand, kid. Take all the time you need."

51

THE ORACLE
CELIA

The familiar song of Port Hein should have given Celia some sense of peace, but instead a deep sadness weighed on her shoulders. Her wrist burned with the distance from her faery companion, but she gritted her teeth. It was only a fraction of the pain running through her body. The burn was a welcome reprieve from the Shadow Sickness.

Celia closed her eyes and sucked in a breath; the smell of salt and brine filled her senses. How long had it been since she'd visited the port city? The mission? It was the first time she'd finally gotten to speak to Eliza since she'd been a child.

It held many hard memories.

"Already bored?"

Her eyes snapped open and drank in her oldest friend; Brandon Thorne had changed, it was clear in the way he watched her with the shadow of knowledge darkening his eyes. The dark shirt he wore looked new, his breeches clean, boots polished to a shine. His hair was longer, curling more around his ears and the nape of his neck, and his skin sun kissed from days at sea.

"Expecting someone else?" she asked, smiling, letting her gaze flicker back to his.

Brandon's cheeks reddened as he shook his head. "Of course not."

Celia laughed and threw her arms around his shoulders. "I have missed you."

"And I, you." He pulled her close; she felt the coiled muscles of his shoulders, breathed in the scent of sea air and sweat. Even the way he held her changed; he tightened his grip around her and sucked in a breath, and something told her it wasn't because he missed her.

As she pulled away, she said, "I could have met you in Laziroth and used a portal to bring you home. Why wait to call on me?"

"I needed the time to think," he replied. Offering his arm, he motioned to one of the several taverns that circled the docks. "Let's go sit down."

She frowned, but linked their arms. "We should return to the palace."

"I need to talk to you, without anyone else."

Her stomach dropped. "Lead the way."

Night danced at the edges of the port city, casting shadows over the buildings lining the docks. Ladies of the night appeared in the mouths of allies to sing for returning fishermen, while soldiers of the king patrolled the docks with stiff backs and eyes searching for any hint of the Dark Master.

Celia swallowed the lump forming in her throat and cast Brandon a quick glance, though he seemed too caught in his own thoughts to pay attention to her. His eyes were cast in darkness, too, heavy with whatever he learnt from the oracle. But he seemed unaware of what had happened in the capital since his departure. The truth twisted in her stomach, begging for release, but she reeled it in.

As they made their way to one of the lonely taverns at the end of the docks, whispers followed them. The news of what happened to Alicsar spread far enough that even after weeks many weren't prepared to speak his name aloud.

Darkness cloaked the tavern at the end of the docks, broken up by the occasional torch, flickering flames doing little to illuminate the space. Celia and Brandon chose a table in the back and were ignored by several of the patrons who chose instead to give their attention to their ale.

Sitting, they waited until two jugs were in front of them, but neither moved to touch them.

"So, did you find what you were looking for in Laziroth?" Celia asked finally, looking up from the sticky table.

Brandon met her stare, and for a long moment, he didn't answer. A storm raged in his eyes, visible despite the dim lighting. "Laziroth." He chuckled, looking down at his scarred hands as he shook his head. "I'm not entirely sure, Celia. I wanted to know if the oracle could help with the dagger, but..."

She tensed. "What did the oracle tell you?"

He released a breath, finally looking up. "Nothing we can use."

She knew that wasn't it. His jaw ticked, and he refused to look at her. "But you found something?" she asked, cocking her head. Brandon looked away, the hand resting atop the table clenching into a fist.

He was quiet a moment, then shook his head. "Nothing I want to repeat."

"Brandon..."

"Celia..." He looked up, meeting her stare. "I can't."

"Davis is dead, Brandon. Alicsar is *gone*. Eliza is a mess." She paused sucking in a breath. "Did you find what you needed?"

He looked at her for a long minute, the storm in his eyes raging. "Yes."

Bile rose in her throat, but she swallowed it back. "She really needed you."

"I know." He sighed, scrubbing a hand over his face. "Celia, I know."

Looking away, Celia pulled the untouched jug of ale towards her, but she made no move to take a sip. "We failed. We didn't get the dagger. She blames herself and I don't know how to help her. I failed too. I failed *her*."

"Celia..."

"I did." She heaved a sigh. "Eliza has had so much pressure upon her shoulders, and she was not coping. She still isn't. She blames herself for the dagger, for Alicsar, for her grandfather. I am afraid for her. And I wish you had been there when she needed you."

Brandon reached for her hand, pulling it from the mug. "I had to go. What I learnt..." A spark of fear entered the darkness of his eyes. Her heart stuttered in her chest, stomach churning.

She looked from the mug to him. "I hope it was worth it."

He nodded. "It was. I know what I must do to help Eliza. From here on, I will not abandon her."

For a moment, all she could do was watch him. There was more she could ask, more she could push for, and yet she found herself hesitating. If she tried, would he lock himself away again, turn into the same man she met on the docks after the last time he was in Laziroth? It took him many year to return from that, to return to the man she met during the *Idrindis* ceremony all those years before.

Celia cocked her head. "There's more to this story, isn't there?"

Brandon bowed his head. "Most I won't share, but..." He looked up. "I found Dragon Riders."

Her eyes widened, and Brandon nodded. "They're being taken to safety, like northern Cadira if the pirates do as they promised, then we may be able to catch up with them."

"Pirates?" Celia pulled back and crossed her arms. "What in the Goddesses name did you do?"

A crooked smile crossed his lips. "A story for another time," he replied, leaning back in his chair.

Celia narrowed her eyes, but a smile twitched at her lips. "Alright, Brandon Thorne." She stood from the sticky table. "Then we ought to return to the palace. I have someone you need to meet."

~

They returned to the palace under the cover of night, the twin moons of Cadira a pair of watchful eyes that followed them into the palace proper. The silence surrounding the castle turned the hairs on the back of Celia's arms, a shiver dancing down her spine. The ache from the Shadow Sickness seeped into her bones, but only a slight tug at her abdomen and lower hips reminded her of its presence.

Brandon paused at the doors and looked up. Though the sky was clear, a breeze carried the promise of rain. "I should go and see Eliza," he murmured, scrubbing a hand through his tousled hair.

Celia shook her head. "She's still in New Orleans, mourning. She doesn't want to come back yet."

Brandon turned to face her, the conflict of his choices darkening his eyes. "Will she though?"

"Of course," Celia replied quietly. "She had me schedule a meeting with King Bastian. She has something planned, but she hasn't told any of us what that is yet."

They walked the quiet halls; servants made no sound, as if afraid to disturb the silence. There were no more visiting nobility or dignitaries. There were only a few who occupied the palace, at the king's request.

Black flags of mourning hung in intervals throughout the halls, for the prince who had been taken once more.

"Well, well, well." Brandon and Celia stopped as Amitel appeared on the grand staircase. "Look who finally came back." Bitterness highlighted his tone as he took the final steps to the landing.

Brandon stiffened as they eyed one another. Celia hadn't expected Amitel to be at the palace; the last she'd seen him, he'd been in New Orleans, reluctant to leave Eliza's side. Caden and Darius, at the behest of Lennox and the visiting Blood Witches, had remained in the busy mortal city to watch over her, despite Kay's protests.

The warlock cocked his head. "Does he know what happened?" Amitel asked, eyes flickering to hers.

Celia nodded. "I told him."

Jaw clenched, Amitel shook his head. "Well..."

From the corner of her eye, Celia watched her friend, who seemed inclined to say something more, but she stepped in, offering both men a smile. "How about we go to my rooms?" She met each stare, challenging them to continue.

Amitel let a smirk play on his lips as he bowed at the waist. "Whatever you want, darling Celia."

She rolled her eyes. "Brandon?"

He said nothing, but nodded.

Celia guided them up the grand staircase to the wing once occupied by Eliza and Alicsar. Like the rest of the palace, the halls were empty and dark; no one had made their way through to light the sconces along the walls.

Amitel waved his hand and they ignited, lighting their way. They said nothing to one another, not even when they arrived at her door.

Celia pushed her way through and found Soh curled on one of the lounges, her feet tucked beneath her, a book in her hands. She looked up as Celia entered, a smile tipping her lips, but her dark eyes went from the Blood Witch to Brandon. A frown replaced the smile that made Celia's heart stutter.

Brandon hesitated in the doorway, hand hovering over his sword. Amitel dropped into the lounge across from Soh and stretched his longs legs out in front of him. He moved like a cat as he discarded a black coat.

"Soh, this is Brandon Thorne, previously of the Brotherhood," Amitel introduced, waving a hand. "Brandon, this is Soh. Celia found her escaping the Wyld Hunt."

Brandon's gaze cut to her; Celia self-consciously touched the thin, white line around her wrist. "I wanted to help. Arawn put a bind on us, so that we cannot leave one another."

"I suppose a lot also happened while I was gone," he mused. Closing the door behind him, Brandon took another hesitant step into the room. "It's a pleasure to meet you, Soh."

The Faery bowed her head, dropping the book onto her lap. "And you, Brandon Thorne."

Celia clutched her hands in her lap as she took a seat beside Soh. "Because of the bind, I can't return to the mountains," Celia said, looking down at her fingers. "We have decided to go in search of more information about this magic."

"Surely the Blood Witches would know how to help." Brandon perched on the edge of the small table sitting between the two lounges. "They would, wouldn't they?"

"There is some magic not even the High Witch can undo," Celia replied quietly. "But we are not leaving just because of that. I don't think the High Witch wants me close to Eliza, not anymore. With the bind she'd have good reason to keep me away—and possibly punish Eliza for my foolishness. Now—" She shook her head, releasing a heavy breath. "It is what I must do to help her."

"There are other cities," Soh continued. "Ones that may reveal more about what happened to Azula's followers and how the Ecix is connected to the dagger."

Brandon frowned. "What is she talking about?"

"Oh, we learnt a *lot* during your time away," Amitel said, sitting up. "Things the Blood Witches might try and kill us for."

"Eliza will only be allowed so much access to her past. We hope to uncover whatever is possible without them always watching us." Celia looked between Brandon and Soh. "We will leave as soon as Eliza has made her decision."

"She won't have much of a choice," Amitel said, leaning forward. "You know she's going to be forced back to the mountains. No prince, no treaty. The king has no grounds to keep her locked away."

"It's true," Celia replied, turning away from Amitel and meet Brandon's stare. "She'll have to go back."

"What exactly did you find that was so dangerous?" Brandon asked quietly. "What aren't you telling me?"

Celia sucked in a breath. Her gaze fell to her hands, and she rubbed her fingers, the words caught in her throat. "I learnt from Isolde that in order to find the dagger, Eliza would need to learn about the Original Ecix," she started, pressing her hands into her stomach to stop from fiddling with them. "There's nothing about the Original with the Blood Witches, and since Eliza left, they've been hoarding texts from the scholars. Isolde is worried that the witches are trying to keep Eliza from knowing her past, and from what we learnt in the Fae

Territory, we are too."

Brandon scrubbed a hand over his face. "Isolde never spoke of an Original Ecix," he murmured, leaning forward, resting his elbows on his knees. Something in his eyes darkened.

"Isolde would have known that the witches were watching her, and she was quite crafty," Amitel said, leaning back. "She wouldn't give her secrets away that easily."

Celia shifted uncomfortably as Brandon spared the warlock a glance. "She only told her secrets to her grimoire." Brandon looked away and stared down at his hands. "And that's hidden."

"Where?" Soh asked. "If the last Ecix knew what we needed, then perhaps we should be going after that?"

Celia tensed as Brandon's darkened gaze fell on Soh. "To do that," he murmured, "we would need to return to the Labyrinth Mountains. *Eliza* would have to return there."

"I think it's what she wants." Celia uncoiled, casting Soh a quick glance from the corner of her eye. "Eliza wants the truth, no matter what. She'll go with the Blood Witches if she has to. Train with them, live with them, so long as she gets what she wants."

The air between them grew thick; she hadn't told Eliza yet her plans to leave, was afraid of how her sister would take it, but she knew Eliza needed her out in Cadira, searching for answers. The Blood Witches were hiding things from her—from them all.

Celia feared the witches would shelter Eliza from the reality of her situation, that they would not tell her the absolute truth. It had taken much prying from Isolde for a morsel of her past... Celia couldn't begin to imagine what it would be like for Eliza.

"And what about you, Amitel?" Brandon asked, sparing the warlock a glance. "Where will you go?"

Celia tensed as Amitel met Brandon's eye. "I plan on doing whatever Eliza needs me to do."

Brandon said nothing as the warlock picked up his coat, and left her suite.

52

TO DO WHAT IS NECESSARY
ELIZA

Eliza studied the king's office with new eyes, and a mind still clouded by loss. After days spent locked away with nothing but her own thoughts to keep her company, there was a sense of relief that washed over her about being in the king's company.

In the span of moments, she had lost her grandfather, and her husband.

In the span of moments, everything around her had crumpled.

But he had also lost so much. His son was gone again, probably dead for all they knew. Eliza had no doubt he had joined Xeb and Alastor wherever they were, wherever the Dark Master had taken them. To the ruins of Valonde? Or some other hidden location that she had no hope of finding?

It wasn't hard, now, to know that the Dark Master had been playing them all since the beginning. He had allowed Eliza to take Alicsar back, allowed her to search for the dagger—and fail miserably.

Everything, from her finding the prince to the marriage, up until the wedding itself had been planned by the Dark Master himself. But for what, she didn't know.

He had taken from her again, not her life this time, but the life of the person she loved most. Her grandfather was gone. The Dark Master had taken Alicsar, ripped him from her hands, because she thought she could protect him.

He had made her feel weak—again.

Eliza let her gaze pass over the wall of old tomes. The fire crackled, its warmth spreading throughout the room. For the first time in a long time, she was alone with the king.

Bastian watched her with keen eyes, his back as straight as a rod. It was hard to read his expression, whether he was mad at her for failing, or if he pitied her for her own loss. For once, they were kindred souls.

"I heard you made a decision," he said finally, voice gruff yet still booming.

She gave a small nod. "I have."

His gaze never left hers, but he nodded. "I understand."

Perhaps there was a hint of sorrow in his voice, though she couldn't understand why. Was he disappointed in her choice? Sad that she'd decided remaining in the capital wasn't in her best interest?

Was it because she was his last connection to his son?

Her stomach twisted, tightening as the words stumbled from her lips. "The Blood Witches want to ensure my safety. They know it isn't safe here anymore. And..."

The king raised a brow. "And?"

She swallowed thickly. "There is nothing more I can do here, to help you, or..." His name wouldn't cross her lips. It was unfair, but she blamed him. He hadn't been responsible for her grandfather's death. He'd been taken, stolen once again, like he had when he'd been an infant.

People had died then, too.

For the first time since she'd entered his office, the king broke her stare, bowing his head. "It seems even fate has been toying with me. I was never truly going to get my son back, was I?"

Tears burned in the back of her throat. "I have no doubt that he loved you, loved being here."

The smile that stretched across the kings face didn't reach his eyes. "Thank you, Miss Kindall."

She pursed her lips. "I'm sorry that I can't stay." It took a lot for her to pull the rings from her finger and set them down on the desk. The king tracked her movement, looked somewhat surprised. "I should return these."

He shook his head. "No matter how hard you try, you won't escape what happened, Elizabeth. You won't escape my son."

She swallowed thickly. What had happened would haunt her for the rest of her life. He didn't have to worry about that.

"But those are yours," Bastian continued, motioning to the wedding band and engagement ring, "because even though my son might be gone again, you are still his wife."

"But we didn't—"

"He would want you to have them." His dark stare met hers. "He cared for you, deeply. He thought of you as more than a friend. He made a bargain with me, one to stop this union. And he did that because he was in love with you."

Eliza sucked in a sharp, cooling breath. Hesitantly, she reached for the two rings, and found some comfort in their weight. But she didn't put them back on. Instead, she slipped them into the pocket of her jeans, the material so unfamiliar now after spending so long in cotton breeches and thick tights—all of Cadiran make.

"I will keep looking," she said quietly, unable to meet his stare. "I won't let the Dark Master win." *I won't let him take anything else from us.* For the longest time, she'd resented the King of Cadira, for taking her away from her family, for making sure her memories of Cadira were hidden so that when she returned, she'd be able to search for his son without asking questions. She still resented him for using her family against her.

And yet she understood. Deep down, she always had.

He was a desperate man searching for answers, searching for a son taken from him. He'd already lost his wife and daughter, a girl who was somehow connected to Azula's dagger, who remained in the spirit realm for whatever reason.

So, Eliza understood.

Bastian must have seen it in her eyes, because when she finally braved his stare, she found herself watching as his onyx eyes glassed over.

The king blinked, sucking in a sharp breath. "Thank you," was all he said. Now, he wouldn't look at her, instead glaring into the fire like it would answer all the pleading questions that likely sat on the top of his tongue.

Eliza curled her hands into fists. "Until we meet again, King Bastian."

He nodded and said nothing as she left.

~

Black flags of mourning lined the streets—for soldiers killed in the fight, for the Keeper who died protecting the would-be Princess, for the prince who had yet again been taken by the darkness that swept over Cadira.

Eliza hadn't been paying attention to it all before, but it was hard to miss the creeping darkness that finally attacked Cadira's heart. Like a poison with no antidote, it spread throughout the streets, tendrils of hopelessness and anguish overshadowing the love and happiness that had once overtaken the city only two weeks prior.

She tugged the hood of her cloak lower on her head as she wandered through the streets of the capital. There was a deafening silence permeating the cobblestone paths. The rolling of carts were dimmed, the whinnying of horses and bray of donkeys almost non-existent. She'd never seen the city so... *dull* and lifeless before.

Those she passed had their heads lowered. Women shed silent tears for the dead and stolen, while even children joined the sombre mood, their laughter diminished.

A shudder crept down her spine. Not even the spirits made an appearance on the streets of the capital, gone—but for how long?

Eliza ducked down an alley and found herself chest to chest with Thorne.

"Hey," she whispered. Her friend looked down at her in surprise, his dark-grey eyes widening as they roamed down her—from the patchwork cloak, over the jeans she barely managed to hide, down to her boots before they met hers.

"Hey."

She gave him a tight-lipped smile and tried to ignore the burning in her throat.

He had finally returned, but at what cost? She'd been warned of his reappearance, giving her enough time to prepare what she needed to say to him.

But staring up at her commander, all those words, the prepared speech and the anger at leaving, disappeared.

Instead, she threw her arms around his midsection and buried her head in his chest. Soft cotton grew damp with tears.

Thorne didn't hesitate to wrap his arms around her; she felt his head drop, face in her hair. "I missed you."

She sucked in a breath, choking on sobs. "I missed you too."

They stood in the alley for what felt like hours; Eliza wrapped in his arms, breathing in his familiar scent, letting his warmth sooth the raging anger and sadness that pounded on her chest.

When she finally pulled away, the tears had dried. "Is everyone here?" she asked, crossing her arms over her chest.

Thorne took a step back and nodded. "They're all upstairs."

"Good."

They strode down the alley in silence; she couldn't help but wonder what he was thinking about. She had no idea what had happened, what he'd seen.

Eliza was thankful that Celia had been the one to explain their journey to Azula's city, how Darius and Caden had come to join them, explained why they suddenly had one of the High Fae in their midst, how they'd even travelled to the Fae Territories to find Azula's dagger, only to come back empty handed.

Amitel had assured her he knew everything.

She wished Thorne had been by her side, like he'd promised.

But his promises to her... Isolde and his love for her, for the dead Ecix that haunted Eliza's dreams, *she* was the one he wanted to protect, to love. Eliza saw that now. She'd known it from the moment she'd learnt who she truly was.

Eliza stopped him before he could open the door that lead up to his apartment. The commander shot her a look that she couldn't quite read. "I just want to talk to you for a second, before I face everyone."

He bowed his head and stepped away from the peeling wooden door, saying nothing.

She sucked in a sharp breath. "I don't want you to feel any obligations to me, Thorne." His eyes widened—in shock or anger she couldn't tell—but before he could speak, she cut in. "I know you feel *something* towards me, but your love for Isolde overshadows that. And I don't want you to feel like you have to choose." Carefully, she reached for his hand and laced their fingers. "You are one of my closest friends, and I don't want to lose that. Most importantly, I don't want to lose you."

She paused and searched his eyes for something, but he'd closed off completely. His hand was limp in hers, and she sighed.

"I love you," she whispered, staring down at their hands. "You are my closest friend. And it hurt *so much* when you left. You walked away because of Isolde."

"Eliza—"

Finally, she released his hand. "I don't want to stand in her shadow. I'm *sick* of being lied to, or only told half-truths. It's killing me, Thorne." She swallowed down tears. "I've lost so much already, and I'm tired. I'm so fucking tired. I lost one of the most important people to me, and you weren't even here. I lost Alicsar, too. I didn't love him, not like I do you. But he became my friend. He loved *me*. Not some ghost who looks like me."

His voice was barely a whisper as he said, "I'm sorry."

She closed her eyes and nodded. "I know, Thorne. I know."

Stepping away from him, she started for the door, but his next words stopped her before she could open it. "I love you too, Eliza."

She pursed her lips and looked skyward, where storm clouds gathered above them. Thunder rumbled in the distance, like an omen. But she didn't reply, and instead entered the apartment where everyone waited. She wiped her eyes and blinked away tears, straightening so she didn't look so *fragile*.

Thorne stayed a couple of steps behind her as she climbed the stairs, reaching the landing where Amitel waited. He leaned against the wall beside the front door and didn't need to ask, but she read the question in his eyes: *are you okay?*

She gave him a small nod. His eyes drifted from hers over to Thorne, who stopped behind her, the warmth of his chest pressed against her back. A small army of butterflies descended in her stomach, but her heart ached for what he could never give her.

Eliza cleared her throat as she side-stepped Amitel, entering the apartment. Despite the fire crackling in the hearth, the living room was cold, the chill of winter seeping through the brownstone exterior and into the warm wooded space. A small kitchen took up one corner of the room, while two doors—one to a bedroom and a bathroom, she imagined—sat to either side. A lounge sat in front of the fireplace, where Celia and Soh watched the flames, while Darius and Caden took up residence by a window the overlooked the streets.

Amitel entered directly behind her, then Thorne. A suffocating silence took over as all eyes landed on her.

Celia, with her ebony hair plaited away from her face and cerulean blue eyes softening, stood and approached. Without a word, she threw her arms around Eliza, encasing her in a warm hug that almost broke her. "I'm glad you're here," Celia whispered in her ear.

The words burned in Eliza's throat, so she said nothing as her friend pulled away.

Eliza coughed, clearing her throat, and started at everyone. *Friends*, she thought, meeting every gaze. They might not have started out that way, but along the way... Swallowing the lump in her throat, she said, "Thank you all for coming here today. We don't have long, but I appreciate you all."

From the couch, Celia gave her an encouraging smile.

"I am returning with the Blood Witches to the Labyrinth mountains," Eliza started, wringing her hands. "Because we lost Alicsar, there is no need for me to be here. I'll use whatever time I can while training to search for Alicsar—and the Dark Master."

"The Blood Witches won't allow that," Caden warned, crossing his arms over his chest. "That won't be your responsibility anymore."

Eliza shrugged. "Then I'll do it in my free time. This all started because of me—because of the Ecix. It's about time I do something, anything, to make this all *stop*." She turned to Celia and Soh.

Her sister hesitated for a moment before saying, "We won't be joining you with the convoy."

Celia stole a glance at her bound companion. There was heat in their stares—one that was hard to miss, even to Eliza, who had no real concept of romantic love—and after a moment, Soh nodded. "We will go to these underground cities. Perhaps there will be answers to our questions as well."

"We aren't safe with the Blood Witches," Celia said. "But we can do more outside of the mountains. We'll find answers. We can travel to the Courts of Light." When Celia turned back to face Eliza, there was no way she could miss the flush that crept up her neck and into her cheeks. "We'll find the dagger. Or at least an answer as to why we weren't able to get it in the first place."

Nodding, Eliza smiled. "Thanks."

"And I will return to face the Brotherhood," Thorne said from behind her.

Spinning, Eliza's eyes widened. "What?"

"I wouldn't bother," Caden replied, snorting. "They'll kill you for deserting."

But Thorne's eyes were on her, gauging her reaction, or maybe he meant it. "I'm not leaving your side, not again." He shook his head, dark locks tumbling over his forehead. "Even if that means making amends with the Brotherhood."

Caden snorted again, but Eliza ignored him. When she'd laid it all out for him, she hadn't expected... Swallowing the lump in her throat,

Eliza relented, because she knew he would do it no matter what she said.

Darius, who had been quietly standing in the corner, cleared his throat. "The warlock disappeared."

When she tore her eyes from Thorne, she searched the living room like he would magically reappear, but he didn't.

Disappointment and frustration curdled in the pit of her gut, along with a sadness she couldn't place. Amitel had been there for her, after the wedding and after the funeral, but he was gone—again, disappearing with no word. Where would he reappear? When she least expected it? After she'd had a chance to let go of their friendship?

But it didn't matter. Tonight would have been the her chance to say goodbye, and he'd taken that from her.

And she was sick of having things taken from her.

~

For the first time since arriving in Cadira, Eliza thought she could taste spring in the air.

A soft breeze picked up strands of her hair and carried her in Amitel's direction, the whisper of his magic winding through the busy streets. Eliza picked her way carefully around the mourners, a hood covering most of her face, but the wedding haunted the people of Cadira just as much as it did her.

Lowering her head, Eliza picked up her pace. Amitel's magic grew warmer, spreading over her skin like sunlight. A tingle ran through her body as she approached a section of the lake new to her; a balcony overlooking the water lay empty save for a single person, whose golden hair danced in the breeze. Wrought iron railing lined the balcony, two wooden benches covered in snow on either side. The laughs of children carried from the iced-over lake, dim in the wanning afternoon light.

Eliza swallowed the lump in her throat and slowed her pace, inching closer. She hadn't bothered masking her magic; Amitel knew she was close, but her heart raced with each step.

"Why'd you leave?" Eliza asked, coming to a stop beside the

warlock.

Amitel lowered his head, shoulders hunched. "I thought perhaps my time was up. And honestly, I don't think I could have handled Brandon Thorne's self-righteous arse."

Eliza snorted and stepped up beside him, resting her arms against the railing. "You didn't have to leave, you know," she replied softly, nudging his elbow. "I could have used you in there."

He didn't look at her, instead lifting his face to the sun. It washed over his golden features, bathing him in its warm light. "You don't need me, Eliza."

She couldn't ignore the strange stutter of her heart, or the yawning pit in her stomach as she watched him. there was something strange about her feelings towards Amitel, something she couldn't explain.

"But I do need you."

Amitel's head snapped towards her, wide eyes meeting hers. Red swirled and danced with the gold in his irises, conveying the doubt and guilt playing in his mind. "Eliza..."

She pressed her lips together, and though her heart leapt into her throat, she pushed past her own fear. "Please. I need you there. Or I'll have no one."

His eyes softened, the red retreating. "Celia, or Brandon—"

"Celia has to find a way to break the bind," Eliza whispered, "and Thorne... he can't be there all the time. He's going to try and get back in with the Brotherhood, but..." She hesitated, looking away. "I need you there to help me with *them*."

Closing her eyes, Eliza wondered if she'd made the right choice going after Amitel. What kind of danger would he be putting himself in if he followed her to the Labyrinth Mountains? What might the witches do if she brought him with her?

She opened her mouth, but his soft voice made her pause. "Are you sure?" he asked, and when she returned her gaze to his, she almost couldn't breathe.

But she forced herself to nod. "Please."

Amitel closed his eyes, lips parting as he released a sigh. Lowering his head, she waited.

"Alright," he said, the spring breeze ruffling his hair.

A smile tugged at her lips, and they stood there overlooking the lake as children played, and spring edged closer to the kingdom, and an ember of hope ignited in her chest.

EPILOGUE

The sun beat down on the small island, blanketing the land in a warm breeze that ruffled the leaves of trees that should be long dead, picking up the scent of ancient fruits and deadly flowers. White sand greeted his black boots, while the crystal blue ocean lapped at the shore. In the distance, sirens sang their haunting tune, far off the rocky coast where ships sank to their deaths.

A portal swallowed him, taking him underground. Sweat beaded on his upper lip, but he preferred the warmth over the bitter cold of Cadira.

Dark stone beneath his feet met iron cells. Magic shimmered around the bars, the perfect little prison he'd created.

The half-Fae he'd picked up from New York watched him, arms chained above his head. He was only alive so long as his lover did as commanded.

There were others; a Blood Witch frozen in her own body, a sleeping spell created from the blood of a necromancer—not Elizabeth

Kindall, but another. A knight of the Brotherhood slept in another cell. He'd given up after three years.

And humans. From the mortal world the Ecix loved so much. Picked up and thrown in the darkest of the cells. They huddled together, like they would one day be freed.

He had ideas for them.

A door in the back of his prison opened on creaky hinges to reveal a darkened room. His most prized possession was finally awake.

He wondered how his little spy would react.

He slipped into the room unseen, let the door click shut behind him. In the shadows, he waited.

The boy had changed in his time at the palace. But he'd foreseen the boys love for the Ecix. Had hoped the prince would fall for her, like many fools before him.

Prince Alicsar bucked, restraints whining, clanging against the stone slab where he sat. He made a sound of disgust as Alastor, a new toy he couldn't wait to play with, held him down by the shoulders, using all his weight against the young, stolen prince.

The Dark Master stepped out of the shadows and donned a simple pair of black leather gloves. With the light of the Valondian sun burning through the small window above Alastor's head, the Dark Master was in full view of the prince.

Alicsar stopped, eyes widening as he took in the Dark Master's form. "It's you," he whispered, shock claiming his young features. He bucked again as anger consumed him, but the Dark Master raised a hand.

The prince slumped in his seat, a spell immobilising him. But he was fully aware as Alastor moved to stand beside a table of sharp instruments and a spell created by the Dark Master himself. Every move made, the prince followed with his eyes.

The Dark Master motioned for the God of War. "Let's begin."

And so, the stolen prince screamed for a saviour who would never find him, and cursed the gods unable to save him, and throughout it all, the Dark Master smiled for the revenge he sought—and the witch he would soon kill.

READ THE COMPANION NOVELLA...

THE LAST ORACLE

OF

LAZIROTH

FIND OUT WHAT HAPPENED TO
BRANDON THORNE...

SHADOWLAND SAGA BOOK 2.5

STEPHANIE ANNE

WANT TO STAY UP TO DATE WITH ALL
THE IMPORTAL INFORMATION ABOUT
THE SHADOWLAND, RECEIVE
EXCLUSIVE CONTENT, AND MORE?

SIGN UP TO MY NEWSLETTER AND RECEIVE A FREE SHORT STORY ABOUT ELIZA!

THE SERIES CONTINUES...

THE ASCENT OF THE ECIX

SHADOWLAND SAGA BOOK 3

ABOUT THE AUTHOR

Stephanie Anne grew up in different parts of Australia before her parents settled down in a small, beachside town in Northern New South Wales. There, she developed her love of reading and began penning The Lost Prince of Cadira.

Now, Stephanie lives on the Gold Coast with her family and two fur babies, avoiding the sun and spending her time drinking coffee, scrolling TikTok, and working on her next book.

https://www.stephanieanneauthor.com/

Acknowledgments

First and foremost, I want to thank you, the reader, for taking a chance on me and the Shadowland. Without your continued support, I wouldn't be writing this. Since the release of *The Lost Prince of Cadira,* working on this book has been a struggle. For three years, I've worked on this book, agonised over it. For over a year, I let it sit and stew in a corner because of how much it stressed me out.

But here it is, finally finished, and I did it with the help of so many people! I need to give thanks, firstly, to my mum, Jenny, and sister Emily, who have supported me through this adventure, who continue to be my biggest fans. And to my critique partner and amazing friend, Dee Atkins, who spent hours with me going over this book.

Thank you to my proof reader, E. Rose. And an even bigger thanks to my cover designer, Celin, who always gives me the absolute best!

My alpha readers, Jenny D. and Leeva, who helped me through some of the hardest parts of this book, and reminded me why I even started this in the first place.

Thank you to my amazing team of beta readers: Jenny D., Leeva, Jenny R., Dee B., Fran, Hope, Jess, Nida, and Robin.

Thank you to Lyra Parish (The Courtney Project on YouTube) and the live sprints that helped me finish this dang book (& the novella).

I can't wait for you to return to the Shadowland, and continue Eliza's journey. Thank you again, dear reader.

www.ingramcontent.com/pod-product-compliance
Lightning Source LLC
Chambersburg PA
CBHW050109120726
47904CB00004B/1281